Hard to HANDLE

K. BROMBERG

PRAISE FOR K. BROMBERG

"K. Bromberg always delivers intelligently written, emotionally intense, sensual romance . . ."

—*USA Today*

"K. Bromberg makes you believe in the power of true love."
—#1 *New York Times* bestselling author Audrey Carlan

"A poignant and hauntingly beautiful story of survival, second chances, and the healing power of love. An absolute must-read."
—*New York Times* bestselling author Helena Hunting

"A home run! *The Player* is riveting, sexy, and pulsing with energy. And I can't wait for *The Catch!*"
—#1 *New York Times* bestselling author Lauren Blakely

"An irresistibly hot romance that stays with you long after you finish the book."
—#1 *New York Times* bestselling author Jennifer L. Armentrout

"Bromberg is a master at turning up the heat!"
—*New York Times* bestselling author Katy Evans

"Supercharged heat and full of heart. Bromberg aces it from the first page to the last."
—*New York Times* bestselling author Kylie Scott

"Captivating, emotional, and sizzling hot!"
—*New York Times* bestselling author S. C. Stephens

ALSO BY
K. BROMBERG

Hard to HANDLE

If life can remove someone you never dreamed of losing,
It can replace them with someone you never dreamt of having.
-Rachel Wolchin

PROLOGUE

Hunter

"YOU HAVE NO CLUE what you're talking about!" Rage fires, as I stare at my agent and verbally reject every rebuke he's throwing at me while silently agreeing he's right.

"I don't?" he yells. "What the hell was that stunt then? Fighting against the opposition is one thing, Hunter, but punching your own damn teammate?"

"Is it that he's my teammate or that he's another one of your clients you're trying to pimp and sell to the next highest bidder? My guess is, it's that. My gut tells me it's because he's your newest golden ticket to a higher commission and, since the press already caught wind of the fight, that pristine reputation of his might be a little tarnished." I shift on my feet and move a step closer. "Ever stop to think how the press already knows? Huh? Ever think that maybe Dyson picked a fight with me, staged the bullshit so he could get his name out there on social media? It's hard to live up to your self-proclaimed wonder-boy status when someone like me outperforms him every damn night, hands down, and steals what he thinks are his headlines. What is it they say? No press is bad press? Seems to me like he's looking to play off that."

Finn Sanderson chews his lip as he stares at me. His hair, his clothes, his everything, are in their usual styled perfection, but there's a flicker of uncertainty in his expression that I can't quite read. His dark eyes never leave mine as they stare and assess and scrutinize.

He draws in a deep breath and purses his lips as the silence falls stagnant. "What's going on with you, Hunter?"

Here we go again.

"What do you mean, what's going on with me?"

"Exactly what I asked. What the hell is going on with you? You're about to smash three long-standing records within a ridiculously short time frame. That's unprecedented. You used to play with finesse and poise, and now you play like a feral cat about to—"

"About to what? Seek and destroy? What does it matter? My numbers are better than ever."

"I was going to say you play like a man ready to win at all costs. Even if those costs include collateral damage."

"Sometimes winning requires that."

His chuckle is low and condescending at best. "At what expense though? Your teammates? Your club?" He shows his frustration with a subtle shake of his head. "They're putting up with it because you're winning, but that'll only go so far. You've been in this game long enough to know that losses happen and the tide can turn."

"I know, a whole twelve years in the league, and knocking on records it took others a lot longer to hit makes me a relic." I don't hide the sarcasm. Instead, I play it up so he knows how ridiculous he sounds.

"Winning will create tolerance . . . but your antics off the ice are going to cost you in ways you've never imagined."

"Fuck this." I say the words, but I know he's right. The problem is, I can't find a flying fuck to give right now.

"If that's how you want to be, fine." He shrugs in indifference. "Then no one is going to be cleaning up your messes in the press. Not the brawl you started at that hole in the wall. Not airing your grievances to the press about the bullshit in the locker room. Not the snubbing of fans as you walk by—"

"Glad to see you believe the press over your own client," I say.

"It was on video. It's kind of hard to dispute the fact that you walked right past a kid in a wheelchair holding out a sign for you to autograph." *Fuck. I never do that. Never.*

I used to be *that* kid. In many ways, I still am, so the fact I missed seeing him makes it all the worse. The notion that the press is using it against me only adds insult to injury.

I replay the scene he's talking about. My mom on my cell freaking out about Jonah and refusing to let me talk to him because she said I'd upset him. Her insistence laced with guilt, the ever-constant reminder of what happened, whose fault it was, and how it made us into the people none of us wanted to be. How I was ducking my head down, finger to my other ear, so I could hear her. The flash of the cameras still in my eyes like a thousand bright lights glittering at once. The weight of the game still heavy in my mind highlighted by all the opportunities I couldn't convert into goals. My teammates behind me, Dyson with his loud mouth and shitty attitude, which I was trying to tune out completely.

And I didn't see the kid.

I wish I had.

I know how it feels to hope and want and dream . . . and then to live that dream but at so many costs.

"Once the public turns the tide against you, you'll have a helluva time getting them back."

"And what about you, Finn? Has the tide turned against me with you?"

His eyes hold mine as he chews his gum with vigor, but he doesn't voice the fucking thoughts I can see in his eyes.

"Really?" I ask, exasperated and disappointed when I shouldn't be either anymore. "You've been with me since the get-go. Represented me right out of college through the trades and renegotiations of my career. It's been twelve years and now . . . now, you want to walk away because I'm having a tough time?"

I walk toward the window. There's a world beyond this hockey arena, but it's not like I can see it. I've lived my life with one goddamn goal since the accident, one goal since being traded to the LumberJacks two years ago, and now with time running out, it's the only goal I can focus on. It fuels the anger that's always been there but has now surfaced. The guilt that owned me but now eats away at me. The tears that threaten burn bright, but I blink them away as I try to find my way back to the man I used to be months ago, all the while knowing he doesn't matter.

He never has.

"And that history is why I'm standing here asking what's going on with you."

"I didn't snub that kid intentionally. You know that's not me. I wouldn't have—"

"I don't know much these days other than it seems you have your head up your ass," he says and folds his arms over his chest.

"There used to be a time you defended me. There used to be a time when you stood up for your clients. Seems to me you now love chasing after everybody in a jersey with potential to maintain that name of yours instead of taking care of those who you stand on top of to make that name of yours glow in neon."

He winces, but he doesn't bite with the anger I was hoping for. "I've got three sponsorships waiting to be yanked from you with one more fuck-up, Maddox. I have management calling, asking me why their captain—*my client*—is the problem and not the solution here. They want me to tell them what's eating you and to figure it the fuck out because if you don't, your upcoming contract negotiations won't be pretty."

"Ah, the threats. The bait and switch to lower my contract when any other team out there would kill to have me." My words are straight bullshit, because I don't want to play anywhere else. I want to be here, with the LumberJacks. I want to be on a team where hockey rules the management's decisions instead of money like so many of the big teams.

And more than anything, I want to be known as the star who turned down those huge contracts to play for the *Little Engine That Could* Team and then helped win that team a Stanley Cup.

I have my reasons. But he's never cared to ask what they are.

As if on cue, my phone alerts a text, and I don't even bother to look. I don't acknowledge its buzz. I already know the gist of what it's going to say and *fuck*, the last thing I need right now is to see how I've disappointed one more person.

"If you don't like the threats, then how about Hunter fucking Maddox shows back up, huh? He's been missing for the past three or four months and this angry, spiteful asshole in front of me is someone I can't quite figure out."

"Can't figure out or don't care to so long as I'm bringing in the cash? There are guys out there doing far worse with a lot less threats and consequences."

"But you're Hunter Maddox. You're the guy the National Hockey League hung its hat on to bring it back from the strike and subsequent lockout."

"They sure as fuck did," I counter, "so how about you remember that and start giving me the benefit of the doubt."

"When you start jeopardizing my other clients with your acts of stupidity like a roid-raged asshole, I have no choice but to put them first."

My hands clench and the unrelenting anger and hurt and confusion that's toyed with my mind over the past few months, hell, *the past season*, fights just beneath the surface.

Obligations.

Guilt.

Responsibilities.

"Good to know where you stand. Is this conversation over? Is the *let's tell Hunter he's an asshole lecture* complete?" I ask, not giving a shit if it is or isn't.

"Sure. It's done. Let's not make it a *let's tell Hunter if he pulls more shit like this again, I can't be his agent* lecture."

His words hit my ears, their gravity, their *everything*. "You threatening me, Finn?"

He holds his hands up. "Just telling it like it is."

It's my turn to laugh. The sound is riddled with disbelief and a healthy dose of *fuck you.* "I'm one of the first clients you ever signed—one who took a chance on you when you were wet behind the ears and no one else would—and you threaten to drop me after all these years, just like that?"

"Something has to snap you out of this funk." His eyes are clear, his voice serious, but he has no clue *this funk* feels like it's permanent.

"Threats don't do it for me."

"Everyone has a line they have to draw in the sand, and one more stunt is mine."

"Good to know." I stare at my agent, the person I thought was my friend, and wonder when the fuck he became a greedy asshole who was only out for himself.

Then I wonder if I even care, because it's hard to find any emotion these days other than anger.

And without another word, I leave.

1

Dekker

MELODRAMA AT ITS FINEST.

It's the only thought that runs through my mind when I take a seat at the conference table in the back office of Kincade Sports Management.

Brexton sits with her arms crossed over her chest, and her resting bitch face in full effect. Her foot bounces where it's crossed over her knee, and she scrolls through her phone with complete disinterest.

Chase sits ramrod straight, her business suit crisp and pressed and everything else about her perfectly styled to match. Christ, even the leather cover of her notepad matches. Perfection in a sickening fashion.

Lennox inspects her fingernails. They're too long and too red, but I'm sure she has her reasons for looking like she wants to claw someone's eyes out with them.

Let's hope this time, it's not mine.

I sit back and wait and watch and wonder.

Aren't we all the perfect picture of disdain? I'd rather be anywhere—anywhere, like even shopping—than sitting right here with them right now. I'm more than sure they feel the same way.

Thrilled was the last thing we all probably felt when we got the call to be here.

My competitors.

My rivals.

"Ladies." Kenyon Kincade's voice rumbles when he walks into the room. Our heads turn and only two of us nod in response, but all of us watch him.

The same paranoia that has me questioning why he'd invite the chaos by inviting us all in here at the same time, has me eyeing his movements closely. Is he moving slower? Is there something wrong with his health?

Fear tickles its way up my spine in a way I've never known before.

"Thank you for coming." He clears his throat and takes his time taking a sip of his coffee, hissing when it scalds his tongue. "I know it's a rarity for you to all be in the office together, but humor this old man in wanting his four daughters in one place, at the same time."

Brex bites her tongue while waiting for him to get to the point. Patience has never been her strong suit, and he takes note of it with a nod of his own.

"Why did you ask us to all be here, Dad?" Taking the lead as per usual, I ask the question we're all wondering.

"I've made a lot of mistakes over the course of my life. Even more so when your mother died, when I was left alone at thirty-something to raise four girls without much experience. I did the best I could, but by the way you guys prefer not to be in the same place together at times, it feels like my best wasn't good enough."

"That's not true."

"Then what is it, Lennox?" He calls her out. "Why can't the four of you get along?"

I think of the years of competition for his attention. A single dad with clients we felt were more important than we were at times. Not by any fault of his own, but more because of his caring nature. We wanted his attention. We lived for it.

And the bittersweet taste of being the oldest still stings. Stepping in to be a mom at fifteen when you're not the mom, fosters a lot of resentment. Telling your siblings what needs to be done inside a house ruled by estrogen doesn't exactly make for long-term peace.

Lennox flips a lock of hair over her shoulder and meets his eyes for the first time. The only man who can tame her constant snark and fiery temper. "We can get along just fine." There's a muffled snort somewhere, and I fight not to look up and glare down whoever it is . . . because I'm not the mom, and I never wanted to be.

"You fight like cats and dogs," he says.

"And we love like lions," she says and we all snicker. "We're just very different people."

His laugh is boisterous and takes us all by surprise. "Maybe it's because you are all so much alike."

When each of us physically bristle at the thought of actually being like the other, he holds his hands up to stop us. "Sanderson is killing us."

The name of our rival agency.

"As in Finn Sanderson?" Brex asks. "What do you mean?"

He purses his lips and takes his time meeting each of our eyes before he speaks. "Twelve clients over the past year. That's what he's taken from us. I'm not sure if he's undercutting our commission or if he's stroking more than just their egos, but it's not acceptable to me."

And my father's tone says it all—he's worried.

Shit.

"Are we in trouble?" Brexton asks, concern weighing down her voice as she sits forward in her seat. "Is something wrong?"

He looks to where his hands are clasped in front of him and his pause in response sets the mood.

"Dad? Is everything okay?" I ask, my voice shaky as worst-case scenarios fill my head. Is he sick? Is he hiding something from us? He's been the unbreakable pillar of strength to this family. Slayer of Boogie Men and the King of Bear Hugs for teenage broken hearts. He's been my strength in dark moments, and I can't imagine him anything other than redoubtable . . . larger than life. But not now.

When he looks up, his smile is forced, his eyes somber, and that feeling of dread settles in me again. "It's fine. I just . . . this is all I have to give you girls—this company, my reputation . . . *each other.*" He twists his lips and nods. "And lately, it feels like I've done a bad job at fostering and preserving all of it."

We all meet eyes across the table. While the four of us may be fiercely competitive, Brexton was right—we love like lions and will fight to the death to protect each other. By the looks on my sisters' faces, right now is one of those times.

"Is it because of your doctor's appointment the other day?" Lennox asks, disquiet flooding every syllable, as she voices the one thing I think we're all wondering but are afraid to put words to.

"We need to take care of Sanderson." It's all he says, and a quick glance at Lennox tells me she's just as worried as I am.

"I think your meaning to that term and my meaning are very different," Chase says, blasé as can be, when I know the simple mention of her ex-boyfriend has what he did to her flooding back and boiling her blood.

"Don't worry, Chase. We'll post your bail," Brexton murmurs.

While we all laugh, it's our father's lack of response that's most noticeable. He takes his time sweeping his gaze around the table, making sure to stop on each one of ours in that way he has that tells us he's about to say something profound like he used to do when we were kids and he wanted to make us feel like adults.

He stops when those bright blue eyes stop on mine. "What is it, Dekker?" he asks as I twist my lips in thought and mull over my assumptions.

"*Of course, he asks Dekk,*" Lennox says to the singsong tune of my other sisters murmuring, "His favorite one," like they used to do when we were kids.

"You're just jealous," I say with a megawatt grin to annoy them.

"Jealous of your shoe collection, maybe," Chase teases.

"Ladies," my dad warns. "You have the floor, Dekker."

I clear my throat and speak. "Obviously the gloves are off when it comes to stealing our clients. Sanderson doesn't give a shit about decorum or professional courtesy or—"

"—or anything else other than money or how far her legs are spread."

If I were taking a sip, I would have spit out the water in reaction to Chase's remark. It's a rarity to see any kind of emotion from her, so I nod slowly in response. She's still hurting all this time later. "That too."

"You're the dork who dated the competition," Lennox says and rolls her eyes as we all laugh. I nudge Chase, hoping Lennox's comment will ease some of the anger in her eyes, and am glad when a smile creeps onto her lips.

"What are you thinking?" my father asks me, attempting to bring us back to the topic at hand.

"If he has no morals and he's a prick—"

"A savvy prick," he adds.

"Exactly. So why can't we be the same way? As much as I want back the clients he stole from us, we need to think bigger than that." I tap my pen against my pad. "Maybe we all work together and try to land a huge name."

"As much as I'd like that"—he shakes his head and chuckles soft-ly—"I'm not quite sure you four working together in that capacity is a wise move. Remember the last time we tried that?"

Brexton shifts uncomfortably, as Dad glances to the wall to his right where the hole in the drywall from her fit of rage has long been patched up. We've since banned paperweights from the office.

"I think we should steal his clients in turn," I suggest.

Lennox snorts, and the sound about sums up everything about the suggestion: it's impossible, it's ludicrous, *it's freaking genius.*

Plus, it's the easiest thing to say—I'm going to steal some of the top athletes in the world away from their current representation as a *fuck you*—but implementing it is a whole other ball game.

But the slow crawl of a smile across my dad's mouth tells me he was thinking the same thing. "Agreed. Fighting fire with fire is the only option . . . especially when it comes to him."

"What did you have in mind?" Brex asks.

"I think we should tackle this on four fronts. Each one of you with an athlete to win over to our side," he says.

"Besides more clients, what's this going to prove?" Lennox asks, despite it being obvious to me.

"People look at you and they can't help but notice your overall appeal. They see the former beauty queen"—he looks at Lennox—"the Olympic athlete"—then Brexton—"the girl who graduated top of her MBA program"—then Chase—"and the lawyer"—he meets my eyes—"and they forget the most important thing of all, that my four girls are just as damn dogged, professional, unflinching, and successful as their old man was."

"*Was?*" I catch the word immediately.

"Is." He waves a hand my way without meeting my eyes. "Slip of the tongue."

"Dad—"

"You have all been successful recruiting clients thus far, but it's always been under the umbrella of my name. It's always been my company. Now I think it's time you make Kincade Sports Management yours."

Silence falls as each one of us wonders why this sudden push, and I hate the answers I assume.

"Should we assume you have it all planned out as per usual?" Chase asks, making Dad's smile widen and the sadness clear from his eyes.

"Of course, I do," he says. "We divide and conquer. When have you ever known me not to have it all worked out?"

He always does.

"What do you need from us?"

His grin is lightning quick, and it's the first true glimpse I've seen of my tenacious, work-addicted dad since he walked in here.

"You're up first, Dekk." He looks to my sisters as they start their singsong "you're the favorite one" again. "I'll get to you next, but yours"— he points a finger my way—"might be making it easier on us with his current antics."

Current antics?

Words no sane agent ever wants to hear.

Shit.

This is not going to be good.

2

Dekker

"HUNTER MADDOX."

Definitely not going to be good.

Every single nerve in my body reacts viscerally to the two words that fall from my father's lips.

Thoughts run rampant as I try to process what he's implying. As I try to fathom how he could think I'd be the right person for the job when Hunter's the one who broke my heart.

But how would he know? Texts late at night telling me where to meet and when. Quick romps in hotel rooms when we happened to be in the same city at the same time. Zero promises given of anything more than the physical. How would anyone know when I played our whole sexcapade off as a casual thing I had no attachment to?

Even to Hunter, himself.

But I'm looking at my father, and he's not backing down.

"This is a joke, right? You're playing with me?" I ask in a half-laugh, half no-damn-way tone.

"I wish I were." At least there's contrition in his voice when he says it, and I wonder if in his father-sense he has an inkling that my casual dating of Hunter had grown into something more in my heart. "I know you two had a thing a way back and—"

"A *thing?*" I snort, realizing I'm reacting off my own emotion and not from something he knows. His lifted eyebrows say as much. "Yes. Sure. Something like that."

"I saw you talking to him at the ESPY's a few months back. I didn't realize there was bad blood between you."

Not bad blood.

More like unresolved feelings.

"This is just a bad idea all around."

"Personally or professionally?" And it's that tone—the one that says I need to suck it up, be tough, and professional—that's a reprimand in itself, but I don't respond. I'm busy wondering how I'm going to make a man, who despite aggravating me in all other ways, devastated me sensually and brought out an explosive sexuality I never really knew I had, come over to Kincade Sports Management. "Any way you look at it, Dekk, he's one we have to have."

"Why?" It's one word but it's loaded with so much tension.

"Because this is his year."

"His year to what?" I snort. "Be an ass and ruin what he has going for him?"

"To win the Stanley Cup."

"I disagree—"

"Hear me out," he says with his hands up. He speaks quietly, and that tells me he's put way more thought into this than I have. "Hunter's been in the NHL for twelve years. Ten with various teams and then the LumberJacks came along and decided to build their hopes on him because he's that freaking good."

"They can build their hopes on whoever they want, but it doesn't mean it's going to happen." I rise from my seat and pace the room as I think. "There's that thing with the kid in the wheelchair the other day. The one he snubbed. There are rumors about fights in the locker room with teammates. That management isn't happy. That—"

"So, you have been keeping tabs on him."

My feet falter as I let his words settle in the room, because anyway

I respond means I'm on the defensive when I shouldn't be about a man I don't care about.

"I keep tabs on a lot of athletes."

"I see," he says in that fatherly way that is part all-knowing, part maddening, and nothing I want to address. "The question is why is he acting out? Why has he had an excellent career with a pristine reputation for almost twelve years and then all of a sudden he doesn't?"

"I'm not a psychologist, Dad."

"No"—he leans forward in his seat—"but you know him better than anyone else in this office."

Shit.

He's right in every aspect, and yet I want to argue and reject his theory because I've moved on and don't want to revisit a man who broke my heart.

"Make Lennox go after him," I say, offering up my sister while at the same time hating that she might. "Give me a different athlete to bring over." Panic flutters in my chest at the mere mention of Hunter and the vivid memories of him that might still fill my fantasy bank.

"Hunter and Lennox?" He chuckles. "The two of them together would be oil and water."

"Well, so were we," I throw back as I attempt to fathom why my dad would ever assume I'd be the right one to go after Hunter.

More like a match to gasoline.

But oh, that one time with oil was so damn fun.

"We can use your history with him to our advantage."

"Using it to *our* advantage is one thing. What about what it means for me?" I ask, giving away what I was hiding—that he meant more to me than casual.

Snapshots of memories flicker through my mind like a tape reel. Volatile and deliciously addictive sex always highlighted—or rather low-lighted—by our inability to remain civil to one another. And despite that, I still fell for him. I still wanted to try to have something more with him.

He still let me walk away from him without a word.

"He's who we need, kiddo," my dad says, ripping me out of the documentary in my head. "Statistically speaking, he's phenomenal. He's angling to surpass records—goals, assists. He's one of the fastest on the ice out there and his stick-handling skills are unrivaled."

"You forgot that he's an asshole." I smile sarcastically.

"Aren't we all in some way or another?" He raises his brows and returns the same smile. "Look, if he stays injury-free, he might just be one of the next greats. And having him as a client could be a huge draw for us."

"Or he could implode and we could be stuck scrambling to salvage his career."

"Then let's swoop in and save him from doing that because, sure as hell, Sanderson isn't."

"It's not that easy."

"It is, Dekk. He's coming up for a contract negotiation after this season that could net him a substantial pay increase. Pair that with his poor conduct and his closing in on some long-standing records, and we could help him get there. *You* could help him get there. I've watched him, admired him, for a lot of years, but lately, I can tell he's struggling."

"I am not a nursemaid, Dad."

"Don't I know it." His chuckle fills the room. "I'm not asking you to be one. All I'm saying is visit him. Talk with him. Travel with the team during their next road stretch and see if you can figure it out. Sell him on the fact that you understand him when it seems Sanderson is just a stat chaser these days—picking up clients with the brightest stars, not necessarily the most talent. And you know what happens to bright stars."

"They burn out."

He nods, his eyes holding mine as they turn serious. "We can assert that he'll receive more by going with us. Drop names, and give him examples of the contracts we've increased during negotiations."

"And that's why you think he'll leave Sanderson?" I snort. "The only effect my appearance will have is him walking the other way."

Or wanting to have sex. And that just can't happen, not if we're to have a professional relationship as my dad is sitting here telling me we need to have.

"You underestimate yourself, Dekker. You always have."

Silence falls as our eyes hold. The hum of my sisters chatting in the main office filters through to us in muffles, but it's him that holds me rapt.

"Dad? What's going on? Is the business in trouble? Was everything okay at the doctor's the other day? I mean . . . where is this all coming from?"

His smile is slow and soft, much like his voice when he speaks. "It's just time for you guys to step up. Nothing's wrong," he says, but I don't believe it. "Make sure you go in with a game plan. Don't underestimate Hunter. You need—"

"Trashing bars, fights with teammates, snubbing kids . . . *can't wait.*" I sigh.

"And he's been the NHL's MVP two years running, so I think this year is his to win the Hart Memorial Trophy. You keep pointing out the bad, but none of it is affecting his success on the ice. Find out what has affected his behavior off the ice. That's not like him, and you know that."

He's right. I do know that. *I've never seen him ignore a fan before. Especially a kid.* But I can't get emotionally involved. Not again.

"Right now, you need to focus on getting your stuff packed and making travel arrangements," he says as he pushes his chair away from the table.

"*What?*"

"You heard me. You'll have plenty of time to think about how you're going to approach him on your flight to Chicago tonight."

"Tonight?" I say the word but it takes me a second to digest it.

"Yes, tonight."

"You expect me to just pick up and go, like that?" I ask, like this is something new and I haven't done it before in the past. But this is Hunter we're talking about. This is my secret weakness and my silent heartbreak. "I have plans with Chad tonight. His work event is a very big deal. I can't just—"

"Yes, you can. I'm sure he'll understand." His smile is tight and his expression is stern. "It's not like he bends any of his business obligations for you."

"And there's the dig," I mutter.

He stops in his tracks and turns to face me. "Not a dig, at all. He's just a man who'll never commit, and for the life of me I can't figure out what you see in him. He's successful and handsome if you go for that sort, which you usually don't—"

"Which sort is that?"

"The kind who doesn't like to get his hands dirty." He holds my glare. "He may look the part, honey, but I don't see a single ounce of fire in your eyes when you're together. If you want to be friends, be friends, because he sure as hell is *friends* with a lot of people."

"My life. My business," I say in warning, but hate the pang I feel knowing he thinks I'm settling. Companionship should be okay in any form . . . even if it's a few nights out a month, some nice dinners, some mechanical-esque type sex. The kind of relationship—and I use that word very loosely—where commitment has never been discussed nor really wanted.

"True. Your business. I'm sure Chad will understand. It's not like he hasn't done the same to you for his job before." He grabs the handle to the door. "Like I said, you should have no problem making that flight tonight to catch the LumberJacks game." He opens the conference room door and looks back over his shoulder. "Good luck."

3

Hunter

DAD: *Sloppy play tonight. You're not controlling the team like a captain should. Your shot percentage has taken a nosedive. Your assists went up but nowhere near what your brother's were.*

4

Dekker

IT NEVER FAILS ME.

The excitement of a game and the roar of the crowd never fails to boost my mood, clear my mind so I can think, and give me that rush of adrenaline to remind me why I love my job.

The crowd bustles inside the sports bar, The Tank. Drinks flow freely while all the TVs are tuned to ESPN. The talking heads on SportsCenter are promising highlights of the game I just watched in person after the break.

"Is it true the teams come hang out here after games?" a twenty-some-thing asks as she sidles up beside me on the barstool. Her dress is Lycra and hugs every glorious curve of her body, no doubt in the attempt to catch the attention of one of the players.

Someone will definitely bite, especially after the high of tonight's win.

"It's rumored this is the bar the visiting teams frequent, yes," I mur-mur and give her a smile, when I know damn well they'll show. Callum already confirmed he'd meet me here. Where he goes, they all go.

"Have you ever met them? I mean, I love hockey—like, *love it*—but the players are a whole other sort of obsession. And the Jacks have so many hot guys. I mean, what I'd give to . . ." Her words trail off as her desperation comes through. Every part of me wants to let her know they'll use her for the night and never call despite the promise to. But one look at her again and I realize she already knows this and is okay with it.

There's no use being overprotective when she's obviously walking in willingly.

"They're pretty cool guys. Fun to party with, not so much fun to date."

A raucous cheer goes up in the bar followed by a cold rush of air as the doors open. I don't turn to look but between the rise in chatter and Lycra girl's sudden fluffing of her hair, I know the New Jersey LumberJacks have arrived.

I don't turn to watch them give high fives to their overeager fans hoping for a few seconds with their heroes or the women hoping to get more than that with their short skirts and tight tops. They'll make their way to the back corner where they can monitor those coming in and out of their space so if fans get a bit overeager, security can cut it off.

The Tank is known for its dark beer, its unfettered access to the hockey players, and its carefree atmosphere.

All those things good and bad, depending on the night.

I keep my attention on SportsCenter and appreciate the quick service of another glass of wine.

"Should I worry that you're showing up in person?" a deep tenor says beside me as a hand grips my shoulder and squeezes.

"Callum Withers." My smile is genuine as I take in my client's grin and the red mark marring his cheekbone from his fistfight in the game tonight. "Someone has to come and scold you for getting in schoolyard fights."

"Just part of the job, *Mom*." His chuckle is infectious and at complete odds with the severity of his features—dark colors and sharp lines.

"Is that so?"

"Yep." He holds a finger up to the bartender and doesn't have to even say what he wants, his regular status here when they're in town ensuring immediate service.

"You enjoy all that time in the penalty box?"

"Dickman's a dick. It's even in his name," he says, referring to the member of the opposing team he traded punches with on the ice earlier. "He had it coming to him for blindsiding Hunter on that play. It was uncalled for and total bullshit slashing him like that."

"It was definitely dirty," I say, glancing over his shoulder to where the rest of the team is, looking for the man in question.

"Everything that asshole Dickman does is dirty." He snorts and takes a sip of his beer. "So, tell me why you're making house calls when we're on a road trip. There has to be a reason."

Yeah. One I don't want to acknowledge.

5

Hunter

UNABASHED.

Unyielding.

Uninhibited.

Those three words describe the woman sitting at the end of the bar to a goddamn T.

I take in her black high heels, her pale pink sweater and black slacks, and the sweep of her pale hair sitting atop her head. She's elegant but feisty, gorgeous but unassuming, composed but so damn infuriating . . . and nothing if not all-business.

And not a single one of those things diminishes the firsthand knowledge I have of every inch of her body.

Dekker Kincade.

Jesus, even my balls draw up at the thought, sight, and memory of her.

But I stop mid-sentence, mid-lift of my beer to my mouth, mid-everything when I catch sight of her sitting at the bar, talking to Callum. Sure, her back is to me, but I would know that curve of her shoulders in a heartbeat.

"There a problem?" Frankie asks.

I shake my head and turn back toward him, trying to remember what the hell I was saying but find myself at a loss.

Damn Dekker.

She always did have a way of owning my thoughts when I'm not a guy to be owned by much of anything other than hockey . . . and family.

But my eyes slide back to where she's sitting. I hate the way Callum's hand rests on the back of her chair and how he throws his head back and gives that cheesedick laugh that's too loud and not real.

Yeah, he's her client, but it's not a hard jump to assume he'd fuck her if given the chance.

Hell, every damn guy in this place would.

I know. I'm one of the lucky bastards who have.

Lucky? Is that the right word, because I've seen her for a whole five minutes and the shit that the sight of her has stirred up is insane.

Over-the-top sex. Hours on end of never being able to get enough. An intensity as she stared at me from the hotel doorway and told me our . . . *friends with benefits* had run its course.

I convinced myself it was because she had found someone new.

I pretended I didn't care.

But fuck if seeing her sitting there right now doesn't tell me otherwise. It's been almost three years since . . . since the end of whatever we were, but seeing her now, I remember every sigh, every moan, every goddamn thing.

And hell if I'd complain about getting lost in her again for a few hours.

I try to focus on what Frankie is bullshitting about, but my mind and eyes keep going back to her. Back to what we left unfinished and to my sudden need to see her again, talk to her again . . . to see if she's feeling that same damn attraction still.

"Right?" Frankie asks, pulling my attention back to him. Fuck I'm being a prick to him.

"Yes. Right. I—uh . . . I see someone I need to talk to."

Without waiting for a response, I make my way across the bar. It's packed tonight with an abundance of puck bunnies wanting attention and lots of guys buying us drinks to celebrate the victory.

It should be sad the visiting town is excited when we beat the hometown team, but our run has been insane lately, and fans always like bandwagons to jump on.

"Hell of a game, Maddox," is yelled to my right, and I lift my beer in acknowledgment but keep my course.

"Withers." Callum looks up when I call my teammate's name and lifts his chin in greeting before continuing whatever it is he's telling Dekker. "Maysen needs you," I say when he finishes.

"About?" He meets my eyes, but I don't give Dekker a glance.

"Hell, if I know, but he's looking for you," I lie.

Impatiently, I wait a few seconds for him to wrap shit up with Dekker, all small talk, and then slide onto the barstool beside her after he vacates it.

Lifting my finger to Donnie, the bartender, I motion for another beer and then tip the bottle toward Dekker's glass to ask for a refill for her too.

"You're a long way from home it seems," I murmur as her subtle perfume—summer and sunshine—fills my nose.

"Just doing my job." Her voice, *Christ*, it's soft with a hint of a rasp and feels like fingernails faintly scraping over my skin.

"What? No, *go to hell?* No, *drop dead, Maddox?* No, *what hotel room can we find so we can use every surface?*" I turn to look at her now. Those dark brown eyes a little too big for her face but in all the right ways. Her soft lips and straight nose with a row of freckles dotting across the top of it. But I know better than to be fooled by those freckles. I know Dekker Kincade is a straight-up sex goddess that may have on occasion made me want to beg for more. I'm not ashamed to admit it. "You feeling all right?"

"Funny," she says with a roll of her eyes.

"I try." I hit the side of her knee with mine. "You're here for work and not pleasure, then?"

She lifts a lone eyebrow and a ghost of a smile paints those lips of hers. "It's always about work."

"Not when it came to us, it wasn't."

"There was no us," Dekker asserts, and I snort in response.

My chuckle is low and knowing and the way she adjusts her shoulders tells me she knows what a lie that is. "You're right. There was no incredible sex. No nail marks down my back. No bite marks on my collarbone." I shrug. "I don't know about you, Dekk, but I think we did pretty good in the pleasure department."

"Too bad we couldn't seem to master the playing nice part when it came to everything else."

"Maybe volatility is our thing," I say, the adjective the only way to describe us in the bedroom. Volatile in desire. Volatile in need. Volatile in temper. "Remember that rooftop bar in Los Angeles?" I ask, knowing she does. "It was a hot summer night. You were in that little sundress and we stowed away to the corner of the patio. I had to put my hand over your mouth to muffle your moans so we didn't get caught." I hum in appreciation of the memory. "God, that was hot."

She averts her eyes and shakes her head ever so slightly, but she doesn't refute me. She remembers how incredible that night was—the sex on the rooftop, the thrill of not getting caught, the sex at the hotel that followed. It was the only time we had met someplace other than a hotel room, and it left me wondering why we didn't do it more often.

She ended things the next time we met up.

"You played well tonight."

Her voice draws me back to the present. I smirk at her attempt to change the topic and lean down so my lips are near her ear. "You can sit here looking all prim and proper and professional, but I know your panties are getting wet and the ache is burning a little brighter, because you remember just how damn good it was and how damn good we were."

She clears her throat and shifts in her chair to unsuccessfully gain some distance from me and turns to look at me without an ounce of fluster in her expression.

"You played well tonight," she repeats.

My grin widens. *That's how she wants to play this?* She wants to act like seeing each other doesn't cause old embers to spark? She wants to act like a tiny part of her doesn't want to revisit that? Then again, she's the one who walked out and ended things, not me. And yet . . . the fact that she's acting like there was nothing between us bugs the shit out of me. I've never forgotten her.

Has she forgotten me?

I lean back and cross my arms over my chest and take my time responding as I struggle with the need for her to remember. "How I played? That's subjective."

"Subjective?" She laughs and the sound slices through the sexual tension that's as automatic now as it used to be when we shared the same space. "Two goals. Three assists, and you had one hell of a block to help Katzen when he was recovering from his first block. But you know, it's *subjective*." She rolls her eyes and pulls a laugh from me as my eyes roam down the sweater and its V-neck that shows nothing but hints at everything.

Damn.

"But I missed more than I made," I say and realize we're actually being civil to each other when normally we're at odds.

The crowd cheers as a highlight of one of my goals is shown on the closing credits of SportsCenter. I glance around at the crowd, at my teammates who are milling about, and try to figure out why she's here.

Because I know it's not for me.

"So you're here, why?" I ask. "You miss me that much?"

A shadow glances through her eyes and as quickly as it's there, it disappears. "Don't flatter yourself."

"Oh, it's official business then." Our eyes hold for a beat. "I can help you mix pleasure with that business."

She tips her glass toward me. "Thanks for the drink, but—"

"Keep your money." I push the cash she's sliding across the bar top back toward her. "And your attitude."

"That was a new record. Us being civil." Her smile in response is all snark. "It was good seeing you."

I grab her wrist to prevent her from walking away. "Back to that again?"

"Back to what?" She pulls her arm back but remains where she is.

"You walking away without an explanation."

Her glare is enough to tell me she gets the dig. That she remembers just as clearly as I do that last time we were together. "I wasn't aware my presence here in Chicago meant I owed you an explanation."

She's sexy when she's stubborn. She always has been. Maybe I forgot just how much . . . or maybe the years have added to her confidence and her confidence merely adds to everything about her.

"So let's see," I say, completely ignoring her comment and loving that it's pushing her buttons. "You're working, but you weren't in the clubhouse before or after the game like I've seen you do in the past." I lean back in my stool and study her. "You have clients on the team, but you're not partying with the team." I chuckle. "You're flying under the radar. That means you're here trying to steal someone."

"Who died and made you the Jacks' official detective?"

"Private Dick reporting for duty." I give a mock salute and earn a glare from her. "And, babe," I say, strictly because I know it pisses her off, "you forget that I know you."

"I'm not your babe, you don't really know me"—I lift a brow at that but she just continues—"and I prefer the word *recruit*."

"Recruit. Got it. Isn't that kind of like using the word borrow instead of steal?"

"More like asshole instead of prick," she says, but I don't buy the innocent flutter of her lashes for one second.

"I always did like that mouth of yours," I murmur as I tip my bottle of beer, but keep my eyes on hers.

"Are we done here?" she asks but makes no attempt to move, which answers my question. She *is* here for a player.

"So, you're not after Callum, since he's already your client." I stand up and crane my neck. "Maybe it's Heffner." I tip my beer to the other side of the bar where our burly defenseman is chatting it up with a few ladies. "Nah. He's not easily swayed and has a perfectly solid and long-term contract. Finch, then?" I ask. "He doesn't seem too happy with his agent, so I'm pretty sure if that's why you're here, the struggle to get him over to your side wouldn't be too tough."

"Thanks for the intel. I'll file it away in my need-to-know, but uh, who says I'm here scouting anyone?"

"You're here to get laid then?" I flash a grin and hold my arms out to my sides. "If that's the case, here I am."

"Don't flatter yourself." She takes her time uncrossing and then recrossing her legs, and I take in every long inch of them as she does.

"You're just here for the night then? Flew in from New York to catch a game, then sit at a bar and talk to the guys afterward, but you're—uh—not recruiting?"

There's the slightest hitch in her movement and it's her tell. She's definitely here to steal a client.

"Just came here to enjoy the atmosphere of a winning team, a player who's on top of his game"—she lifts her chin to me—"and get a break from the monotony of things for a bit."

"How's what's-his-name?" I ask, thinking of the guy I saw her with the last time I was in New York. Or was it at the ESPYs? Regardless, he was too slick, too pretty, and nothing like who she needs.

She was on his arm but her eyes were firmly on me.

Definitely not a match made in paradise, and I'm a dick for being happy about it.

"Well, considering I was supposed to be at his work event with him tonight." She shrugs with a lift of her eyebrows . . . but there's something more there she's hiding.

"So what? He can't adjust to his girlfriend's successful career because it reminds him he has a little dick?" The words come from nowhere, and I'm surprised by the pang of jealousy that hits me over the thought of them together.

She opens her mouth to defend him but her hesitation speaks volumes. "When my dad ordered me here, Chad decided—"

"Chad?" What kind of name is Chad?

"Yes. Chad," she says with a resolute nod. "He said he was sick of me putting work before him—"

"Probably like he does to you."

She takes a gulp of her wine. "So, he is no more."

"I'm sorry," I lie.

"No, you're not." She forces a smile. "You hated him."

"I never met him."

"But you still hated him. I could tell in the way you glared at him during the Corporate Cares Charity Gala when we ran into each other." She eyes me above the rim of her glass.

I laugh and tilt my head to the side. "You're right. I did hate him. He wasn't good enough for you."

That and I can't stand the idea of any other man touching you.

"Says the man who doesn't know him."

"I don't have to meet him. No one'll ever be good enough for you, Dekk," I say, our eyes holding. *Including me.*

"Not your business," she murmurs and her words hang in the unsettled air because fuck if there isn't so much unsettled between us. Like why she walked away. Like how I let her. "Besides, you know me, I suck at relationships."

"It wasn't relationship status, was it?"

She snorts. "Not even close."

And there's something about the way she says the words, almost as if she'd been trying to talk herself into believing it was more than whatever they thought it was for so very long, that she almost feels a relief that she can stop bullshitting herself now.

"So you came all this way to take a spin around my cock for old times' sake, then?" My words are meant to ease the tension—*partially*—and to see that gorgeous smile of hers.

"Yes. That's it." She sighs. "Do you really get women with lines like that?" she asks dryly.

"I don't have to speak and I get women."

"*Jesus*. And you wonder why we fought all the time." She rolls her eyes for good measure.

"We fought all the time, because you could never get enough of me and because I . . ." I falter over my words, because I prefer not to finish the thought. Maybe because I can't. Maybe because the truth is I was starting to feel things and those things were feelings . . . and feelings are bullshit.

"Because you, what?" she asks, her interest piqued. That slow crawl of a smile does things to my insides that shouldn't be legal.

I take a moment and let the topic die. The last thing I need to do is to get into shit that doesn't matter. How her walking away fucking sucked and was the closest thing I've ever felt to regret. How seeing her here right now is like a slap in the face of how good we were when we were good and how bad we were when we were bad and everything in between.

But more than anything is how she makes me feel, when every other fucking thing in my life is on dull fucking mute.

I look at the label on my beer as the crowd erupts into a Happy Birthday song on the other side of the bar, moving for a change in topic. "You're smart as hell, Kincade. You know if you're sitting in a bar full of Jacks, no one will think twice if any of us talk to you."

"That's your first mistake," she says, her voice low as she shifts to turn and face me. "No one is paying any attention to where I am or who I'm talking to."

My eyes drag over every seductive inch of her before returning to those eyes of hers. "You're a hard one to miss."

"I doubt that, considering half the women in this bar are showing about ten times more skin than I am."

"You don't have to show skin to be sexy, Dekk." My voice deepens and lowers with the words, and once again memories flicker to the forefront of my mind. Tangled bodies and unattached hearts. "We both know that."

She clears her throat and shifts in her seat. "You look good too."

"I look like something the cat dragged in. My cheek is sore from that stick I took to it. I'm limping like an eighty-year-old man from my knees hurting so bad . . . and I'm just all-around exhausted. This beer doesn't help with that, but you being here does."

6

Dekker

I STARE AT HIM. At his dark hair that's a little long, a little shaggy, but fits the man as a whole. At his bright blue eyes that look too closely, and his five o'clock shadow dusting across his jaw. Sure, his cheek is red from the hit he took, but there's something about him that makes you stare.

And savor.

All man, all arrogance, with a hint of boy beneath the surface who's living out his dream.

And he knows me way too well.

This beer doesn't help with that, but you being here does.

I choose not to acknowledge it.

I opt to ignore how it tugs on those feelings that seeing him—*and talking to him*—have drummed up.

The ones I feared would rear their ugly head when my dad told me who my client to win was.

"You do look a little rough around the edges," I say, because it's so much easier to notice the shadows under his eyes and the tension in his posture than to admit the punch in the gut I felt the minute I laid eyes on him. *As always.*

"Candor always was your blessing and curse," he murmurs as he shifts in his chair, and I take in the abrasions on his knuckles from tonight.

"It's why I'm good at my job. I know when to coddle versus when to push."

He chews the inside of his cheek as he surveys the members of his team on the other side of the bar. "So who are you here to push?"

"What's going on with you?" I ask, pushing his comment to the side and his need to know why I'm here. "Things good? Life outside of hockey good?"

He purses his lips and lifts his brows, but it's there for the briefest of seconds—a stutter. Was Dad right? Is Hunter's behavior of late unrelated to him simply being an asshole?

"What is it, Hunter?" I ask, reaching out to put my hand on his arm, sensing something is bugging him.

But his rare drop in his guard is replaced almost instantly. He makes a show of removing my hand, as he stands and places his own on the back of my barstool. My breath hitches as his fingers sweep ever-so-subtly against the skin on my neck. Chills chase over my flesh and I hate the visceral reaction my body has to it—to him. It's as if I still want him even though I know the havoc he'd wreak on my system.

He leans in so the heat of his breath feathers over my ear for the second time in this conversation, but I stand my ground and don't move. "How about I'll tell you what it is, when you tell me why you're here. And I know you won't do that . . . so my secret's safe for the time being."

I stare at him, at the cocky smirk that quickens my pulse, and shake my head. Now is not the time nor place to proposition him about KSM. I knew that coming tonight. I thought I'd hate him on sight after how we left things. But, no. It's not hate I'm feeling. *It's lust.*

"Hunter. I—"

"Ah, if it isn't the Ice King and the Frigid Queen," Katzen, the LumberJacks goalie says as he stumbles over and hangs an arm on the back of my chair where Hunter's just moved his from.

"Hey, Katz," I say but my eyes go right back to Hunter.

"Drunk as always," Hunter says and presses his palm against Katz's chest to push him back.

"Fuck yes, I am. We won. You rocked. I got a little playing time."

He laughs at his own joke considering as their goalie he was protecting the net, saving goals left and right, the entire game. "And shit—you are looking mighty fine tonight, Miss Kincade," he slurs as he draws out the word Miss.

The muscle in Hunter's jaw ticks, and I shake my head to try and stop him from acting on whatever darkness I see in his eyes. With his recent antics, I'm not exactly sure I trust he won't use force to move Katz away from me.

"I'm looking fine every night," I say with a wink, knowing the rumors about him and his drinking are more truth than fiction. Guys like Katz are a dime a dozen and working in this industry has taught me how to take care of myself and push back. "A good agent would remind you that hockey is your job, and that hangover you're angling for isn't going to help your stats any."

Katz makes a hissing sound. "Did you just burn me?" He laughs. "See? That's why we call you the Frigid Queen, cold as ice and not afraid to burn anyone at the stake."

"Dramatics get you nowhere." I chuckle to play off his moniker, but hate that it irks me.

Katz sets his empty glass down and looks from me to Hunter and then back. "You know? You guys make a cute couple. You should really do something about that. The two of you together. You and your captaining," he says, pushing on Hunter's shoulder then turning toward me, "and you and your bossiness." His laugh is obnoxious and over the top. "Like sleep together or make a porn or something hot like that . . . but then again, *coupling* isn't really Hunter's strong suit . . . but it could be *mine*."

In the morning he'll feel like an ass for hitting on me. I know this, he'll know this, but the tightening of Hunter's fists tell me his temper is flaring regardless. His forgiveness isn't as readily available as mine. And I'm not sure if I should be flattered or pissed at his overprotectiveness when he has zero claim on me.

"Hey Katz," I say and rise from my seat, going for shock value to deescalate the tension. "I'd say Hunter is the type to be more into *fucking* than *coupling* . . . and uh, how do you know we haven't already? Those memories of us together. On the kitchen counter. In the nightclub at Mandalay Bay. In the press box before a game." I groan overdramatically. "Those are what keep me satisfied on those cold, lonely nights."

"What?" Katz screeches, body jolting, as I put an arm around his shoulder.

"*Get real,*" I say and push him away playfully, refusing to meet Hunter's eyes, knowing one glance and Katz will know the truth. "I'd *never* sleep with a hockey player. They're all stick and no finesse. A discerning woman likes slow. She likes skill. She likes to know that once the goal is scored he still has more in the tank."

"Stick. Skill. Finesse," Katz murmurs.

"Damn straight. Stick. Skill. Finesse." I stand on my tiptoes and press a kiss to his cheek, my voice lowering as I say, "I've yet to find a hockey player who can deliver that."

"Maybe you've dated the wrong hockey players, then," Katz replies.

"Maybe I should be worried that you're more concerned with Hunter's between-the-sheets tendencies instead of his on-the-ice skills."

"Fuck off," he says with a wave of his hand but with a grin a mile wide. "I like you, you know that?" He nudges Hunter and shakes his head. "She gives as good as she gets."

Hunter bristles at the double entendre that Katz probably has no clue he managed.

"That's no way to talk to a lady, Katz. Remember what I said. *Finesse.*" I look around the bar and then back to the two men—one drunk and careless, the other tense and on edge. "It was a pleasure, gentleman, but I must be heading out. I expect to see that finesse on the ice next game."

"And you're here why?" Hunter asks with just the hint of a smile curling his lips. One that screams arrogance and sexiness and makes me wonder if he's trying to figure a way to get me back in his bed tonight.

No way.

No how.

This will be a strictly professional trip.

"I'm traveling with the team for the next however long. Call it customer maintenance." I shrug coyly. "That's why."

And without another word, I walk out of the bar with my head held high while holding on to tonight's small win.

Hunter Maddox came to me.

That's a start.

7

Dekker

I FEEL SO ALIVE as I walk the streets of Chicago. I stay among the crowds, milling around on my way back to the hotel.

My cheeks are cold but the chill isn't enough of a sting to ease the hurt from Chad's rant, which I really haven't had much time to process. I've been in go-mode since I left the office, what feels like days—not just hours—ago.

But his words linger. *"For what it's worth, you're cold-hearted, Dekker. Lack the sort of passion I want in a woman."* They hurt more than I'd like to admit.

First, him calling me cold-hearted and then Katz calling me the Frigid Queen. What the hell?

I haven't always been unresponsive. Uninspired. Passionless. But, I did realize that while I wasn't in love with Chad, I also wasn't *in like* with him either.

Maybe the thing with him was more of convenience.

Who knows.

I'm done.

We're done.

Life moves on.

The doorman to the Thompson Chicago greets me as I step into the lobby of the luxury hotel. The dark brown décor is the perfect mixture of modern and old-world with its reception desk on one side and its elegant bar on the opposite end of the massive space. Classical music plays softly in the background, accompanying the soft hum of chatter from the bar's occupants.

Glancing that way, I recognize a few players relaxing at the tables off to the right, and wave in greeting when one of them recognizes me.

"You good?" Heffner calls out.

"Yeah, thanks. Just tired. Good night, guys."

With my coat wrapped tightly around me, I head toward the bank of elevators and push the up button. It dings within seconds and after I enter the car and push my floor, a hand stops the door from closing.

"Hold up."

When I look up, I'm stayed by the intense eyes the color of the sky. I despise the thrill that shoots through me at the sight of him—at the complication of him—but it doesn't make the ache it leaves me with any less potent.

Crap.

He doesn't say anything as he steps beside me, but rather holds my eyes and leans a shoulder against the wall. I refuse to retreat.

The doors finally slide closed.

"You don't date hockey players?" he asks, repeating my words back to me, as he cocks his head to the side.

"Nope."

His chuckle is a low rumble that's equal parts smooth and rough and reminds me of what his hands on my body used to feel like.

"Nope?" He reaches out and tucks an errant lock of hair behind my ear. "I seem to remember you dating a hockey player before." He lowers his voice so it's a seductive whisper and takes a step closer to me. "The one whose memory and stick skills keep you satisfied on lonely nights."

I open my mouth and then close it, knowing there's absolutely nothing I can say to take back those comments. Even worse, I can't pretend those words were a lie . . . because they're not.

"Stick. Skill. Finesse." His eyes light up with so much more than humor when he stares at me. Desire swims with lust, and the sight of it shouldn't surprise me, but it unnerves me.

"I was just . . . I was putting Katz in his place."

"Was it true though? How exactly did my memory keep you satisfied on those lonely nights?" There's a ghost of a smile on his lips with an intensity in his eyes that demands an answer.

Sexual tension thickens in the elevator as a floor dings, the door opens, but no one gets on.

It doesn't matter if someone did though because nothing would break his focus on me.

And I feel it all the way to the apex of my thighs.

Memories of him—his skill, his prowess, his finesse—own my mind, and I can't divorce myself from them and the man standing before me.

No matter how much I tell myself I need to.

The urge to reach out and touch him is real, which I hate.

The door shuts.

"Not true," I murmur.

"Ah, that's where I think you're lying, Dekker." He closes the distance with another step. Our chests are all but touching as he braces himself, placing one hand on the wall beside my head. "Your lips and eyes aren't matching up there. Sure, you're telling me you don't think of me, but your eyes"—he emits a guttural hum in the back of his throat—"they're telling me you can't stop thinking about me . . . because as you know, I'm the triple threat."

"Triple threat?"

"All stick, all finesse . . . all *stamina*."

I roll my eyes at his macho, chest thumping. "See? That's why whatever it was between us never worked—"

"You mean sleeping together?" he asks.

"Yes. That."

"Can you not say it? Can you not say 'having sex with you,' because that's what we did." He leans in so his lips are near my ear, so one hand can trail a finger down the line of my jaw, and whispers, "We had a *lot* of sex. *Incredible* sex. *Mind-blowing* sex. *Incomparable* sex."

"Sex is sex," I lie as my nipples harden at the thought of us together, the palpability of our attraction still volatile in nature even all these years later.

"Not ours."

I lift a lone eyebrow to meet the dare in his eyes and know it's a mistake.

"Then I'll remind you."

His lips are on mine before I can process his words, a torrent of desire owning my thoughts—*and* my body.

Good sense tells me I should resist him, but the heat of his body and warmth of his tongue fires everything inside me that dear ole Chad never could.

Funny how I never noticed it until now.

Hunter's hands don't touch me, but stay positioned on either side of my head. His body doesn't meet mine, but brushes ever so subtly.

But his lips own mine. How they move, how they possess, how they control.

And as much as I want to say I'm helpless to the onslaught of desire they bring me, I also want to own every damn sensation they summon within me. The chills chasing, the adrenaline coursing, the ache simmering, and the desire mounting.

There's comfort in the familiarity and a thrill of newness simultaneously.

Need wars against want as he launches an all-out assault on my senses with his mouth.

The man can kiss.

How did I forget how devastating his lips were when they connected with mine?

"Dekker," he murmurs. The strain in his voice mirrors how I

feel—flustered and aroused, dashed with a mix of regret.

I lose track of my senses, of my resolve, and with lust leading my thoughts and the memory of him urging it along, my hands are on him. His chest. The back of his neck. His ass.

And it's maddening that his only reaction to my touch is to push and hold the door close button on the elevator so we're not interrupted. To pause this from ending but to do nothing to further it along.

Does he not feel this? The unsated need? The desperate desire? The damn *everything* that makes me want and need and not be ashamed in the least?

My hands are on the buckle of his belt.

On the button of his waistband.

On the zipper of his pants.

When I cup him, he groans into my mouth. When I slide my hand between the fabric of his underwear and begin to stroke the thickness of him, his entire body tenses, his hands fisting against the wall beside my head, and his lips faltering momentarily in their sensual destruction of mine.

I crave the feel of his hands on me.

It sounds so simple yet stupid, but Hunter knows how to touch a woman. My body remembers.

Because I've missed it.

His touch.

Him.

Touch me.

I stroke my hand up him and rub my thumb over the crest of his cock.

Want me.

The nails of my other hand score down his back through his shirt.

Take me.

The ding of the elevator shocks me to my senses, and the way that Hunter jolts back, has me looking toward the door in fear of being caught by a guest.

When I look back to him, he's tucking himself back into his pants, and the smirk on his lips is almost as taunting as his words. "Now you'll know how it feels. Now you know what it's like to watch *me* walk away." His chuckle is low.

"*What?*" I look up to meet his eyes, curious and darkened with desire neither of us can deny.

"Good night, Dekker. It was good to see you again."

When he strides out of the elevator, I stare after him with shock etched in every muscle of my body.

That shock morphs to embarrassment. The embarrassment churns to anger. That anger fuels self-loathing.

The dig is real, and the sting from it hits harder than it should.

But I caused this. He kissed me, yet I overstepped every damn line there is.

You almost just gave him a blowjob in the elevator.

I didn't, but my mind *was* there. The want *was* there. The goddamn urge *was* there.

I let the door close. I let the car ride to my floor. I let the doors open. All the while my mind reels, and my temper simmers from the utter mortification of what I just did.

Each step I take toward my room is emphasized by my thoughts.

How could I be so unprofessional?

Step.

How could I let him play me like that?

Step.

How could I let those unrequited everythings I feel when it comes to him resurface?

Step.

How could I be so weak?

Even worse, how can I stand here trying to put my key card in the door and question how I'm going to carry out my dad's professional wishes when they clash with my personal desires?

This is bad.

So very bad.

"This can't happen. You can't let this happen," I mutter as I move into the room. "We're not good together. We can't be good together. Not even for a night." *Shit. Shit. Shit.* "This was a huge mistake. Christ, the last time . . ."

I kick my heels off and fling them carelessly into the hotel room as my mental chastisement for what I almost let happen reigns.

For what I wanted to happen.

The last time . . .

I undress with trembling hands, and my need to take back everything that just happened owns my every thought.

But I can't. I know, I can't.

And I hate that a small, unprofessional part of me doesn't want to.

The last time . . .

Those three words keep repeating in my mind as I climb into the shower.

As I crawl into bed.

As I try to clear my head and not think about him when the taste of his kiss still lingers on my tongue.

The last time . . .

The last time almost broke me, because it was only after I walked away that I realized I'd fallen in love with him.

8

Dekker

3 years earlier

"DEKKER." HUNTER GROANS MY name and every part of me aches as he pushes his way into me.

Our fingers link and our bodies churn with a deep-seated burn that neither of us can put out. Time after time. Hookup after hookup.

We may be in a new hotel, in a different city than usual, but dammit, Hunter knows exactly what I need, and how I need it.

It's been a shit day. An even shittier week. And the only thing I looked forward to was this.

Him.

That thought scared the shit out of me but didn't deter me from showing up, and it sure as hell didn't prevent me from holding myself back when my heart constricted in my chest when he opened the door.

There's something different about tonight, though.

"Fuck. I needed this." A kiss to my lips. A grind of his hips. "I needed you." A pull out as his teeth nip my collarbone and the head of his cock slides along every damn nerve.

Something's definitely different.

Sure, the carnal hunger was there for our first round tonight. The clothes yanking, hands possessing, can't-get-in-me-quick-enough desperation that we thrive on.

But now—this second round—is so very different.

The sex has shifted. Less greed, more need. Less fervor, more finesse. Less guardedness, more vulnerability.

He moves in and out of me with silent strokes. His lips are on my skin, the heat of his breath against my ear.

When he pushes up and meets my eyes, gone is the usual cocky smirk. Gone is the humor that usually lights up his face. He's intense and serious, and my breath catches when our eyes hold and he moves.

There's an intimacy I'm not used to from him.

An intimacy I've slowly begun to crave and fear at the same time. One that spooks me and fulfills me in ways I'm too overwhelmed to contemplate in the moment.

So I avert my eyes. I lean up and take my own nip of his collarbone as I move my hands from his and scrape them up his flanks. "Let me ride you," I murmur into his ear as my hand slides between us and my fingers circle around him at the hilt of his cock and squeeze.

I take control, pushing us back into familiar territory. Into the physicality of our motions. Into the carnality of our movements.

He emits the sexiest groan when I turn my back to him, straddle his hips, and lower myself painstakingly slowly on top of him. He's heaven, hell, and everything in between as the stress of the week releases with each inch of him I accept until he bottoms out inside me. When I begin to rock my hips, I lose myself to him.

I lose myself to him.

His hands grab my hips and help guide me up and down.

I ignore the look in his eyes from moments ago and how being with him has made me feel lately.

Our moans fill the room, one after another.

And how wanting more from him scares the ever-living shit out of me.

I let my head fall back and we give ourselves over to the pleasure and desire and fall under its all-consuming haze.

Getting close to someone means getting hurt.

There are no sweet words whispered afterward. No soft kisses or snuggling.

This is how we are. We are *let's meet in a hotel somewhere*, work ourselves into an exhaustion of sexual satisfaction, and then part ways before we fight or spar or whatever it is we do that makes us want to get away from each other. But as I stare at myself in the bathroom mirror, there's a churning in my stomach and an ache in my heart.

This doesn't feel like enough anymore.

The question is, why?

I see my flushed cheeks and swollen lips. I see the truth staring right back at me.

I've fallen for Hunter Maddox. I've fallen for him when we agreed this was casual, when I don't let myself get close to anyone, and when he doesn't do relationships. I've fallen for him when we agreed to meet at hotels instead of our places so we'd prevent this from becoming routine or take the excitement out of it. I've fallen for him when I've never allowed myself to fall for anyone.

I'm an emotionally unattached girl. It's easier this way. It prevents the hurt of knowing it's going to end badly.

But his eyes . . . the way he looked at me. The tenderness in his touch when we're typically fire and brimstone and bruises and teeth marks . . . there's something more on his end too.

Panic sets in.

Full-blown panic . . . because this isn't us. This isn't what we agreed to. And hell, I'm looking at his actions through love-colored goggles so of course I'm going to read too much into everything. Of course I'm going to when I'm the one who went and fell.

I bring a hand to my chest as if it's going to allow me to catch my breath, when I know it's not going to do shit.

When I know falling for Hunter isn't going to make him want any more from me than the hot sex we find ourselves in. Even if he did, we'd crash and burn into an ugly mess before we even began.

How did I let this happen?

I take my time getting dressed. Each item of clothing I put on, I talk myself out of my revelation. I haven't fallen for him. This is just sex. We'd never work. He doesn't do relationships.

I almost believe it, until I walk into the room and see him. His pants are pulled on but unbuttoned, his chest is bare, and a bottle of beer is in one hand when he looks up to meet my eyes. Every part of me wants to go and kiss those lips, run my fingers through his hair, and tell him I want more with him. Six months flew by and doesn't seem like enough.

And then the truth is clear. My heart already hurts. My head is already spinning. The words I need to say—to tell him I've fallen for him—die without ever finding sound. He's not in this like I am. He's not ready for more.

His eyes narrow. "Where're you going?"

"I've got stuff to do," I stammer.

"Like . . ." He takes a few steps toward me.

I want to wake up next to you. At my place. At your place.

"Just things I forgot I needed to do. Deadlines."

I want to learn about what it is that clouds your eyes and makes you go quiet.

"Deadlines?"

I want quiet nights with a glass of wine and you beside me.

"Yes." I gather my things in measured movements, when all I want to do is shove them in the bag so I can rush out of here and let the tears fall. Even worse, I can feel the weight of his stare at my back, and I know he's standing there watching me and wondering.

"Hey? What's wrong?"

With a deep breath, I turn to face him. Standing a few feet before me, he's throwing a shirt on, his hair has fallen over his forehead, but his eyes home in on mine.

Tears burn as my thoughts tumble and fight against the want to say them and the knowledge that they'll only end in being hurt.

"Nothing." I offer a tight smile.

"Dekker?"

I shake my head and swallow over the lump of emotion lodged in my throat. "This was a mistake. *Again.*" He chuckles over this ongoing banter we always have. I don't sell the lie as well as I think I do, because his head tilts to the side. "But"—I look down to my purse strap in my hand and take a deep breath—"I don't think we can do this anymore." *Because I hate saying goodbye to you.* "We always said we'd know when this had run its course, and I think it finally has. You know, you and me and this." *Because it's easier to walk away now than to confess my feelings for you and be destroyed when you reject me.*

"What do you mean this has run its course?" He takes a step toward me.

"Just what it sounds like." I offer a laugh that has no resonance. My smile warms but only by sheer force when I take a step toward him. "Don't you think it's better to part ways now, like it is with us . . . actually liking each other?"

Confusion etches the lines of his face as he leans his hips against the dresser behind us. "If that's what you want."

Ask me to stay.

"I think it's for the best." I nod to reinforce my clipped words.

Tell me this is more than sex.

"Okay then." He runs a hand through his hair and blows out a breath that fills the room and suffocates my heart. "If you're sure. I mean . . ."

Agree that I forgot our rules—no emotions, no obligations—*and tell me you want more than this.*

In what feels like the hardest thing in the world, I step up and press a kiss to his cheek. I let his arms slide around me and pull me into him. It's the kind of bear hug that you can lose and find yourself in. It's the kind that tells you you're loved and that the person cares for you.

But his words don't come.

Not when he leans back and gives me that lopsided smile that makes my heart melt.

Not when I walk toward the door, my heart screaming to tell him the truth.

Not when I turn back one more time and look at him.

There's something in his eyes I can't make out, something I wish I could read, but I know I'm staring through jaded eyes. Eyes that want to believe he doesn't want me to leave for more reasons than the incredible sex. Eyes that want to believe he has feelings for me too.

Isn't that the irony though? I want him to feel about me how I feel about him, but if he did, if he professed how he wanted more, I'd run the other way.

I learned about love the hard way.

I learned how you could love someone more than the whole world but that doesn't save them from death. It won't save you from being alone.

My soul knows that love always ends in pain and loneliness.

9

Hunter

THE PUCK HITS THE plexiglass that separates the crowd from the ice with a *crack*. The arena is a ghost town at this godawful time in the morning, so the sound ricochets off the walls and echoes back to us.

"You losing your touch, Maddox?"

I swing my stick back and then let my arms jerk forward without responding. The puck hits the upper left corner of the net, and I glare at Maysen.

"Does that look like I'm losing my touch?" I ask.

One after another, I land puck after puck into the back of the net, but nothing abates the anger and restlessness I feel. Nothing diminishes the feeling that I'm a hamster on a wheel. Nothing eases the goddamn ache Dekker left me with last night but that I refuse to admit.

But walking away was the right thing. Putting her in her place so she doesn't think I'm naïve about why she's here, or that I'd fall right back into how things were when she's the one who walked away.

Was that the whole point of last night then? A subtle stab at revenge? I can't make sense of it—my need to talk to her in the bar, to remind her I was there, and then leave her hanging in the elevator.

Shit. I'd be lying if I denied it wouldn't have been a hardship to fall right between her thighs.

Groaning at my own stupidity, I go back to my practice shots. Trying to work myself into a frenzy so my head can go to that silent place where I don't think and just do.

There's a rhythm. Grunt with the swing. Smack the stick to the puck. Thud as the puck hits the net.

Grunt. Smack. Thud.

Maysen lifts the bottle of beer to his lips, and my eyebrows lift.

"Hair of the dog?" I ask.

Grunt. Smack. Thud.

"Shit, if it were the hair of the dog, I'd be sliding back between Sadie's . . . or was it Sandy? Maybe Shelby. Fuck if I remember what her name was, but if that's the case, I'd be all up in her because she straight wore me out. I need this shit," he says and lifts the bottle of beer in the air, "to simply get me through the morning."

Fucking Maysen.

Normally I love the asshole. Right now, not so much.

Perhaps it's because he got some and I didn't.

Then again, after seeing Dekker last night—after tasting her—just any ole puck bunny wouldn't have satisfied me. Not that they've satisfied me for a long time.

Since Dekker.

Stopping to catch my breath, I rest my hand on my stick and take in the arena around me. Years upon years of blue and red pennants hang from the rafters while images of the team's history play out over the uppermost walls. Defining moments in the franchise's history. Defining moments in the league's history. And while I shouldn't care about any of it, it's a history I never thought I'd get to be part of and now hope to leave my own mark on as well.

And that, in and of itself, makes me a prick.

How can I be grateful to play here when Jonah can't? How can I be happy when I'm the one who took his place?

Christ. Isn't that why I play for the Jacks? I could have been on any playoff-contending team but he told me to play here. He told me this was the decision he would have made. And since I play for him, I did what he suggested.

Who knew it would work? Who knew I'd be the starting block management built the franchise around and that in my second year here, we'd be in playoff contention?

Always the big brother, always looking out for me.

Even after what I did to him.

But that's why this is so fucked. Sanderson is already threatening that contract talks are going to be brutal when they were the ones who begged me to come here . . . and then not keep their promises. *Why can't I just play the game I train every day for?*

I close my eyes for a second and breathe it in. It's by far my favorite time in any arena, when the nineteen thousand or so seats are vacant, and it's just me and the ice and a game I'm lucky to be gifted at.

Nothing can beat the roar of the crowd as you're dancing down the ice, weaving between defenders while trying to control the puck, but there's something about the silence that is more profound. Almost as if the silence reflects the magnitude of it all.

So how come I'm feeling that less and less?

How come most days, this gift feels more like a curse?

Why have I come to rely on these early morning sessions with just me and the puck and the silence of an absent crowd to attempt to keep my head in the game?

"What is it?" Maysen asks.

I shake my head and eye his beer. "That shit better be cleared out of your system before game time."

Grunt. Smack. Thud.

"Relax, Captain. The game is over twelve hours away and I've got an IV set up at noon. You know, I feel like I'm coming down with something"—he fake coughs—"so I already set it up with the doc to give me more fluids to replenish—er, flush my system."

"How are you even any good?" I joke, knowing full well, I'd never pull a stunt like that.

"It's in my genes."

"You wish it were in your jeans." I roll my eyes.

"*Jealous?*" he asks, when we both know my stats run circles around his.

"Drink the fuck up," I mutter.

Grunt. Smack. Thud.

"Mind telling me what the hell is up your ass, Maddox?" he asks again, his skates cutting across the ice the only other sound between us.

"I do mind and it's nothing," I grumble, refusing to look his way, but swipe his beer from his hand as he skates past and help myself to the rest of it without asking. As much as it tastes good, it also isn't what I want.

It seems I don't know what I want these days.

"Nothing?" His chuckle resonates.

"Yeah, nothing. Why?"

He moves his jaw from side to side as his eyes question me with things I don't quite understand. "Just trying to figure out what's going on with you."

His words cause me to pause. "What the hell is that supposed to mean?"

"We just thought—"

"*We?*" I bark the word out. "So that's what this is? The team designated you to come play the shrink with me?"

"Not like you couldn't use one," he mutters under his breath.

"What the fuck is that supposed to mean?" Now he has my full attention.

"It's . . . we're concerned."

"About yourselves? About the team? About me? What exactly are you concerned about?" I demand, the stick in my hand and the pucks lined up waiting to be shot now forgotten.

"You're playing dangerously. Over the past two years, you've become the man we look to for leadership—*to lead us*—and now in the past four months, you're like a one-man show out there. While that's great for your stats and the scoreboard, it fucking sucks for team morale. You're not better than us"—he pauses and emits a laugh of contrition—"well, maybe a little . . ." He chuckles. "We're on your side, Cap, and when you're on the ice, your play suggests you don't know we're even there. Sure, we're winning, but at what cost? So again, what's your fucking deal?"

His words are like a slap to my face. A slap I've anticipated but that doesn't lessen its sting. "Good to know my team thinks so highly of me."

"No one thinks more highly of you than you do yourself."

My hands tighten on the beer bottle. "Where the fuck do you get off . . ." My words fade as I check myself before I say something I'd probably regret. Hell, I'm the leader of this team. I shouldn't be the one being put in his place.

But can you fucking blame them, Maddox?

"We all have a stake in this. That's where we get off talking to you." He blows out a breath in frustration. "You're the big shot the Jacks took on to build this franchise to its full potential. And it's fucking working. We're tearing up the league and closing in on a playoff berth for the first time in this club's history."

"And the problem with that?"

"What the fuck is your endgame? You *were* here for the long haul. The franchise player, but now . . . now it seems you want the fuck out. You went from being our captain who pulls us together, who's led us to this point, to acting like you're a one-man show."

"Bullshit."

"That's exactly right. It is bullshit, but on your part. Hell, if you put as much effort into the game as you do your anger, we'd already have a fucking playoff berth clinched."

"Or maybe you should do it without me." I throw the baseless threat into the air between us but have never felt as strongly about the statement as I do right now. A man can only keep going for so long.

"That's how you're going to be, Hunter?" He shakes his head and I feel his disappointment—and fucking hate it. "Come on. We're just concerned for your well-being."

We hold each other's stares for a few seconds as I try to process why I'm so pissed off by this. As I try to figure out why I should expect them to have my back when I've been a selfish prick for the past however long.

The hardest part about processing it all though is knowing how I should feel and still giving a shit less.

"Tell me something, Maysen . . . if I'm playing like a one-man show, being selfish but we're still winning. . . which one do you want me to be?

"Because I assure you, if I started passing the puck more and shooting less, I'd have one of you on my ass asking me what the hell was going on in the opposite way."

"Oh, so none of us have earned our own spots on the team, Maddox? That what you're saying?" And when I don't answer, I hear him mutter, "Asshole."

Yep. That's me. *Grade-A asshole.*

I throw the empty bottle across the ice in frustration and turn back to my row of pucks without saying another word.

My head is filled with so much shit I can't see straight, think straight . . . anything. It's so fucked.

You're the one who fucked up, Hunter. You owe it to him to fulfill his dream. You owe him.

I'll never stop owing him.

Grunt. Smack. Thud.

His talent was unmatched.

Grunt.

My one-man show isn't even good enough for him.

Smack.

My dad's words . . . they fill my head, fuel the anger, feed the rage, expose the hurt. The goddamn everything.

Thud.

"Since when do we drink when we work?"

Catching me off guard just as I hit the puck, Dekker's voice rips through my flustered concentration, and the puck goes sailing into the stands.

I hate that I don't want her here.

I despise that I do want her here.

And when I turn to where the sound of her heels clicking on the concrete of the tunnel leading up to the ice, I hate myself even more for *remembering*. How good we were in bed, how explosive—almost violent with lust.

Fucking incredible.

She stands with the beer bottle I chucked onto the ice in one hand, her other hand on her hip, and rocking a pinstriped pantsuit that looks part *time to party*, part *don't fuck with me*.

Totally in control when last night she was anything but.

Maysen is behind her as he walks down the tunnel toward the locker rooms. I was so pissed, so focused, I didn't even realize he'd left.

Lucky for me, now I don't have to address the bullshit he was hoping to resolve. Unlucky for me, I'm being stared down by a much tougher opponent, and the look of disappointment on her face isn't one I really care to acknowledge.

I already have a mother.

I already own guilt.

"Should I be worried there are more bottles hidden elsewhere?" she asks and shifts her weight.

"You know us hockey players, Dekk. If there's a rule, we're going to break it. You want to strip search me?" I lift my hands above my head. "I might have a stash somewhere on my body you can find."

"Drinking on a game day? At eight in the morning?" She lifts a lone brow and ignores my comment.

"What? Last night you were all about touching me and today you're not?" I tsk. "My, how things change."

Anger fleets through her expression, followed closely by embarrassment, but just as quickly as it's there, it disappears.

Hmm. Seems what I did last night got to her more than I thought.

"The beer?" she asks, giving a stoic glance from the beer bottle in her hand and then back to me.

"Sometimes you just need to relax." I shrug. *What does it matter? What do I care what she thinks of me?*

Why is she here?

"You going to call the LumberJacks management police on me?"

10

Dekker

I STARE AT HUNTER. At his shirt plastered with sweat and how it clings to his body, despite the chill of the ice his skates are standing on. He has his warm-up pants on and is without a helmet, his hair curling at the ends from the sweat.

And all I see in his eyes is anger I didn't put there. Or maybe I did. Rejection can do that to a man . . . but there's something more here. Something I walked in on that doesn't make sense.

"Don't give me that look, Kincade," Hunter mutters as he skates over to the penalty box where his electrolyte drink sits.

"What look?" I ask.

He half laughs, half snorts and meets my gaze across the distance. "Disappointment. Disproval. Disdain. I'm the king of all of them, so save your breath—or in this case—your glare, because it's not going to work with me."

"Are we working on emotions that start with the letter D today?" I ask. A hint of my embarrassment and anger over how I acted last night creeps into my voice, but I mask it with sarcasm. "If that's the case, I'm more than impressed with your answers thus far."

He clenches his jaw in response and then skates back over to line up more pucks so he can shoot them. And he does, one after another, each shot taken with laser precision and a healthy dose of fury behind it.

He goes through the first ten lined up and then stops to catch his breath.

His talent and skill are undeniable, but so is the beer bottle in my hand.

"Just because you're the captain and star of this team, doesn't mean management won't frown upon this," I say, unable to let this go.

"Fuck the management."

His comment surprises me. Always a team player and public mouthpiece for the team, I've never heard him talk like this.

"Those are some strong words," I say.

"The iron fist they seem to hold me with is even stronger."

"Iron fist?" *Where is this coming from?* "I believe they pay you a healthy sum to put their jersey on every night and play a sport that you love, so unless they're handcuffing you to a locker afterward and forcing you to not eat or drink for days, I think you're being ridiculous."

"Handcuffs, huh?" His eyebrow quirks up, and his constant need to distract from the gist of our conversation tells me I'm hitting too close to home.

"What's going on?" I ask again.

"We'll just say we're not seeing eye to eye at the moment," he mutters and then slaps a shot off and hisses when he misses.

"No one likes a player who's hard to handle and honestly, Hunter, you're becoming hard to handle."

"No one likes unsolicited advice from someone who has no bearing on his career, either," he counters, the rebuke stinging but deserved.

The problem is, I do care about him. Doesn't he get that's where my hostility stems from?

And only a crazy person would say that, Dekker.

I put my hands up in surrender to both him and my own thoughts. "You know I only want the best for you." I take a few steps in his direction in the first row of the stands. I'm close enough to catch the hitch of his movement and to see uncertainty flicker in his eyes. It's almost as if he needs to talk but doesn't see me as someone he can trust. *I hate that.* "What is it, Hunter?"

"Nothing. It's . . . never mind."

But I see it, and he knows I see it. The question is what do I see, though?

"Twelve years in the league. You're thirty-two, in the top twenty of all-time best scorers and you still have years left to play. Made it there faster than anybody else."

"You make a habit of studying people's stats who aren't your clients?" he asks.

"It's my job to know who the best of the best is." I only speak the truth but hate that it probably comes off like I'm kissing his ass.

"What's your point, then?" he asks, but his tone is different, quieter, more reserved.

"No point. I just know you've been running full steam since you entered this league. Straight off NCAA championships, where you still hold some records, right into the NHL."

"Every kid's dream, right? So many would kill to be in my shoes. Save it. I've heard it all. I've thought it all, and I leave everything out on the ice every damn time I play."

I nod slowly, letting him know I hear him, but I don't buy what he's saying. I'm missing something. "But you're angry."

"And your point?" he snaps.

"It's affecting your game. Your life."

"You don't know the half of it," he mutters as he skates past me.

"I know a change of scenery is sometimes needed. I know that stars can sometimes burn out. From what I've seen—"

"You don't know what you're talking about," he says, his skates cutting into the ice as he stops right in front of me, the plexiglass the only thing separating us.

"I make a living knowing what I'm doing. Just like you do." I shrug, trying to act as unaffected as possible by his nearness. Trying to pretend my pulse isn't racing as my body remembers his kiss last night. Trying to hide the flush on my cheeks over how I overstepped.

"I'm sorry about last night," I say quietly. "I overstepped. I . . . your point was made. Again. I apologize."

Our eyes hold, question, dismiss, and right when I think the conversation is over, his lips turn up in the slightest of smirks. "Same hotel as the team?"

The mental whiplash lasts only seconds as I refuse to give him the satisfaction of knowing he threw me. "Why am I staying in the same hotel?"

"Yeah."

"Convenience."

That cocky grin spreads wider as he just shakes his head ever so slightly and takes a step closer so his skates hit the barrier between us.

"What?" I ask, relieved by the sudden levity. This verbal sparring is exhausting.

"Just trying to figure you out."

"Didn't you know? I'm an open book," I tease.

"An open book inside a block of ice."

"Amusing," I mutter, unnerved by his intense scrutiny and hurt by his dig, even though it's more accurate than not. Those eyes of his hard to look away from.

"I'd say it's amusing too, but I'm the one who's always on the other end of whatever game you're playing."

"What the hell is that supposed to mean?" I shift on my feet. This is the last place I need to address why I'm here in Chicago. The mood has changed, the moment lost to speak to him. "You know what? I'm not going to be your verbal punching bag. By the way Maysen stalked out of here, you're pissed at him. Fine. Be pissed at him, but not me. I know that look in your eyes, and I'm not going to be the one you toy with so you feel like a man in control again."

I stalk toward the players' opening, the click of my heels only rivaled by the slice of his skates on the ice. And just as I reach the entrance to the tunnel, Hunter is there, his hand on my bicep pulling me back toward him.

"A man in control again?" he asks, his fingers adjusting his grip as his chest brushes over mine. "I'm always in control."

"That one seemed to touch a nerve, did it?"

"Maybe you should ask yourself how in control you are, huh?" His eyes flit down to my lips and back up to mine, the warmth of his breath hitting my lips. I can all but taste his kiss again but know that mistake will not be repeated.

No way.

No how.

Not after last night.

"Let's move on to adjectives that start with I. Irritable, much?"

His chuckle is that low rumble that tells me he's ready to play. That's the last thing I want right now. "*Irritable*? How about *indecisive*?"

"Who, you?"

"No, you," he sneers and takes a step closer.

"Not in the least."

"No?" His eyes flicker from my eyes to my lips again. "This was a huge mistake," he says, pretending to sound like me last night before clearing his throat. "Right back to that phrase, huh?"

"What do you mean?" I tug on my arm to no avail.

"I mean, it's amazing how convenient it is for you to fall back on that line. You said it the last time I saw you and you said it last night."

I did? I try to relive the moments, knowing I said it in the elevator but not remembering the time before. All I remember is trying to keep my emotions under check so Hunter Maddox had no clue I'd failed at the causal dating—er, sex situation—we'd found ourselves in. Sure, we fell into bed that first time, then verbally fought our way out of it, only to fall back into it more often than not over the course of six months.

But we weren't dating.

You could have asked either of us and we would have confirmed that. We were benefits buddies. The call we'd make when we were in the same city, at the same time—hell, even when we weren't we'd arrange to be. That's how great our sexual chemistry was.

The problem? Even though we couldn't be in the same room longer than thirty minutes without fighting—unless we were having sex—I became addicted to him. His gruff way, his cutting sense of humor, and his . . . well, his cock and fingers and oh-so-gloriously skilled tongue. But I can't see that in him now.

"Cat got your tongue, Dekker?" he asks, and leans in so I panic he's going to kiss me. Panic I'm here in the arena with the team nearby and Hunter is body to body with me. But I don't move. I don't back down. I refuse to let him feel like he has the upper hand again like last night. "Because the way I see it, this is your MO. We'd have incredible sex, you'd get up and say, 'Shit, that was a mistake,' and then collect your clothes or kick me out of wherever with a lame excuse about how you had somewhere to be until we'd see each other again. We were always a mistake. Every time. Until the next time that is."

I hate that the boyish smirk and arrogance in his eyes owns my every reaction—even after all this time.

I hate that I know he's right. If only he knew why . . . but he didn't stop me from walking out three years ago, so he has no idea what it took to leave.

"Are you saying we weren't a mistake?" I ask through a laugh to try and find my footing.

"'Till next time." He releases my arm and runs his hand down the length of it.

"There will be no next time."

"Yes, there will," he says and begins to put skate guards over his blades.

"No, Hunter, there won't." I straighten my spine. "Last night was completely unprofessional of me. It was—"

"That's never stopped you before," he says, and I swear to God I see the moment it clicks, because his body falters in motion moments before his eyes flash up to meet mine. "And here I was thinking you'd come here to finish what we started last night. Have an early morning of brunch sex for old time's sake before telling me what a mistake we were . . . but it's *unprofessional* of you. Let me guess, you didn't come here for that part of me . . . you only came for the other part of me. The part that would make us sleeping together unethical."

"You're crazy," I mutter and wave a hand at him as I backpedal.

"It'd only be unprofessional if I happened to be the person you were here to recruit. It would only be immoral if you were sleeping with your client, because that would mean others might worry that you're giving me preferential treatment . . ."

"You need a new agent." It's the closest I'm going to get to telling him the truth in this environment.

He throws his head back and laughs. "And why's that? Why the concern all of a the sudden?"

"Because Sanderson isn't doing you any favors."

"And how would you know what he is or isn't doing for me? Unless of course you were asking around and trying to figure out how to woo me over to your side."

"I'm here to check up on my clients," I say and glance over my shoulder as the trainer walks past with Katzen following closely behind, no doubt to work on that hamstring that's been giving him trouble. "And you're reaching."

"Am I?" Hunter asks as he walks up to me, our bodies back in the same position as last night in the elevator—almost touching.

I nod, not trusting my own words and hating that he's the only man who can make me tongue-tied. The one thing my dad always emphasized to us was time and place. Never make an offer, a proposition, an anything to a potential client if the timing is off or if the place has you at a disadvantage. I walked into the arena this morning thinking I'd have a chance to talk to Hunter alone, since everyone knows he prefers his mornings solitary and his practice hard.

What I didn't expect was to walk in on whatever was happening between him and Maysen, a beer bottle on the ice, or Hunter to have me on the ropes so to speak with his comments.

Ones I have to figure out how to maneuver.

"Yes," I reiterate. "You're reaching."

"So then why not give in to what we both want?"

My mouth is as dry as his eyes are intense. "What's that?" I barely get out.

The groan he emits might as well be for both of us because it rumbles in the space between us. "Shall we finish what we started last night?"

"I told you, we're not sleeping together. Things have changed. I've changed from who I was three years ago."

"You may have changed but the chemistry is still the same. Time didn't put a damper on the want."

"You're being ridiculous." I take a step back only to bump against the wall. Of course, it's there, because why wouldn't it be, right?

"I am? Because I mean, if you're not here to try and steal me from Sanderson, then there would be no reason for us *not* to walk down memory lane."

"You mean sleep down memory lane?" I ask.

"There's that smile."

Shit. Don't do that, Hunter. Don't be playful. Don't be charming. Don't be nice.

"While this has been amusing—"

"There's that word again."

I sigh in exasperation. "I have work to get to."

I expect Hunter to stop me—he's a man who typically gets what he wants after all—but he doesn't, so I walk down the hall toward the visitor's section in the bowels of the arena.

"One thing, Dekk."

"Yeah?" I turn to face him. He's standing in the opening, the rink at his back, his stick in one hand, and the smug expression on his face fitting perfectly. If I could take a picture, the image would be him to a tee.

"Why'd you come this morning? If it wasn't to steal me or fuck me . . . why waste the trip?"

Shit.

"I told you, I'm traveling with the team for the next stretch."

"That didn't answer my question of why you came looking for me."

Bastard. He wants an answer? All right.

I walk back toward him and stop as he strips his shirt over his head. Where there would normally be an undershirt and pads, there is nothing but skin. Defined, sculpted muscles beneath his olive-toned skin with a tattoo on one shoulder and a war story of scars on the rest.

Scars I've traced with my fingers. Tattoos I've nipped with my teeth.

When I drag my eyes away from the sight in front of me, I'm met with a raised eyebrow and that damn amusement again painting every single muscle of his face.

Definitely a bastard toying with me.

"I wanted to come here and thank you."

"We've talked all this time and those words haven't graced your lips so I doubt that's the reason."

"No. Maysen was here. I was thrown with the beer bottle," I fumble.

"Beer bottle is in the trash. Maysen is gone." He puts one hand on his hip and raises his eyebrows. "What did you want to thank me for?"

I clear my throat. "For reaffirming that Chad wasn't right for me."

"How'd I do that?" he asks.

And what I meant as a completely innocent comment on the fly— one I somehow didn't get out correctly, now just screwed me. How do I answer this? How do I tell him that I felt more alive in the few moments his lips met mine than I did the whole damn time Chad and I dated? *Dated?* Maybe more like were companions.

Because now I'm stuck staring at his blue eyes that are questioning me and I can't really give him an answer without showing my cards. *Professionally and personally.*

"Because . . . I . . . uh missed his call last night when we were in the elevator," I lie. And internally roll my eyes. *I missed a call?* Pfft.

"I'm not following you." His smile widens.

Shit.

"Um, a man who wanted to fight for me would have called back. He would have—"

"Kissed you like I kissed you? Is that what you were going for?"

"No. Absolutely not." *Yes. That's exactly why.*

"You keep thinking that," he says and then holds his hand up to someone over my shoulder. "Hold up. I need you to look at something." He takes a few steps so that he's shoulder to shoulder with me. "It was definitely the kiss."

"Hunter—"

"You're welcome."

Without another word, his skates clomp down the carpeted hallway toward the visiting team's quarters, while I watch after him wondering how in the hell he just got the upper hand in this conversation when I'm the one holding all the cards in a game he doesn't even know we're playing.

But isn't that us?

Well, him and me.

There is no *us*.

There won't be an us.

There can't be an us. Not even a one-night-stand us.

Hell, Hunter maneuvered me right where he wanted me to be—me answering his questions while I forget to get answers to mine.

Something is going on with him.

The agent in me wants to figure it out so I can manipulate it to my advantage—take care of the problem, negotiate the issue away, and show him just how good I am at my job.

The woman in me worries about *him*, because you can only push so hard, so long, without burning out.

11

Dekker

KINCADE SPORTS MANAGEMENT
Internal Memorandum
New Recruit Status Report

*denotes urgent status

ATHLETE	TEAM	SPORT	AGENT	STATUS
Carl Ryberg	n/a	Golf	Kenyon	Meeting set up
Jose Santos	D-Backs	Baseball	Chase	In talks
Lamar Owens	Bulls	Basketball	Lennox	Negotiating
Michelle Nguyen	n/a	Soccer	Brexton	Negotiating
*Hunter Maddox	Jacks	Hockey	Dekker	

I GLANCE AT THE first page of the weekly status sheet in my inbox and twist my lips. What do I type? What answer do I give? Haven't approached him? He doesn't know? I kissed him?

I want to kiss him again?

Shit.

Instead of typing anything, I close the email and don't respond. It's too soon for me to type anything.

12

Hunter

"HEY MOM. JUST CALLING to see how Jonah's doing." I lean back against the pillows propped against the headboard behind me. Different day. Different hotel. Same life.

Her nervous chuckle unnerves me. "He's fine. Just has a cold. Probably from all the germs. I went to the store to buy things to prepare us to come and see your game. I probably got the germs there and somehow brought them home to him."

Christ, it's always my fault he's sick, one way or another.

"There are germs everywhere. You can't really avoid them."

"When it comes to Jonah though. He's fragile and—"

"Can I talk to him? Can you put his headset on him?"

"You know sometimes that thing doesn't work."

"Then can you put the phone up to his ear?" I ask, running a hand through my hair as I stare out the window.

"Your father asked if you've been getting his texts. He says you're not responding."

Another no when it comes to Jonah. I shouldn't be surprised, but I am. *Thanks, Mom.*

And my father's texts? I don't think I've responded in ten years, and yet he keeps sending them as if he doesn't notice otherwise.

Then again, it's not like they notice me much at all.

"How should I respond to his texts?" I ask. "Thanks for the negativity? The criticism? How exactly should I respond?" I chuckle, the toxicity I endure to talk to my brother is ridiculous.

"He means well. He's the reason you're there, you know."

"Jonah, Mom? Can I talk to him?" Exasperation hits an all-time high.

"Yes. Sure. I can't remember the last time you called for him."

Two days ago.

Two fucking days ago. And two days before that.

There's shuffling on the other end of the line as she goes through the process of connecting his headset to the phone line so he can hear me.

"Okay, it's connected," she says, her voice distant.

"Hey J." I suddenly feel calm and pause after my greeting because in my head, I can hear him talking back, I can feel my twin responding. *God, I miss him.* "Just wanted to call and check in. I'm sure Mom is driving you crazy with her fussing and repeating the same thing over and over. I get it. I totally do." I close my eyes and listen to the ventilator for a beat. "We're playing Rampage tonight. Those guys are fucking assholes but yeah, I'll keep my stick up like you taught me. It's going to be a tough one. Ferguson knows how to play me. It's like he knows which line I'm going to take before I even know myself. And their double team defense is strong. We've been working on a way to overcome it. It's like a play you would have made up. Perfect in every way for them and harder than fuck to defend against for me."

So I talk to my brother for the better part of an hour like I always do, caught in that indecision that I'm being an ass for talking to him about things he'd kill to be doing and treating him like he's gone completely.

The worst part about it is that I call him because I want to, because he's the only person that quiets the anger. But as I hang up, I wonder if my calls only feed his.

13

Dekker

SOMETHING'S OFF.

I can't put my finger on it but watching Hunter play, the difference is noticeable from the last game to this one.

There is none of his intuitive anticipation of where his opponents are going to play several passes before it happens. There's no showmanship as he dodges defenders left and right while keeping the puck in action. There's a loss of the ferocious determination to get the puck in the back of the net.

Normally I can't take my eyes off him because his ease of play enthralls me. Tonight, I'm all but cringing every time he gets the puck. It's almost as if he's the star kid on the first-place hockey team that's creaming the last-place team so the coach has told him to hold back and pass twelve times before he attempts a shot.

But he's not shooting.

No, instead he's passing it off and then falling back when normally he's the heart of the offense.

If the Jacks were in their own arena, the crowd would be booing him after every pass. This crowd here senses something is off and has been cheering each and every one, because it's to their advantage.

Someone has knocked the king off his reign-of-terror throne and it's not pretty.

I welcome the distraction from the scoreboard when my phone buzzes at my hip.

Lennox.

It's sad that I'm immediately on the defensive before I even answer the phone.

"Hey, Len," I say, walking toward the back of the press box and pushing a finger to my other ear. "What's up?"

"Just checking in."

"For?"

"No reason," she says, but a lifetime of living with her tells me she's fishing for information.

"So you just called to say hi?" I can't remember the last time one of my sisters did that.

"Yes . . . and, never mind."

And here we go.

"What is it?" I honestly don't have the bandwidth to deal with her today.

The crowd goes wild as the opposition scores, and I crane my neck from where I stand huddled in the back to watch the replay on the Jumbotron overhead. Lucky shot.

"Who scored?" she asks.

"The Patriots."

"Boo," she says, and I smile but then remember she's playing coy.

"What is it you needed, Len?"

"I just wanted to see how it was going with Maddox."

"I've talked to him but haven't *talked* to him yet about us."

"Us?"

"KSM," I explain in annoyed exasperation.

"Yes. Sure," she says but doesn't sound anything like she does. "It was pretty shitty of Dad to make Maddox your recruit."

I open my mouth and close it, wanting to say so much—agree, commiserate, talk about what it felt like to see him for the first time—but don't. "It's business. I can handle it."

"Keep that in mind."

And now my back is up.

"Excuse me?" I snort.

"You two were more than sex."

"Thanks for the analysis, but you're wrong. That's all we were." *Were my feelings for him really that transparent?*

"That came out wrong. What I mean was I know he hurt you."

"I've been hurt a lot. It's not a big deal."

"Easy to say, hard to do," she murmurs.

"Your point?" I ask, ready for the conversation to be over.

"If you sleep with him, this whole thing is over." I should be stunned by her direct nature, but I'm not. Subtlety is not Lennox's strong suit. Silence is my response. "Not to be the party pooper . . . or should I say pretty kitty pooper, but if you sleep with him—"

"No worries there."

"—then our other clients will think he's getting preferential treatment—"

"Are you actually lecturing me?" I ask through a laugh. "After you slept with Hardy and that entire debacle? Seriously?"

"It's not the same. This time it matters."

She pauses as the arena plays a song that the crowd chants along to and I welcome the distraction.

"And who exactly are you busy trying to woo over to Kincade?"

Her pause has me leaning over as if I can hear the words she's not saying . . . and I wait.

"I don't exactly know yet."

"What do you mean you don't know yet?"

"I mean, Dad said we need to recruit one at a time so it looks more subtle than a hostile takeover, or some weird father analogy like that."

I stare at the game unfolding before me—at the loss the Jacks are being handed, no thanks to Hunter. "So I'm the only one who's—"

"Teacher's pet always gets to have fun first," she says in a singsong voice. She called to gloat . . . or to make sure I'm not fucking up things for her because let's be honest, when's the last time she thought about anyone or anything but herself?

If KSM were to fail as a business, how would my sister survive without all the fancy social functions that go hand in hand with being a sports agent? God forbid, it would thrust her out of the limelight she thrives on.

I'm far from naïve and know her concern is genuine but skewed for selfish reasons.

But what the hell is my dad pulling here? While he has some logic to avoid an all-out war with Sanderson, why was it so pertinent that I pick up my life on the fly and do this?

"I've got to go," I murmur.

"No. *Wait!*"

"What?" I snap. "What more can you possibly have to say that's not duplicitous in its meaning?"

"Look, all of that came out wrong. All of it."

"I don't care anymore, Len. I've got a game to watch and a client to schmooze."

"Hear me out." It's the tone in her voice and the fact that I've been like their mom that prevents me from hanging up.

"You've got two minutes."

"I know you like him, Dekk. And I know how you get when someone gets too close to you," she says. I'm still not following her. "Because of Mom, because of the hurt we experienced, it's easier to push someone away when you love them than to see where it leads."

"There is no talk of love here." I snort at her ludicrousness.

"But there was when you walked away from him last time." Her voice softens and she speaks before I can interrupt her. "You can interrupt me all you want, you can tell me you didn't have feelings for him, but I was staying at your place that night when you came home. I know that look you had, and I know you were hurting and maybe, just maybe, it's because you were too chicken to tell him how you felt. You were too scared that if he said he had feelings for you too you'd have to face your fears. That you'd have to let someone in."

I forgot about that. That she was there at my place when I got home. The twenty questions she peppered me with asking what was wrong. The twenty shrugs I gave, telling her I was perfectly fine. The scrutiny of her stare and how irritated I got when her voice turned compassionate, because it only made the tears I was fighting burn brighter.

Damn my father for giving me him to recruit.

Old feelings are better left dead and buried.

"Len—"

"All I'm saying is if you choose to sleep with him—if you choose to risk him as a client and what Dad's asked of us because of it—that it better be for more than just sex. It better be because you're going to put yourself out there and tell him how you feel this time."

"I have to go."

"I'm sure you do," she says quietly but doesn't argue.

I end the call.

I sit back in my seat but don't see a minute of the game before me.

It better be because you're going to put yourself out there and tell him how you feel this time.

I'm used to the panic that comes with the thought, but I'm not used to someone else seeing it or knowing it . . . and I'm not sure how I feel about that.

What I do know is that what started out feeling like a wild goose chase to acquire Hunter has turned into so much more.

I knew that the minute I laid eyes on him.

I knew that there was going to be a casualty in all of this.

And most likely, it was going to be my heart. *Shit.*

14

Hunter

"WHAT THE FUCK WAS that, Cap?" Frankie asks and deliberately bumps my shoulder as I stride past him in the locker room.

I keep walking and ignore the inferno raging within me to take a swing at any of these fuckers. Guys that were friends—teammates—and now calling me out. I did exactly what they fucking wanted—became a pansy-assed passer instead of myself—and of course, it's not fucking good enough.

"You not feeling good?" Katz asks.

"Your ankle bugging you again?" Callum questions. "Your knee?"

But I keep my focus on my locker, because it's so much easier than facing the bullshit in here and their subtle digs at how I played.

Maysen's shoulder hits mine and I refuse to respond to the look in his eyes that says, *this is how you let us down.*

"You trying to throw the game?" another voice yells from the back just as I hit my locker. "How much money'd you bet against us?" There's laughter that follows the joke, but I know it wouldn't have been said if it wasn't thought of first.

Do they really think I'd bet against my team?

Screw this.

Like fucking clockwork I don't want to acknowledge, I open my locker and the first thing I see is the screen of my cellphone lit up like a goddamn Christmas tree. Text after text after text telling me what a disappointment I am to the Maddox name, no doubt. How Jonah would have never played this poorly. One after another hit the screen and goad me like the eyes of my teammates at my back.

I don't pay any attention to them. I never do.

At least that's what I tell myself.

I round on the locker room to find every teammate staring at me, defeat in their postures, and fury in their expressions. They're sweaty and spent in partial stages of undress but all of them are laser-focused on me. In anger. This isn't right. This isn't how it was when I decided to come here two years ago. They had welcomed me and my aggression, knew I was here to lift the game—the team—to Cup level. And now the bastards think I could throw a game . . . *fucking pisses me off.*

"What's the problem?" I shout, hands out, fight welcome. "Is that not what you were asking for when you sent Maysen to talk to me today? Be more of a team player? Pass to make sure every goddamn one of you got to put their stick on the puck? You wanted a fucking Kumbaya session, boys, and you got it." I stand on the bench. "What? You don't have a right to stand there and look like someone pissed in your Wheaties when you got exactly what you asked for."

They all gawk at me, the rookies on the team shrinking into themselves, the hardened fuckers like me standing their ground.

"What do you all have to say now?" My voice reaches a fever pitch, and I hate the fucking tinge of panic in it. I hate that even though I did exactly what I set out to do, I'm still sick to my stomach over it. Staring at the people I've devoted blood, sweat, and pulled muscles to, I loathe the look of disappointment in their eyes and that it's directed at me.

"Mad Dog—"

"Don't Mad Dog me. Don't act like you guys didn't send Maysen to lead the charge in telling me I'm too selfish, too aggressive, *too me*, be-cause guess what? When I'm not, none of you stepped up to the fucking line and played the damn part." I throw my gloves into my locker with a thud. "Maybe you all oughta start asking yourself the question, why the fuck not?"

My hands tremble with anger, and I need to get the hell out of here before I do something I'm going to regret. Before I fuck up more than I already have.

I'm losing control and there's no worse feeling in the world.

None.

"Maddox. In my office." The voice of Coach Jünger booms through the locker room and while I look at him, everyone remains staring at me. "*Now.*"

"This is total bullshit." I jump off the bench, kick the foot of my locker, and stride toward the door Jünger is holding open for me.

When it slams behind me, I stand there as he takes his time walking to the other side of the desk before resting his hips on the counter at his back. He looks at me with the same disappointment that everyone else did.

"You want to tell me what the fuck that was all about?" he asks and tosses his clipboard on the desk with a thud.

"The team thinks I've been showboating. Had a delegation deliver a talk to me this morning over it . . . so I gave them what they wanted." There isn't an ounce of fucks given in my voice, but inside is a goddamn hurricane of emotion. "I gave them mediocre Maddox."

"And you think you're paid the big bucks by the big dogs upstairs to deliver mediocre Maddox?" He crosses his arms over his chest.

"It's not our arena so I'm not quite sure where the big dogs are, but I'm pretty sure they're not upstairs."

"That's how you want to respond, smart-ass? Let's try again."

"Just trying to keep the team chemistry alive."

"The fuck you are," he shouts and walks over to snap closed the blinds that allow everyone in the locker room from seeing in before turning to face me. "I don't know what the fuck is going on in your life, and it sure seems like you don't want anyone to know, so you give me one reason why I shouldn't go against the GM's request I received five minutes ago to bench your ass for the next three games."

"Because you want the Stanley Cup as much as they do and benching me isn't going to help a goddamn ounce with that. We're running out of games now and without me on the ice, the team's just not the same. *You need me.*"

"We don't need what you did tonight."

"My half-ass is better than some of their full bore."

"Your arrogance isn't becoming." He says the words but nothing else, because he knows I'm right.

"Withers is in a shooting slump, Frankie is in his own head too much after that suspension, and Maysen, God love the fucker, but shooting isn't his strong suit right now . . . so yeah, I've been an asshole. I've got shit going on that no one needs to know—"

"Who'd you get pregnant?"

My laugh echoes off the walls. "Hilarious."

"You off the oxy?" he asks, his face suddenly falling some to match the gravity in his voice.

"I'm good."

"You sure? You've had injury after injury this year without taking a day off. Cortisone shots help, but I know Oxy is even better to take the edge off. Is that it? Are you hooked on—"

"It's not drugs, it's not women . . . fuck, Jüng, it's just *shit*, okay?"

"Things okay with your brother?" he asks, his voice lowering as sympathy edges his gruff tone.

"Of course," I lie. Because what else can I do? Tell him, no, things are shit? That Jonah's struggling more and more, getting sick time and again and doctors think his time is limited? That I'm the reason Jonah's there, and dealing with it is more bullshit than he could ever imagine? I walk toward the window and back before he can see the reality of my thoughts, before he realizes that this sport I've been *blessed* to play has single-handedly saved me and ruined me simultaneously. "He's fine. It's my teammates pulling crap like they did this morning that isn't exactly helping."

"And what about the crap you've pulled the past few months? The lashing out. The fights. The thumbing your nose at the people who sign your checks? The you're too good—"

"I've never said I'm too good!" I shout and take a step toward him, realizing more than ever that everyone around me doesn't understand, and it's making me feel even more suffocated. I lace my fingers at the back of my neck and exhale a loud sigh in frustration.

My exhale fills the room as he settles in his spot against the counter again. "You're too valuable to be fucking up like this. It looks like you don't give a shit about anyone but yourself."

I'm the last person I care about, I want to scream. *The last person. Don't you see that? Don't you see I'm punishing myself? Don't you see that no one gives a fuck about me, and I've never felt so goddamn isolated in my life?*

"I'm not going to bench you, Maddox. Whatever you're dealing with needs to be dealt with though, or else I'm not going to be able to protect you from the people signing that gigantic check of yours or the teammates who can make you look even worse if they start talking to the press." He holds his hands out to the side. "It's your call."

I nod, unsure what else to do or say because my head feels like it's not connected to my body. The thoughts are there but the normal emotions I should feel—shame, grief, chagrin—aren't attached.

"That's all." I can't get out of there fast enough, but the minute my fingers are on the door handle, he speaks again. "Hey, Cap?"

I turn to face him. "Hmm?"

"You need anything, I'm here, okay? It's never as bad as it seems."

Yes, it is.

"Thanks."

"I'd avoid the main exit on the way to the team bus. I've made the locker room off-limits from the press tonight. Wasn't sure what was going to happen in here and we like to keep our fights within the family. But uh . . . the press is out there in droves, clamoring for answers."

"Noted."

15

Hunter

DAD: *Such a waste to have ability and potential and refuse to use it.*

DAD: *Disgraceful. Absolutely disgraceful.*

DAD: *You get a chance that should've been your brother's and that's how you play?*

DAD: *You're lucky they don't boo you out of Jersey when you get home.*

I STARE AT THE texts. At the criticism and negativity and am reminded, as I am after every game, how I'll never be Jonah.

How I'll never live up to my father's standard of perfection even when I bust my ass day in day out and he criticizes from the sidelines.

With a swipe of my thumb, I clear the display. I know the words will eat at me as I fall asleep tonight.

Sleep.

That's what I want. To fall into an oblivious sleep and to put this fucking piss-poor night behind me. To try and forget. Just fucking forget.

I take a glance around the locker room. Most of the team has cleared out by now. Thank God they left me alone after Jünger's dress-down. I'm in no mood to talk to them, or anyone, so I head to the back tunnel just like he suggested and hope everyone continues to stay away.

16

Dekker

"I HAD A FEELING you'd be coming through this side of the tunnel," I say the minute I see Hunter walk out of the doorway. His head is down, his sweatshirt hood pulled out to shadow his face, and his posture can either read absolute defeat or unfettered anger.

Or a mix of both.

His feet falter as he stands in the middle of the tunnel. We're in the bowels of the arena, and there is no one in sight but the two of us.

He lifts his gaze to meet mine and words, emotions, everything seem to fall when they do. He looks beaten down and confused, and I want to reach out and hug him, even though I know that's so inappropriate. It's like the fire in him from earlier this morning has been extinguished, snuffed out.

We stare at each other in the dim light for longer than we should as a million things I should say come to mind and then fade. He won't listen. It'd be unwanted, unheard, lip service.

And I have never given lip service to clients just to make them feel better, so why would I attempt to with him? If I lie to them about things we both know aren't true, how would they ever trust me when it really matters?

"Leave it, Dekker." His voice is a soft rumble as he walks past me.

"Hunter!" I hate the desperation that rings in my voice but can't help it.

But he doesn't stop.

He keeps on walking.

"THAT SIGH OF YOURS is heavy, Dekk. It always is when you're over-thinking things. What's on your mind, kid?" My dad's voice sounds like comfort coming through the line and as much as I'm frustrated at him, a smile turns up a small part of my lips.

"Are you trying to set me up?"

"What?" he asks. "Don't be ridiculous."

But I'm not being ridiculous.

It's all I thought about as I wandered through the tunnels of the arena waiting for one of my clients on the opposing team to finish with his press interviews so I could have a quick check-in with him.

My conclusion was this. "I'm the only one of the four of us you sent to recruit, Dad. Lennox told me you haven't given the rest of them clients to steal yet."

"Because it's not the right time."

"I call bullshit." I fold my arms over my chest and stare out the window of my hotel. The skyline of the city is dotted with buildings and lights in the moonless night.

"Hunter was the most urgent. He's up for a contract negotiation in a few months and with them so close to competing for the Cup, it's a good time to be ready to poach."

"Uh-huh."

"What?" He sounds like the voice of innocence. "Did you piss him off? Is that why he played like shit tonight?"

"That right there!" I all but jump. "You never watch hockey, it's not your sport, but you watched tonight's game? That's suspect."

"It was on the TV while I worked through some contracts." His chuckle fills the line. "And, sweetie, I watch all sports."

I chew the inside of my cheek as I listen to him turn the water on and then off, now wondering if my thoughts ran away with me earlier. "You're up to something." *I know it.*

"How about you be *up to* telling me what's going on there?"

"Nothing to report," I say, willing to give him a reprieve momentarily, because I do want to talk to him about Hunter.

"But your silence says you have thoughts."

"I do." I nod. "I think he's definitely burned out and can't see the forest for the trees."

"Meaning?"

"Meaning, there's a catalyst that's causing it."

"Like?"

"Getting to the playoffs? His future with the Jacks? Something," I murmur more to myself than to him.

"So what are you going to do?"

I lean my hip against the back of the couch and eye the sandwich I brought back for a very late dinner and think for a second. "Make him fall back in love with the game somehow. He's too important to the franchise and maybe he's feeling the pressure."

"That's what I would do."

Is it stupid that such simple affirmation from my dad still makes me grin ear to ear?

"Now to figure out what to do."

"You'll sort it out. You always do," he says. "It's getting late—"

"Not so soon, Kincade. Nice try. Now about you picking me to go after Hunter." I purse my lips and wait for an answer.

"I promise you, it's because I know you're the right one to handle him."

My mind flashes to the other night. To my hand wrapped around his cock and my tongue slipping through his lips. To how bad I screwed things up and how much Hunter called me on it.

My cheeks fill with heat as I fumble over what to say to my dad. "I'm not one hundred percent sure I believe you."

His laughter fills the line. "Good. Then it'll keep you on your toes. Night, Dekk." Without another word, he hangs up on me.

All I can do is laugh into my empty hotel room and shake my head. The worst thing about my dad is also probably the best thing about my dad. I can never stay mad at him.

I'm spending too much time with my thoughts.

Way too much time.

But the one lingering thought remains as I eat my sandwich. If Lennox saw how I felt about Hunter when I rarely acknowledged that we were together, wouldn't my dad have too?

That's the million-dollar question.

17

Dekker

KINCADE SPORTS MANAGEMENT
Internal Memorandum
New Recruit Status Report

*denotes urgent status
***denotes Dear Dekker isn't answering us and we're going to raid her chocolate stash while she's gone until she does.

ATHLETE	TEAM	SPORT	AGENT	STATUS
Carl Ryberg	n/a	Golf	Kenyon	In talks
Jose Santos	D-Backs	Baseball	Chase	face-to-face mtg
Lamar Owens	Bulls	Basketball	Lennox	Contracted. YES!
Michelle Nguyen	n/a	Soccer	Brexton	Coming to KSM Tues.
*Hunter Maddox	Jacks	Hockey	Dekker	*** *Hello? Anybody home?*

18

Dekker

"WHEN YOU ASKED ME to take a ride with you, should I have known you were planning on kidnapping me?" Hunter asks from his place beside me in the passenger seat. "Or is this your attempt to finish what you started the other night?"

As much as I want to make a witty comment, I just flip the blinker and smile.

It took me half the morning to figure out how to make Hunter realize he was burned out. Even trickier is showing him without mentioning the words.

Athletes are superstitious. They don't shave if they're winning. They don't step on lines when they walk on the field. They wear the same, but washed (hopefully), undergarments if they had a great game in them. And they never speak aloud certain terms: no-hitter, perfect game, burnout, etcetera.

So I had my work cut out for me to show and not tell.

Even more so, I don't know if Hunter even knows he's burned out so if I did tell him, I'm assuming he'll fight me on it.

And fighting me is exactly what I don't want.

When I asked him to take a ride with me, I'd already made the promise to myself that no matter what he did or said to antagonize or irritate me, I was going to smile and let it go.

We could get along outside of the bedroom.

I was determined to prove that to myself on a personal level and to him on a professional one.

That's the only way I have any chance of convincing him I know what's best for him and once he knows that, trusting me as an agent would fall into line.

Heading east on Wheelock Street, I glance his way. "I never said how far the ride was going to be."

"Good thing it's an off day or else I'd be missing my game," he mutters, but there's humor in his voice as the lights of the college come into view on our left and the arena is just coming into our sights on our right. It's dark outside, but co-eds mingle on the sidewalk and common areas as the streetlights cast their glow around them.

"When in Hanover, right?"

"When in Hanover, what? Kidnap a hockey player and take them to . . . where in the hell are we exactly?" he asks.

"Dartmouth. We're at Dartmouth College to be exact."

I see the jolt of his body. "Okay." He draws the word out as I pull into a packed parking lot and get lucky and find a space right off the bat. "I was never good at school, Kincade. You're making me get all itchy just thinking about having to sit in a classroom."

"What? You hate having someone tell you what to do and how to do it? That's a shocker." I shift the gear into park. "Here, wear this." I reach into the back seat and toss a baseball cap at him and wait for his response.

"No way!" He shakes his head and throws the LA Kings hat off his lap like it's a hot potato. "Are you crazy?" His laughter fills the cab and I pause and take it in. It's not a sound I hear often from him. "I can't wear that."

"Why not? You'd be supporting the NHL." I pick it up and try to put it on his head.

"No," he cries and grabs my wrists as I struggle with him playfully. "I will not be a traitor. I will not."

"I'm going to take a picture and post it all over social media."

"Never," he shouts as he begins tickling me to distract me from my efforts. I squeal as I fall awkwardly across the center console so that my chest is on top of his.

Breaths panting and lips inches from each other in the small space, our eyes meet and hold as the protests die on our lips.

"Dekker." My name is a quiet assault to my ears even after all the shouting. In those two syllables, I hear so many things. Are they real or am I making them up?

Kiss me.

The thought is in my head as I struggle to slow my thoughts. As I fight the urge to lean in and taste him.

But his lips are right there. His body is warm and inviting beneath my hands pressed to his chest. And the memory of just how good we can be together is front and center in my mind.

His eyes flicker to my lips and then back to my eyes.

A horn blares in the aisle behind us and we both jump back like two kids caught necking in the school lot.

"Saved by the bell," he murmurs into the silence of the cab as he turns the Kings hat over in his hand. I sit with my back against the door and watch his fingers play over the embroidery.

"You ready?" I ask the question, but neither of us move as we sit in the silence.

"Why are we here again?"

"Here as in the car or here as in more of a philosophical way?" I dodge.

"Dekker?" he growls, and I laugh.

"Because sometimes a change of scenery is good for perspective." The comment is innocent but the insinuation is there, and the way he looks over at me, blue eyes shielded in the shadows, says he caught it.

"What exactly are we talking about here, Dekker?"

Chills chase over my skin as we stare at each other. Nerves. They run rampant as I debate how honest to be with him.

We're talking about you needing to remember why you play the game.

We're talking about you needing a new agent who appreciates you.

We're talking about you and me deserving a second chance.

But none of those reasons fall from my lips. Nope. Instead, I chicken out and give him the answer that will satisfy him. For now.

"I need to watch a prospective client's game. I thought you might want to watch him and provide some feedback."

He narrows his eyes and shakes his head. "What?" The word comes out in a disbelieving laugh.

"Humor me," I say and turn to look in the back seat. "I think I have a beanie. Would a beanie work?" I ask as I begin to rummage through the travel bag I have there.

"Why do I need a hat?" he asks as I produce a nondescript black beanie.

"Voila!" I hold it up. "You need a beanie because you're not here to be Hunter Maddox, the hockey god. You're here to be Hunter, an average guy with an even more average-sized dick who's going to enjoy a game simply to enjoy a game."

He eyes me for the longest time and I wait for him to say something, for him to express the caution fleeting through his eyes, but he nods and slowly slides the beanie over his head. "But it's more than average in size. This beanie-wearing guy might be average, but his dick definitely isn't."

I laugh. "I should've known you'd say that."

He shrugs. "Average guys need all the love they can get."

"Let's go, bigger-than-average Hunter," I joke and open the door, needing the blast of the cold air to shock me to my senses from realizing that we're actually getting along. And from thinking how much I want a second chance with him . . . despite how he hurt me the first time.

But is it hurt when you both go into a situation with the same expectations and yours change? How is he to blame for that?

Jesus, Dekk. Get over it. *Get over him.*

But it's been three years and obviously, I haven't. What exactly does that mean?

Our shoulders bump as we walk through the lot like other college co-eds on their way to one of the biggest games of their season against Dartmouth.

"Wait." Hunter tugs on my hands and stops me so I can look at him. "Why in the hell do you have a Kings hat in your car?"

"I have clients on most teams."

"So, what? You dress the part at their games?"

I shrug and offer a coy smile. "Sometimes."

"You've been on the road with us this whole stretch. I've yet to see you wear a LumberJacks hat."

"I'll only wear one once they've won the cup."

"Ohhhhhhhh," he says and then bursts out laughing. "Fucking brutal."

But his laughter as we head toward the arena is all I focus on.

It's all I hear.

It's all I want.

19

Dekker

"YOU SURE YOU DON'T want one?" Hunter asks as he slides a pint of beer onto the table. The tavern is dim with Dartmouth paraphernalia lining its walls and teeming with college students excited after tonight's win.

We found a seat in the back corner where we can blend into its dark edges and hopefully have a drink incognito. I'm surprised we've skated by this far, pun intended, without anyone recognizing him.

"You drink. I'm the designated driver tonight." I take a sip of my Diet Coke and laugh.

"What?" he asks

"I'm just thinking of how confused that poor lady was until we convinced her you're Hunter Maddox's twin."

His smile is tinged with sadness and I hate that I put it there. Maybe I was too caught up in the moment during the game to see it then, but I definitely see it now. "I'm sorry. I didn't mean—how is your brother?" I ask, feeling like a heel. There's not much I know about Jonah Maddox other than Hunter thinks the world of his twin, and that he became a quadriplegic after a car accident in their teens.

His brother is a topic Hunter rarely speaks about. In interviews and relaxed conversations, he keeps anything about Jonah close to his vest. I'd probably be the same if it was one of my sisters, let alone a twin.

"He's fine." He takes a sip and looks around at the patrons having a good time. "You were quick on your feet with that lady, Kincade," he says. "Thanks."

"You have to be in this job."

A cheer goes up in the bar as some of the Dartmouth hockey team walks in and Hunter's face lights up at the sound of it. He watches the Dartmouth forward I was scouting walk in and shakes his head ever so subtly.

"Give that kid a couple of years and he'll be getting the same reception when he walks into The Tank after a game."

"You think?" I ask, even though I already know the answer—the kid's that good. But more than anything, I'm happy Hunter's engaging with me on this.

"Yeah. The kid has it. Skill and that star quality that has you on the edge of your seat waiting to see what he's going to wow you with next."

"Kind of like another forward I know," I murmur with a lift of my brows. I catch the hitch in his movement as he brings the beer to his lips. But he lets the comment go. He doesn't push or prod or live for the praise that many athletes I've repped need to continually boost their egos.

Hunter's different. He'd rather fade into the background than be the center of attention. I've always been curious why a man so brash in personality and bold in his play, hides from the limelight. As if he's not worthy of such praise. Ridiculous.

"Your dad doing good?" he asks. "Your sisters still a pain in your ass?"

I nod, surprised he's asking. Small talk was never our thing and this feels surprisingly normal, but maybe we're stepping into new territory. "They're always pains in my ass but isn't that how it goes?" I laugh and think of Lennox and our conversation the other night about the man in front of me, and I have a sudden pang of homesickness. Sure, we fight and annoy each other, but there's a comfort in knowing they're there. In knowing we might tell each other we hate each other one moment, but the next, they'd have my back if I needed them to. "We're all just super busy, always all over the place to tell you the truth."

He chuckles. "Is that your polite way of saying you guys still don't get along?"

I run my fingers up and down the condensation on my glass and let the water pool around the coaster. "It's not that we don't get along." I sigh and try to put it into words so that someone on the outside of our family dynamic might get it. "I mean, we all care about each other but there's a lot of resentment there. I—it wasn't my choice to be the mom when my mom died. I was the oldest, so with my dad off all the time with clients, trying to provide for us . . . sure, we had a nanny, but the discipline and rules and shit fell on me for some reason."

"That had to have been hard losing her when you were young."

I avert my gaze from his and look at the bubbles moving up the side of my Diet Coke. What no one truly understood was that I was never allowed to grieve. To have her be there healthy one day and the next be gone when the aneurism hit without warning. I remember feeling so damn lost and alone. I had responsibilities and emotions way beyond most teenagers, but no one knew I cried myself to sleep every single night. No one saw me turn over the pillow because the case was soaked from the tears I shed.

No one knew how desperately lonely I was.

"It was devastating." I scrunch my nose to abate the tears and then push away the sadness as I've learned to do. "For all of us."

When he meets my eyes, there's a compassion I've never seen before from him and as welcome as it is, I'm glad when he breaks the moment by speaking. "Why haven't your sisters realized you were just stepping up?" he asks. "They're old enough to know better."

"I'm sure they do . . . and we're all working on healing from the trauma of it all, but we're so damn different. It's like each one of us are different directions on a compass that will never see eye to eye except in those rare moments. For us though, it worked. I mean, our individualism was good because it gave our dad something to have with each of us . . . but it also caused a competitive dynamic that was toxic in a sense."

"Something will happen that will make you all realize none of the differences mean shit. You'll realize the fights are love disguised. The competition is fate's way of making you want more. The laughter is something you'll hold on to in your darkest moments. And eventually, you'll reach a point where you appreciate each other and the rest will be white noise."

I stare at him, his poignant words so unexpected, and wonder where this wisdom comes from. There are so many things I want to say to him, least of all how beautiful his comment is . . . but I know that's not something he'd readily accept. "Maybe we should already realize that after losing our mom. Then again, maybe we're just a houseful of stubborn women who'll figure it out someday."

"Hey man," a waiter says as he slides a fresh beer across the table before patting Hunter on the shoulder. "It's on the house. Your secret's safe with me. Enjoy your beer in peace."

Hunter laughs and shakes his head. "Thanks, man. Appreciate it." They shake hands and then the waiter moves to another table.

But when I look back to Hunter, he's leaning back in his seat, more relaxed than I've seen him this whole road trip, and a soft smile is on his face as he studies me.

"What made you think to bring me with you tonight?" he asks after a beat.

"Just a hunch."

"A hunch?"

"Yeah. Like I said earlier, sometimes it's good to get a different perspective on things."

"You're talking in circles, Dekk. You tend to do that when you don't want to answer something."

"Tell me," I say. "From the last few hours, what's the first thing that comes to your mind?"

"Besides the fear you were kidnapping me?"

"Besides that," I say with a nod.

"Tennis balls," he says through a laugh.

The same laugh I've heard all night. While he pointed things out to me about the game. Insights I might never have caught as I wouldn't have known. When he took the tennis balls the people sitting next to us offered and tossed them on the ice as is the school tradition upon the team's first goal against their rival Princeton.

He was booing and laughing and pointing at the torrent of balls bounding around the ice. It was the most carefree I've heard him, and another clue that I might just be right about him being burned out.

"It's the craziest thing I've ever seen, and that's coming from a man who's had the damn octopus flung within feet of him during a game against the Red Wings."

"I've been to the Dartmouth-Princeton game a few times. Sometimes for fun, others for recruiting purposes. It's the best when those tennis balls get tossed. Chaos and comradery. There's nothing like a rivalry, like playing a sport simply because you love it, like being a part of something so steeped in tradition."

"Ah," he says and tips his glass up, but his eyes don't leave mine. "Is this where we return to talking in circles?" His tone is playful but his eyes warn me to tread lightly.

I could have figured as much.

"No circles. I just thought after the last game, you needed a night away from the guys."

"So you took me to more hockey." There's amusement in his voice.

"I did." I shrug unapologetically. "It was an off night before the team moves on to Boston, I had to check out that kid, and so I thought . . . why not bring one of the best along."

"The best? You keep complimenting me, Kincade, I'm going to start thinking you actually mean it."

"Maybe I do." Our eyes meet, hold; there's a silence between us that stretches with equal parts comfort and flirting.

"That's why you kidnapped me?" He reaches out and tucks a piece of hair behind my ear. "And here I thought it was for you to use me for your own devious pleasures."

"Devious pleasure?" I laugh, but hell if that slow, sweet ache doesn't come to life at the apex of my thighs thinking about Hunter and pleasure.

"So good it's dangerous."

"Jesus!" I laugh. "Yes, that's it. I kidnapped you and then twisted your arm so I could take full advantage of you."

"Tasered me too."

"Was it that bad? Is going with me so brutal that tasering is the only option?"

He leans forward and puts his elbows on the table, and for a moment I think he's going to kiss me. I freeze and then feel ridiculous when he does nothing more than murmur, his voice a low rumble. "You want to know the best part of the game?"

"Hmm?" I'm surprised by his sudden change of topic but entranced not only by his voice, but by how content he seems.

"Everything I do, everywhere I go, someone wants something from me. Time, talent, notoriety, you name it. Do you know how nice it was to go to a game and just enjoy it? To be amazed by talent and laugh at tennis balls and to sit in the stands where no one knew who I was or demanded something of me?"

"I can't imagine," I murmur and feel like a traitorous asshole, because *I* want something from him.

"Part of it's the Cup, you know."

"What do you mean?"

"That's why Ian and the Jacks gave me such a huge contract," he says, referring to the LumberJacks general manager. "It's on my shoulders to deliver the Cup in return."

I laugh at the ludicrousness of that. "Any agent worth their salt wouldn't agree to those terms." I shake my head and place another mental tic next to why Sanderson is an asshole. Commission, first. Client's well-being, second. "What happens if you don't deliver?" I ask, and the only response I get is the twitch of that muscle in his jaw. Curiosity owns me, and while I understand that companies acquire benchmark players to build on, no one can guarantee a Stanley Cup.

"It doesn't have to be written in the contract to know what's expected of me," he says answering my unspoken question.

"Winning is expected of every player." I laugh, but it falls when I see the gravity in his expression. "That's why you play the game, right? That's why every player is out there on the ice. No one forms a team hoping they'll be mediocre."

"The teams without the big purse strings do."

"You're missing my point, Hunter." I shake my head and lean back and stare at him. Now, he looks like the weight of the world is on his shoulders, and I wish I could take it all away. "Do you know how many exceptional players never won the Cup? I can list a ton of them."

"So can I, and my name would be one of them."

"Your career has been phenomenal. Even if you never win the Cup—"

"Don't bullshit me, Dekker. You can be the greatest there ever was, but if you don't ever win, it doesn't mean shit. The greats win the Cup. More than once. So that was our deal. He paid me a ridiculous amount of money, and expects me to build the team around me that will help win the Cup for the first time in franchise history."

"You're staring down your first playoff berth. I'd say the team you built around you is working just fine." But at what cost, I wonder. "What is there, fifteen games left in the season?"

"Yes."

"That's a hell of a lot of pressure," I murmur more to myself than to him.

"You have no fucking idea." He sighs. "And we're almost there. We're so close I can all but taste it . . . but, fuck if I know if we can do it."

"What do you mean?" I ask, reaching out and putting my hand on his to stop him from pulling away.

"Never mind. It's nothing." His smile is tight as he downs the rest of the beer. "It's late. We should get going. It's a long drive back."

I sigh as he scoots his stool out and goes to close out his tab, because I feel like we were making genuine headway. The positive in this? My hunch was right. Hunter Maddox has reached his emotional limit, and he doesn't know how to admit it to himself.

Instead, he's angry. He acts out. He burns the candle at both ends. For a man who prefers to fade into the background, he's the face of a team who I think is going to take center stage in the coming weeks.

How is he going to handle it? Because if his reaction to the pressure he's under now is any indication, it's not going to be good.

Will helping him realize he's burned out help the situation or hurt it?

20

Dekker

"JUST SAY IT."

The fight he's angling for, the one I can sense in his tone of voice and how he's pulled into himself and thoughts since we parked, I don't really have the energy to give.

"Say what?" I ask as I glance over to Hunter as we walk through the parking lot toward the hotel entrance. It's been a long drive, it's late, and I'm beat.

"Whatever the fuck it is that has been on your mind since we left the bar."

"Who said I had anything to say?"

"You've always been shit at hiding your emotions. You think you're so good at it—a hard-ass—but they're on your sleeve when it comes to me."

"You're such a liar."

"Huh. Then I guess the last time I saw you *before*, when you walked out of the hotel, I misread you and had you pegged all wrong."

"What's that supposed to mean?" Caution vibrates through me.

"It means you walked out because you broke the rules."

My feet falter, and I have a hard time swallowing as his words hit my ears. "Broke what rules?" I feign ignorance.

He takes a step closer to where I've stopped and stares at me. I'm glad for the cover of the night, but I don't think it's going to mask the sudden anxiety I have about where he's going with this. "You tell me."

Our gazes hold in an awkward dance where it seems he doesn't want to follow through with whatever accusation he'd planned. I don't want to open Pandora's box.

I'm not sure what's worse, him telling me he knew I had feelings for him or me realizing he knew *and* let me walk away without saying a word.

I shake my head when I realize why he made the comment. Such a Hunter thing to do. Dodge. Deflect. Turn the topic around to the opposition by changing the subject so he doesn't have to answer and be the one to open himself up. Classic fucking Maddox.

I'm glad I didn't say anything. I'm glad I didn't give him the distraction he was angling for and answers he might not have realized.

"Tell me something," I ask, bracing my hands on my hips.

"Nothing good ever came from a sentence starting like that." He crosses his arms over his chest, already on the defensive.

"You're the one who came after me, so why can't I ask you a question in turn?"

His exasperated sigh fills the silence around us. "Look, it's been a good night. We had fun. We didn't kill each other, which is always a bonus when it comes to us, and while it's a good thing, it's also kind of unnerving because *it's us*, right?" He chuckles but there's an exhaustion to it. "Just let whatever it is go that you need to know and don't ruin the night, okay?"

"What do you do in the off season?" I ask.

He laughs in protest. "I'm not doing this, Dekker. This isn't the discussion we're having."

"Just . . . humor me. Please. I . . . please." I reach out to grab his arm to stop him when he begins to walk, but I see the minute his shoulders fall and know he's going to give me an inch here. "It's not a trick question. It's just . . . what do you do in the off season?"

"Practice. Work out. Practice some more." His arms fall to his sides.

"And in your downtime?"

"Study hockey, film, opponents, weaknesses." He says the words like

I should know this—*and I do*—but I need him to hear it. I need him to listen to himself and realize his single-minded focus.

"And what else do you do besides hockey?"

"What is it I do?"

"Yeah, besides twenty-four/seven hockey, what else do you enjoy doing?"

The crooked grin that crawls over his lips and the way his eyes scrape down the V of my shirt and back up has me shaking my head.

"We could go upstairs and I could show you exactly what I enjoy."

While my body reacts viscerally to his words, my head remembers his complete rejection from the other night.

"I'm sure we could, but that's not part of this conversation." I shake my head. "Seriously. What do you do besides hockey and the one-night stands?"

"Two-night stands."

"Funny. I'm serious."

He stares at me. "Plenty."

I bark out a laugh but the sound settles as he stares at me.

"You asked me why I took you to the Dartmouth game tonight. You asked me to stop talking in circles . . . so I've stopped . . ." Every part of me prepares for the fallout from what I'm going to say. My shaky inhale reflects it. "You're burned out, Hunter—fucking fried—and you need to recharge your engine somehow—"

"No, I'm not." He physically rejects the words as if taking two steps back from me is going to help do that.

"It's okay to say it. There's no shame in it."

Another partial laugh. An opening of his mouth and then shutting it, but I see the sudden panic in his eyes. I hear it in the vibrato of his laugh.

"This is the last thing I need right now. Do you know that? Do you get the shitstorm I'm about to walk into tomorrow?"

"Tomorrow?"

"Do you know—fuck," he barks, his body tense, the can of worms

I've opened expected but unknown. He walks a few feet away and laces his fingers on the back of his neck. "This is the last damn thing I need. Why couldn't you leave well fucking enough alone, huh?"

"Hunter. I'm sorry. I don't know what you're talking about, but I—"

"You're goddamn right you don't," he thunders as he glares at me, probably oblivious to the couple on the other side of the parking lot. But I care and hate to know what they're thinking as they glance our way several times. "Do you know how stupid that sounds?"

"How stupid what sounds?"

"That I no longer *love* hockey."

His words stagger me. Burning out because of the relentless nature of the sport and trying to be your best versus hating that sport are two completely different things. But standing here, seeing him struggle, I know he can't see the difference or separate himself from it . . . and it breaks my heart. There are tears in his eyes weighted with a mixture of shame and confusion and anger. It's almost as if uttering those words—that he's lost his love of hockey—is an admission that his identity has been stolen, and he's not sure how to navigate his way back to it.

I struggle between offering him tough love or sympathy and know that it seems that neither is going to cut it. Taking a step toward him, I try to reason with hm.

I no longer love hockey.

"You don't mean that—"

"You're goddamn right I do," he shouts, arms out to his sides. "But it's so much more than that. So much more than I could ever explain."

It's that little break in his voice on the last word—and the defeat that eats up his posture—that nearly undoes me and makes me want to wrap my arms around him to take away the hurt that owns his eyes.

"Try me." I take a step closer. "I'm here. I'm—"

"You're what? You're going to waltz in here with your positive attitude and magic wand and put everything back to fucking perfect again? No offense, Dekk, but it's the last thing I want or need from you. The shit that's broken can't be fixed. The damage done can't be reversed. All I can do is ride the fucking wave and make the best of it."

"At least let me be there for you." His laugh is hollow and raw and eats away at me. I get he's a man not used to talking about feelings, but he needs to know. "Just know it's a normal thing that most professional athletes experience at one time or another during their career. I mean, how can you not burn out? How can you play day after day and—"

"That's enough!" His voice thunders through the parking lot. His words suggest he's not listening, but the expression on his face—fear and uncertainty—shows me that he hears me. He knows I'm right. He's just too proud and stubborn and masculine, too scared to admit defeat. Like many, he sees it as a sign of weakness.

As a sign of failure.

But failure of what is the question?

"Who do you think you are, playing shrink with me?"

"I'm the furthest thing from a shrink." I take a step toward him. "We need to help you remember why you loved the game in the first place."

"Who's this *we*, crap?"

"You. I mean you. I just thought I could help—"

"So that's what tonight was about, right? It wasn't about just letting me go watch a game. It wasn't about letting me get away from the guys for a bit and be me, and not just a captain. It was to show and make me see that I can love the game in a different way." The protest dies on my tongue when I see the tears of frustration glistening in Hunter's eyes. "Like I said, there are always strings attached. Always an ulterior motive. Always something someone wants from me and this time, no fucking surprise, it's you—"

"Will you listen to yourself?" I shout.

"What? The alternative is listening to you?" His voice beats mine out.

"I don't want to fight. All I want to do is help you however I can. Saying you're burned out isn't an admission of—"

"Isn't an admission of what? You don't think I know millions would kill to be in my shoes? You don't think I know how fucking crazy it sounds for me to complain about living the dream? Who the hell needs a break from the game or thing they love? Who the hell says fuck you to the thing that has defined and saved them?" He walks a few feet the other way and the low, guttural chastisement he emits is heartbreaking. "I'm thirty-two years old and every goddamn day is a grind. Every day is me chasing a ghost I'll never surpass in certain eyes. Each day is me faking it for the fans that I'm the person they think I am. *Christ.* How many days will it be until they see I'm a fraud? Until they realize I'm smoke and mirrors and only trying to live up to the expectations others have of me?"

He's saying things I don't understand now, but I don't interrupt. I close my mouth and let him rant on things I can only partially comprehend but emotionally can fathom.

He's like a little boy. One who hears the truth but rejects it on principle.

"Hey." My voice is calm and soothing as I step beside him. My hands itch to pull him into a hug, to touch him somehow, to calm him. "I know you don't want to hear this, but I really need you to. I understand everything that you've said. The why. The how is it possible. The *what an ass* I *would be to feel this way.* And all of that's valid to someone on the outside . . . but you're on the inside looking out, Hunter, and what you feel is valid too. I mean, isn't that why you're struggling? The *how can you complain* or be sick of it when it's most people's dream job . . . but it's just that, *a job.* You can be the best in the world at something, be on top of your game, and still burn out. It's human. It's—"

"And I'm sure you have the cure for it, right?" Gone is the emotion etched in the lines of his face. His mask has been put back on, feelings under lock and key. The anger replaced by sarcasm. The confusion traded for denial.

It takes everything I have not to grab his shoulders and shake him to make him listen to me. I'm frustrated and hurt that he's shut down.

"I don't have any answers. All I can say is that you need more balance.

You need to be Hunter Maddox, the guy who likes to watch movies or cook or I don't know what it is you might like to do, but you can have an identity that's outside of hockey while still being Hunter Maddox the hockey star to everyone else."

"Oh, don't look now, but here comes Detailed Dekker and her perfect answers for everything to the rescue. Well, news flash, I don't need to be saved. I don't need them or their pressure. I don't need fucking anyone, and I sure as hell don't need you."

His words hit me one after another. Most making sense, some not, and I concentrate on who he means by *them*, but refrain from asking.

His shoulders heave with anger as our eyes hold. The white smoke from his breath disappears.

When I speak, my voice is the antithesis of his. It's calm, even, unemotional. "That's not what I was trying to do. All I was—"

"Save it, Kincade. Fucking save it." He waves a hand at me and shakes his head. "I've had enough of this shit. Thanks for ruining tonight when I told you to let it go."

Without another word, he turns on his heel and heads to the entrance of the hotel.

That whole conversation was a disaster. Total and utter disaster.

And I'm not a single step closer to figuring out what it is that weighs so heavily on his shoulders.

21

Hunter

"WE DIDN'T GET A chance to speak to you after the other night's game, any comment on the marked difference in your performance or were you just having an off night?"

The game feels like light years ago already. What was it? Only three days? Four? Fuck if I can remember.

Through the blinding lights I can just make out my agent, Finn Sanderson, at the back of the press briefing room. His arms are crossed over his chest, his back is against the wall, and it seems like his eyes never leave me.

Management called in the big guns to control me. Jünger must be worried I'll let him down and not heed his threats.

Hell, maybe they were smart considering we're in my hometown and avoidance is at its finest.

"Everybody has an off night. Apparently that game was mine," I say, giving the company line Sanderson drilled in my head right after his numerous threats about how if I keep my shit up, I'm going to be benched or suspended and lose him as an agent. While I'm pretty sure his warnings about losing endorsement deals are a load of crap said to instill fear in me, the benching me part might be true enough. "Let's hope I can shake off the bad juju and get back into the groove tonight."

"Are you worried how that loss is going to matter to the Jacks in the standings?"

I move the microphone back and try to find who asked the question but have a hard time seeing through the lights.

"Every game matters. Every win, every loss. I've been playing in this league long enough to know a one-goal loss in the first week of the season can be the determining factor to how your season ends when you never realized it. Lucky for us, the Nomads lost too so we had an even night on paper."

You're burned out, Hunter—fucking fried.

Dekker's words replay in my head for the millionth time since they passed her lips, and I try to shake them off. I know it's true. Obviously, she knows it's true.

But goddamn it, the reason why is something I can't fix.

I've tried.

Jesus, have I tried.

"Mr. Maddox, over here." The female reporter's voice rings out and knocks Dekker's voice from my head. I blink a few times into the light and then hold my hand over my eyes so I can look in her direction. "Hello. Hi."

Rookie reporter. They always ramble when they're new.

"Hello."

"Um, yes. Um . . . Vida Henson with Sports Worldwide. You seem to have been on a tear lately. You're closing in on two NHL records in rapid time. Are you doing anything different this year to make such strong improvements to your game?"

Yeah, my brother's dying.

"Good question."

And I helped kill him.

I stare at the lights and shake my head as I fight back the truth that haunts me every day of my life. At the crushing weight of it.

"I've been . . . training differently," I lie. "I added on some new members to my team outside of the club to help bring out my potential, and

I—uh—guess they deserve a raise because it seems to be working."

I say a few more things, but I'm distracted.

Maybe it's being back in the same city I grew up in.

Maybe it's knowing I have to go home and face reality.

Maybe it's because . . .

"Mr. Maddox? Randy Girdley with Headline Sports. You grew up not far from here, are there any places you like to frequent when you get to come back home?"

The stretch of road where my life changed forever.

The cemetery to pay my respects.

Dekker wasn't completely right.

It's so much more than being burned out.

I blink a few times as the room shifts and moves around me, and I try to fight those first few terrifying moments when the path my life was on changed forever.

Your game is shit tonight, son. You should be embarrassed of how you played.

Facing my dad.

Yeah, that's another place I can't fucking wait to go, *home*.

I force a smile and let a laugh fall. Anything to draw them away from the truth. "Everyone has their places when they return home." I scoot my chair back and stand.

"Like?" he counters.

"My schedule is always packed when I come here, so I rarely have time to venture from it. Of course, my training and the team comes first, but then there's a visit to Boston's Children's Hospital, some time spent with the kids at the Elite 9 Rink to answer their questions. A few other things to help pay it back or help the game move forward. Busy. Busy." Another smile to sell the lie. "Thank you for your time. I hope to see you all at the game tonight."

I'm through the door to my right as more questions are fired off, my feet moving from one side to the other while I try to settle the discord eating me whole.

Why is this so hard this time? Why does it feel like all the oxygen is being sucked out of every breath I try to take?

Within seconds, Sanderson comes through the same door I just did. "Everyone has their places?" He chuckles. "It came off like you meant a brothel or some shit."

If he only knew.

"I danced in the dog and pony show you set up, isn't that enough? You want me to focus on the game tonight and play my hardest, then isn't it time I go so I can prepare for it? I did what you said and you're still crawling up my ass."

"I asked you this the other day when your GM called me and told me to straighten your shit out and you dodged it, and I'm going to ask you again: what the fuck is going on with you? You answered their questions, but your smile said *fuck you.* The bad-boy act only flies so far. Are you trying to throw away your career, the stats, and records you've almost reached?"

"I played nice. Now I'd like to go study films. The Fishers have a new defense they've been toying with and I need to make sure I've got it figured out," I say of the team we're playing tonight.

He nods as he studies me. "Good to see your head is back in the game."

"It never left it."

"You're the face of this team, Maddox. A lot is riding on you."

My face is, but it should be Jonah's heart and body.

"So you've said," I mutter and look out the window of the otherwise empty room.

"Mind answering why you seemed so distracted? Why you keep moving around like you can't sit still? Jünger was concerned the Oxy you were taking for your knee is—"

"Fuck this." Fed up with the accusation, I go to walk past him and he reaches out and grabs my arm. I yank it the hell away. "Get the fuck off me, Finn. You think I'm using? Then drug test me. I'm clean. You think I'm drinking? Hell yeah, I overindulge a time or two, but not any more than anyone else on this team. Maybe my problem is you guys putting your nose in my shit when I've told you to back the fuck off."

"My job is to have my nose in your shit and right now, it stinks. Straighten the fuck up."

"Noted." I move toward the door.

"I'm riding out the next few games with you, because I fear what you'll do if I don't, so I suggest you make sure we don't have to have a talk like this again."

When I exit the room without a response and turn the corner, I come face to face with Dekker.

Fucking hell. First him and now her. Both on my ass.

"Whoa! You going somewhere in a hurry?" she asks as we spin around so we're in opposite positions now, and she puts her arms on my bicep to steady herself.

"Yeah. I've got shit to do." A ton of it, in fact. Having too much to do gives me an excuse why going to my parents' house isn't an option until after the game.

That and being busy prevents the ghosts this place conjures every time I come back here from haunting me too much.

"Hunter?" I meet her eyes and it's for a split second too long, because I can tell the minute she sees them—the ghosts—because her hand tightens on my arm. "Hey?"

"Yeah? What?" I take a step back.

"I've texted a few times. You're not responding."

Because if you're the only one who's noticed I'm burned out, I'm afraid if you look any closer you'll see the rest of the truths I hide.

"Been busy." My tone is clipped and my feet shift with impatience.

"I just . . . I wanted to apologize for the other night. I didn't mean to push you. I—"

"Done and fucking over with." I offer a tight smile and hate that seeing her makes me feel so damn rattled. Hating her presence and not wanting her to leave. Frustrated, because it feels like a burden has been lifted that someone else knows and unsettling that she does. *That she can see me.*

She worries her bottom lip between her teeth and shakes her head, her eyes loaded with concern I don't want to see. "Got it. Done and over with. Discussion never happened. Night never happened. No need to repeat it."

But it did. The laughter. The Kings hat. The tennis balls. The beer. The comfortable silence. The solidarity.

"Did you need something else?"

"Just know I'm here for you. If there's anything I can do to help—"

"Do you know what would help? If people stopped fucking telling me that. I'm not a cancer patient. I'm not dying. I'm fine."

She stares at me, her jaw clenching and eyes firing with anger.

I'm reminded immediately of three years ago when she stood in that hotel room, her chin quivering but held high as she fought the emotion in her eyes. As she told me our fling had run its course and that it was best we didn't meet again. As she saved me from having to break her heart that was starting to grow a bit too attached to mine.

Because mine was already fucking there too.

The memory is the last thing I need. To be reminded of what it felt like to be cared for by her. To remember how I had spent too much time convincing myself I didn't deserve someone like her—the feelings, the comfort, the simplicity of it all—only for her to save me by doing it for me.

Only to prove to me just how much of an asshole I am. I never chased her, told her she was wrong . . . because I let her walk away.

She struggles momentarily with her emotions before the business-woman façade slides back into place and she takes a step back.

"It makes sense now."

"What's that?" I ask.

"You don't want to hear what I said the other night, but you want to play the victim. News flash," she says, mocking what I said to her. "You—"

"Christ, Hunter." I look up to see Sanderson over Dekker's left shoulder, disbelief and disgust etched in the lines of his face. "You told me you were leaving to get your head in the game. Yet here you are, trying to score a cheap fuck like a desperate john."

Before I can respond with the fury that streaks through me, Dekker spins to face him.

"A cheap fuck?" she asks, and Sanderson's face pales when he sees who I'm speaking with. "I'm sure your clients get great publicity when their agent talks to their fans like that." She takes a few steps toward him, a tsk on her tongue. "For the record, Finn, I'm nowhere close to being a cheap fuck, but you'd never know because I wouldn't touch you with a ten-foot pole."

With that, Dekker Kincade saunters down the hotel hallway without looking back. I chuckle quietly. And then I wonder why she's the only person who can put a smile on my face these days.

22

Dekker

SKATES CARVE UP THE freshly resurfaced ice. The sound is like a symphony of skills and maneuvers you can hear just as easily as you can see.

I watch the LumberJacks go through their warm-ups as the diehard fans arrive early to make sure they catch every second of hockey they can.

A few times I catch Hunter glancing up to where I'm standing in the visiting team's suite. While a small part of me hopes it's because he feels bad for being an ass to me earlier, the rest of me knows he doesn't care.

Hell, the only time Hunter Maddox cared about how I felt was when it came to sensations to get me off.

But I think about his press conference today. About the disconnect I saw him have in his answers and the way he acted when I ran into him afterward.

Guess nothing much has changed about him in that aspect either . . . Even now, I can't figure him out.

"Such a surprise to see you in Boston."

I glance in my periphery to see Finn Sanderson step up beside me, arms folded, the suit he's wearing ridiculously expensive.

"We all have jobs to do," I murmur, not exactly wanting to engage with him, and not just because of his *cheap fuck* comment. I simply don't like the man.

"And some of us are better at those jobs than others, right, Dekker?"

His voice is smooth as silk but I know it's laced with arsenic.

He's pushing buttons.

I don't give him the satisfaction of responding.

"What client are you here to babysit?" he asks.

Every word he utters is a reminder of the clients he's taken from us. How he's slowly chipped away at our foundation and it strengthens my resolve that much more. The Kincades will win this fight.

Now, if I could just approach Hunter to see where I stand.

Then again, if Finn keeps sticking his foot in his mouth like he did earlier today with his *cheap fuck* comment, I'll just keep my mouth shut and let him do the convincing for me.

The guys switch drills, and I watch Callum move through the line. He swears his change to a plant-based diet has made all the difference in the past couple of months and a part of me agrees. It seems to have assisted in the fluidity of his movement and his increased stamina. Regardless of the reasons behind it, I'll take it, because his contract is up at the end of the season and I'd love his stats to inch up to help those negotiations in our favor.

I watch them and Finn watches me.

"Should I be worried you're here to steal my clients, Dekker?" he finally asks.

He's pushing buttons.

I snort in response and check a text that came across my phone to play him a bit.

"Is that a yes?" he pushes.

I turn to face him for the first time. I take in his perfectly styled hair and dark gray eyes and all I can think is how he's too perfect, too polished.

I bristle over how much I despise him but the smile on my face shows nothing but indifference.

"It's a nothing. It's a maybe you should be a better agent and then you wouldn't have to worry if your client might jump ship, because you already know they're satisfied."

"Like yours are?"

"I'll let you stand here and be a petty, insecure agent while I go stand over there in shoes I'm more than comfortable in and with a conscience that lets me fall asleep perfectly fine at night." I start to move to the opposite end of the box.

"Tucking your tail between your legs already, Kincade? I thought you'd fight harder than that to keep your clients."

"Prick," I mutter under my breath and welcome the ringing of his cellphone to interrupt this less-than-stimulating conversation.

There is a commotion at my back, and I turn toward the entrance to see a high-tech-looking wheelchair being moved into the suite. I smile at the person who's strapped into the chair out of kindness, but I'm unaware if he sees me or not. Fearing I'm staring, I offer a similar greeting to the woman pushing it. She's older in age, her hair stuck to her cheek and frustration lining her face.

"Do you need any help?" I offer and move toward them, noting the awkwardness of the chair since its occupant is lying back.

"No. I've got it. Thanks," she says with a slight grunt as she moves him to the end of the aisle where the chair can fit with an unobstructed view of the arena.

And it hits me.

That's Jonah. It's Hunter's brother.

I digest the information, trying not to look their way so I can make the connection completely.

Then I debate walking over and introducing myself to them, but figure I should let her get them situated first so my presence doesn't make him feel like I'm there to ogle or so I'm not in the way.

And the whole time I stand there waiting for them to get settled, eyes watching the Jacks warm-up and their actions in my periphery, she murmurs words to who I assume is Jonah as if she's making sure everything is okay.

"Here we are. You comfortable?" She adjusts his arms. "How exciting.

Aren't you excited to be here, Jonah? I know you've been waiting forever for this." She flips a switch on the chair and it sits up some. "The Jacks are going to win tonight. I mean, you're here. You're their good luck charm."

She talks to him in a soft, singsongy voice, each sentence of hers competing with the gentle hum of his ventilated breaths, as she fiddles with things on the chair.

"Carla. So great to see you," Finn says before stepping around me.

I turn to watch Carla's face light up as she moves toward him and embraces him in a quick hug. "Mr. Sanderson. I didn't know you'd be here tonight. So good to see you."

Finn moves toward the man in the wheelchair. "Good to see you, Jonah. You excited to watch the game tonight? Your brother has been slaying it. I bet he's going to play like a madman tonight knowing you're here."

Carla reaches her hand out and pats Finn's arm, her eyes and the slight shake of her head saying something I don't understand.

Feeling like I'm eavesdropping but forced to due to proximity, I turn my attention back to the ice, my moment to introduce myself lost.

"Are you taking care of my boy?" she asks.

"You know he doesn't need taking care of." Finn laughs. "I'm sure you saw that for yourself."

"We haven't seen him yet. He said you had him scheduled all day. Maybe after the game tonight." There's sadness in her voice that replaced the excitement from moments earlier.

"Maybe."

Hunter looks up my way again and raises a hand in greeting.

"Hi, honey," Carla says loudly as if Hunter can hear her. "Jonah, Hunter says hi."

"Dekker? Have you met Carla and Jonah Maddox yet?"

I take a few steps to where they're set up. "No, I haven't. I've heard so much about you though," I say with a smile and extend my hand, hoping Sanderson just caught the implication that I'm close with Hunter. "Such a pleasure to meet you."

"Aren't you a pretty little thing," Carla says in the warm and most non-condescending way as she shakes my hand.

"Thank you." I turn to Jonah and suck in a breath. And it's not because of his pale complexion or the trach tube or anything to do with his disability, but rather the fact that he's identical to Hunter. Like exact. The hair, the eyes, the nose . . . it's simply stunning. I force myself not to stare at him for that reason alone and offer a smile. "Nice to meet you, Jonah."

He doesn't respond verbally but his eyes meet mine, and I nod in greeting.

"Carla, this is Dekker Kincade. She's the agent trying to steal your son away from me."

Carla barks out a laugh while I try to figure Finn's angle with the comment. "Well, she already has one up on you," Carla says. "She's a hell of a lot prettier."

23

Hunter

HE SHOULD BE THE one out here.

The thought is on replay in my head with each pass.

Each shove of the opposition.

Every whack of the puck toward the goal.

He should be the one out here.

The anger in my blood hums with a potency stronger than any drug I've ever been given. It surges and pushes me to take risks I don't even register and beats the shit out of me when whatever I try to do on the ice fails.

He's not doing well, Hunter. Another chest infection. Another blood infection. He's not able to speak anymore. Dr. Masterson says it's only a matter of time, really.

My mom's comment from months ago echoes in my head and causes the split-second fumble of my thoughts and the puck is stripped away from me. *Shit.*

My head.

It's way too fucking busy to be on the ice. Way too much shit going on.

How can I be down here doing this when he's up there like that?

When he damn well knows what ice feels like beneath his skates? When the roar of the crowd was more his drug than it was ever mine?

When life ended that night for him and finally began for me?

He should be the one out here.

The thought is the cadence of the fists I throw at Brighton for no reason at all—other than he plays like Jonah used to and it pains me to defend against him and remember—and then later at Vladkin for pushing me from behind like so many others have in my years playing this game.

But tonight is different.

Tonight, I can't deny the pain that burns within. I'm the reason he's not in my skates right now.

The reason hockey feels more like a prison than a job. A game.

The guilt.

Shame.

Self-loathing.

C'mon, Hunter. Tonight's your night.

Those words from my twin so very long ago echo in my ears and ring true now.

Tonight is my night.

Every night is.

And I hate every minute of it.

And I'm the reason why.

24

Dekker

I WATCH THE GAME from the nosebleed seats.

It's where I prefer to sit. My AirPods are in, the local announcers are giving the play-by-play in my ear, and the game unfolds in front of me while I'm wrapped in my own world.

"Look, Bob. I'm not going to complain that Mad Dog Maddox showed up to play tonight, but it does look like there's a little trouble in paradise. Unless I'm mistaken, when Withers came up on him before that last period, I thought Maddox was going to take a swing at his own teammate."

Shit.

Announcers are noticing.

How can they not? When Callum came up to get his attention from behind, Hunter whirled on him with his fist cocked back and so much anger etched in his face, his intention was all but unmistakable.

Management has to see it.

Fans won't be far behind.

"Or maybe you read it all wrong," Bob says.

"I know what it looked like to me and that, mixed with his poor performance last game, has me wondering if he's losing his edge."

"Losing his edge? No way. Not Maddox," Bob counters. "Everyone has an off game."

"An off game is one thing, but there have been rumors during the past few months about discord in the team over Maddox," Steve says.

"Of course there is. The tension is just as high as the expectations over us gunning for the Cup. It's bound to surface somewhere. Besides, you said it yourself, they're just rumors."

"Let's hope the boys can keep it together and bring this thing home for us . . . if not, I'm afraid of the fire sale that might happen."

"Fire sale? Are you implying the Jacks will get rid of Maddox if they don't reach the playoffs?" Bob gasps. "That's blasphemy. Boo, fair-weather fan."

Steve laughs. "That wouldn't be my option of choice, but seriously, how much longer can a club like the Jacks keep a player like Maddox?"

"Let's hope forever." Bob chuckles.

"To be the voice of reason—"

"Fair-weather fan," Bob coughs, and they both laugh.

"Seriously. We're a small-time club with only so much money for salaries. If we're not winning and the seats start going half-empty, we'll never be able to afford a player like him."

"I see what you're saying, but he's a sure thing," Bob says. "He's going to get us that Stanley Cup . . . and he's a Jack now. He's one of us and dammit, we love him."

"Sometimes sure things don't pan out."

"The season's not over yet. Give him time."

Yeah, time to succeed or to fail.

"Action coming back in two minutes, folks. In the meantime, I'll hit Steve over the head for those of you already doing it at home for throwing out into the ether that we might have to trade Maddox away."

"Oh, please. All I'm saying is we—the Jacks—are like the little engine that could. We're having a hell of a season. For the first time, everything has clicked and a huge part of that is because of Maddox's leadership and star power—off games like the other night not included. At what point will a club like the Rangers or the Red Wings with their abundance of cash be able to woo him away?"

"Woo him away?" Bob laughs.

"It's a legitimate question."

"He'd stay here. Lucky for us, he chose to leave one of those big-name teams two years ago to come here. I'm sure he has his own personal reasons why, and yes, while he's had a rough patch these past few months, he's brought this team and our city to life like no other player has in recent memory. My money's on the Jacks on this one. They won't let him get away."

"Yeah, well, let's just hope whatever is going on with him sorts itself out. The subpar game the other night against the Patriots where he played like he was handcuffed, and now this game tonight where he's a one-man wrecking crew . . . it's like night and day."

"You can't have him both ways. He's an all-or-nothing guy."

"Food for thought," Bob says. "We're back in action, Jacks fans. The third period is about to get underway with your Jacks up an impressive four to one."

They drone on as the game picks back up while I lean back in my chair, cross my arms over my chest, and try to figure out what to make of today. Of Hunter's press conference, of my conversation with Sanderson, meeting Hunter's family, and how he's playing tonight—somewhere between out of control and brilliant. He's a very rich man, but is out there playing like he's starving. He's been in the penalty box more than I've ever seen him before. There's more of an edge to him tonight, and I guarantee that's part of the reason.

His family.

His brother.

Is that part of the drive for him?

I don't need them or their pressure.

Is he living out this dream . . . for the both of them since Jonah can't? The relentless schedule is enough to burn a man out, let alone have the added pressure of trying to do it for another person. Even his family, perhaps.

Is that what he meant by *them* the other night? Or am I way off base and he just meant *them* in general?

With a sigh and needing a break from my own thoughts, I figure it's a great time to stretch my legs. Standing from my seat, I walk back toward the general manager's box to get a refill on my drink. I'm just about to its entrance when I overhear Finn's voice.

"How can you complain? He's tearing it up tonight. The team's winning and we're one step closer to a playoff berth," Finn says. "Fourteen games and counting, but I think you'll have the playoff spot clinched before then."

"He may be tearing it up tonight, but he's also tearing up the team," the unique voice of the LumberJacks General Manager, Ian McAvoy, echoes off the concrete walls and has me perking my ears up. I'm not one for eavesdropping, but I'm definitely one for getting as much information as possible to do my job and the task I was sent here to do.

Even I understand how lame that sounds—standing here in the hall of an arena when I've had several times to tell Hunter exactly why I'm here but have balked every time.

"After the stunt he pulled the other night, Finn, I'm at my limit. The press conference was a Band-Aid, but don't kid yourself into thinking it fixed everything. The calls I received from the commissioner of the league asking me if he was purposely throwing the game tell me they're watching him."

"He wasn't throwing the game. I spoke in depth with him about what that game looked like to everyone else, and I promise you, it won't happen again."

"It better not. I wasn't too thrilled having to explain to the commissioner that Maddox isn't betting against his team, nor is anyone else for that matter. The last thing we need is a full-blown investigation into the club and whether or not they're betting money on game outcomes."

"That's preposterous," Finn sputters.

"It is, I agree, but can you see what it looks like to the outside world?

The guy goes from a precise, calculated player, to a selfish madman on a scoring streak, to being all but listless the last game, then to whatever you want to call the man down there who we're seeing dominate tonight. I'm all about showmanship, but this is more than that," Ian says, and I can't help but agree.

The crowd's chants echo in the corridor and I miss some of what the men are saying.

"We're nearing the end of the season, Ian. He's probably just running out of gas. I know you're paying him to be who he is, but between all the publicity you're pushing on him, you're taking time away from his game . . . and from some much-needed downtime. He's been pushing hard for months through injuries and without a break—"

"And we're paying him handsomely for his time." He laughs. "Don't try to act like we're not. He's your player, manage him or I will, and you're not going to like how I handle it."

"Is that a threat?" Finn huffs the words out as if he's not buying Ian's warning.

"That's up to you to decide."

They move back into the press box and their voices fade, but I'm left leaning against the cold cinderblock wall stunned at what I just heard.

Why in the hell are they talking about this right now, in the middle of a game? Did something else happen that I don't know about?

As much as I hate to admit it, Finn gave the perfect, placating response.

But shit, is this what I'm walking into if I win Hunter as a client? Threats by his GM and the inability to respond with conviction because Hunter refuses to let me in?

I lean my head back against the wall as the crowd roars and sigh.

~

THERE'S A LOT OF time between the end of a game and when the players leave the locker room to head to the team hotel. Time is spent with coaches, with teammates going over certain plays, with physical therapists treating injuries, interviews with the media in the locker room, and then finally showers and cleaning up.

I know other female agents stride into the locker room not caring that they're going to be hit with a bare ass or better yet, someone's dick, but not me.

I prefer to keep things on a professional level, and I've found that the minute a player knows I've seen him naked, the dynamic changes. It opens the door to the crude jokes and innuendos and those can sometimes ruin a working relationship no matter how nonchalant you are about them.

So, I stand outside the locker room as players begin to trickle out. Some dressed up to go out for their night on the town in Boston, some a whole lot worse for the wear with ice taped to knees and know they are definitely headed to the hotel to order some takeout.

"You ready?" Callum asks as he tosses something in the trash can.

"Sure am." I push my shoulders off the wall where I'm standing. "It's about time I get some time with you."

"Sorry. My schedule's been crazy."

"I get it. Mine always is. Great game, though."

He snorts. "They almost came back."

"But they didn't." I pick up my briefcase off the ground and wonder how a 5-2 score is almost coming back, but let it go. "What do you feel like eating?"

The door to the locker room opens and there's a shout that sounds off before it shuts.

"Party starting early?" I joke with a lift of my chin to behind the door.

His chuckle says volumes but he waits until we round the corner, away from any ears. "It's Maddox. He's . . . I don't know what's going on with him, but it's pulling all of us into it. I don't know if it's family or life or shit . . . I figured you knew since you guys, *you know* . . ."

"Since we . . . *you know*?" I brace myself for the frigid air when he opens the door to the outside for me. "What does that mean?"

"Everyone knows you guys had a thing a while back."

"Is that so?" I laugh outwardly . . . and cringe internally.

"Yeah. Rumor was you were leaving a hotel together."

"So nice to know my personal life is fodder for rumors," I say, playing it off. "We had drinks a few times like three years ago," I lie, neglecting to divulge the sordid details of our quick but fulfilling sex life. "But our interaction didn't give me any more insight on why he's acting how he is than you guys have."

"Yeah, but with you—never mind," he says as we reach my rental car.

"With me, what?" I stare at him over the roof of the car, our breaths turning white with each breath.

"With you, he's just different."

25

Hunter

DAD: *Is that seriously all you had in you? Piss poor performance.*

I STARE AT THE text, at the blinking cursor taunting me, and fight the urge to hurl my cell against the wall opposite me.

It's not his words that get me this time. It's the sudden emptiness that follows them. It's the hurt I felt when I looked up to the box between periods and didn't see him there. It's the knowing he never missed a single one of Jonah's games, but he won't take the time to make mine no matter how fucking effortless I make it for him.

I squeeze the phone and grit my jaw and struggle to control my temper.

Then I type.

ME: *I didn't see you at the game tonight, Dad. I had a ticket saved for you.*

I hit send and lean back against the wall, my eyes closed, and my disappointment heavy.

But why, Maddox?

Why are you disappointed he wasn't here? So he could criticize you face to face?

You need to stop wishing he might care as much about your game as he did Jonah's. You need to stop thinking he's going to be proud of you. You need to stop hoping for miracles.

I look down at my phone again as if he'll respond, when I know he won't, and then reread Dekker's text again.

DEKKER: *Great game tonight. That first goal was tennis ball-throwing worthy. Heading to dinner with clients then to Sculler's Jazz Club after with some of the team. Come celebrate.*

I'm not sure how long I stare at the text before deleting it and heading toward what I know will be a clusterfuck.

Visiting my parents always ends in one.

It doesn't matter that we won the game or that I've taken time out to visit my brother.

It doesn't make a difference that we're running down the playoffs or that my personal bests are beating past ones by miles.

Nothing does.

All that matters is that I'm not Jonah.

That's what it all comes down to.

26

Hunter

I STEEL MYSELF WITH a deep breath before I walk into the house. Everything is the same—the flooring, the furniture, the curtains. It looks like time stopped the day of the accident and has never moved on.

It's hard for me to breathe.

It's difficult for me to think of anything other than how, already, I need to get the hell out of the house with its walls lined with images of a life Jonah and I never got to live together. Because that life—that future we always talked about—never happened.

Reminders of that life we used to have are plastered on every surface as if to remind us all how perfect it used to be.

As if to forget the accident ever happened.

"Hunter? Is that you?" My mom's voice calls out from where she no doubt is sitting with him in his room.

I've offered to buy them a new house a million times, even put deposits down on a few. I explained how much easier it would be having a custom suite built for Jonah and his needs. How it would make their life—and his—so much easier, how it would give him some autonomy when he already feels trapped, but after numerous rejections of the offers, I gave up. They'd preferred to stay here where they can be reminded daily of the ghosts of that day and the butterfly effect I created.

"She's in Jonah's bedroom," my father mutters from his La-Z-Boy where he folds his newspaper with a crisp snap and reveals the blood pressure cuff on his arm. His eyes move from the newspaper in his hand to the television on the wall beside me, but he never looks at me. "Sloppy game tonight, son. Your skill fell by the wayside to your aggression. You need to work on keeping both at the same time."

"Yes, sir." I choke over the words and the resentment they cause. I played a damn good game by any player's standards, and as much as I know it, I also know he's nowhere near finished.

Just like the nights he kept me on the ice way past midnight. My body would be exhausted, my fingers numb, my stomach growling, but dammit, I was nowhere near good enough.

I wasn't Jonah.

And the way he looks at the picture of Jonah in front of him tells me just that: he sees everything Jonah could have been and more. He sees everything I caused. He sees everything I'll never be.

"You're weak on your left side, you know that? You were beat every damn time. You're not checking your shoulder enough like Jonah did, and it's getting you in trouble. You're partying too much. It doesn't seem like you're practicing on your shot and that's for mornings. You're out drinking and hungover. It's showing."

"Yes, sir." I nod—my feet shifting and lips pursing—and take the ridicule without talking back, because whatever I say doesn't matter. It won't be heard. His head is too preoccupied with another star forward, the one lying paralyzed in the next room, who I'll always be compared to.

I take the criticism, I accept the disdain, because I know my dad is hanging on by a thread. I know this is the only way he can cope with the dreams that were killed that day and the future that was robbed from us.

But it doesn't prevent my resentment from festering. It doesn't prevent my hands from fisting.

"There was a ticket there for you, you know. I didn't see you in the box. I thought maybe you'd like to come."

He nods, his eyes never leaving the television. "You know I like to watch my hockey from home."

Not with Jonah, you didn't. You were at every damn game up against the glass cheering and yelling.

In the fifteen years since the accident, you've sat and pushed me, but criticized and judged and disapproved from afar.

I swallow over the rejection that tears into me like it does every time, and let it settle in a place where someday I'll deal with it. *Maybe.* "Your health? It's okay?"

Forced words in a strained relationship.

"Yes. I can't be going anywhere, now can I? Jonah needs me too much."

So do I, Dad. So do I.

But that's irrelevant—I'm irrelevant—because Jonah does. Only one son survived that night and in my parents' eyes, it wasn't me.

I need a dad too, but not according to the man in front of me.

If only I had truly died that night. Anything but a walking ghost who once had a family who loved him.

"Of course." I stare at him for a beat. The blue of the television casts an odd glow on his skin, and I wonder if he really loves this life he lives, or if he's merely going through the motions.

"Maybe I'll see you in the stands at the next game?" I ask like I always do. My, *I love you, Dad, and still need you as a father* plea that never seems to be heard.

"Maybe." The lone word is all he says. All I want is for him to tell me to stay and sit with him, but I take off down the hallway toward Jonah's room.

The old, oversized den we used to sit in for hours playing Nintendo as boys and then later making out with girls as teenagers, looks like a hospital room now. My mom has tried to dress it up, but there's no hiding the reality.

The quiet hum of the television hides my footsteps as I stand there and take it all in. There's a bed on the far side of the room with a lift that hangs on a boom off to one side that helps my mom get Jonah in and out of bed.

The room is decorated in light colors that do nothing to disguise the medical equipment dotting its perimeter. A wheelchair is parked against one wall while on the opposing one a curio cabinet showcases his old trophies like shrines to an era gone by.

Like reminders to Jonah every single day of what he's missing out on in this shitty deal fate handed him.

My mom's back is to me as she fiddles with something beneath the hospital bed, her soft talking a constant, soothing sound she somehow adopted after the accident—almost as if one of us were a little boy complaining about an upset stomach, not a quadriplegic depending on her for his every need.

The last thing I look at in the room is my brother. I'm petrified almost as much as I am desperate to see him. It's been several months but it feels way too long since I have, and every part of me misses everything about him in a way I've never been able to express or understand.

It's the twin thing. The connection that's inherent.

I bite back my gasp when I finally look. He's withered away to nothing now, the shape of his body beneath the sheets barely noticeable. His lungs rise and fall with the help of the ventilator fastened by the trach tube at his throat, and the sound of the machine fills the room in a steady rhythm. His face is pale and his eyes are closed, but there's a small smile on his lips in reaction to something my mom has said.

My chest fucking caves in like it does every time I see him. Guilt and sorrow and anger and so many other damn emotions ride a roller coaster through me until they strangle all the words I normally say.

I feel awkward, as if I'm invading his privacy, while at the same time feeling at home and comfortable with the one person I know better than anyone.

Or used to.

"Hi guys," I say and walk toward them. My mom gasps, her startled smile following right after.

"There you are. You were so busy today I wasn't sure if we were going to see you before you moved on to the next city."

"I'd never miss the chance to see him." I accept the arms she wraps around me, and I fucking hate that I hold her tighter a little longer so I can keep the tears welling in my eyes hidden behind my closed lids. I don't want him to see how I see him. I don't want him to know how bad he's gotten.

And yet, I feel like he already knows. How can he not?

"It's been too long." Her words are barely audible.

I breathe her in. She smells of citrus and vanilla, but she feels so very frail and incredibly strong simultaneously. "I missed you too," I murmur as she pulls away and puts her hands on my cheeks to look at me.

Tears glisten in her eyes but she blinks them away with the sadness that falls momentarily over her countenance.

"Jonah, look who's here."

"You don't need to announce me. I'm not a guest," I tell her as I step to the bed and meet my brother's eyes.

He garbles something unintelligible that I know is a greeting, his attempt at pronunciation seeming worse than the sounds he was making last week when I spoke with him. Even with the speaking valve . . . It feels like everything is on a constant decline.

"Yeah, yeah." I lean down and give him a pseudo hug and rest my forehead against his for a moment, almost as if I'm recharging my twin meter. He's the same but so very different. "You're still the better looking one," I say as I stand back up with my jaw clenched to fight the helplessness I feel.

He gives a partial laugh that ends in a coughing fit. My mom pushes me out of the way as she pulls him up so he doesn't choke.

"You sanitized?" she asks, her voice going into panic mode over me bringing germs into his room.

"Yes," I mumble, feeling inept as I step back and let her help him in ways I can't. Ways that have changed and evolved over the fifteen years he's been a prisoner in his broken body and mind.

"Just rest, Jonah. You're fine now," she says after fixing something on his ventilator. He draws in a deep breath and calms.

"Rrrr," he says for my name with the next struggle of breath.

"Yeah?" I lean down closer so he doesn't have to fight so hard to be heard, and grab his hand even when I know he can't feel it.

But I can.

And I need this connection with him more than anything right now.

"Good." He takes a second and closes his eyes as if each word is a battle to be won. "Gm."

My smile is soft and sincere and hides the emotions clogging in my throat. Our eyes hold—one twin to another, two halves of a whole—and I know his is the only praise I need. His is the one who matters the most.

"I miss you, J."

Tears well in his eyes and slip from the corner to the pillow beneath his head. I hate that he can't wipe them away. I hate that it'd kill him if I did it for him. He may be paralyzed, but I'm still his little brother by four minutes and two seconds and even like this, he holds tight to that tiny bit of pride.

"He's exhausted, Hunter," my mom says as she steps up and adjusts his pillow for him. "His sleeping pills are kicking in and he needs to get to sleep. It's way past his—"

"Yes. Fine." I don't need to be reminded of the Ambien he takes nightly to combat the anxiety that's caused him to have nightmares in the past few months.

The anxiety I wonder is because he fears he's dying.

She steps in front of me to fuss some more while I struggle with what to say like I always do, caught in that need to pretend like everything is normal when nothing is.

It's so very different when we're face to face.

On the phone, I feel like I'm filling him in on the world outside of this damn prison cell—almost as if I'm letting him live vicariously through me.

But when we're face to identical face, it's brutal.

Face to face, I can see his reactions and feel the guilt. If I talk about hockey, I feel like the asshole who's talking about the one thing he loved more than me. If I talk about women, his other favorite love, then it's a stark reminder of the things he'll never get to feel again. And if I talk about trivial bullshit to fill the air, he knows I'm at a loss of what to say to him—my twin—and isn't that worse?

So when my mom clears out of the way, I sit there with him and hold his hand he can't feel and connect without words he can't speak, but still feel a sense of peace. Nothing can rob the two of us of that. *Except of course, death.*

His exhaustion from leaving the house and going to the game is evident in the bags under his eyes, and it's not long before he succumbs to it. His eyes fall heavy and the muscles in his face relax as I whisper to him that I love him.

But even with him asleep, I don't look away. I can't. All I keep thinking is how I packed my schedule today to avoid this emotional bullshit and how wrong I was to do so. This is my brother. He deserves better from me . . . and I should be able to deal with my parents, because this time with him is what matters most.

How many moments like this will I get? How many more times will I be able to tell him I love him face to face? How many more times will I be able to find my calm with him?

Not enough. And yet my pride has kept me away.

As if guilt didn't rule my life already.

Fuck.

I close my eyes and shake my head, knowing I fucked up. Knowing I should have figured he'd be worn out from the game, and that I'd get so little time with him.

"Love you, J," I whisper as he settles into slumber. "Love you more than you know." I can't take my eyes off him. I need to memorize the lines on his face. The same ones we should share. But where I have laugh lines and crow's feet from the sun, his are less pronounced or not even there. Mine show a life lived and his show a life lost. So I visually trace the lines he does have, over and over, needing to map them. Needing to commit them to memory.

The problem is, the longer I sit here, the calm Jonah gives me is slowly eaten away by resentment.

At my parents. At the world. At fucking God and fate and everything in between, because why is he there and I'm here?

Knowing he's completely asleep, I turn to face my mom. She's sitting in a chair at the foot of his bed, her eyes focused on the television show that's on but that I can barely hear.

"You didn't show up before the game like you were supposed to today. I had everything set up for him."

"Hunter." My name is an apologetic sigh that snaps my anger like a livewire.

"I had plans to empty the arena so I could push him on the ice. So I could let him skate again—"

"He's too sick now to let him—"

"He can't get much sicker, Mom." I stand and move to abate the anger. Or try to.

There's no abating shit right now.

"Let him have whatever fucking joy he can. Christ." I shove a hand through my hair and turn my back on the damn case of trophies.

"Oh, you know Jonah," she says with a wave of her hand, as if we're talking about the weather outside. She stands and moves to the seat I just vacated. She takes her time tucking his arms beneath the covers so he doesn't get cold. "He has his routines and when we step outside of the routine too much it's hard, and he gets upset—"

"Upset?" I chuckle without an ounce of humor. "Robbing him of the experience would make him upset." I look out the window to the streetlight's orange glow and try to compose myself. "Next time, I'll just pick him up and take him myself."

"No, you won't." Defiance edges her tone and does nothing to soften the tight smile she gives me. "We're his guardians and will do what we think is best for him."

All I can do is stare at her and her subtle but stinging rebuke and wonder if she hears her own words. If she realizes she may have lost two sons that day, because she gave up on me too. She devoted her life to him, forgetting that I need her too, just in different ways.

My chest aches in a way it never has before. "Maybe I wanted you there early, Mom. Maybe I wanted you to stay after. Maybe I wanted you or Dad to see—" My voice breaks and I fucking hate that it does. "You know what? Fuck it. Just fuck it."

"He has to come first. He needed his medication and I had to get him back and—"

"I know." It's futile. I lost the right to need anything from them the night of the accident.

"We need to keep our voices down. He needs his rest," she says, trying to usher me out of the room.

"I wanted to see him tonight, Mom. And you and Dad." I turn to face her in this house that no longer feels like home to me. "I don't get the time to have with him and you didn't come early like you said you would. You didn't let him meet the guys. You didn't—"

"You just don't understand how things are, *Hunter*." And there it is. My name is spoken with so much derision that I don't think she hears it anymore.

"Yeah, I do. You see me and you see who he could have been. You look in my eyes and know everything changed—your life, his life, my—"

"You don't get to feel sorry for yourself," she bites out, and again, I'm reminded why I kept busy all day with publicity stints for the team. Why I hope every time I come home things might change and then hurt when I realize they never will.

"What about you, Mom? You've fired every nurse I've hired to come in here and help you out."

"No one will take care of my son but me."

"You need to get out more. Go back to teaching or something." Maybe I say the words I know will cause a fight like every other time so I have a reason to leave. Maybe I poke the sleeping bear so I can find my way out of this house. So I can breathe again.

"We've had this discussion a million times. You may have run away . . . but we didn't."

"Ran away?" I cough the words out. "Is that what you called it? Pushing me to be everything Jonah was supposed to be? Letting me know every damn chance you had that I would never be him. That I would never be enough." I clench my fists and resist the urge to punch the wall. "Look at me." I throw my hands out to my side, my voice rising. "I'm one of the best goddamn NHL players on the ice right now and neither of you can see it. Neither of you can acknowledge I've lived up to every one of your fucking goals. And yet, it's still not enough. It's still not Jonah."

"Hunter." My father's voice comes as a low warning from the other room. His constant aversion of anything about to show.

"Honey." My mom repeats the tepid warning in her placating tone. "Don't upset your father. His heart . . . it's fragile."

"It seems everything is fragile in this house," I grit out, running a hand through my hair and blowing out an unsatisfying sigh.

Nothing fucking changes.

"It's been a long day," she murmurs.

"Got it. I know. You're tired. He's tired. It's been a long night, and I should get going because I'm upsetting the balance here." I walk back toward my brother and look at him one last time before leaving. She turns the lamp off so the light from the open door paints a swath across his cheek.

All I can do is stare at him. At his face that was once the mirror image of mine. At the hands tucked away that I used to play catch with. At the memories I hold closer than anything in the world while hating them all too. At the person I've tried the hardest to become.

And wonder, for the millionth time if I'd have been better off being the one in the bed instead of being the one who lives with the guilt for putting him there.

27

Hunter

16 years earlier

EACH NAIL I POUND into the fence does nothing to abate my resentment.

You think you deserve to go, Hunter? You think with sprint times like that I'm going to reward you for slacking and let you go?

Another nail.

Jonah has your time beat by a full second. Christ. There's a reason he's being scouted by the top schools and clubs in the country and you're not.

I drop the next nail as I try to hold it in place with hands shaking with anger. When I bend over to pick it up I realize my jaw is sore from clenching it so tightly.

He's got everything going for him. School. Hockey. That Terry girl. What do you have going for you? What do you do that doesn't require me asking you to do it twice?

I pound the head of the nail so hard into the shitty shed at old man Watson's house that the face of the hammer leaves a round circle in the weathered wood.

So no, Hunter. You can't go to junior prom tonight or whatever the fuck it's called. You'll fix Mr. Watson's shed while he's out of town. You'll pick up your mom from work for me since Jonah's using the other car. Then you'll meet me at the rink at seven o'clock, and you better be ready to skate. Your whole class will

be at the dance, and you'll be here making up for slacking off. Maybe then . . .
you'll learn your lesson.

I drop my arms to my sides and raise my face to the late afternoon sun, trying to catch my breath that keeps getting robbed by the emotions I don't want to feel.

Hatred.

Resentment.

Fury.

Fucking jealousy.

It's not Jonah's fault he's perfect. It's my fault I'm not the fucking golden boy.

He's the one set up with a full-ride already, Hunter. Full fucking ride to Boston College, one of the best hockey programs in the country. And what are you going to do, huh? Stay here and be a bagger at Stop & Shop? Why can't you apply yourself and make us proud? You'll never be Jonah, but you can at least be something.

My hands ball into fists. I fight the urge to punch the stupid wall of the shed, because I'd either break my knuckles or the whole damn thing will collapse, and then I'll be stuck here for even longer.

My cell rings and I sigh.

"What do you want now?" I snap at Jonah.

"Mom's getting off work early and she needs you to pick her up," he says. Laughter in the background has me gritting my teeth. Nothing like a pre-dance beer or two while the girls are at the salon getting ready.

"Get her your fucking self," I mutter.

"Dude. I can't." He laughs at something someone else says. "Please, bro."

"You're the reason she doesn't have her car tonight. You fucking get her," I say. "I'm the one finishing the shit you didn't at Watson's."

"I'll finish it tomorrow. Don't worry about it."

"Can't. It's part of Dad's punishment for me. You know, picking up your shit while you're busy being perfect."

He sighs. I know it's not his fault. I know he's stood up for me with Dad more times than he should have. I know he hates the difference in treatment between us just as much as I do.

But it doesn't change a fucking thing.

He's perfect, outstanding, everything my dad wanted in a son and hockey player.

I'm mediocre, insignificant, the son my dad has never needed.

The failure.

"C'mon, Hunter. Don't be a dick to me. Dad's just being Dad. I'm sure if you turn it on after a few suicide sprints, he'll be wowed by how fucking fast you are. He'll think he's taught you a lesson and then tell you to meet up with us." He shushes people around him and their noise fades. It sounds like he walked into a different room. "Hunter?"

"If only it were that easy."

Easy to what though? Live in your twin's shadow? Never be enough? Love your brother like he's a part of you while hating him from jealousy?

"Look." His voice lowers as someone yells, *I need another brewski*, in the background.

"Nah. I'm out. Get Mom. Don't get Mom. She called *you* to get her, so figure it the fuck out on your own." I end the call and toss my phone on the ground, then squeeze my eyes shut to push the tears back down.

Jonah doesn't fucking care.

No one does.

And when I go to pick up the hammer to finish punishment number one, I catch movement out of the corner of my eye.

I look over to where Terry Fischer plays with the ties of the bottom of what could be called a T-shirt if it had more fabric to it as she walks toward me. Her shorts are short, her legs are sinfully long, and her sandals high. When she rocks back on her heels as she licks her lips and bats her eyelashes, every damn ounce of blood in my body heads south and my mouth goes dry.

"Hey. I thought you were going out to Rick's house for some beers before we meet up for pictures and then head to the dance."

I stare at her—I mean how can I not—eyes blinking and lips parting, before I realize she thinks I'm Jonah.

There's a split second where I hesitate and she continues—her hips swaying, her fingers accidentally twisting her shirt tighter over her boobs— and I keep thinking about my brother.

How much he thinks he loves her.

How he's already lost his virginity to her. (*Hasn't everyone at Hillman High?*)

How he has fucking everything without trying, while I have to work so damn hard at everything . . . *but for what?*

"Jonah," she croons as she stops within a foot of me, laces her fingers with mine, and swings our arms. "What's wrong?" Pouty lips. Cleavage right there. Perfume. "Your daddy make you finish this since I distracted you the other day from finishing?"

Her giggle fills the air and her tits jiggle when she does. I'm mesmerized.

"Yeah." I smile and emit a nervous laugh. No wonder Jonah keeps volunteering to come over here and work on Watson's property.

"You gonna answer that phone?" she asks. I didn't even hear my cell ringing again.

"It's probably Hunter." I roll my eyes. "You know how he is."

She laughs again and twirls a lock of hair on the finger of her free hand. "So . . . you're not out with the guys?"

"I had to finish this. I'm meeting up with them in a bit." I wrack my brain to remember what was supposed to happen this afternoon. "I—uh— thought you were getting your hair or nails or whatever done," I fumble.

"Why?" She leans up against me. "You don't think I'm pretty just like this?"

Jesus. Hell. Fuck. Nerves vibrate through me just as fast as the adrenaline does, and I swear I can smell it coming from my pores.

I've dated girls. Lots of them. I've been to second base a few times, while the guys think I've all but slid home.

But this is Terry Fischer, innocent sweetheart to parents and blow-job queen to the boys of Hillman and the almost-men at the local junior college.

"Pretty?" I lick my lips, my mouth dry as cotton, my dick harder than it's ever been before and my balls ache. "You're so much more than pretty."

"Jonah," she says in a singsong voice as her lips meet mine. The hammer drops to the ground with a thud right beside the cellphone that starts to ring again as her fingers slide around my neck and thread through my hair.

Terry Fischer is kissing me.

Our tongues touch, and she moans loudly as she presses her body against mine.

My thoughts are frantic. What am I supposed to do now? I'm going to hell.

Oh my God, this feels so fucking good.

She thinks I'm Jonah.

Oh shit.

Oh shit.

The kiss grows greedy, if that's even a thing. Like I can't get enough of it or her, and it's easier to get lost in her kiss than to acknowledge the tinge of guilt over how I'm kissing my brother's girlfriend.

"Is old man Watson still not home?" she asks as she looks around the empty backyard before pulling my hand up and pressing it against her breast.

"No." I gulp. I try not to move, because if my jeans rub too hard or she grinds again against me, I swear to God, I'm going to come in my pants.

Gretzky. Crosby. Lemieux. Roy. Howe. Orr.

I try to recite the hockey greats. Anything to get my focus off what her nipple feels like beneath the thin fabric. Hard and soft and her breast the perfect weight as if I know what that is.

"He—he's still out of town."

"Should we do this now? Like you and me? So my hair doesn't get messed up later and my parents don't wonder?"

Jesus.

I'm not Jonah.

Oh my God, he's going to kill me.

She runs a hand over the outside of my pants and my eyes all but roll back in my head. If a cool breeze on any other day is enough to make me stand at attention, her hand is doing so much more than that.

"I—sure—I—"

"I mean, we can do what we did before—with me sucking you and you licking me . . . but, I brought a condom." She holds a foil packet up and my eyes bug out of my head, causing her to giggle as my breath all but stops.

"Yes. Please. Um—"

"You're acting funny," she says as she pushes me toward the patio furniture and grabs my shirt, pulling me toward her to meet my tongue again.

My pulse pounds in my ears. My breathing is shallow as I try to process what's happening. As I realize the next closest house is half a mile away and Terry Fischer is here and wants to *do it* with me.

I guess the rumors were right.

I guess Jonah wasn't lying.

Don't think about Jonah. Don't think about—

"C'mon, J. Feel my panties. Feel what you do to me."

She guides my hand between the flimsy cotton shorts to where it's warm and moist and—

Gretzky. Crosby. Lemieux. Roy. Howe. Orr.

"Ohhhh." My own moan is all I can hear as her hands slide inside my jeans and circle around me.

Gretzky. Crosby. Lemieux. Roy. Howe. Orr.

28

Dekker

THE SAXOPHONE FLOATS THROUGH the air above the steady drone of chatter. Sculler's Jazz Club is crowded for a Thursday night and by the looks of my company—Finch and his wife, Maysen, and Callum—the few drinks have settled and the exhaustion from the game tonight is setting in.

Finch with his uniquely good looks—longer hair with almost clear blue eyes—has his arm hooked around his wife's shoulder. For the life of me, I can't remember her name and am too embarrassed to ask, so I've spent the better part of the conversation making sure to avoid saying anything where I need to use it.

For a businesswoman who prides herself on remembering names, I just don't have it in me tonight.

Regardless, Callum was right. This place that the guys usually meet up at after wherever their adventures take them in the city, is just what I needed. Relaxed and sufficiently off the beaten track that it offers privacy away from fans. The guys can enjoy a drink or two without interruptions for autographs or fear that pictures will be posted online of them when they've had a little too much.

The lounge is dim, and the furniture is dark, save for the stage across from us with its red velvet backdrop and lights angled at the lone man sitting there playing the sax. His tune is melodic and seductive and begs you to relax . . . or make love. I'm angling for the former. We're in the top of the three tiers of seats, and the bar is behind us with its clinks and clanks of glass as it buzzes with business.

Taking a sip of my martini, I close my eyes, and lean my head back to listen and unwind, but as per usual, my head never quiets. Everything I need to do sifts through my mind. Contracts and negotiations and endorsement deals. I understand my father's reasoning in sending me here to recruit Hunter, but in the meantime, I feel like I'm neglecting my other clients who need my attention.

Sure, I can work most crises remotely, but not being in my office makes it difficult. Living in a hotel room that changes every other night makes it even harder.

I tune into the conversation in front of me. Comments about the game tonight, including a few snide remarks about one of my clients on the opposing team, make me smile.

"It's true, isn't it, Dekker? The fucker must eat lemons the way he's so damn sour," Finch says.

I belt out a laugh. "Client info is confidential, but uh, he's got some killer lemon trees at his house," I say with a wink.

He throws his head back and laughs while Maysen stands suddenly, the expression on his face causing us all to turn and see what has his attention.

Hunter stumbles near the entrance of the other side of the club. His shoulder falls into a guy and much like Maysen, we can see the fight coming a mile away.

Unlike Maysen, though, I overheard the conversation tonight between the LumberJacks GM and Sanderson.

The last thing Hunter needs to be doing is getting into a fight.

But before I can react, Maysen leaps over the back of the couch on legs that don't look like he just played sixty minutes of high-intensity and brutally physical hockey, and jogs over to his teammate.

Between the distance and the music, I can't hear what's being said, but body language—Maysen's hands are up and his smile is broad as he talks to the guy Hunter is staring down. A few tense seconds unfold where I'm sure Maysen offers to buy a round of drinks or something to that effect, before he wraps his arm around Hunter's waist, and starts veering him our way. Situation handled.

Thank God.

But what the actual fuck?

What the hell is Hunter thinking?

Disgusted with his immaturity, I turn back to the company in front of me, down the rest of my delicious and much-needed martini, and choose to ignore whatever the hell is going on with him, because I'm off the clock.

At least that's what I tell myself.

I should be prepared for Hunter's flop on the seat beside me a few seconds later, but I still emit a startled yelp when he does.

"It's Dekker the pecker wrecker," he says with a huge grin that would be charming if he weren't drunk or his words weren't shitty. His cheek is red where a punch was landed in the game tonight, and his hair is falling in his face. I can't deny that small tug that hits me at the sight of him.

And I hate everything about that admission.

I have just enough of a buzz going that I'm primed to pick a fight with him. Despite his behavior, how he's shutting me out, the way he's turned me on, the fact that I haven't told him why I'm here, and the career he's trying to throw away with his bullshit antics.

Reason would tell me I shouldn't engage. The last drink I had encourages me that I should.

"Oh, look. It's out-of-control Hunter who's going to get his ass kicked off his team if he keeps his bullshit up," I add with an equally charming smile as I meet his eyes.

"Bullshit?" he scoffs. "Nah, it's just me getting warmed up."

"I'm sure your teammates are thrilled to hear that."

I don't back down from his glare, so the silence settles between us as we stare at each other.

"Where've you been, man?" Callum asks, trying to ease the tension, as he leans back in his chair.

"Just taking care of some business," Hunter says and dismisses him.

"Old friends?" Finch asks.

"Something like that." He stands abruptly. "Can't an asshole get a drink in this place?"

I push myself up. "I'll get it," I say, knowing if I get it for him, I can ask the bartender to make it light. Hunter's so drunk he probably won't notice. "What'll you have?" I ask when I already know the answer.

"Good. I'll have a Bombay and tonic. And uh, glad to know you know how to do your job properly," Hunter says, and I see Finch's wife wince at the comment.

"At least someone does," I say, and he grabs my arm as I start to walk past him.

"Hey," Finch says and stands to reinforce his warning. He glares at his teammate.

"It's fine," I say and shrug out of Hunter's reach before anything can escalate. Getting in a fight with a random person is one thing, but fighting his own teammate is even worse.

The bar is crowded and it takes a few minutes before I can belly up to it. "Another?" the bartender asks.

"No. A gin and tonic. Bombay. And a lot more tonic than gin," I say with a wink.

He nods, understanding what I'm saying. "Got it."

Right when I go to turn around and check on Hunter, he slides into the spot beside me and leans his elbows on the bar top. Our eyes meet and the million questions I want to ask him surface and die right along with my want to tell him about the conversation I overheard tonight.

"Let me guess, you're watering down my drink," he says, his lips beside my ear.

"Should I worry about what kind of trouble you got in tonight before finding yourself here?"

Something flashes through the blue of his eyes, but it's gone before I can decipher it. "I'm not your problem to worry about. Just looking after some fans. Surely you know what that is." He looks at me with such an unexpected bitterness as if to test me. "How much do you want to bet I could walk away from this place tonight with five different phone numbers?"

"If your goal is to be a phone book, then by all means." I roll my shoulders and refuse to give him what he wants. *Another fight.*

"What is it with you, Kincade?" he murmurs just above the music. "All of a sudden you're here, there . . . fucking everywhere. In my face."

"Not what I'm here for. But I'm sure any of those numbers you collect would be willing to be whatever you need for the night." The bartender slides the drink in front of me, and I thank him as I push it toward Hunter.

"You're right. They would." He turns around so he's still beside me, but so his back is against the bar. He makes a show of giving a hum of appreciation when he spots a woman who catches his eye.

I can't figure out if he's being serious or just trying to get a reaction out of me.

"Have at them, Hunter." I choke over my own words. "You sure seem like you're at peak performance tonight."

"What?"

"Nothing." My buzz is gone, and there's no point saying another word.

His chuckle is a low rumble that I can feel more than hear as he turns to face me, but I keep looking straight ahead at the mirrored wall behind the bar. "Why are you here, Dekker?"

"Same reason you are. To have a drink. To unwind after a long day. To have a little downtime."

"*To get laid.*"

"Yep, that's me." I shake my head in frustration. "My every waking goal is how I'm going to end up on my back with my legs spread."

"It used to be."

A million things run through my mind—*fuck you*, being the one that rings the loudest and *only with you* running a close second—but I know Hunter Maddox. He wants to stay angry.

But his words still sting. They still ignite my temper. They still hurt, when I shouldn't care.

Hunter seems determined to ruin or sabotage every part of his life. Why bother being his agent? Then I'll be the one being warned by McAvoy. *And why do I want that?* Surely my dad *doesn't* want that.

"That's a class-act thing to say, Hunter. Be a dick to me." *I don't deserve that from him, and I hate that his drunkenness has disconnected his filter and allows him to be so scathing.*

"Not being a dick, just trying to figure out why the hell you're following the team around like a puppy dog waiting to get a scrap of bone."

I take a sip of my drink, let the alcohol swish around on my tongue before I swallow it, and turn to face him. He remains looking ahead, his profile strong with pride and marred with a disdain I can't figure out. "Let's get one thing straight, Maddox. I chase after no one. I'm a damn good agent who's simply doing my job. If I choose to go out for a drink with one of my clients after a game, that's my own business, not yours."

"Is that what this is, Dekk?" The muscle in his jaw feathers as the melody being played changes.

"What?"

"We fizzled out so I moved on, and now you're back to exact revenge?" *For fuck's sake.*

We never fizzled out.

The thought screams to a halt in the front of my mind and sits there in blinking neon lights.

We never fizzled out because if we had, those feelings I had wouldn't have sparked to life the minute I saw him. They would have had me sneering and disgusted. But then I hear the other part about him moving on. I *had* tried to avoid looking up pictures of Hunter after I left him. To see how quickly and how easily I'd been replaced. *How he'd moved on.* I'm not naïve enough to think that I walked away and he's pined after me all these years.

So yeah, I'm sure he moved on. But I've never wanted that reminder.

Hell.

"News flash. What happened three years ago is dead and over," I say.

"Yes, I forgot. No-nonsense Kincade can move on without ever looking back."

"God, Hunter. There are way more important things you need to be focusing on than me."

"Yeah," he murmurs just loud enough for me to hear, "like that hot brunette over there."

That dig hurts.

"Just like old times, huh?" I ask, staring at him until he slowly turns and faces me, that cocky smirk that usually makes my insides simmer, instead now irritating me.

"Depends on what you mean by old times." He reaches out to move a piece of hair off my shoulder, and I slap his hand away.

"Hockey. Party. *Repeat.*"

"You forgot the most important part." He leans closer so I can smell the alcohol on his breath just above the scent of his cologne.

"Meaning?"

"Hockey. Party. *Fucking.* Repeat."

"Screw you, Hunter," I say, refusing to show that those words and his cavalier attitude are hurtful.

I toss some cash on the bar and head back to our table, needing space and distance from him and his destructive behavior. *Why?* Why does he keep coming to me when it clearly bothers him that I'm here? Why can't he just go after his hot brunette on the other side of the bar and leave me the hell alone?

More importantly, why do I keep engaging?

I think the answer lies somewhere between the two of those answers.

"You jealous?" he calls after me as I step past Finch and his wife on the way to the open seat on the couch. I turn to face him, confusion no doubt etched in every line of my face, as he stares at me above the rim of his glass, his eyes challenging me as much as his words do. "You're the one who moves from man to man, night after night."

"Man to man? Really? It's called entertaining clients, you ass." I laugh at his ridiculousness and when I try to walk between him and the table in the way, I realize now that putting myself in this corner was a bad idea.

"Sleeping with clients is part of the job now? No wonder Chaddy-boy was so pissed that you dropped him to come see me," he says, reaching out to grab my arm.

Finch and Callum both stand instantly with his name falling from their lips.

But I'm faster, my hand stinging as it connects with his cheek.

We glare at each other—his teammates and one of my clients—staring at us, gauging the situation and whatever it is that's happening between us. Patrons on the outside of our seating area turn to watch too as the music picks up in pace.

Hunter may have a ghost of a smile on his lips but there is a host of pain in the depths of his eyes, but I'm past wanting to listen to him now. A moment passes before I see him tuck it all away and that smile falls lopsided and his snark returns.

"This is what this is all about, isn't it? You. Me. Years ago. Relationships aren't my thing, Dekker."

"No shit." I pull my purse strap back up to my shoulder that fell off with the action.

"Not between me and a woman. Not between me and an agent." He chews his cheek momentarily. "Not with anyone."

"Good to know." I angle my head, stare at him, and then go out on a limb with a hunch. "Why are you here? Hockey. Party. *Fucking*. Repeat? Is that why? I figured you'd be spending time with your family. But *you're* out drinking and being an asshole."

Muscles tic in his face as he clenches his jaw.

And there it is.

A reaction that is as sincere as it is threatening.

"Leave my family the fuck out of this," he growls, his shoulders squaring, as he takes a step toward me. "Where do you get off—?"

His teammates take a protective step forward, but I shake my head to tell them it's fine. In fact, I turn toward them and say, "It's late, and I have an early conference call. Thank you for inviting me. It was a great time"—I glance to Hunter—"until it wasn't."

"Do you want me to take you back?" Callum asks, and I shake my head, not wanting to add fuel to Hunter's accusation.

"No, thank you. Enjoy the rest of your night. It'll probably be your last one for a while with the next few games being tough ones . . . so enjoy it while you can." When I go to leave, Hunter won't move so I can walk out of the small space between the table and the couch.

"Just admit it," he says.

"Admit what?" I ask.

"Why you're here."

"Lay off, man," Finch says and tries to pull Hunter by the arm out of my way, but he shrugs off his teammate's arm without a look his way.

I shake my head subtly, the gravity in my voice matching the look in my eyes. "Honestly? I'm not sure why I'm here anymore." More than a small part of me wishes I wasn't. I've been his verbal punching bag one too many times since I came here, and I'm done.

It's one thing when it's just the two of us, but now he's doing it in front of his teammates and all that does is undermine my professionalism. If I stand by and take it, I look like I have no backbone, and they'd wonder how that would translate to me fighting in contract negotiations for them.

On the other hand, when I do engage him and stand up for myself, it just devolves into an insult-fest that looks unprofessional and immature.

I feel like I'm in a no-win situation, especially when I see he's not going to change.

Before I showed up here, I thought I could fix whatever was going on with him and win his trust in doing so, but now . . . now, I don't think anything I do will help him.

Is this where I call my dad and tell him to pick someone else for me to recruit?

That I refuse to put up with Hunter and his constant picking of fights to prevent us from having any real conversation? Or do I stick it out to prove to my dad that I'm tough and can handle even the most difficult of clients? *But this isn't about my father's lack of faith in me . . . because I know he believes in me.* KSM needs a Hunter Maddox in its client list.

I feel like I'm at a loss either way, but my dignity is stronger than my pride, and I'm done.

I look at Hunter one last time, and his expression falls as I stare at him a second longer before skirting around him and walking out of the club.

29

Hunter

"WHAT?" I SNAP AT the guys when they stare at me after she walks out.

"What the fuck, Cap?" Finch asks and the look on his face—disgust and disappointment from a man I'm supposed to lead—hits me harder than his words.

I don't wait for them to say anything more or rebuke me or what-the-fuck-ever it is they want to malign me with and head to the bar.

It's much easier to drink to cope than to stand here and replay everything that happened at my parents' house—the things I know will never change—and the fight I got into at the first bar I stopped by on my way here.

When will this pain and guilt and need to destroy everything go away?

When will the things I do ever be good enough to outrun the clusterfuck of emotions that have been running rampant over the past few months?

It's simpler to down the first shot of gin. To focus on the burn instead of the argument I had with my mom and the disinterest and then criticism from my dad. From the words I wanted to shout at them—that I'm still alive and still their son, and isn't that enough?

But I know why they are how they are.

I know why our lives have all changed.

I know that I'm the one who set forward the events that caused all of this.

The second shot I swallow in one gulp burns just as bright as the first.

Thoughts of Dekker fill my head. I can't get them out. Not her before. Especially not her now.

Her presence is torture. It's showing me something I thought I wanted. Something I forced myself to walk away from because I knew I didn't deserve her.

And just when everything is turning to shit, she's back again. A sinner and a saint, and fuck if I know which one of those parts of her I'd love to drown in.

You're a piece of shit, Hunter.

I think of the words I spewed at her.

Grade-A piece of shit.

Not like that's anything you didn't already know, but now you can't deny it.

The accusations I made just so she wouldn't look too closely or see the truths about me.

Hockey player. Royal fuck-up. Commitment-phobe. *The reason Jonah's dying.*

I scrub a hand through my hair and down the third shot in as many minutes, landing the glass back on the bar top with a slap for emphasis.

Fucking Dekker.

I shake my head but she's still there, still owning my thoughts, still making me want her.

But she's here.

And I think she's recruiting someone.

But who?

Me? She's ballsy enough to make that kind of move without a blink of an eye.

Maybe the rumors are true that Sanderson is fucking people over. It's not like he's doing me any favors right now.

Would I move over to KSM? Would I let Dekker represent me? Her track record's phenomenal . . . so why is it people are jumping ship to Sanderson? What exactly is he promising these new clients that us old ones aren't seeing?

The question is, if she represents me, how is it going to work when I sleep with her? Because I *am* going to sleep with her again.

That was a forgone conclusion the minute I saw her standing in Tank's last week.

And with her by-the-book attitude, I'm going to enjoy every damn minute of bending her to my will.

I chuckle to myself and look around, catching the eye of a blonde at the end of the bar. Tall, nice rack, good smile, *come fuck me* eyes.

She'd do for the night.

But Dekker would be so much better. We may be oil and water, but between the sheets, hell, we're a goddamn masterpiece.

I rest my hips against the bar and watch the sax player do his thing—fingers pressing on keys, sunglasses shading his eyes, body moving to the rhythm he's creating—and let myself fall under the haze of the shot I've just downed.

I'm still watching him while the blonde studies me, and all I can think about is a different woman: Dekker Kincade.

The fourth shot is much smoother, simply because I no longer taste it. I'm distracted though. Preoccupied.

You better stop thinking about her, Maddox.

The question is, do I really want to?

Maybe she's the distraction I need right now.

Perhaps she's the something I can get lost in—the chase and the challenge and then the reward—that will get me out of my own head.

But I know more than most, a little bit of Dekker was never enough. Nights of wanting and needing and pretending, are my proof of that.

But why would she want you after the bullshit you put her through tonight? The crappy comments and accusations?

Surprise, surprise. You fucked up again, Maddox.

I pull bills out of my wallet and set them under an empty shot glass. Time to go. To stop thinking. To sleep this off even though my thoughts have already sobered me enough.

Shit. What a waste of good alcohol.

"Hey there." The smooth voice belongs to the blonde from the corner of the bar and as much as I need to get lost in something for a while, she's not her.

"Have a good night." I take a step away but her hands grab one of mine and pull it toward her as she tries to lace her fingers with mine.

Interest doesn't even flutter to life.

"Don't be a party pooper." She pouts and then paints a siren's smile on those glossed lips of hers. "I saw you looking. I know you're interested."

Doesn't she know that subtlety goes a hell of a long way?

I laugh a few notes. "I'm interested in a lot of things. Going to my hotel right now is one of them." I pull my hand from her grasp. Her fury can be heard in the stomp of her foot.

"I could give you a lift."

"I'm more than capable of getting there. Thanks though." I give her a smile and take a step back.

"You're the first guy to say no, you know."

I turn back to look at her. "That line in itself is the reason I'm walking away."

She mutters something I can't hear and don't fucking care because the sudden movement tells me I'm still buzzed enough. I laugh as I push the door open and breathe in the frigid air.

That's a slap to sobriety right there.

It's when I step a few more feet under the covered entrance that I see Dekker near the carpark. She's standing with her arms crossed over her midsection, shivering from the cold, as she looks from her phone to the car that's pulling up and back again in what I can only assume is checking the Uber drivers.

The shit feeling I had inside about what I said returns at the sight of her.

But so does my resolve to want to lose myself to her—in her. *Please don't say no to me.*

30

Dekker

"DEKKER."

His voice is the last thing I want to hear right now. I'm tired, have had enough alcohol, and more than enough of his bullshit, so I pretend I don't hear him. Besides, I've already decided I'm done with this. Done with him. Turning my back to the entrance of the bar, I check the ETA of my rideshare again.

It's almost one o'clock in the morning. How in the hell is the only driver checking in to pick me up over five minutes away?

"Dekk!" Snow crunches beneath his boots at my back and my hands fist in response. "Look. I'm sorry." His words slur and I hate the sound of it. Hate that in the fifteen minutes max that I left him at the bar, he's drunk more to shut out whatever the hell is going on with him. And even worse, I hate that I care. "You know how I get. You know—"

"No," I shout as I whirl to face him. "I don't know how you get and I don't care how you get. Even if I did, that doesn't give you the right to—"

"Come on," he says and tries to put his hands on both of my arms.

I shrug out of his grasp and step back. "Let's get one thing straight. You are not allowed to talk to me like that. Ever. It's bullshit and demeaning and nowhere near close to the man I used to lov—know."

His head startles as my words hit him. "Maybe you didn't know me at all, then."

There is no thought to my next action other than anger and hurt and frustration. The three mingle and meld in the second I reach back into the planter filled with snow at our side, scoop up the biggest heap of snow I can find, and throw it at him.

He mutters a curse as the handful hits him squarely in the face. It falls like powder to his chest and pieces stick to his eyelashes as he blinks it away—but there's no expression on his face, no rebuke on his lips, just eyes staring at me with an intensity that makes me question what his reaction will be.

"Mature, Kincade," he finally says as a car pulls into the drive at his back.

"That's my car."

"You're not going anywhere until we get a few things straight," he says with a stream of white from the cold highlighting his breath.

"Like you have any right to tell me what to do."

He grabs my arm as I walk past him and I get lucky, because when I swipe the planter again, I come up with another handful of snow. We stand there with his hand on my arm and my other arm cocked back, ready to fire.

"You wouldn't dare," he taunts, his smile finally returning, even if it's just a trace of one.

"You don't know me very well, then," I say, seconds before I launch the snow at him.

When it's midair, he lunges for me, but I don't see how much hits him because I'm off running down the sidewalk like a ten-year-old kid without a care about slipping on black ice or wet clothes or waking anybody up.

"Paybacks are a bitch, Kincade." He laughs as his footsteps thump behind me.

"You've got to catch me first." My screech fills the air as I jump over the small hedge that borders what looks like a park area under the blanket of snow. It's desolate at this time of night—morning—whatever it is—and I'm just grateful that Hunter is drunk. Otherwise, he could have easily caught me by now.

"It's an all-out war," he shouts as the first ball of snow hits my shoulder. Another yelp escapes as I swoop down to make a snowball of my own while trying to hide behind a piece of the play equipment.

"I'll win." I peek my head up and duck just in time to avoid being hit by a massive snowball. It lands with a thud behind me and pieces of it hit against the leg of my pants.

"Like hell you will."

I toss two in a row to where he's hiding behind a bench and shout in excitement when one lands on his back.

"Son of a bitch!" He laughs as I prepare more ammo. "That one's going to cost you," he says as he runs in my direction.

"No," I shriek as I run to the opposite side of my hiding place that now is his and throw two more blindly at him.

"Missed me. Missed me!"

Now you have to kiss me.

The childhood taunt repeats on my mind as I run to where I think he is . . . only to find him gone.

"Hunter," I call in a singsong voice as I look behind a shrub where I swear he is. Crap. "Hunter?" I follow footprints in the snow but am not sure if they're mine or his. "Come out, come out wherever you are."

I turn around when I hear a sound to be met with a snowball in the middle of the chest. "Argh!" I laugh as I brush it off my jacket only to look up and see him walking toward me, grin lighting up his face, and another monster-sized snowball between his hands where he's toying with it. "Do you really want to throw that?"

He nods and takes a step closer. "Do you surrender?"

"*Never.*"

He takes a bite of the snowball in his hand and there's something about him right now—the soft yellow of the park's lights overhead, the boyish grin on his lips, and the careless snowball fight—that momentarily lessens the insult and injury of the crap he said earlier and reminds me why I find him so damn irresistible. "I'm still furious at you."

"And you're even prettier with all that snow in your hair."

Shit. Don't do that, Hunter. Don't . . . break down my defenses that are weak enough already.

"You owe me an apology." I make a stand with my hands on my hips and my feet firmly planted, more than sure there's no way he's going to throw that at me.

"That's what you want to say right now when you're at my mercy?"

I've been at your mercy since I first laid eyes on you at Tank's.

Another laugh falls from my lips—nerves mixed with an anticipation I can all but feel—as I take a step in retreat. "One hundred ninety-two goals in this season alone. Twenty-three shy of Gretzky's single season record. One hundred twenty-four assists. That's fourth all-time in a season and you still have over ten games left to play. Too bad you weren't a baseball player, because all of those pretty stats don't do shit to bolster my confidence that you're going to actually hit me when you throw it," I tease, his arm pulling back faltering slightly.

"All-state third baseman right here." He lifts a finger and points to himself. "I'd have probably ended up hating it too though in the long run. *Tag.* You're it."

I'm distracted slightly by his comment about *hating it too,* so my reaction time is off.

Shit.

I cry out in shock as the snow hits my cheek and explodes in a puff of dust all over my face and down the collar of my jacket.

"That's it. You're mine now, Maddox."

The war begins. One snowball after another, we act like little kids having a snowball fight in the front yard instead of two adults in the dead of night in some random park in the middle of Boston.

"Time out," I finally pant as my lungs burn and toes numb, my hands going up to form the time-out sign.

Hunter stops in his tracks, hands on his knees but eyes trained on me and a smile owning his face. "I never figured you for a quitter."

"I am not a quitter," I say and then wait for him to get a few feet closer before I launch the snowball I'm hiding behind my back at him.

He charges after me. I shriek and run, but I'm no match for him before he tackles me to the ground.

"No!" I laugh out, as he takes a handful of snow and tosses it on my face.

"You play dirty."

"Always." I giggle as he cuffs both my wrists. "No," I groan as he pulls himself up to his knees so he's sitting astride me with my hands pinned to both sides of my head. "Get off me." There's no heat behind my words, because as fun as the snowball fight was, as exhausting as our wrestling match becomes, all of a sudden awareness hits both of us as I stare up at Hunter, inches from my face. There's clarity in his eyes that I haven't seen in forever.

The cold of the snow beneath me begins to seep through my jacket but the smile on my lips feels so very good. The heat and weight of his body against mine even more so.

"Where's that cocky mouth of yours now?" he asks as his gaze flickers from my eyes to my lips and then back up.

"This wasn't part of the snowball fight," I all but whisper.

I hold my breath as he leans forward, his lips near my ear. "There aren't rules to a snowball fight. You don't get to control it, Dekk."

"I know . . . I just—" But I'm at a loss at what to say, and then can't find any words as Hunter brushes his lips over mine.

"Missed me. You missed me," he whispers. "Now you've gotta kiss me."

He leans down to kiss me again. It's gentle and tender and unexpected, since there has never been anything like it between us before.

Hunter isn't gentle when it comes to kisses. He's possessive and demanding and steals the breath from your lungs with the dominance everything about him holds over your senses.

But he just stole my breath with the simplest of kisses, and I'm not quite sure how to feel when I know I want to feel everything.

So when he releases one of my hands and runs his fingers down the side of my cheek before kissing me again, I don't fight him like I should.

I don't think of KSM and what's right or wrong professionally. All I think about is wanting to forget.

Who I am. Who he is. The possible repercussions, and the throwing my own principles out of the window to just enjoy the moment.

The warmth of his lips.

The tenderness of his touch.

The taste of him on my tongue.

The sense of calm mixed with desire that he's evoking in me.

How is it possible to want all of this without there being any fall-out—professionally or emotionally?

The kiss ends, but the whirlwind of emotions sparking back to life inside me doesn't.

"Now who's playing dirty?" I murmur, my mind as scrambled as my hormones.

But when desire darkens his eyes and turns up the corners of his lips, I realize what we're doing. Here. In the snow. One hundred feet from where his teammates could be coming out of the club at any moment.

I'd like to think reason takes hold, but it doesn't. Nerves do. Pure, flustered nerves have me saying, "Snow angels," in a spontaneous burst of words as I roll out from under him.

"What?" He laughs the word out as he runs a hand through his hair to shake the snow out of it and shifts to sit on the ground.

"Snow angels," I repeat, "Come on"—I tug on his arm—"make an angel with me."

"There are a million things I want to make with you right now, Dekker Kincade, and making snow angels isn't one of them."

Our eyes hold as I'm mid-angel—arms above my head, legs spread out—but I love watching his defenses crumble. I love that he gives in to the moment and plays with me when he flops on his back and starts making angels.

Our laughter is loud as it rings through the night, dotted only by the sound of buses air brakes and a horn way off in the distance.

The sound of our swishing stops and silence descends over the park. We stare at the stars in the sky above, clouded intermittently by the curl of white from our pants of breath.

"Christ," he sighs, as his frozen hand finds mine at my side in the most casual of ways. "Why was that so fun?"

"Because being a kid again is always fun." I giggle without caring how stupid it sounds.

"It's easy to forget."

"You know . . ."

"And here it comes," he says. How easy it is to get his defenses back up.

"Nothing is coming." I pause to choose my words as best as I can. "In fact, you don't even have to respond, but if you need a friend, I'm here."

His silence is deafening, but then again, I didn't expect him to up and spill.

But I said it and I'll let it rest. I know by the tightening of his hand on mine that he heard me.

"Truth." One word. It's all he says, and a part of me dies at the sound of it.

"Nah. I'm not playing this game with you. I remember what happened the last time you asked me that," I say, and I do. It was the first time we hooked up. He asked me if I thought people could do friends with benefits. I told him no. He told me I was stubborn and questioned my resolve. The insults we flung at each other were heartless, the angry sex we had afterward, mind-blowing.

Truth.

That one word was the start of our six-month benefits-only affair. The one I walked away from with a broken heart he may or may not have known about.

So why would he say it now? Is he trying to get us back on an even footing? Or is he trying to cause a fight to push us further apart?

I'm not sure which I would be more surprised at.

"It's not what you're thinking"—he chuckles—"although that might be fun too, considering we're actually being civil to one another."

"At the moment," I murmur. "You forgot to add that we're being civil with each other *at the moment.*"

"Truth," he says again, ignoring my comment. "Why are you here, Kincade?"

"Truth?" I murmur, knowing we need to have this conversation but afraid if I admit what he already knows then the moment will be ruined. I improvise. "Only if you tell me what's going on with you first."

His sigh is long and drawn out and is at odds with how relaxed and comfortable we are with each other . . . excluding how cold we are. "Is this all there is, Dekk?"

I open my mouth and then close it as I hunt for the words to appease or soothe or commiserate. But all will sound placating. Nothing will answer a question I'm not quite sure he's getting at. "What do you mean?"

"You said it earlier. Hockey. Party. Fucking. Repeat. Is that all there is?" I want to brush away the pain I can hear, but know I don't have the right to.

"No. It's not. Maybe it's what there is for you right now—what you want there to be—but there is so much more."

"Says who?" he asks. God, he sounds lost.

"Says . . . says whoever it is you listen to, I guess." My answer is stupid and feels inadequate at best but without knowing more, I don't know how to help him. I don't know how to put to rest whatever it is he's struggling with. "Maybe you just reach a point where hockey, party, sex, repeat, isn't enough anymore. Maybe that's when you realize you want more."

"Maybe I don't deserve more." His words fade off as my surprised laugh breaks the silence.

"That's ridiculous. Why would you even say that?"

"You were right."

"About?"

"Being burned out."

My breath catches. I exhale as softly as I can so he doesn't hear it. I know how hard this admission is. "Okay."

"It's . . . it's a long story, but you were right."

"I never needed to be right. I just needed you to know it's okay if you are." I squeeze his hand to reinforce my words. "If you ever want to tell the story, I'm a good listener."

I focus on the swirl of white from our breaths above as a small part of me sags in relief inside. Not because I'm an agent trying to make a breakthrough with a client, but because I'm a woman finally being let in by a man I can't help but care about.

Finally, a breakthrough.

"Hey?" he says after a beat.

"Mmm?"

"I appreciate the romp in the park, here . . . but uh, there are parts of my anatomy I'm fearing I'll lose to frostbite." His laugh is forced, but I also know this conversation has given more of himself than he's ever given me before, so I don't push.

I let him help me up to a standing position. We laugh and threaten more snowballs as we dust the snow off each other's backs and admire our sloppy angels.

But it doesn't go unnoticed to me that he doesn't ask for my truth in return.

It only makes me wonder. *What is he afraid of?*

31

Dekker

"YOU'RE KIDDING ME?" MY teeth chatter and my body shivers.

Even with the heat on high, the constant blowing of my breath into my hands, and Hunter's arm around me in the rideshare, I still can't feel parts of my body as I stand in front of the reception desk in the lobby and stare at the after-hours clerk.

I'm sure we look like drowned rats—hair plastered from the snow, clothes wet, boots making squishy noises on the expensive floor.

"We're so sorry, Miss Kincade," the clerk repeats, as I stand where he stopped me to tell me the news.

"What seems to be the problem?" Hunter asks as he comes in behind me.

"It shouldn't be more than an hour or two," he explains as his eyes grow wide when he realizes who he's speaking with. "I'm sorry, Mad Dog—er, Mr. Maddox. A pipe has leaked on Miss Kincade's floor. The rooms are fine, but the hall is closed off so we can fix the problem quickly."

"Then move her to a suite," Hunter demands, and I should be miffed he's speaking for me, but I'm too freaking cold to care.

"We're completely booked. I don't have any vacant—"

"You don't have rooms set aside for emergencies like this? You don't—"

"We do, but they're all taken already. We can try to find and comp you a room at a neighboring hotel. Just give me a moment to—"

"It's fine," I say with a tight smile, on which I'm more than certain are blue lips.

"My room then," he says.

"No, I can wait," I stutter, more than cognizant of the unrequited sexual tension continuing to reverberate between us, even when we're half frozen.

"Don't be ridiculous." He rolls his eyes and puts his hand on my back to usher me to the elevator as the clerk stares at me, waiting for me to tell him anything more. "You can at least get out of these wet clothes so you can warm-up."

"That's what I'm afraid of," I say drolly and lift my eyebrows.

"You're a pain in my ass," he mutters and then turns to the clerk. "She'll be in my room."

"How should we inform you so we don't wake you up in case you're asleep?" the clerk asks.

"Text her cell," Hunter says as he gives him my number from memory that has me quite surprised. He wraps an arm around my shoulder and runs a hand up and down my arm.

"Please," I finish for him when he doesn't say it.

And without waiting for a response, Hunter directs us to the elevator. We're in his room within minutes—top floor, great view of the city, but all I can think about when he closes the door behind us is getting warm.

He turns the heat on as high as it can go. I'm stuck in that dilemma between wanting to take my jacket and my wet clothes off and not being in my own room.

"Sooooo cold," I say as I rock back and forth under a vent with my face tilted up and eyes closed.

I hear the click of something and then the sound of ringing. "Hi. Yes. This is room eight-oh-five. I want to order two hot chocolates, two grilled cheeses, um . . . and any dessert you have that's hot." He murmurs something. "I don't care if the kitchen's closed. Figure a way to get it made and I'll make sure to tip accordingly."

"Hunter—"

"No. It's the least they can do after not having access to your room." Then he turns back to the voice on the other end of the phone. "Yes, we're one of those rooms . . . thank you so much for your help. I appreciate it." He hangs the phone up. "It'll be about thirty to forty minutes."

"What are we going to do?" I ask with a chattering laugh as the heat stings my face. "Have a frozen picnic?" It does sound perfect though.

"Why not? Get out of your jacket," Hunter says as I hear a zipper and then a thud as his falls to the floor.

He moves into my line of sight, and of course he didn't just remove his jacket, but his shirt too. Him standing before me shirtless in all his chiseled ab perfection doesn't do anything to help erase the kiss on my lips and his taste on my tongue from the park.

At least he's sobered up now. There's that.

Refusing to give him the satisfaction of staring at him or acknowledging that he's half-naked, I focus on undoing the buttons of my jacket. "Crap," I mutter, my fingers so numb I keep fumbling with them as my teeth chatter and my body begs for some hot water to sink into.

"Let me."

"I've got it." I slap at his hands when he reaches out to push mine out of the way and help me, but it does nothing to deter him. Within seconds, he has the front of my coat opened and is yanking it off my shoulders and then fighting to get my hands out of the bunched ends of the sleeves as if I'm a little kid.

"There," he says as it drops to the floor before enveloping me in his arms. I accept the warmth—even though his body is as cold as mine—and accept the rare moment of magnanimity from him after the night we've had. It feels like an apology without words, and I didn't realize how much I needed this from him until now.

I close my eyes momentarily and absorb the feel of it.

This is a bad decision all around. Me. Here in his room. Our past.

Our future.

Christ.

It's a double-edged sword that reminds me just how good the good is when it's with Hunter and how there's no way I can let myself fall back into this trap when I have to try and win him over as a client.

"I can't. Hunter, I can't," I say as I push against his chest and step back even when he tries to keep me close.

"You'd rather freeze?"

I eye him. "Last time—we weren't—"

"Shh," he says and holds his very cold finger to my lips. "Don't ruin the moment. More civility is afoot."

A sigh falls from my lips that matches the shake of my head. I stare at him. At the breadth of his shoulders and the wave to his hair. At the blue of his eyes and the lopsided smile. At our past, and what I'm trying to make our future. I take in the whole and let his words from earlier hit my ears again. *Is this all there is?*

"This is too complicated," I say when I finally find the words.

"What is? You standing here in my hotel room? It's only complicated if you make it," he says, batting around words with double meanings that I try to ignore. "Besides, you're the one to blame here."

"Me?" I laugh the word out. "How am I to blame?"

"You're the one following us from city to city on this road stretch."

"Okay." I draw the word out and toe my shoes off one by one, trying to buy time to figure out where he's going with this. Is this his way of realizing what he said to me in the park and being uncomfortable that he had a moment of vulnerability?

"You're the one who hit me with a snowball."

That's definitely what this is.

"I'd do it again." I laugh and play along. "And your point is what?"

"Why exactly do you know my stats?"

"What?"

"My stats. In the park you recited them off the top of your head like you'd been studying them, so I wanted to know . . . why do you know my stats?"

Here's my chance. To finally be honest . . . professionally. But because he just opened up to me, was real, I loathe to ruin it. I'd be lying if I said I didn't want him to share more. He's standing there shirtless. We just shared a kiss that's still very fresh in my mind and on my lips.

Shit.

How did we just go from a fight in a jazz club, to a snowball fight full of laughter, to a kiss loaded with things I don't want to acknowledge . . . to this? I answer with caution. "I know your stats because it's my job to. I told you that the other day when you asked me the exact same question."

"But I'm not your client."

"I know a lot of athlete's stats who aren't my clients."

He takes a step closer to me. "Why?"

"Because what you're paid is commensurate with your stats and status and draw to a crowd, and that affects all my clients. If you're the benchmark, we know where to go from there."

He cocks his head to the side and stares at me as he says, "Hmm. I thought maybe you were following the team because you missed and wanted me. Because you were sick of those memories keeping you satisfied on lonely nights and wanted the real thing as a refresher." A slow, steady grin slides onto his lips as his eyes reflect thoughts I'd be better not to remember.

"I do like you. Like this," I explain, pointing to him and then me. "But with you clothed and me clothed and—"

"Liar." He unbuckles his belt.

"I'm not lying. How can I be lying?" My words tumble out in a frantic mess as my libido and my head argue with my visceral reaction to it.

He unbuttons his pants.

The body is definitely winning out over the head right now.

"What are you doing?" I practically shout because yes, I may have seen him in all his glory many times before . . . but I've also experienced what that glory feels like and holy hell, I do *not* need to be reminded with a high-definition visual.

"I'm freezing," he says as nonchalantly as possible as he shoves his pants down his hips so he's standing before me in his boxer briefs and a body gorgeous enough to want to reach out and touch and feel its realness.

"Hunter?"

"What?" He chuckles. "You can stand there in your wet clothes and freeze to death because you don't trust me . . . but I'm getting in the shower."

Heat. It sounds so damn good as my teeth chatter. I suddenly forget him standing before me and remember the wet clothes I'm still swathed in.

"No one said I didn't trust you." *Liar.* "But I'm not taking a shower with you."

"Suit yourself, but oh, it's going to feel like heaven sinking in a nice, scalding hot bath."

"Bath?" My ears perk up. "I thought you said shower."

"Plans change. Now it's a bath."

"Oh," I moan the word out.

"Yep. I plan on filling it until it starts to cool and then refilling it again."

My eyes virtually roll back in my head at the thought. "That's wasteful."

His chuckle is a seductive sound. "But it'll feel oh-so-good," he hums.

"And bad for the environment."

"Currently, feeling my toes and my nuts trumps my inefficient use of water."

I take a step toward him as my body shivers. "You're keeping your underwear on, right?" I ask, shoulders straightening as if the thin cotton will be a deterrent from us touching each other.

Or wanting to.

"If that's what you want. I mean"—his eyes roam up and down the length of me—"you'll need to do the same because there's no way I want to see you naked either," he teases.

I stare at him—my body begging me to accept and my head knowing it's the worst idea ever . . . but I'm so damn cold.

"Fine." I strip my shirt over my head and do everything to ignore the hungry way his eyes scrape over the black lace of my bra beneath, the muscle twitching in his jaw. "Quit looking at me like that," I scold.

"I'm not looking at you in any way. Not your curves or your ass or . . . God"—he mock shivers—"why would any man be turned on by you?" His words are playful, his smile even more so.

"Go turn the water on like you promised." I flick my finger in that direction as I question whether the wet clothes or fighting my attraction to him is worse torture. "I'll be right there."

He gives me one quick flash of a grin before heading toward the bathroom, giving me a view of his ass, hamstrings, and back. I have no shame in staring at and appreciating it.

When the sound of the water echoes out of the bathroom, I shimmy out of my jeans in record time and thank fate that I wore some lacy boyshort panties instead of the thong I originally grabbed.

That decision just made my life a whole lot easier.

Or at least I think it did until I enter the bathroom to find him standing to the side of the massive tub, bubbles starting to form in the water, and the lights of the sleeping city twinkling outside the wall of windows the bathtub is positioned in front of.

Hunter glances up, and I'm not going to lie when I say it gives me the slightest thrill to see the hitch in his motion when he sees me standing there in my bra and panties.

"No funny stuff," I warn as I head toward the tub.

"No worries, Kincade," he says, but I don't believe him. "I'm well aware you're on the straight and narrow."

"I have to be. It's my business."

"What is?" He takes a step toward me. "You being here in my bathroom is business?" He gives a frustrated shake of his head. "It's always business with you. Every time. It used to not be that way. You used to take every ounce of that pent-up perfect professionalism you wear like a shield of armor and destroy me in bed with it until we were spent. Until we were satisfied. Every damn time. You used to like to walk on the wild side with me. You used to—"

"Not anymore." I shift my feet, needing to stop his words, the memories I can all but taste, and the poignant ache they create. "I have too much at stake now."

"And what exactly do you have that's at stake?" he asks as we stand a few feet apart, eyes warring and bodies wanting.

Too many things.

Way too many things.

My company.

My heart.

My dignity.

He takes a step closer and dips so we're eye to eye. "What is it, Dekk? What happened to change you? What is it that dimmed your fire?"

You.

The answer pops in my head without any hesitation, and I stagger because how can I say that? How can I think he's the reason I've become cautious when before I would have jumped in with both feet with him without a thought?

"My fire's still there." I offer a smile that I don't think he believes.

"Prove it," he breathes, as he closes the remaining distance between us. It feels like it's in slow motion as he reaches out to brush an errant strand of hair off my cheek, and I almost let myself sink into him.

"Whatever," I say as an out and stride past him toward the tub, simply to avoid his touch, and the dare I can already see him trying to set me up with. Nerves dance beneath the surface as I stare at the world beyond but somehow end up meeting his eyes in our reflection in the glass.

It hits me how much I'm flirting with danger.

In my standing with my clients.

In the reality of my life.

In what the hell I'm doing here in my bra and underwear in Hunter's room, when I know even if we did do something, he'd wake up in the morning without anything changed when everything would have for me.

He turns the water off but his chuckle at my lack of answer snaps me to the here and now. To the want and the need sparring against the reason and sanity.

I take an even breath and turn to face him and his inflammatory comment.

Walk away and make a stand, Dekk, or stay here and know what's going to happen.

His hand is on the nape of my neck in an instant and pulls me to him so his mouth meets mine the same time our bodies slam into each other's.

And every damn thing I felt in the park is magnified times a million.

Where the gentleness of the park confused me, the violent desire of right now is the Hunter Maddox I remember.

This is the one I can feed off.

This is the one that's purely sex, only need, and completely animalistic.

One hand holds my neck hostage to allow his lips to take what they want, while his other fists in the back of my panties and twists tightly so the fabric cuts against my skin.

Push him away.

He tugs on my bottom lip with his teeth.

Tell him no.

The hardness of his erection grinds against me.

Oh my God.

The firmness of his chest beneath my palms.

I missed this.

The hunger in his every action.

I missed him.

His breath is ragged when he rips his lips from mine, eyes blazing into mine, as we stare at each other, hands still owning the other's body in some way or another.

"Goddammit, Dekk," he groans. "Don't fucking toy with me. Tell me you want this. Tell me you need this as much as I do."

His voice sounds like how I feel—desperate, needy, ready to detonate.

The knowledge that I can break the control of a man like him, is beyond explanation. I want him. How he sates all desires. How he devastates all reason.

Him.

More of him.

Now is the time to feel every ounce, every inch, everything, he's willing to give me.

Chills chase up my spine as I stare at him and anticipate and debate and throw caution to the wind.

Who cares about hot chocolate and grilled cheese now?

It's my lips that meet his this time. It's my teeth that nip the tattoo on his shoulder. It's my fingernails that score their way down the side of his torso. It's my hand that slides inside the waistband of his boxer briefs and encircles his rock-hard cock. It's his body that tenses beneath my touch.

There's intensity to our actions, an urgency. A need to hurry up to the endgame and slow down at the same time.

I ache and burn and yearn every place Hunter's hands touch and his stubble scrapes.

We are a mass of hands and lips and grinds as we stumble the few steps to the bed. His underwear comes off as we walk. His fingers unclasp my bra as I shove down my panties.

I lied the other night.

I don't care about finesse when it comes to Hunter. I care about his hands gripping, his hips thrusting, his teeth nipping, his cock sliding.

My body vibrates as his hands take and claim and knead my breasts, my hips, my ass.

"Dekker," he groans, his lips against my breast, my skin vibrating under the strain of how he says my name. His hand fists in my hair, and he pulls my head back so I'm forced to look in his eyes as he stands back to full height.

My body is raw and wanting, and the seconds we waste as he stares at me, as his eyes wander up and down every inch of my body, has me itching to reach out and take what I want.

I open my lips, swollen from his, to speak, to tell him to destroy me in the most delicious of ways, but there's something in his look that tells me he needs this as much as I do . . . but for such very different reasons.

"Turn around," he orders and I obey, anticipation held with bated breath.

He puts a hand on my waist as he pulls me back against him, my ass meeting his thighs, the firmness of his dick undeniable against my lower back. He moves the hair off my neck with his free hand and his teeth scrape over the skin there as his other moves between my thighs.

"Fuck, Dekk. You . . ." He kisses the juncture of my shoulder to my neck. "This." His fingers slide between my thighs as one of his feet knock mine wider. "I'm going to fuck this sweet pussy of yours." He parts me, and his groan when he finds me wet for him has my nipples hardening. "With my fingers." He tucks them into me and my body convulses in reaction, anticipation for the next touch already building. "With my tongue." He slides his tongue up to my ear and dips inside, the combination of his coarse stubble and warm tongue making me gasp. "With my cock." He uses his hand to slide it between the cheeks of my ass and I tighten around his fingers in response.

My body is strung so tight, my need at fever pitch, my want dancing across my skin in goosebumps.

His hand grips the back of my neck again. "Tell me you're ready for me. Tell me you want me. Tell me to fuck you," he growls into my ear.

But I don't speak—can't—as his fingers continue their slow, delicious torture to the nerves and pleasure points between the apex of my thighs. My head falls back on his shoulder as I moan with another maneuver of his fingers. "Hunter." His name is a long, drawn-out plea to give me what

I need and to never stop.

"I know this body. I know what you need. So goddamn wet," he groans. "I've wanted you from the moment I saw you. Now, bend over."

My pulse races as I do as I'm told. His hands caress down my hips before one slides up and down my slit, allowing the room's cool air to hit my most sensitive flesh.

But more arousing than his touch is his hum of approval, of desire, of greed that owns the room around us.

I rest on my elbows in eagerness and then jolt when I feel the soft swipe of his tongue over my clit, stopping to dip in my center, before moving up over the tight rim of muscles atop, before going back the way he started.

He's deliberately slow, and his tantalizing torture has me squirming and widening my legs so he can have whatever part of me he wants.

I'm his.

Completely.

"Please," I moan.

A chuckle is his only response as he withdraws all touch from me. Then I yelp as his hand connects firmly with the side of my ass.

But the sting is quickly forgotten, the temporary pain gone as I hear the telltale rip of foil. He takes a moment to protect us before he slides the head of his cock up and down my slit.

"Sweet hell, Dekker," he moans as he slowly pushes his way into me.

My muscles resist with the sweetest of burns until they heat and accept and tighten from the fullness. It's my moan in the room now. It's my command for him to move. It's my ass pushing back against him telling him I'm ready.

With both hands on my hips, he begins to move in and out of me in measured, controlled strokes.

Each one a slow seduction to my nerves.

Each one an assault on my senses in the best way possible.

Each one another stroke closer to his control snapping.

And I can feel it happening, just as surely as I can feel my own orgasm begin to build.

His grip becomes tighter on my shoulder. His thrusting is more powerful, the slap of his thighs against mine louder. The sounds he emits more guttural, more unhinged.

Combined, they turn me on in a way no one else has ever been able to before, but I push the thought out of my mind and fall into the moment. Under the haze of pleasure. To the sensations he evokes.

I reach my hand between my thighs and brush my finger over my clit. The drag of his cock inside. The tease of my fingers on the outside. The gruff groan of my name. The ability he gives me to feel, to be, to give in.

It's heady and powerful and damn it to hell, he allows my body to build and soar and ache until the sensations reach a crescendo that I can only close my eyes, bow my head, and hang on to for the ride.

My body detonates—fractures into a million pieces as the orgasm slams into my every nerve, my every muscle, my everything.

My hips buck.

"Take it all."

My hands grip the comforter beneath me.

"Come for me, Dekk."

I cry out as my body tenses with pleasure and then sags with its release. I'm awash with warmth and bliss as my knees buckle, but Hunter's hands hold my hips up as he continues to drive into me. As he milks every ounce of pleasure out of me before picking up his pace.

I'm still under the fog of my climax, still trying to catch my breath and gain my faculties, but I don't have a chance to because it's Hunter's turn now.

His hands bruise and hips slam against me until his feral groan echoes as he empties himself into me.

"Hell," he murmurs as he bends over and kisses my shoulder before wrapping his arms around my waist and holding me into him.

We stay like this for a few moments as our breathing evens and our hearts decelerate. Just as I'm trying to figure out what happens next, he slips out of me when he straightens up, and heads for the bathroom without a word.

32

Dekker

THE KNOCK ON THE hotel room door has me jolting to attention like a kid caught doing something she shouldn't be doing.

"*The food*," we both say in unison as if that singular idea can suddenly bring back the disjointed feeling we both have in the aftermath of what happened between us.

"Here." He tosses a robe my way as he strides past me to where his suitcase is. "Just a second," he calls to the room service person on the other side of the door. Within a few seconds, he's stepping into a pair of jogging pants, as I slide the robe on.

"I'd kill for anything hot." He laughs the words out, his hand tapping my ass, before he opens the door. "What do you have for us . . .?"

Hunter's words fade while my hands still tying the knot in my robe. *Callum.*

Eyes wide, jaw lax.

Shit. Shit. Shit.

"I'm—I'm sorry." He jerks back a step. "It's late." His eyes go between the two of us again as he stammers. "I didn't mean to interrupt—"

"You didn't. Nothing happened." More than flustered, I take a step forward, well aware that the room behind us suggests the contrary. Our wet clothes litter the space, landing wherever we took them off, and the bed is a rumpled mess. "We had a snowball fight. We were wet." The words come out messily as I gesture toward the clothes strewn about. "Freezing. There's a pipe leak in my hallway. On my floor. We thought you were room service bringing us food to warm us up."

"Relax, Dekk," Hunter says as he reaches up and puts a hand on my bicep. "You're a big girl. You don't have to explain."

But I do have to explain, I want to say. Callum is a client, and now that he thinks we're together, my integrity and reputation are at stake.

"I just . . . it's not what he thinks it is," I mumble, hating that Callum can't even meet my eyes.

"I wanted to make sure you got back okay," Callum says to me, eyes lowered. "I tried your cell but didn't hear anything." He pauses and then turns his attention to Hunter. "And you, Maddox. You took off from the club without a word and were drunk as shit . . . Forget about it." He looks from Hunter to me and then back. "You're obviously okay. Both of you."

"Yep. Sure am," Hunter says, that half-cocked smirk on his lips not doing me any favors to dispel the situation.

"I'm just waiting for my room to be ready."

"In a robe," Cal purses his lips and nods. "Got it."

"Cal, wait," I say and step past Hunter. "I promise it's not what it looks like."

"It's your business, not mine."

"Perfect timing," a voice says behind Callum, and we all startle at there being someone else in the hallway at this odd hour of the morning. There's a rattle of dishes on a tray—glasses and silverware, before the room service person steps forward, pushing the tray in front of them. "Mr. Maddox?" he asks as he looks at the two men.

"Yes. Thank you." Hunter steps forward.

"Some hot chocolate. Grilled cheeses. Some hot apple turnovers. And I think a few more goodies. It's all on the house of course for the inconvenience we've caused you, Miss Kincade."

"Thank you." I nod and give a tight smile, more than relieved to have an innocent bystander back up my story with Callum.

"Maintenance just told me your room will be ready in five minutes. I was asked to escort you down there to make sure all your things are okay and to your liking."

"Oh." I hold the top of the robe closed and wonder if this is a blessing or a curse.

The blessing being that Hunter and I have never done that after part of sex before. It used to be sex, clean up, exchange a few words, maybe not . . . and then one of us would leave. Sure, we enjoyed each other, but there was nothing else between us.

The *curse* being that we've never done the after part of sex before either.

I glance back to the clothes on the floor and wonder how I retain my dignity while I scramble to pick them all up.

Callum assesses the situation and nods. "It's late," he says before shuffling down the hall toward his room, a few rooms down.

Hunter moves a hand to my lower back as the server moves the cart into the room. "Stay and eat?"

I shake my head, suddenly in a state of limbo—embarrassed, worried, confused. "I'm fine. I've got to go to my room—he said so—and . . ."

"Dekker."

"No, It's late. I should go make sure my room and things are okay."

"I'll walk you down there."

"No. I've got it." I step away from him, suddenly uncomfortable in everything. Needing space to clear my head and the emotions I know are most likely one-sided. At the situation I've just put myself in.

Shit.

"Dekker?" he asks.

"It's fine."

"I'll take her down," Hunter reasserts.

"No," I say with more force than I should before turning to the hotel staffer. "Can you give me a minute? I'll be right there."

The staffer nods and I shut the door to buy me a few minutes to gather my stuff.

"Dekker?" Hunter says as I move around his room like a madwoman gathering my wet clothes and shoes.

"It's fine. We're fine," I mutter and smile.

"So you've said."

"If Callum talks—"

"Then what?" Hunter asks, his voice resonating around the room. "If he talks, then what's the big deal? You're a grown woman who can have sex with whomever she chooses. Why does it matter?"

"Because it does." I fight the sudden burning of tears and hate that they're there. Because I don't cry over men. I don't cry over things that can never be. And I certainly refuse to cry over Hunter Maddox.

"Gotcha." He sighs as he moves with me through the room. "Ah, I forgot." He tsks as I survey the room one last time. "This was a mistake, right? It shouldn't have happened. It can't happen again. Yadda, yadda, yadda."

I expect to meet his eyes and find amusement in them, but there's nothing but a gravity that unnerves me. I can't tell if he's angry or confused, but it's something I've never seen before, and that in and of itself has me needing to get some space from him to figure out why there's an awkwardness here.

"Hunter . . . I'm here for work and—"

"I wasn't aware you were on the clock at two in the morning."

"It's not that. It's just—"

"Just like old times, huh? Great sex. Poor communication. It's best you leave before the fighting starts." He takes a step forward and presses a kiss to my forehead. "Good night, Dekker."

I stare at him as he opens the door. The second course of rejection from him tastes just as bitter as the first time. Maybe even worse.

The hotel clerk in the hallway rocks on his heels as he senses the discomfort between Hunter and me. I give him a half-smile and then turn back to face Hunter. Our eyes hold unspoken words exchanging between us—I'm sorry. *Why is it like this? Why can't we figure out how to do this right?*

At least that's what I think they say, because I second-guess every single one of them as I head to my hotel room.

Maybe this was the best way to end tonight.

Hockey.

Callum knocking on the door. The room service man shortly after.

Party.

Maybe a quick exit where neither of us had to talk about what's next, and how we move on from here is for the best.

Fucking.

Because I just screwed up by sleeping with Hunter.

No *repeat.*

And the worst part? I know that I did, but I wish I was still in the hotel room with Hunter right now.

33

Hunter

THE CURL OF STEAM comes off my coffee as I sit slumped in the chair where I moved it in front of the windows of my hotel room.

The city of Boston waits to wake up as I replay the last twenty-four hours in my mind and anticipate the sun to light up the sky.

Sleep was hopeless.

It is most nights as of late.

I've watched film of last night's game twice. My notes are taken. My critiques of my performance ten times worse than my father's. Maybe next game I can prove him differently.

Who can sleep when the world is burning down around them? When my brother's dying, my parents live in an alternate reality, and I'm constantly fucking up one thing after another.

When I simply don't want to care anymore.

It's the white noise I've grown used to living with. The constant. The things I'll never be able to change but will always try to.

"Christ," I mutter and roll my shoulders, my body exhausted but my mind going a million miles an hour.

The lone difference tonight in my thoughts is Dekker. For the first time in as long as I can remember, the shit in my head is quieter. Or maybe not quieter, but not as choking. The anger, the guilt, the unease . . . they took a backseat for a snowball fight, her hand holding mine in the rideshare, and then the incredible sex soon after.

Or maybe it's the relief in finally admitting to someone an ounce of my truth.

Either way it—us together—was *like* old times and yet so very different.

Is that what's bugging me? The *difference* between us this time?

I already knew having sex wasn't going to sate the hunger I had for her. I already knew one taste of her, one thrust into her pussy, and I'd only want more.

That's how it has always been with her. That's how it always will be.

What I didn't expect was for the same damn heartache I had when we broke things off last time to return with a goddamn vengeance. The heartache I didn't have to admit to last time because she walked out before I could.

But there was something different than that tonight. Something new.

I let the coffee scald my tongue when I drink it. I let it hurt and burn, as I force myself to acknowledge the one thing I pretend I don't notice. *Experience daily.*

I have women at my fingertips, fans are everywhere I go, and I have teammates around me almost every waking minute of each day, but fuck if Dekker walking out of here tonight without a glance back didn't make me realize how fucking lonely I am.

How alone I feel.

Daily.

"You're crazy. Fucking crazy, Mad," I say to the empty room as I acknowledge that tonight was most men's dream. Hell, it used to be mine too.

Great sex with a gorgeous woman who walks away after it's over and doesn't ask for anything more—not even a kiss goodnight.

Sex without strings.

But fuck if I don't feel invisible strings tying me up in the biggest fucking knot I've ever seen or felt before.

One that has her at the goddamn center of it.

Get over it, Maddox. Get the fuck over it.

I don't get attached.

I don't get the privilege to have feelings for someone.

I don't ever allow myself to want more.

But hell if what she did for me tonight—made me laugh, made me feel carefree, and then fucking owned every urge and need and want and inch of my body—doesn't make me wonder what it would be like to have that on the ready. If it's something I could get used to.

Drawing in a deep breath, I swear this room still smells like her—her shampoo, our sex—and that makes it hard to stop thinking about her. To stop wishing she were still here. To stop replaying her bullshit ghosting act and the way it felt watching her walk away.

"Let it go," I murmur and lean my head against the back of my chair, willing sleep in any form to come.

I close my eyes and try to quiet everything. All thoughts. All hopes. All dreams.

And in that limbo state between being awake and falling asleep, I have a moment of clarity I'm sure I won't remember once I wake in the morning.

She slept with me tonight and bailed.

Why?

To get back at me like I did her that first night in the elevator? To show why I should have chased after her three years ago? That's not like her, though.

Then what could it be?

Because Callum saw us? Because what had just happened between us was more than obvious?

Why the fuck does that matter?

He's her client, I'm not.

There's no line of professionalism that was crossed when it shouldn't be. There were no favors promised. Just pure, insanely incredible sex.

So why . . .

Shit.

Because Dekker Kincade is here to recruit *me.*

That has to be the only logical answer.

And I say logical, because I can't swallow that she bailed because she's embarrassed for people to know we were together. For Callum to know we had slept together.

The question is: is that why she slept with me? To maybe slide into my life between some bouts of good sex, some pillow talk . . . where she convinces me to leave Sanderson and change to KSM?

That would mean she just slept with a potential client. That would explain why she bailed right after.

I reject the notion but hate the thought that lingers. The one that screams all I am is a client to her.

A number she wants to nail to her wall, a fat commission check she'll win over to her side and then forget to pay attention to. First the Dartmouth game and then tonight.

It's the easiest thing to believe.

So much easier than believing maybe I deserve her. So much easier than believing she cares for me.

Because the last time she blew me off like this was after a bout of sex, when she got dressed and walked away, visibly upset without divulging why.

I didn't chase her. I never asked what the hell happened but just figured our time was up. It was probably a good thing because the minute I feel things, I bail too. And I was starting to feel things.

But now I'm remembering the shitstorm it made me feel and hating it.

And that's a sign that I need to back the fuck away and head whatever shit I'm feeling off at the pass.

My life is hockey. It's about being the best. It's about outrunning ghosts that will forever be a part of me.

Her job is profiting off athletes like me. It's about getting the biggest roster. It's about acquiring them like tokens and cashing them in when all is said and done.

She's using me, and that gives me a justified reason to be pissed and push her away when I'd fucking kill to have her sitting beside me right now, quiet and comfortable waiting for the sunrise.

But I can't let that happen.

I don't deserve her.

I don't deserve anything.

She used you, Mad. She just showed her cards. She's in this for her. She can ply you with comments about how she wants to be your friend and be there for you if you need to talk, but the endgame is you being her client.

Another person to use me.

Another person to see me as a commodity.

Maybe if I keep telling myself that, I'll stop wanting her as badly as I do right now.

Maybe I'll find some other way to not be lonely.

Is this all there is?

34

Dekker

THE SUBTLE SORENESS BETWEEN my thighs is the first thing I notice when I snuggle deeper beneath the covers to hide from the sun streaming through the window.

Last night is more than a distant memory. It's more like an in-the-face reminder of a pickle I need to figure my way out of.

I slept with a potential client. A current client all but caught me in the act. And then I had a moment of panic.

A huge moment of panic that only took some tossing and turning in bed when I couldn't fall asleep to figure out.

What I felt for Hunter—the reasons I pushed him away the last time we were together—came back clearly last night.

And I wasn't sure how I felt about that. How can I purport to be this strong, independent female who puts up with no one's shit, and after I spend one night with a man, I still have those same feelings? How can I be proud of myself when he was an ass to me at the club and I turned around and did what we did? How can I do any of this when I haven't been up front with him about why I'm here?

I'm a chicken.

Isn't that what this comes down to? I'm an overthinking, nervous-nelly chicken who doesn't have the guts to admit that I not only screwed up by sleeping with him for professional reasons, but also because I know I'm not gutsy enough to tell Hunter being fuck buddies isn't good enough for me anymore.

I'm not the same person.

Three years does a lot to mature a person and after Chad, maybe I want something more.

Maybe, my dad was right—not that I'll ever tell him.

Hunter Maddox. Complicated and multi-layered, incredibly gifted, a god in the sack, yet troubled by something significant.

I'd ask myself what I want from him but I already know. *Just* sex won't be enough. *Just* being a client might never work.

Oh what a tangled web I've woven.

But at least I'm sexually satisfied for what feels like the first time in forever. There's always that very shallow tidbit to fall back on as the sky falls and more clients leave KSM, because one of their lead agents sleeps with clients and presumably gives them better treatment than all her other clients.

Even worse, they'll start thinking that sleeping with my clients is part of the KSM package.

Shit. The more I think the worse this gets.

I groan and flop onto my back, trapping myself in the comforter when I do.

"Woman up, Kincade," I mutter. Tell him the truth. Explain why this can't happen again. March up to him and say, yes, he's the player I'm here to recruit. And yes, we slept together. *Christ, Dekker,* he already knows that part. But maybe tell him it happened once, I own it, but I can't let it happen again because I want to win his trust as a client. And once he's a client I can't cross that line.

I take a deep breath and fight the urge to slide back into sleep like only a person whose body feels satisfied knows, when it hits me.

Oh shit. Oh shit. Oh shit.

I fling the covers off me and scramble to grab my laptop like a mad-woman. I'm logged in within seconds, the connection accepting about the same time I'm patting down my hair and pretending I don't look like I just woke up.

"So glad you could join us," my father says through the connection as it goes from pixelated to clear where I can see him and my three sisters sitting at the conference table at the offices.

"Sorry. Late night."

Brexton's chuckle fills the room. "I hope he was worth it," she teases and has no idea how true that statement is.

"Funny," I feign. "I went with a few of the Jacks to a jazz club and then came back here to find a pipe had burst in the hallway. Late night," I overexplain when I need to just stop.

"Ha. Dare we ask *whose* pipe burst, exactly?" Lennox asks, staring at me through the screen.

There's absolute silence and then my sisters and I break out into laughter.

"Ladies," my dad says as he tries not to chuckle. "That's enough. We've already run through the status of all of our clients . . . your tardiness allowed you to miss that part, so you're up, kid. That status report remains blank so I'm beginning to get worried here."

"I'll update, but did we talk about what clients they're going after yet? Because I'm still miffed at my urgency and not theirs to pick up and leave."

"Considering Maddox is the one tearing up the charts and making scenes, I agree with Dad that it was important for you to be there now. Get him on the upswing so you can show him why you'll prevent him from falling," Chase says in her clipped, professional tone as if she has no stake in any of this.

"Always the pet," I mutter, knowing that's what they say about me.

"And she finally admits it." Lennox laughs, to which I hold my hand up to the lens and flip her off.

"So has Hunter been receptive to your advances?" he asks, and I cough in response to fight the smile on my lips.

"We haven't gotten to that part yet." I bite my bottom lip as they all stare at me.

"Hence the blank status report," Chase mutters under her breath.

"And why not?" Lennox prompts.

"It hasn't been the right time."

"In two-plus weeks' time, you haven't found a measly moment to corner him and ask if he's happy with his representation?" Chase asks.

"Look, I'm here because you guys feel like he's a ticking timebomb you want me to manage. I have to use caution. His game is stellar, but he's a disaster off the ice, so I'm trying to be the one to be there to fix his fuck-ups right now. He's burned out, and I'm trying to help him see that. Trying to help him see what he fell in love with again."

There's a snort in the conference room and they all glance to Brexton, and I can only imagine what she said.

I clear my throat and continue. "I'm trying to show him I'm the one there when Sanderson's not or is too busy with his other clients. I'm trying to make it be me who Hunter calls when he needs something. When he needs someone to understand him," I say, knowing it's so much more than that. To them, this is our career and business, but to me, it's wanting to see him get over this. "I'm at the games with the praise, but it's the off of the ice part that will win him to my side."

"Smart. Let him get comfortable—umm . . . more comfortable with you," Chase says.

"Knock it off, you guys. Hunter and I happened over three years ago. We're both mature adults who've moved on," I lie.

"I hear Sanderson was there," my dad says before a fight can start.

"He was." I nod. "His warning was delivered and ignored." Their chuckles fill the room.

"And you?" my dad asks. "How are you holding up?"

How do I answer that with the four people who know me best? How do I mask my expression so they don't see I'm kind of a mess this morning, torn by emotions I can't even name myself?

Because now that he's asked, it's ten times harder to pretend it's not there.

Now that he's brought it up, all I want to do is crawl into his arms and get a fatherly hug that tells me it's going to all work out in the end.

"I'm good. Fine," I reiterate. "My goal is to get Hunter alone this week between the next set of games and pitch our case."

"Rumor is Finn's not happy with him," Lennox says.

"Rumor is a lot of people aren't." I pull my hair up in a clip, suddenly more aware than ever what I probably look like to them. "And I intend to exploit that to my advantage."

My father nods, his hands steepled in front of him, and lips pursed. "He's our in to Sanderson, Dekk. He's the influencer or whatever term you young kids use these days. He's the one who sets the bar. Get him over and it'll be easier to pull more hockey players who want to be him." He leans back in his chair and, as he looks me directly in the eyes, I feel both his challenge and confidence *in* me. "I know you can do it."

35

Dekker

"THIS SEAT TAKEN?" I ask when I spot Hunter in the hotel lobby Starbucks.

He barely glances up from his iPad as he stands abruptly. "Now, it is. Have at it."

Ridiculously, I think he's standing to pull out my chair. Instead, he starts to walk away.

"Hey," I say after him, surprised and dumbfounded by his reaction. "Hunter."

"What?" he snaps as he looks back at me.

"I've texted and you haven't answered. I thought maybe we could talk, you know—about—"

"About what? Our *mistake*?" He scrunches his nose up and my insides twist at that stupid phrase. "No thanks. I'm sure Callum or another one of the guys will be along shortly, and I don't want to fuck up your reputation with them because you slummed it with me."

"Jesus Christ. Are you kidding me?" I stare at him dumbfounded, hands out, head shaking.

"Nope. I'm not kidding in the least." He takes a step toward me and lowers his voice. "You wanted sex, you got sex. You want to take the temperature on a new client, then put your damn toes in the water. Sleeping with him and bolting for old time's sake is a dick move."

His words sting and hurt and I stare after him, blinking. There's obviously so much I don't understand about last night.

I walked away trying to protect my heart.

He watched me walk away thinking I was using him?

I've really screwed up almost every aspect of this.

"You have this pegged all wrong. *Me* all wrong."

"Morning," Katzen says as he strolls into the coffee shop and then stops and looks from Hunter to me and then back. "We still working on that coupling thing?" he asks obliviously. "Because if you are, I think there should be a lot more lovin' and a little less fighting." He holds his hand up in mock surrender and laughs when Hunter glares at him. "Just saying."

"Whatever," I say with a roll of my eyes and a forced smile.

"I've got a phone call with Sanderson," Hunter says and holds his phone up as if that's his answer to why he keeps walking and doesn't engage.

Or maybe to throw it in my face who his agent is.

"Who pissed in his Wheaties this morning?" Katz asks with an over-ex-aggerated flip of the bird to his teammate.

"No idea," I murmur.

Me.

I did.

I'm the one who pissed him off and screwed this up.

"Well, shit," Katz says, sliding into the seat in front of me. "If he's not going to sit with a pretty lady, then I definitely will. I'm around way too many jockstraps these days and not enough G-strings."

I throw my head back and laugh. "If you're looking for G-strings, you're sitting at the wrong damn table," I say but then shift in my seat, considering the black lace one I put on this morning.

36

Dekker

ATHLETE	TEAM	SPORT	AGENT	STATUS
Carl Ryberg	n/a	Golf	Kenyon	Contract Mtg
Jose Santos	D-Backs	Baseball	Chase	Declined representation
Michelle Nguyen	n/a	Soccer	Brexton	In talks
*Hunter Maddox	Jacks	Hockey	Dekker	**********
Vincent Young	Rams	Football	Dekker	First contact initiated
Garrett Zetser	n/a	NASCAR	Lennox	Face to face meeting

********* It means our dear sister is ghosting us. Dekker, Dekker, Dekker, Dekker . . . quit ignoring us.

THEY'RE BEING LITTLE BRATS, but their comments on the scouting memo give me a much-needed laugh.

And then I hit send, leaving the status for Hunter Maddox blank. Serves those nosy little punks right.

37

Dekker

I SIT IN THE press booth in whatever damn city we're in and answer my messages. One after another. Email and phone call after email and phone call.

But I work through them as the Jacks practice on the ice below and work on a new defensive play that just might work in the coming weeks.

It would be smarter to work in my hotel room, but I'm distracted. Not by work that desperately needs my attention but rather the man on the ice who has consumed my thoughts since he left the coffee shop the other day.

Who am I kidding? He's consumed it much longer than that, but I'm not counting that part.

Maybe it's because we've never had a chance to be alone since then, my texts have gone unanswered, and my phone calls sent to voicemail. I've even thought about sliding a note under his door, but just my luck, a teammate would find it and more shit would hit the fan.

We really need to talk about why I left, about why I'm here, and about what his perception of it is.

This could all be solved with decent communication—in fact, if it were one of my friends, that's the first bit of advice I'd impart—but it's not as easy as that.

The minute I tell him why I'm here—whatever's happening or has happened between us can be no more. Then he becomes a client. Then I must put professionalism before him.

And the struggle between pleasing my father and owning what I want makes the path not so clear-cut.

"You sure are spending a lot of time with the team."

I startle and look back to see Ian McAvoy standing with his arms crossed and shoulder leaned against the doorframe.

"The same can be said for yourself," I reply with a smile, hoping he'll smile at my joke. He doesn't. "Most GMs aren't fond of road trips."

"And most GMs' teams haven't been pulled from the depths of the hockey dungeon to the top of the division within two years."

"True." I nod, shut my laptop, and lean back in my chair to wait for him to talk about whatever it is he wants to talk about. Ian isn't one to hang and chat without having an objective in sight.

"Should I believe the rumors?" he asks.

"Depends which rumors they are."

"Why you're here."

"I have clients on your team. We're heading into unknown territory for some of them, and I want their heads in the right place come playoff time."

"And what about those who aren't your clients? Shouldn't it be said I need them to be left alone so their heads are in the right place too?"

"Let's not beat around the bush, Ian. If you've got something to say, then say it." I rise from my seat, never wanting to be at a disadvantage. Him standing over me puts me at a disadvantage.

"What do you want with Maddox?"

I purse my lips and watch the team practicing. Hunter moves with ease, and then something is said among them so their laughter floats up to Ian and me.

"He's not my client if that's what you're asking," I finally say, wondering if Ian would be having this same conversation with me if I were a man.

"I'm well aware he's not your client." His shoes squeak on the concrete floor as he takes a few steps past me and braces his hands on the desk the next row up. "It just seems like you've taken a special interest in him."

I draw in a deep breath and let the sigh of frustration be heard. "I have a vested interest in this team. Callum is coming off an injury, Stetson is trying hard to fight his way onto the roster, and Guzman is doing his thing. Like I told you when I cleared my being here beforehand, it was a good time to check on some clients. If something has changed, just come out and say it."

"I've known your father a long time, Dekker," Ian says, looking back at me over his shoulder from behind his glasses.

"So have I." My response sounds like I'm trying to be funny, but I'm not. I already know where he's going with this, and my guard is up.

"I've never seen him doing something like this."

"Like what? Road trip with a team to check in on clients? Funny. He's the one who insisted I come."

"It's different," he says.

"How so?"

"You're a woman. The team acts differently with women agents around. They—"

"With all due respect, Mr. McAvoy," I say and step beside him as Hunter scores a goal and the rest of the team taps their sticks to the ice in response. "This is my job, not a bar where I come to hit on men. I've never been anything but professional. I don't venture into the locker rooms to keep it that way, while male agents go in and out like a revolving door. Your implication is bullshit and unfounded," I lie through my teeth.

"Don't fuck with our season, Kincade. Maddox is a huge part of it."

"He's an old friend. I'm allowed to reach out and make sure he's okay, considering it seems like he's dealing with some shit. That's just the person

I am, so you can either appreciate the help in taming your out-of-control star, or you can tell his agent to do his job himself. While I may be able to heed your threats, they only succeed in pushing your star further away."

"I need the Cup."

"I have no doubt Maddox is going to lead this team and get it for you."

38

Hunter

I SIT ON A frozen metal bleacher in the freezing fucking cold and stare at the players.

My attention is rapt on the two kids on the ice. Two boys who are laughing as much as they're practicing. Two boys who every now and again skate past each other and wrap an arm around the other's neck in brotherly affection.

My decision to come here to try and remind myself how it used to feel rewarding.

You're burned out.

I watch them with tears burning in my eyes.

Two kids having fun. Learning to play a sport and love a game that has been humming in my blood for as long as I can remember.

Two kids pretending to be someone like me when all I want to do is go back and be like them. Innocent. Unjaded. With my brother back at my side.

Fucking fried.

What are you going to do, Maddox? Lie down and die? Walk away from the game?

Or win the Cup for Jonah with the club he told you to play for? Win the Cup he should have won in a game he was always so much better at?

My insides are a fucking jumbled mess. Shit stirred up I don't want to acknowledge. Shit Dekker's presence brought to light.

Fuck.

And thinking of her—hell, I feel like that's all I've been doing is thinking of her—screws me up even more.

I scrub my hand over my face and breathe out a huge sigh as the boys' laughter floats over to me.

"Nah-uh. Dad's never going to let us be on the same team," the taller of the two says.

"Why not?"

"Because then we can't both be stars, silly." He pushes his brother from behind so he's shoved forward, and they both start giggling hysterically and look over to where their dad sits in his truck, engine running, heater probably on, as he eyes the crazy man sitting by himself in the bleachers to gauge if he's a creeper.

I don't care, because all I hear is what the big kid just said: *because then we can't both be stars.*

Such a simple solution we never got the chance to figure out for ourselves.

The loneliness hits me even harder watching them, but so do the memories. The laughter. The secrets. The bond we shared on and off the ice.

It never mattered that he was the star and I was the second string. It only mattered that we were there together. It only mattered that we understood each other. It only mattered that I played the sport I loved with the brother I loved more.

I lift my head to the clear sky and close my eyes for a beat.

I'm so sorry, Jonah.

I'm going to win you that Cup you deserved.

I'm going to break every record in your name, because I know you already would have.

I'm trying to be the star for both of us before one or both of us burn out.

"You can't go yet, J. Don't go until I finish the job you asked me to finish.

Don't leave me yet."

When I rise from the bleachers half an hour later, I don't have all the answers, but I have more determination and clarity.

39

Dekker

"HEY."

Hunter stops midstride and glances over to my car where I've pulled up beside him. "Go away, Dekk."

"What's that supposed to mean?" I keep driving slowly beside him as he keeps walking.

"Just what it sounds like. I don't want what you're selling."

"Lucky for you, I'm not offering anything," I mutter. "We need to talk about the other night."

"There's nothing to talk about," he says, still refusing to look my way.

"There's not?" There's a whole host of shit we need to talk about.

"Nope."

Nope? What the hell? I slam the rental car into park, hop out, and jog up beside him, but he still refuses to look my way.

"Hunter? What the hell?" I grab his arm and he turns on me with confusion and anger etched in the lines of his face.

"You're wasting my time, Kincade. I've got practice to get to. You know, *my job*. I haven't been avoiding you, I've just been throwing myself into perfecting my game. As an agent, you should appreciate that in a client."

His smile is tight and his words are cutting.

"I do, but I also know avoidance when I see it."

"What am I avoiding?" he asks and takes a step back and crosses his arms over his chest, throwing the ball back in my court and of course now that he has, I just stare at him.

Answer the question honestly and sound like a needy female. Lie and sound like a flustering idiot.

"Me." I choose honesty and feel so stupid saying it, but it's true, and it's better if we face this now rather than later.

"Bullshit," he sneers.

"You're not avoiding me?" I ask on the defensive.

"Nope. Don't think so highly of yourself. I have a Cup to win. I have a team to lead. I have consequences if I let them all down."

"You've always had a Cup to win." I take a step toward him as he takes one back. "I don't under—Hunter, talk to me."

"About what? How we got drunk. How we had a laugh or two. Then how we fucked." He throws his arms out to his sides and raises his voice. "Just like old times, huh? No harm, no foul—mistake made and realized until the next time."

His words should hurt, but for some reason, they don't. Maybe it's because it's been two days since we slept together and this is the first time I've been able to actually talk. It's been two days of overthinking and wondering if the sex was just sex or blowing it out of proportion to second-guess every nuance of his and wonder if there could be more. But now that I'm standing here, he's made it clear what the answer is, and I'm not exactly sure what to say.

"I—I just thought we should talk about it."

His chuckle is raw and brutal. "About what? The snow angels? The shit I said in the bar? Or someone seeing us together?"

"Because it could affect my job."

He chuckles and scrubs a hand over his jaw. "I expected more from you than that. I really did." The disappointment in his voice is like a knife to my heart. Here he is handing me the key to the door I need. But I know the minute I unlock and open it, everything I want will fall out of reach.

"I can't give you more." It's the only thing I can think to say as my professional world wars against my personal one.

"Why?" This time, he's the one who takes a step closer to me. This time, he's the one staring and demanding and wanting to know.

"Because I can't," I whisper.

"That's what I thought," he says and starts to stride off.

"Hunter. Wait." He keeps walking. "Truth. *Truth*," I shout, and this time he stops but doesn't turn around. I stare at him, the bright lights of the arena he's playing in tonight in the background. "I can't admit to you why I'm here because the minute I do, whatever happened the other night can't happen again. I can't tell you what you want to hear, because there's a blaring red line in the sand and once I cross it, all those things about you that made me want to come back to your room over and over once I left that night have to be buried and gone." My breath hitches on what feels like a sob, but it's really my fear in admitting the truth to both him and myself.

It's the fear in admitting that I had fallen for Hunter Maddox before, and being here, sleeping with him, just reinforced that I never got over him. That I chose mediocre options in the interim who never dimmed his sparkle, but rather made it shine brighter.

He turns slowly and stares at me, eyes burning into mine in a way I've never seen or felt before. The muscle in his jaw feathers as if he's trying to control any and all emotion from playing across his stoic face.

The hope I had that he might hear me drains away slowly.

I throw my hands up in a shrug and surrender whatever else I can't express. "I don't know what to do. I don't. My dad sent me here to win you over to the agency because you're you, and any agent would be crazy to not want you on their team. Now that I'm here, I don't know that I can follow through with it. I know you're struggling with something, and I would do anything to help you through it. But if I offer you that, you'll always be wondering if it's because I'm personally invested or because I want to profit off you professionally. The answer is I care, when it seems you don't want anyone to. So you tell me, Hunter, what am I supposed to do?"

The first tear slips over and I shove it away with the back of my hand as I stand before him, intentions exposed, emotions on the line, waiting for him to respond.

"I've got to get to practice."

He turns his back on me and walks toward the entrance.

And I watch him.

Every single step.

But this time through the blurred tears.

I now have my answer.

He walked away.

Decision's been made.

He left me.

I'm done.

It's time to go home.

40

Dekker

I STARE AT THE memo and wish I could add more, but I can't. I've failed. My dad had faith in me, and I blew it.

KINCADE SPORTS MANAGEMENT
Internal Memorandum
New Recruit Status Report

*denotes urgent status

ATHLETE	TEAM	SPORT	AGENT	STATUS
Carl Ryberg	n/a	Golf	Kenyon	Contract Mtg
Desi Davalos	n/a	Basketball	Chase	Contact initiated
Michelle Nguyen	n/a	Soccer	Brexton	In talks
*Hunter Maddox	Jacks	Hockey	Dekker	Recruited, no response
Vincent Young	Rams	Football	Dekker	Face to Face Meeting
Garret Zetser	n/a	NASCAR	Lennox	In talks

I look at it one more time, and then I hit send.

41

Hunter

DAD: *Worst game I've seen you play all year. Why isn't your head in the game, son? Think of everything we gave up for you to be there and prove you deserve it.*

ME: *Fuck you.*

I STARE AT THE text. At those two hostile words. At the cursor flashing. The pressure is mounting. I feel the exhaustion everywhere. Just. Fucking. Everywhere.

The suicide drills and the endless shooting challenges he made me perform until late into the night.

No breaks.

No sympathy.

Only the weight of the world on my shoulders. Only the knowledge that I'm the reason Jonah left that night. I was the catalyst who put him in the car and robbed *them* of *his* spectacular career.

I'm the *mediocre* brother forced to live out the dream Jonah no longer could.

Because living for Jonah is the only other thing they have. Even though I'm still alive and have dreams of my own.

And living for someone else is so exhausting, so daunting, so goddamn frustrating.

The cursor blinks.

The same two words I've wanted to respond with after every game I've ever played professionally.

Two words.

They say so much.

I'll never fill his shoes.

I'll never be as good as he would have been.

But I'm me. Fucking *me*. A man who rose to the challenge and have lived *my* every moment so that Jonah knows I'm sorry. That I'm so god-damn sorry for what I did that night. For how I lied. For not being re-sponsible. For not being the one who took the keys.

The guilt is why I've always deleted those two words.

The guilt is why I've never thought I deserved anything—the praise, the accolades, the love.

The guilt is why I punish myself.

But hell if walking away from Dekker yesterday didn't shoot that all to shit.

Fuck if looking up in the owner's box and not seeing her there—as I have the past three weeks—wasn't a blow to my concentration. I thought of the ten other things I should have said to her instead of the one sen-tence I did.

The hurt in her eyes when I didn't acknowledge a fucking thing she said.

"You good, Mad Dog?" Callum asks as he walks by. I lean back against my locker, dropping my phone in my lap.

"Yeah. Just . . . that was a brutal fucking game." I glance at the bag of ice Saran-wrapped to my knee and shake my head.

"It always is. The Bandoliers are fucking thugs."

"Not going to argue."

"You were an animal out there."

I nod and replay the game in my head in the flash of time. All I can see are the shots I missed, the times I was stripped, the bullshit fouls called.

"Meh. I beg to differ, but it's not worth the argument."

He checks the bottom of his skates and busies himself before turning to look at me, eyes intense. "She leave?"

He doesn't have to say who *she* is, and I'll save him the bullshit of pretending I don't know who he's talking about. I have more respect for him than that.

"Not sure. I don't keep tabs on her." But I was looking. I was wondering.

"Huh."

"You got something to say, Withers?" I ask.

"Nothing you're going to listen to," he says. "Shit. We finally get to go home tonight. My bed is calling me."

"I'm listening," I say, ignoring his color commentary.

He pauses, stuffing his gear into his bag and stares at me. "She's obviously under your skin."

"What the hell is that supposed to mean?"

"It means, I've never seen you give a fuck about anything other than hockey and your family . . . but you give a fuck about her."

I blink and try to hear him—really hear him—and then like always, play it off. "I think that punch you took to the head tonight was harder than we all thought." I chuckle to sell the lie.

"You're indifferent with women. They're a dime a dozen to you because they're everywhere you go—"

"Whatever."

"But Dekker challenges you." He hefts the bag over his shoulder and walks a few feet toward me.

"Your point?" I ask.

"It's a good thing she does." He reaches a hand to my shoulder and squeezes. "She's a good person, Mad. She deserves to be treated right. Whatever happens, just remember that."

And without another word, Callum walks out of the locker room to our transport waiting to take us home for the first time in what feels like forever.

But I sit in the empty locker room. There are a few guys still in the trainer's room getting worked on and their laughter filters out to me, but other than that I'm alone.

So goddamn alone.

The worst part? The only time I haven't felt lonely is when *she's* around. Fucking Dekker.

Closing my eyes, I think about what Callum said. About Dekker and what she deserves and wonder what I've never allowed myself to wonder. About me and what I don't deserve, but hell if the moments spent with her haven't made me want. *An us.* About the opportunities I've passed up, the dreams, the happiness I told myself weren't merited.

Christ.

So fucking alone.

But this time when I stand to head to the bus, I don't delete the text like I normally do.

This time, I hit send. Finally.

42

Dekker

"IT'S MIDNIGHT. WHY ARE you here?"

I laugh as Brexton props her shoulder against the doorway of my office and debate how much I should tell her. "I guess the same could be said for you," I respond.

"I forgot a contract I need for the morning. Less traffic to get it now than to fight rush hour, and you know how I love my sleep."

I smile softly and wonder why brusque Brexton is being so kind.

"Smart," I say and look out the window to the city beyond. The Manhattan skyscrapers and their lights dot the distance. A city still alive, while I'm struggling with so much turmoil.

I walked away from Hunter, from my time with the Jacks, without saying a word. I walked away, knowing full well I left my heart behind. I came back home with the bitter taste of rejection on my tongue and knowing I was letting my dad—my sisters—down by not finishing what I set out to do. Letting Sanderson win.

"Wasn't there a game tonight?"

I nod and exhale a sigh. "Yeah, but . . . I decided to skip it. I have a shit ton to do and being in the press box isn't going to do anything toward getting Hunter to sign with us."

"Huh." She makes that stupid sound I hate that says *I don't buy a word you're saying,* and then twists her lips in thought as she studies me. "So you finally told him KSM wants him?"

"Something like that." I look at the papers on my desk and relive everything—my confession and his nonchalance—and wish my mom were here right now, as I've wished many times over the last fifteen years, so I could get her advice. I think I just screwed everything up. "He didn't react, so I'm not sure what to make of it."

I'm not exactly lying—he didn't react—so why do I avert my eyes and blink back the tears that threaten?

"Humph." She moves to the window of my office and looks out. Her hands are on her hips as she scans the skyline. I study her. "It never went away, did it?" Her voice is soft, gentle almost, when she's never gentle.

"What never went away?" My mind is thinking of clients and contracts I missed while I was on the road trip. What didn't I—

"The way you feel about Hunter."

I freeze and am grateful her back is to me so she doesn't see. Like with everyone else, I want to deny. Deny their observation. Deny my feelings. Deny it all. *Especially now. Why can't I tell the truth?*

"You're delusional."

Brexton takes her time moving to my desk before setting her hip on it. "I may be delusional, but I also know you have a habit of running the other way any time you get feelings for someone."

"I do not."

"Yes, you do."

My guard is up, my defiance front and center. "Name someone."

"Chad."

"What-the-hell-ever. Next."

"I'm being serious. You were fine with Chad—content with him—because you didn't feel anything for him. He was safe. He allowed you the appearance of having someone without you having to get emotionally involved." She picks up a trinket on the corner of my desk—a hockey puck given to me from a client a long time ago—and weighs it in her hand. "Chad is the latest casualty. Before him that software salesman who wore his pants too tight—"

"Come on. He wasn't that bad." She eyes me until we both start laughing and I nod. "Yes, I guess he was . . . but his pants were too tight for a reason," I say to try and get the focus off me.

"At least he had that going for him," she says and shakes her head. "And before him was the baseball player. Then Gene Harsket. I never understood what you saw in him."

"Brex—"

"No, I need you to hear me. To listen to me. I need you to see that you make a habit of being emotionally unavailable because you refuse to put yourself out there. You refuse to be hurt."

I open my mouth and close it, because it hits me how very right she is. And then to make matters worse, why can she see that when I can't?

"Look." She waits until I meet her eyes, and then it's a struggle for me to keep them there. But I do, and she continues. "It's okay to have feelings, Dekker. Mom died, and we all retreated into ourselves. It's natural to pull away and not want to be hurt when the last time you really loved something, you were devastated."

I clear my throat and rise from my chair, needing to abate the restlessness her words cause me.

"You're making me think I failed at this big sister thing. You're the one giving advice."

Brexton steps up beside me but we both stare at the streets below for a few seconds. "That's the thing, Dekker. We love that you're our big sister, but you became our mom and in doing that, you never allowed yourself to grieve. You never allowed yourself to rage. We did, and you were too busy holding us together to be able to do it yourself . . . so of course any kind of attachment scares you."

"I grieved."

"Sure," she says. It's her way of telling me she doesn't believe me.

"I did. I raged and screamed but I had to do it in a pillow so you guys wouldn't hear me." The wave of memories hits me. The loneliness. The fury. The unknown. The sadness.

"Okay, then why don't you let yourself love?"

I laugh despite the tears welling in my eyes. "Grieving for Mom and falling in love with someone are not mutually exclusive."

Her arm goes around my shoulder. "It never went away, did it?" she asks again.

I blink away the tears, but one escapes down my cheek as I think of how heartbroken I was three years ago when I walked away from Hunter, and how similarly I felt this time with his nonchalance and nod. "The first time, he didn't ask why the abruptness of it all. Why we went from seeing each other as much as we could to nothing."

"Maybe because he had feelings for you and felt scared about them too. If you bailed that easily, why is it hard for you to believe that he could do the same? If you're afraid of love, why is it unfathomable that maybe he's afraid of it for other reasons?"

I lean my head on her shoulder and breathe deeply, hearing her words but not wanting to believe them.

"What happened this time, Dekk?"

I let the silence settle as I struggle with telling her the truth. Their problems are my problems but my problems are no one's problems. So, I usually keep everything close to the vest.

"What happened this time?" I repeat. "He's like kryptonite to me." I give a self-deprecating laugh. "There's something going on with him he won't talk about, and of course, I want to try and fix it."

"No surprise there."

"No, I mean . . . I went there to do my job as an agent—what Dad asked—but when I saw him, I knew he was wrestling with something." I continue to explain his acting out, his hot and cold, his being completely burned out and finally admitting it.

"So you slept with him."

"Mm-hmm."

"And then what?"

"And then I bailed to my room. It was much easier doing that than trying to sort through my feelings with him sleeping right beside me."

"But you felt something, right?"

"I felt fucking everything," I admit without hesitation and know how stupid it sounds. To run away from those kinds of feelings, but the fact that she doesn't point it out makes me feel a little better.

"And when you confronted him?"

"He acted like I was asking him about the weather."

Brexton turns to face me and puts her hands on my shoulders so I'm forced to look at her. "The question is, what are you going to do about it, Dekker? Are you going to let him walk away a second time when you know damn well he's the only one who's lit your fire emotionally and sexually?"

"Christ." My cheeks flush.

"No. I'm being serious. What are you going to do? Rob yourself of the chance of seeing what happens because you're too chickenshit to try?"

"That's not fair."

"Why isn't it? Maybe what's not fair is how we've let you sneak by doing this and not really living for anything other than work and a false sense of security with people who put water on your fire like Chad." She gives a little shake to my shoulders. "So the question is . . . what are you going to do about it?"

"There's nothing I can do about it. I can't ask him to be a client and want to have a relationship at the same time. I can't–"

"Fuck that." She waves a hand at me. "We'll figure it out. Dad will have to deal. There are always solutions to every problem. We can handle him."

"But that doesn't fix the other problem."

"Other problem?"

"Like how other clients would perceive me sleeping with a client I'm going after."

"Then he's not with the agency or we pass him off to one of us to represent. Done. Next excuse." She flashes a dazzling smile my way, and

I groan because the next one isn't so easy.

"You can fix all the things in the world on the professional side, Brex, but nothing will make Hunter see me as anything other than a no-strings notch on his busy bedpost."

"I think you're wrong."

"Good for you." I move back toward my desk and the stacks of paperwork, hoping that if I ignore her, maybe this conversation will go away.

"If Hunter didn't have feelings for you, do you think he would have gotten all butt-hurt when you left after Callum saw you that night?" She lifts her eyebrows and crosses her arms over her chest. "Do you think he would have been more of a dick and less dismissive when you confronted him in the parking lot? You made him feel like you put work before him . . . and I'd say that screams that he has feelings for you."

I see what she's saying but . . . "You weren't there."

"You're right. I wasn't. But if you want him to see you as more than a notch—which I already think he does—then force him to."

"He closes off emotionally before anyone can get too attached. It's like he doesn't feel like he deserves to be cared for or loved."

She coughs through a laugh and throws her hands up. "The irony."

"Shut up." But I laugh with her this time as my mind spins and whirls and contemplates if she could be right.

Could Hunter have feelings for me but not know how to show them? Could he be just as fearful of letting someone in as I am? If so, how do I push him past that—how do I push myself past that—to give us a chance?

"Say I buy into what you're saying—"

"You do. And you should."

"Then what do I do next?"

One side of her lip curls up. "Nothing. He'll come to you."

"That's a solid plan. Real solid," I say in frustrated disbelief. Just when I start to believe her, she pulls something like that? My sigh is loud.

"No. I'm serious. You've laid the groundwork. You were honest with him. You told him you wanted him personally and professionally and why the two can't mix. But he's a rule breaker, Dekker. He's going to push boundaries just because he can. He's going to want to be macho and masculine and prove he can have you and eat his cake too."

"I think you're crazy."

"And I think I'm right."

I stare at my sister, so similar and yet so very different from me, and wonder how she can be so sure. And I consider the many exchanges between Hunter and me. Over the laughter, his ability to be serious with me, and I wonder how I never saw it before. How angry he was when he accused me of *meeting* with my clients night after night. How he let his guard down ever so briefly with me on the hard-packed snow amid angel wings we had made. How his smile lit up when the ice became littered with tennis balls at the Dartmouth game.

And more so, I wonder how I've been harboring feelings for a man for over three years and never took charge of *them*, when I seem to grab everything else by the balls.

Because you're scared, Dekker.

You're scared because you know he's the most real thing you've ever felt and it terrifies and exhilarates you.

"I don't know," I murmur. How and when did my little sister become so wise?

"I do." She leans forward and drops the puck on top of the paperwork I keep staring at. "It may take him a few days—a week, or two—but with radio silence from you, he'll realize how much he misses you. How much he's gotten used to you being around, and how puck bunnies look boring to him now."

"You have an active imagination." That's just the visual I need in my head. *God, I hope he ignores the puck bunnies.*

"Either that, or I've had a client or two go through something similar before going *holy shit*, I'm going to lose her." She clucks her tongue as if she had some play in these revelations. "He came back for you this time around because he wanted to see if the feelings you both walked away from were legit. He's pushing you away now, because they are."

I lean back in my chair and close my eyes, letting her words settle and take root as she moves toward the door.

"Hey, Dekk?"

"Hmmm?"

"Falling for someone is never the plan. One day, you just wake up and it's there in full-freaking, high-definition color. You realize those un-anticipated butterflies you got when you saw him, those frustrated late nights overthinking and overanalyzing every interaction, those automatic, genuine smiles when you received a text from him . . . they all add up until they become love. It's the little things that add up. It's the unseen that touches your soul. It's the unexpected that makes you fall in love." She moves to the doorway. "I've got to jet . . . but you know I'm here for you. You know we only want the best for you."

I look at her through eyes blurred with tears and nod. "Thank you."

She smiles and then turns her back.

I listen to the door of the outer office click shut, to the lock engage, and to her footsteps down the hallway to the elevator.

When I put my feet up on my desk, lean my head back, and close my eyes again, I carefully examine her words.

I wonder what would have happened all those years ago had I not run from him that night. If I had just been honest instead of chickening out.

Is Brexton right?

If I wait, will he come?

43

Hunter

NO TEXT.

It's the first time in years that I look at my phone after my game and see nothing from my father.

There's relief and an odd constricting of my chest. Almost as if I don't know how to process my post-game cool down without the anger generated by them.

As if not having that negativity I've been a slave to for so very long feels like I've lost a part of me. As if it's no longer worth comparing me to Jonah . . . leaving him to him and me to me. *Untethered.*

I sit on the bench with the guys moving around me and simply stare at my phone.

This has nothing to do with Jonah, Mad, and everything to do with you. This is you realizing you can love your brother but not be beholden to our parents over life's fate.

Over fate's blind arrow shot in the night to ruin one person's life and change another's.

"Dekker? Hi." My ears perk up the minute Callum answers his phone, and fuck if I don't check my texts again to see if I missed one from her.

Nothing.

Almost as if she said what she said to me—confessed two things that could change my life in numerous ways like me sending that text to my dad did—but I'm afraid to face it.

Let her represent me instead of Finn. He's dogged and well-known, same as Dekker, and yet, I feel like she has more than just her bottom line in mind from how I've seen her manage Callum. I've seen her patience with him, Guzman, and Stetson, and I've talked to other players who she's secured endorsement deals for. All professional, no bullshit, all results.

And when it comes to me. Maybe . . . maybe there's even more than a bottom line and deals.

Maybe she could love me.

Fuck if that's not a hard thing to think out loud. Fuck if that's not the thought that has had me tied up in knots for days.

What am I going to do about it?

Live in the past . . . or realize I can't change the past and can only move forward?

Shit.

She followed us around the damn place and now that we're right in her backyard and our home turf, she couldn't bother to show up? A damn subway ride away from Manhattan to Jersey, and she couldn't make it?

If she wanted me that badly, wouldn't she have shown up? Tried to win me over?

So, you tell me, Hunter, what am I supposed to do?

Dekker's words replay in my mind. The confused desperation in her voice, the pleading in her eyes, the defeat in her posture . . . fuck. It killed me.

Why am I thinking about this now?

Why am I sitting in a locker room with my teammates and not celebrating being one game closer to clinching a playoff berth?

"Yes, it looks that way, doesn't it?" Callum says as he walks past me, his finger pressed to one ear, his cell to the other. *Because of her.* "But don't say the word. Don't fucking jinx it." His laughter rings out.

The playoffs.

She called him to talk about the playoffs.

Sanderson doesn't call me to talk about my games.

Shit, he doesn't call me unless it's to make me get in line. Unless it's negative and unsupportive, much like my old man's.

Fucking hell.

I lean my head back on the locker behind me.

Deal with her after the playoffs.

Deal with my representation and all the shit in my head and my questions after the playoffs.

Accomplish the one thing you need to—that you promised Jonah—and then maybe you can carve out more of a life for yourself.

"Hey!" I pound my fist against the metal locker behind me and the sound echoes across the chatter in the locker room. All the guys turn toward me as I climb on top of the bench.

Their hoots and hollers fill the room and mask my own groan as my knee aches from bearing weight on it.

"Speech. Speech. Speech," the guys begin chanting.

I motion with my hands to quiet down as I look at my teammates looking up at me. I looked at this team not very long ago and saw limitations and incompetence. *Just like my dad sees in me.* But when did I last congratulate *them* for a job well done? When did I last praise *them* for kicking ass? When did I last lead *them* off the ice like I do on the ice? The pressure to do right by them isn't as great as my own drive to do this for Jonah, but it's still there. In their smiles. In the excitement mixed with anticipation in their eyes.

"Way to kick ass and take names, guys. One more win and one more game down." I let them cheer, some fists going in the air. "I just wanted to give a shout out to the defense tonight. Killer job, guys. To the fresh legs off the bench, we needed you more than you know. To the guys up top—shit, you made it easy to do our jobs tonight. In short, keep it up."

"Great job, Cap," Katzen yells out from the back of the room, and I nod in response, because this isn't about me.

This is about them. It needs to be about them.

"One more thing," I say and hold my finger up to quiet them down. "I know I've been shit to deal with, play with—unpredictable as fuck. I'm sorry for that, but I promise you, my head's back in the game. My priorities are straight. And fuck if they're not fixed on winning the Holy Grail."

The small room explodes with noise and a palpable excitement as I climb down from the bench to finish getting my gear off.

"Glad to see you back, Cap," Jünger says just above the fray, then pats me on the back as he walks past me.

And each one of my teammates follow his footsteps.

A punch to my shoulder. A push to my chest. A bump of fists.

Each one stops and tells me in their own way that they're in it with me.

That they're ready to win it all.

And fuck, so am I.

44

Hunter

16 years earlier

I JOLT WHEN TERRY stands at the front door of the house, her dark-blue fancy dress with sparkles and her hair up in some flashy way that makes her look as old as you should be to do the things she did to me earlier.

Swallowing over the sudden panic mixed with immediate lust that hits me, I walk toward the screen and thank God I took a shower and changed.

At least she'll know I'm Hunter.

At least she won't realize I tricked her earlier.

On my best day ever.

Terry. Losing my virginity. The euphoric bliss over it feeling so much better than jerking off. Soap and warm water have nothing on what a girl feels like.

On my worst day ever.

How I've been beating myself up the past few hours over it. I know Jonah's going to find out what I did somehow—how I betrayed him—and shit's going to hit the fan.

I already know my parents are going to rail. Jonah's going to throw punches. I'm going to be dead. Absolutely fucking dead.

I'm guilty as hell. I feel like shit, but I also wonder why out of the two of us who are identical, why he's the one who gets everything while

I'm left to pick up the scraps?

"What are you doing here?" I ask as I lean my hip against the jamb and stare at her. "I thought you were with Jonah at the dance."

She shrugs. "We were all supposed to go as a group. Gannon called though and said Jonah had to leave to do something. Pick someone up or something." She looks over my shoulder. "He's not here?"

"No one is," I say, ignoring the pang of guilt over making him get our mom.

"I'm all dressed up and nowhere to go." She smiles and fiddles with the hem of her skirt with one hand showing me more of her thigh.

I look behind me and debate asking her to come in. I know I should, but Jesus, isn't that inviting a disaster to happen? "I can call him. See where he is."

"I left him a text telling him I'll be here. I'm glad we're alone though, because I—uh"—a slow smile spreads across her red painted lips—"wanted to make sure what happened earlier stayed between us. I really like your brother and all, and I'd hate for him to find out that we—"

"Wait. What?" I shake my head as if my ears aren't hearing properly. "You knew I wasn't Jonah? You—"

Her laugh floats out freely, as I stare at her as if she's crazy. I should be thinking more along the lines that she's easy, that she's a bitch for doing that to my brother . . . but I'm sixteen, and that's my convoluted first thought about the girl I just lost my virginity to.

"Of course, I knew." She rolls her eyes. "I . . ."

Her words fade off as we turn toward the police cruiser that pulls into the driveway—its flashing lights are on but the sirens are off.

It's as if my body just tuned into everything around me—everything that has been faded by the high of sex—and there is the worst feeling in my gut and chest. *I can't breathe.* I don't know how I know it, but something bad has happened.

Even worse, when I walk toward the police car, an officer is practically carrying my mom out of the passenger seat of the car. She looks as boneless as her complexion is pale. Her face is swollen from tears but her eyes look completely hollow.

"Mom. Mom!" My voice breaks as I run to her.

"Jonah. Thank God you're okay," she says as she clings to me. I look at the officer, and then try to pull my mom off me so I can look her in the eyes.

"It's Hunter, Mom. It's me. What happened? Tell me what happened?" I yell at her as she stares at me with a slack jaw, almost as if she doesn't believe I'm me.

"Hunter?"

"Yes. It's me. What happened?"

"But you were the one who was supposed to be in the car." She grabs my hand and yanks me to the cruiser as the ever-present dread begins to weigh me down in a weight I've never felt before. "We need to get to the hospital. We need to—"

"What the hell happened?" I yell. Every part of me goes silent that moments ago felt off. And that scares me more than anything.

"There's been an accident, Jonah."

"Hunter. Mom, it's Hunter."

"An accident. Your brother was in an accident."

"What do you mean an accident?" I look at my mom and then to the officer. "What does she mean?"

"Your brother crossed the median and hit another car head-on." His voice is serious but his eyes, his eyes tell me they've seen way too much, and I fear what he's going to say next. I focus on the shield on his chest. The badge with the sun and rays of sunshine engraved on it. The letters of his last name, as I recite them in my head over and over and over . . . because if I stop, he'll tell me my brother is dead.

He'll tell me that my brother was drunk driving. That he was the responsible one. That when I refused to go get Mom, he went. *He couldn't refuse. He couldn't say no. He* drove to pick up our mom even though he'd been drinking.

Because I didn't . . .

I was the screw-up. *I didn't pick up the fucking cell.* His missed calls. Calls to tell me he couldn't drive because he'd been drinking. And the officer would know. He'll tell me that while I was having sex with my brother's girlfriend out of spite, I caused this. *I fucked up.*

"Is he okay?" I can barely speak as my body blankets with goose-bumps. My words feel like they have to be pried from my mouth as I stare at him and hope and wait and already know.

"He's at the hospital. This officer—he picked me up from work to bring me there—to get you on the way—it's very serious, Hunter. Your brother. He's—and the other driver . . . she didn't make it."

I try to process.

I try to fathom.

I try to comprehend.

But none of it makes sense.

Except . . .

I caused this.

I'm the one responsible.

I'm the vindictive one.

I'm the one my mother thought she'd left at the hospital. *Alone.*

And then . . . I can't sense Jonah. I can't feel my twin.

I stare at the police officer as if I don't hear him, as if I don't want to hear him . . . then the bottom drops out.

45

Hunter

SOMETHING'S AMISS.

My head's foggy.

My thoughts are lost.

I try to concentrate, but every time I try to manipulate the game plan, I fail.

Maybe I'm coming down with something.

Maybe this is burnout showing now.

⌐

"TOUGH GAME TONIGHT."

I glance over at Maysen and nod. "Sorry. I . . . was fucking up left and right out there."

He shrugs, probably surprised that I'm not arguing or being defensive about it. "It happens, man." He pats me on the back as I head toward my locker. "At least we still won."

"True." I nod. I hate knowing I didn't contribute. Hate knowing that if there was a text from my dad, which there hasn't been for the last couple games, exactly what it would say.

"At least we have a few days to shake it off."

"My body could use it," I tease and throw my gloves into the locker, sighing when I see my screen light up with Dad on the message ID.

"I knew he wouldn't be able to resist for long," I mutter.

With a deep sigh, I pick up my phone. Panic hits when I see the three words on the screen.

DAD: *Call. It's Jonah.*

Within seconds, I'm out of the locker room, trying to find a place where I can hear and talk and have some privacy.

My mom doesn't pick up on the first call. I end it and try again.

"Hello?" She sounds like a ghost of herself.

"Mom? Mom. What happened? How is he?" My words sound strangled from part panic, part disbelief, part *just when I was trying to figure out a way to live for me, I'm sucked back into the darkness of shame.*

And of course, the self-loathing is like an old enemy—unabashed, relentless, and unforgiving.

"He coded. He—"

"He what?" I bellow. How the fuck do I get out of here?

I can't breathe.

"He coded and the ambulance came and . . ." The vibrato in her voice, the pure fear, hits me harder than any punch I've ever taken. "They revived him. He's at the hospital."

"Why? What happened?" *I need to get out of here.*

"Another bacterial infection in his lungs. His body, Hunter . . . it's broken and can't take much more. The doctors say his immune system is always on the defense and they were lucky to bring him back this time." She emits a sound I never want to hear again.

It's raw and abraded and sounds like her heart has been ripped from her chest.

"Mom. But he's okay now, right? He's resting and—"

"Yes. He is. He's under observation and will come home tomorrow most likely."

"Okay. Okay." I repeat the words over and over, almost as much for me as for her. Almost as if I need to talk myself into believing that every-thing is going to be okay when I know at some point it's not.

"Your father's heart," she murmurs almost in the same fashion as I just said okay.

Two people lost in the miserable grief and confusion we know is coming but want to deny.

"Yes, I know. His heart is okay?"

The same heart that went into cardiac arrest the night he found out about Jonah's accident. The heart that never fully recovered, but that only sparked to life when he pulled me onto the ice so he could somehow do something—boss someone else around and drive them into the ground, make them be what he thought Jonah was going to be—to save himself.

And I let him. Night after night. Day after day. Hour after hour. I let him break me down on the ice to punish me for what I'd done—for ignor-ing Jonah's request, for being the reason Jonah got behind the wheel drunk, for killing the innocent driver he hit. I cried and burned and prayed . . . with no idea if my brother would die that next day. My other half was gone. *I was alone.* In agony, I begged and bled and sucked it up because coaching me was the only thing keeping him going. Punishing me was the only way he knew how to manage the dreams he had for Jonah. *Dreams he'd never had for me.*

"I don't know what to do," she whispers. "What am I going to do?"

"I'll be there as soon as I can."

I find the exit just as I end the call and shove through the doors so they slam back with force.

I welcome the cool night air as it fills my lungs. As it burns my lungs and assaults my skin with its temperature and its indiscrimination. Taking huge gulps, I try to catch my breath from the thoughts that rob it.

Jonah's time is running out.

I felt it tonight. I felt *him* tonight.

That's why my game was off.

The other half to my whole was coding.

Struggling to breathe.

And I can't fix him.

I can't fix anyone.

46

Dekker

KINCADE SPORTS MANAGEMENT
Internal Memorandum
New Recruit Status Report

*denotes urgent status

ATHLETE	TEAM	SPORT	AGENT	STATUS
Carl Ryberg	n/a	Golf	Kenyon	Signed
Desi Davalos	n/a	Basketball	Chase	Meeting next week
Harry Osgood	Rays	Baseball	Brexton	Contact Made
Michelle Nguyen	n/a	Soccer	Brexton	Contract under review
*Hunter Maddox	Jacks	Hockey	Dekker	No change. Unresponsive
Vincent Young	Rams	Football	Dekker	In talks
Garret Zetser	n/a	NASCAR	Lennox	Coming to KSM next wk

47

Dekker

THE KNOCK ON MY front door startles me. The papers on my lap from when I fell asleep on the couch flutter to the floor with the jolt of my body.

I'm in that just-woken-up, confused and freaked-out phase where I wonder who in the hell is knocking on my door at one in the morning.

Who the hell did the doorman let in on my list that would come at this time of night?

Chad? My sisters?

Oh my God. Something is wrong with my dad.

My pulse pounds wildly as I run to the door, every horrible scenario playing out in my mind in those thirty feet. It's when I look in the peephole though that every part of me stops and freezes.

Hunter.

I almost want to laugh at the sight of him. I put him on my approved visitors list three years ago with the hope that one night he might make his way to my place. To fight for me.

I never took him off.

When I open the door and come face to face with him, my smile falls.

His shoulders are slumped, his face pale and hollow, and his eyes troubled.

"Hunter? Is everything okay? What are you—?"

He steps into me and holds on for dear life. His arms go around me, his face is buried into the crook of my neck, and his body shudders with an emotion I can physically feel.

"Hey. What happened?" I ask. His actions have taken me by surprise—especially from him, his need so palpable that I immediately slide my arms around him, hands running up and down his back, and my lips pressing a kiss to the side of his head.

We stay like this as he holds me, and I feel helpless.

"I just needed you." Those four words said in his broken rasp as the heat of his breath hits my shoulder, are all I need to hear for my heart to constrict. There *is* much more between us than just sex. So much more shared than a physical act meant to bring two people together.

"I'm here," I murmur to him. "I'm here."

My mind races over scenarios—he was cut from the team, something happened to his family . . . over and over—as we stand there in this silent desperation.

"Christ, Dekk." He runs a hand through his hair as he walks to the windows and then back to me. His shoulders sag. He stares at me with total defeat.

"Are you okay?" It's one of a million questions on my mind and the safest of them all. He'll talk when he wants to.

"Yeah. I think." Tears well in his eyes and the sight of them—of a man completely vulnerable when I've never seen him that way before—undoes me in ways I can't quite fathom.

They say he trusts me.

They say he needs me.

It's a poignant thought that gets thrown to the wayside to be thought about later when he's gone and I'm alone . . . but right now, *he needs me*.

"I was going to go home . . . but . . . it's just. I didn't know where else to go." His voice is barely audible, his admission mixed with the confusion in his eyes, enough in itself to tell me what he needs. To remind me out of the blue of something my mom used to say to us when we were at a loss for words. "*I needed you.*"

Those three words slide around my heart and embed themselves in my soul.

He came to me.

He needs me.

"Come with me." I reach a hand out to him and even though he stares at it with question in his eyes, he takes it.

I lead him down the hallway of my apartment toward my bedroom. If I'd told anyone I was taking Hunter Maddox to my bedroom with no intention of taking my clothes off, they'd think I was mad.

But I am.

And he's so lost in his own head, in the heartache overwhelming him, that he doesn't think twice when I turn the covers of my bed down, climb in, and pull his hand for him to join me. With his eyes on mine, trying to relay a story his lips won't yet speak, he toes off his shoes and climbs in with me.

His arms go around my abdomen, he lays his head on my chest so I can rest my chin on it, and he holds on.

We lie like this without saying a thing, just me providing comfort and him taking whatever it is he needs, until his breathing evens out, and eventually he falls asleep.

With my hand running up and down the length of his back and the realization of how damn good it feels to be needed, I slowly drift off to sleep too.

48

Dekker

I WAKE WITH A start.

The sun is streaming through the blinds I never closed last night and the bed beside me is still warm, but I remember everything about what happened.

There's a thump in my living room and I slide out of bed, groggy, still sleepy, and still concerned for Hunter.

"Hunter?" When he doesn't answer, I head down the hallway just in time to see him walking toward my front door. He looks back over his shoulder and our eyes meet. "What are you doing?"

He still looks like hell—eyes red, brow furrowed, like he hasn't slept in years, when I know for a fact he just got a solid seven hours.

"I—uh—I've got shit to do."

"Hey," I say when he turns his back on me again. *He was going to skip out without saying a thing.* Hurt flickers through me that I try to justify and rationalize, and then give up all hope on. "What's going on?"

"It was a moment of weakness."

"What was?" I ask, but I already know the answer.

"Me coming here."

"Weakness?" I laugh, the irony not lost on me that his *weakness* is akin to my *mistake.* My temper fires on a dime as I study him. He's obviously still upset, but his choice to skip out is his way of using me . . . what feels like again. "You want to know what weakness is?" I take a step closer to him. "It's me baring my soul to you. It's me standing in a parking lot in front of an arena somewhere telling you exactly how I feel. That I'm willing to put my professional aspirations—ones dictated by my father and to benefit my family—aside, because of and for you. It's me standing there telling you that it's you. *It's always been you.* The one I walked away from three years ago because I was too afraid of how I felt for you, and the one I walked into this time still afraid but with a job to do. It's you, you asshole, and once again, I shouldn't be surprised that you're going to take the chickenshit way out and sneak away instead of face me and talk to me."

I suck in a ragged breath, because my body is trembling and my temper is wired as I stare at him and wait for a reaction—anything other than the pained look. *He's going to do the same thing as last time and let me go.*

"You don't get it," he says with a shake of his head.

"Then make me get it," I shout, closing the distance between us. After how he made me feel last night—suddenly afraid of losing him but knowing if he lets me push him away again, he wasn't good enough for me in the first place—I'm fed up. "You don't get to walk in here like you did last night and need me and then leave without saying a word."

"Or what?"

"Or it will never happen again." My voice is a low, threatening warning.

"What's that supposed to mean?" He laughs the question out.

"It means I'm not yours to use, Hunter. I'm the shiny toy in the store you can't have. You visit every once in a while so you can take me down and play with me so long as you put me back on the shelf when you're done."

"Fuck this, Dekk." He gives a shake of his head as he moves toward the door. "You wouldn't understand. You wouldn't want to understand."

"Then make me," I scream, as I stalk after him. "Make me understand. Talk to me and tell me what I need to know, because I'm here, real and bleeding emotion while you're standing there acting like it's not a big fucking deal when it's everything to me. When I'm realizing you're *more* to me than I want to admit."

"Dekker." He stops with his hand on the door and hangs his head, my name an apology I don't want to hear.

Tears well in my eyes. Just as I realize what I want—as I realize I want to see where things can go with us and, fuck yes, it's scary and the end isn't known and hurt is probably preordained . . . but I want to take a chance and figure that out.

Hurt reigns.

Embarrassment surges.

Anger wins.

"Then go. Get out. If you can't face me, I don't want to see you again either." Emotion drives my words as my heart jumps in my throat, and what's at stake hits me full force.

He turns and looks at me. His big body framed in the small entryway, and I swear to God if the tumultuous emotions in his eyes could be expressed, I'd be drowning in them. Every single one.

"You don't mean that." His eyes hold mine, the lines etched in his face so full of sadness that I look away when I speak my next words, my temper faltering despite my self-worth holding strong.

"I'm done being used. Just done." I turn my back on him and walk to my bedroom.

Let him leave.

Let him walk out.

Each time I repeat the words my heart hurts. Each time I say them in my head, I'm reminded how damn gullible I am. First to fall back in bed with him, then to let Brexton's words take hold and grow and evolve over the past two weeks. I began to believe that a true connection—a future—could be possible. The revelations last night with him in my arms making me think he realized there was more to us too.

And now this.

I brush my teeth with a vigor that might make a dentist cringe, but it's easier to focus on my hygiene than to chase after him in the hallway to the elevator like a lovesick woman with zero self-worth.

It's only when I dry my face off, when it's buried in the hand towel that I let the tears that have worked themselves up slip over. It's only when I let the disappointment hit me, and the hope I had worked up in my own mind to dissipate.

I stand there with my eyes closed and try to suck it up.

"Do you know what it's like to feel like you don't deserve anything?" Hunter's voice shocks my eyes open, and a gasp falls from my lips. *He didn't leave?* "Do you know what it's like to live a life where your every step, your every thought, your every action is driven by how you can make amends for the wrongs you created?"

I take a step toward him, shaking my head as I try to follow him. "What do you mean?"

"I mean, how do I deserve this life? How do I deserve someone like *you* when for as long as I can remember, I was told I don't? I made myself think I didn't." His voice breaks and the pain, God, the pain, is so palpable I can feel it ricocheting in the space between us. "How do I let you walk into and be a part of my life when everything I've done up until this point, every person I've pushed away, everything I've walked away from, is another way to punish myself for what I did to Jonah and my parents."

My body jolts at his admission and so does his. I watch him physically reject the words he just said, almost as if it's the first time he's ever heard them.

And just as quickly as I see it, Hunter pulls away physically by turning on his heels and jogging toward the door.

"No. Hunter," I call after him, and luckily, he's distracted by the emotions or else I never would be able to catch up to him and stand in front of the door like I do.

"Get out of the way, Dekker." His face is a mask of fury and shame, and it breaks my heart to see such distress in his every muscle.

"No. I'm not letting you walk out this door. I'm not letting you believe for another goddamn second that you don't deserve the success you have, the accolades you've achieved, or the love and affection you deserve." I'm breathless when I finally finish speaking, but I feel like I'm on borrowed time to keep him here and make him believe what I've said.

"No, I don't." He shakes his head and looks at me like a little boy wanting to believe but not trusting that he should.

"Yes, you do," I say and take a step forward.

"You don't know what happened. You don't understand—"

"Then make me understand. Sit down and tell me everything and get the weight you're carrying off your shoulders."

"I don't know if I can," he says in a whisper.

I don't care that he feels a million miles away from me, I take another step toward him and place his face in my hands. He tries to pull away, but I don't let him. "I know you're a good person, Hunter Maddox. I know you bust your ass day in and day out chasing a ghost no one can see, and I know it has to be a merciless burden that you carry." I wipe the lone tear that escapes his eye and slides down his cheek. It's devastating to see. But it's also a sign that maybe I'll be able to get through to him. Maybe I can help him. "Please, talk to me."

49

Hunter

I STARE AT DEKKER, and my body and mind revolt.

I'm terrified that if she sees what I did, she'll walk away for good and never come back.

Her eyes tell me to trust her and her words tell me to believe her, but fucking hell if that's not hard when all I know is regret. When all I feel is guilt.

I took away their star, their life, their hope.

"Hunter? Come on, talk to me. You can trust me."

My pulse pounds in my ears and my chest feels like it's on fire, like the space around my lungs is constricting and squeezing the breath out of me.

Betrayal comes with telling someone. A betrayal to my misery, to myself, to the way I've lived my life, and fuck, it's a hard thing to let go.

I open my mouth and shut it, the words so very hard to utter, that day so godawful to relive, but I know I need to.

I know that if anyone can help me, it's Dekk. She walked away from me before, knowing I would hurt her if she told me how she felt. I knew it. She knew it. It was so much easier to pretend like her leaving was no big deal.

But now? Shit, she's the only one who thought I was worth pursuing. *Being my fucking punching bag.* She's the only one who cared enough to dig beneath the surface despite my shitty attitude. Not Sanderson, who has a stake in my well-being, but Dekker.

She made me admit that I've burned out.

She forced me to acknowledge that I care.

She made me believe in the possibility of more.

I start rejecting the thought, and then try to push that ingrained response away.

I nod. It's slight, but it's there.

"It was supposed to have been me that day," I finally say.

Her breath hitches. She gently takes my hand and leads me to the couch. Her papers are still where she left them last night, her laptop still open and no doubt the battery dead, but she sits me down in silence. She waits until our knees are touching and our eyes hold before she asks the one question that can break *and* free me. "Who was supposed to have been you that day?"

I stare at her for as long as I can before looking down to where I'm winding my thumbs around each other . . . and I tell her my story.

All of it.

Terry Fischer, and wanting to get back at Jonah for my dad's punishment.

Jonah driving buzzed to get my mother because I'd refused to.

The young mom of two little girls he killed in the accident when he crossed the median strip.

The way my mom became frantic in the driveway that day when she realized it was Jonah in the accident and not me.

My dad's heart attack when he found out about Jonah.

And then life after.

The endless hours on the ice where my dad tried to make me be my brother. How I felt—and probably still feel—like it's the only way we survived from the drastic change in our lives.

But did we heal?

My mom hasn't lived a day since then. Her every waking moment is for Jonah. My dad lives for him too, but also for me to actualize the dreams I robbed Jonah of.

And me? I've lived, but every accomplishment, every defeat, every critical text has been to reach my one goal, to win the Stanley Cup, because that's what was expected of Jonah.

Not of me.

Not for me.

But for them.

For him.

Because as stupid as it sounds, it's all I'm good for, and it's the only amends I can make.

50

Dekker

WHEN HE'S FINISHED WITH his story, with the guilt that owns him and has owned him for sixteen years, tears are on my cheeks and so much sadness is in my heart.

There's also a healthy dose of anger too, but not at him. No way. His decision that day was of a young kid lashing out at a harsh father's favoritism. It was his way of rebelling for being made to miss a teenager's rite of passage. While consequences are consequences, the ones his father put on him that day, and Hunter's decision to refuse to collect his mom, are in no way worthy of a lifetime of devastating guilt and a life sentence of penance.

And he's borne the burden daily. Bullied to believe he must attain the things his brother *may* have achieved, because who knows? Jonah may have had an injury. He may have gotten into a different car at another time with alcohol in his blood. Who knows? But to be made to feel *less than* when *he*, Hunter Maddox, has achieved nearly every accolade possible, *is* the captain of an NHL team, *is* one of the highest paid hockey players in the US. It's . . . it's criminal.

The hardest thing to process though, is how to make Hunter see and comprehend the reprehensible injustice. It was Jonah's choice to get behind the wheel and drive drunk. No one knows what the future held for Jonah, so how could he be responsible for robbing him of something that hadn't happened yet?

But his words were so powerful. A life led with guilt and regret. Wanting to take back something that happened so long ago, when there's no way he can know what would have happened if he were the one in the car that day either.

"Hunter." I shake my head. "There is so much to say, so many comments I want to make; I don't know where to start." I reach out and lace my fingers with his, the tears on his cheeks dried long ago, but the pain they leave behind so very visible.

"Don't say anything. Please. I don't deserve any sympathy. I don't deserve to feel better or to rationalize it all away. I've spent years doing that. I've spent nights slamming the puck into the net as hard as I can to help and it doesn't, because when it all comes down to it, look at me and the life I have, and then look at Jonah and the life he's been left with." He goes to pull his hand away, but I hold on tight to it. "I definitely don't fucking deserve it."

"Survivor's guilt is real." My voice is a whisper, a small offer in the giant chasm that one incident left.

His chuckle is hollow. "It's so much more than that." He shoves up off the couch and moves to the windows to look at the morning outside. The city as it comes to life. His hands are shoved in his pockets and his shoulders are squared, as if he's about to go on the defensive after everything he's confided in me.

"You didn't make Jonah drive drunk that day, regardless of what happened before he grabbed the keys. You didn't steal his career, because who knows what could have happened—I mean, professional athletes are injured all the time. And you sure as hell don't deserve to live a life paying for things you had no control over."

My words hang in the air. My only hope is that they somehow cling to his soul and add some balance to the harrowing grief and guilt and gravity that have domineered it for so long.

"Maybe I hated him because he was better than me at everything."

"Siblings hate each other as much as they love each other. That doesn't mean you wanted or willed this to happen. That rivalry is a normal thing. There's jealousy one minute and horsing around the next. There's tattling to your parents one second and then sneaking into her bed the next to giggle and tell ghost stories when you're supposed to be asleep. It's a yin and yang that no one else understands unless they have a sibling."

"I was jealous of him. Plain and simple. Of the girls who fell at his feet. Of the constant praise he got on the ice. Of the grades that came easily, while I studied all the time . . . of fucking everything."

"Of the things your father pitted you against each other over." I'm quiet when I speak, afraid I've overstepped, but I heard the animosity when he shared his story. "That doesn't mean you're at fault. That doesn't mean you don't deserve to have a life. That doesn't mean you don't get to love and be loved. To laugh and have someone to laugh with."

"It's the fact that he was better than me," he says with a shrug, as if he didn't hear me. I don't take offense, because maybe he didn't want to *hear* it yet. It may be background noise to his thoughts right now but when the emotions settle, he'll remember what I said, and I hope he'll know it's true. "Maybe that's why I resented him. He was always perfect, and I was always the one who needed more work. Hell, maybe I secretly wanted the spotlight and was sick of being in his shadow." He chuckles, but there's so much sadness in the words. "Christ, that sounds stupid. We were the same in every way, but that he had more talent in his little pinkie than I did in total played a part."

"I find that hard to believe," I murmur.

"Go dig up our high school records. He still holds a couple that were made through our junior year. Could you imagine what he would have done if he had one more year?" He turns to look at me now, the city and morning sunshine at his back.

"I hear what you're saying, Hunter, but these are all normal things kids go through. I can tell you athletes peak at different times. Some people have natural talent while others have more heart and have to work harder to get it. But none of this"—I point to the space between us where the reasons I've pointed out are hovering like neon signs—"is why Jonah is paralyzed."

"How can you say that?" He raises his voice, but it loses its gusto on the last word.

"Because you didn't make Jonah get behind the wheel," I say so he might hear me again. "Sure, you were pissed at him and didn't get your mom like you were supposed to. Yes, you were duped by his girlfriend, who apparently wanted to brag she'd slept with both twins, but *you*, Hunter Maddox, didn't cause this. You didn't make him slide behind the wheel. He was already drinking, knowing he was picking up Terry Fischer and taking her to the dance. He had your mom's car, yet *he* was drinking." I pause, watching him contemplate something it seems he never considered—or rather, let himself consider. "And," I continue quietly, "you sure as hell aren't the reason your parents can't seem to step away from being Jonah's caregiver and be supportive parents to you."

Because that's the other crucial part of this he's not addressing. He not only lost his brother that day in the everyday sense he was used to, but he also lost his parents. They became so busy taking care of and cruelly coronating Jonah, that they forgot they had another son living and dying for the affection and approval any kid craves from their parents.

And the look on his face says I just hit the nail on the head with the other part of this whole tragedy—the little kid in him deserves love and affection instead of expectations and blame.

"But—"

"You didn't give your dad the heart attack, and you sure as hell don't deserve to live your life trying to make up for something you had no control over."

"Stop. Please, just stop," he says to me, covering his ears to prevent my words from hitting them.

"No, Hunter. No." I step toward him, toward his disbelieving eyes and shaking head. "I'm not going to stop, because you need to hear this." I reach out and grab his hands from his ears so he can hear me and whisper, "You need to hear you're not at fault. You need to stop drowning in guilt and burning in anger that's not yours to bear."

His eyes well and his chin trembles, and every part of me wishes I could convince him of the truth in my words. "You don't understand. No one does." He jerks his hands out of mine as his anger takes hold as his moment of vulnerability and need give way to self-loathing and fury. "It's like every time I see him there in that goddamn prison of a chair or bed, I hate myself even more. Do you know what it's like to sit there and know what he could have been? The incredible things he could have done? *I do.* I know a fraction of what he feels because it was like that when I was a kid. Sitting by while your brother did everything you were dying inside to do, but couldn't. No one was ever as good as Jonah. In our house, at our school, at our church. Not a single fucking person was."

"Is that why you're always angry?" I ask, trying to connect dots on a chart I can't see.

"You're goddamn right, I'm angry." His voice thunders around the small space, his hands fisting and his shoulders tensing. "Don't you get it? I've been running so damn long trying to chase the ghost of who he could have been, that it's the reason I'm burned out. That's why I hate the game I used to love but can't say a damn word, because who the fuck am I to complain? I make millions a year. I have records I'm chasing. I'm living the damn dream. All that's left is the Stanley Cup, and I'm going to win it if it kills me, because it's the least I can fucking do for him."

"But what about you? When do you get to have a life? When do you get to have someone to go home to at night? To wrap your arms around her and then lose yourself in when shit gets too tough? To laugh with, to fight with, *to live with.* When do you get to live, Hunter?"

51

Hunter

SHE DOESN'T UNDERSTAND.

That's all I keep thinking as she watches me and says things to me I don't want to hear.

As I reject what I know are truths that she keeps saying, keeps repeating, keeps trying to rewire in my head.

When do you get to live, Hunter?

But there is so much anger, so much sadness, so much goddamn everything, it's hard to hear anything through it.

"You know the irony in this? I have all of this"—I throw my hands up—"to thank my dad for." I laugh, but there's no humor. "I wouldn't be here if it weren't for him and his punishments. That's the fucking blessing and curse, now isn't it?"

"It's whatever you want it to be. Make what used to be your curse, now be your blessing." They're words meant to fix but nowhere near as easy as they sound.

I know it.

She knows it.

And yet she says them anyway.

"If it were only that fucking easy."

"It's not easy. You're right. But it's also bullshit you've been made to feel like this life of yours isn't for you."

"I got out as fast as I could." I switch gears as the thoughts hit me. As if I need to purge everything at once. Maybe once they're out in the open they won't fucking hurt as much. "I love my brother more than the whole goddamn world. Hell, the twin thing is real—the connection, the feeling each other's pain—but looking at him is like a torturous, never-ending slap in the face. One minute I'm pissed at the fucking world, the next minute I'm pissed at myself . . . so the easiest thing for me was to get out, to not go back home. He's their world, and I'm just the fucking mistake."

"How can you say that?" I refuse to see the sympathy that fills her eyes even though it's sincere. "Look at the man you are, at the accomplishments you've made. Look at—"

"All they see is the one decision." I've never spoken truer words. Saying them out loud feels like a burden has been lifted from my chest. "All I see is him slowly dying, bit by bit, day by day, infection by infection. Christ, he's barely a shadow of who he used to be. He can't talk or eat or fucking do anything without my mom doing it for him. What kind of life is that, Dekker? What kind of fucking fate did I hand him?" My voice breaks and my shoulders shudder. "Like I said, all they see is the one decision."

"That's not true," she says, but I can see her struggle with wondering if it is. "You leaving them to have an NHL career made Jonah become their world. He's who they think about first and last . . . so it's natural for them to put him first now, but don't think they're not proud of you. Don't think they don't watch your games on TV and smile knowing that's their son. Don't—"

"Stop," I shout. I hate the tears that burn in my eyes. Tears I can't hide. I hate the silent hope her words are offering, but more than anything, the lifting of the weight that has been so damn heavy on my shoulders. *That I've carried alone.* I don't . . . I don't know how to stop believing. "Just. Stop." *Please.*

"Stop what?" she shouts getting in my face. "You have to learn that it's okay to be loved. You have to learn that you're not to blame. Winning a Stanley Cup is not going to take away the sting of what happened. It's not going to—"

"But Jonah will know that I didn't fulfill my promise to him and time is fucking running out."

When she reaches out to lace her fingers with mine, it takes everything I have to accept the gentleness of her touch. It was so much easier last night with the darkness around us to accept it versus now that she knows the truth.

But I crave it. And hate it. And feel like I don't deserve it, but all I want is to pull her into me and lose myself in her . . . but this time, not to forget. Not to use sex to numb the pain. This time it's because I want to feel. *I need to feel.* I need to think that for the smallest of seconds she's right, and I'm not to blame. That I deserve this.

That I deserve her.

"Dekker." Her name is a whisper on my lips, her touch a balm to my soul.

She frames my face and stares at me as she leans up on her tiptoes and presses her lips to my cheeks, kissing away the tears I wasn't aware I'd shed.

"Dekk." Gruffer.

Her eyes on mine. Her hands on me. Her words for my soul.

Our foreheads are pressed against each other's as her exhale is my next inhale, and her fingers tighten in the fabric of my shirt. The realization hits me.

All I want is her.

All I need is her.

She quiets the demons.

She sees me—the real me—and that scares the ever-loving shit out of me.

I lean forward and press my lips to hers. "Let me lose myself in you. Please. I need you."

They're the toughest words I've ever spoken. They're also the most honest.

And when she kisses me back, when she opens herself up to me after I bared every demon I have and she didn't back away, I'm overwhelmed.

She lets me set the pace. She lets me take what I need. Every sigh, every touch, every moan. She lets me evoke them from her.

She lets me be in control when I've felt out of control for so very long.

My hands slip inside her pajama bottoms to find naked skin. The strip of curls atop her pussy, the wet heat when I slide between her lips, the arousal that coats my fingers as I tuck them inside her. My groan is swallowed by her kiss.

How can I still turn her on even though she knows the truth? How can she still want me?

The thought is like a vicious eddy in my mind but with each touch, each sigh, each tightening of her fingers on my skin, it becomes more of a possibility. More of a reality.

The dance to undress is slow. There is no seduction needed. There is no desire needing to be awakened.

It's me as I grab her hips and sink down on the couch.

It's her as she lowers herself painstakingly slowly onto my cock and stills so I'm forced to feel everything about her. The warmth. The wetness. The tightness.

It's us as our eyes meet, fingers entwine, and Dekker leans forward to kiss me ever so slowly before begging to rock her hips over me.

Pleasure builds within. My balls tighten. My cock swells.

It's the shame that I'm now setting free.

Her tits bounce with each grind. Her teeth bite into her bottom lip. Her juices begin to cover wherever she touches.

It's the hope that I can believe them.

I reach out to touch. My thumb and forefinger over her nipple. My fingers bruising into her hips. My cock hitting the very depths within her.

And *it's the knowledge* that someday I might be able to.

Our pace is slow and sensual, her giving me everything I need, and God, she's so fucking sexy. Sitting atop me, working me out, with those innocent eyes and those vixen lips.

There's a connection I want to shy away from but she doesn't allow that. When I break my eyes from hers—to take in her fingers as she slides them between her lips and begins to rub slowly, to watch the pink of her flesh as it stretches to accommodate me, to watch her back arch as I run my fingers up the crack of her ass and tease the tight rim of muscles there—she moans my name and brings me back to her. To the emotions swimming in her eyes and the connection the two of us have that is so much more than the physical.

Hell yes, I need to lose myself here, but she's also showing me that I feel so much more.

She's showing me how to be found.

She's demonstrating that it's possible to find more than simple sexual gratification.

As my orgasm slowly builds, as our pace begins to pick up, as the frenzy starts to peak, I'm overwhelmed with a surge of emotions that bring tears to my eyes. When I try to turn away, when I try to close my eyes, Dekker leans forward, my name a moan on her lips before breathing life back into me with her kiss.

And I'm gone. Done. Restraint breaks and I empty myself into her— my head thrown back, my hips pushed up, my fingers gripped tight.

Jesus Fucking Christ.

She's a savior and a sinner, and I'm not quite sure which one I need to hold on tighter to.

But I do know one thing. *I want both.*

52

Dekker

MY HANDS ARE THREADED through his hair as we lie in my bed. His head is on my stomach, and the covers are thrown haphazardly over our bodies.

I know he has to leave soon. He'll need the time to take the train back to the Jacks arena in Jersey and get ready for his game tonight, but we don't talk about that.

We don't utter a sound about what he confessed to earlier and what we shared in the sex we had after that. Because it wasn't just sex. It was so much more than sex and I think both of us have our reasons for being scared to admit to it.

So we lie in my bed, where we've been for some time, and let things settle around us in a way that it no longer feels like confused chaos but more like something we might be able to work with. Something we might be able to make something out of.

"He's dying. My brother." They're the first words he's said, and I'm sure they're probably the hardest ones he's had to admit to himself.

Yes, everything else earlier was difficult, but admitting your brother is dying means you're acknowledging it. It means you're realizing it.

"I know," I murmur as I lift his hand and press a kiss to the palm. "I'm here for you. I'll be here for you when the time comes."

It's all I say. It's all I need to say, because that's the crux of everything.

Hunter's anger. His urgency. His defiance.

He made a promise to his brother and he's worried Jonah might not make it to see it come true.

That's why this all makes sense.

53

Dekker

HE PLAYS WITH QUIET confidence tonight.

There's steadfast arrogance to his touch that is trademark Mad Dog Maddox, but there's also a peace to him that I haven't seen in the longest time.

I know part of it is playing in his hometown arena for the first time after a long road stretch. The fans, the chants, the support.

But I like to think a part of it is because of what we shared in the past twenty-four hours. What he confessed and learned and heard.

I bring my fingers to my lips, the tenderness in the kiss he gave me before he left this afternoon still a memory there. The look in his eyes—gratitude, understanding, and something much more profound I cling my hope to—makes my heart feel so much happier tonight.

Wrapped with a blanket around me that smells like him still, I watch him clinch the LumberJacks first ever playoff berth, hoping somewhere in the suburbs of Boston that Jonah watched it too.

54

Hunter

DAD: *It's about damn time. Good thing you had that Maysen beside you tonight or your three points would have never happened. Gonna need a lot of practice if you think you can make it through to the finals.*

DEKKER: *Incredible. Every minute of every period you were phenomenal. Congratulations on clinching a berth to the playoffs!*

THE ALCOHOL IS FLOWING freely in Dante's Inferno, our hangout after the game. The bar is dark and crowded, but we're able to stay in the back room where the servers know us, know our drink orders, our occasional tendencies to get rowdy, and our penchant for leaving large tips.

I lean my head back against the booth and close my eyes. My legs are stretched out and my ankles are crossed, and the two texts keep running through my mind.

Oddly enough, one stands out more than the other. For the first time in forever, something is drowning out the negative.

"Hey Cap? You good?"

I look over to Katzen as he slides into the booth opposite of me and smiles. "I'm well on the way to being drunk so there's always that."

"Aren't we all?" He laughs that obnoxious laugh of his.

"You had some incredible saves tonight, Katzy."

"And you played like I haven't seen you play in a long fucking-ass time." He lifts his beer to his lips and mimics my posture on his side of the table. Then he angles his head to the side and just stares at me.

"What?" I ask.

"What happened? Did you figure out the answers to life's problems? Meet the Messiah? Eat some really good pussy that cleared both your head and your pipes? What?"

"Jesus," I say through a laugh and just shake my head, unfazed by my goalie and his crassness.

"Whatever it is, don't change it." He smacks his hand on the table with a resounding thud that startles me. "Superstition and shit."

"Fuck off."

"No, I'm serious. It's nice for us all to sit and celebrate instead of one of us having to keep an eye on you, worried you're going to throw a punch at some dude or fan or who the fuck knows who because they pissed you off."

"Huh." I don't know what to say to that if I'm honest. But suddenly I realize how much my poor behavior has affected my team. Has it really been that bad that one of my teammates has had to babysit me after every game? Even the ones we win?

Fuck. *And yet, they've stuck by me.*

Nothing showed me that more clearly than all the punches of encouragement they've thrown at me since I first stood up in the locker room and congratulated them last week. Is that the difference tonight? That *I* can celebrate? That I can believe *I* played a good game and led my team well?

The dynamic, the comradery, the whole of us. That's something I should feel guilty about. *Shit.* That's a hard pill to swallow.

Katz yells something else, but I miss it, no doubt distracted by my thoughts, the alcohol, and the noise level of the bar. "What?" I ask just as Maysen runs to our table.

A long, drawn-out, "Fuck yeah! We made the playoffs, baby," is yelled into the room as he slides two shot glasses our way. "Shots!"

I laugh with him. I drink with them. But the whole time I keep thinking about what Katz said and wonder why I played differently tonight.

But deep down, I know.

The weight was still there on the ice, just not as heavy as before.

The guilt was still there that I'm moving to the playoffs, I'm shaking champagne bottles in the locker room and not Jonah, but I could start to see around it.

The resentment of my dad's text was softened by the one right below it from Dekker.

Numerous changes in such a short time, but Christ, it feels so much better. I feel so much better. And that showed in my game. And in how I relate to my team. The emotions—sadness, guilt, anger, pain—are still there, but they're not as . . . loud. Consuming. After being bottled up for sixteen years, they feel lighter somehow. The change feels sudden, but I know it's been gradual . . . and because of one person.

One person who saw and believed in me.

I shove up out of my seat.

"Holy shit, you okay, dude?" Katz slurs as he looks my way, his eyes half-closed, and a stack of empties on the table between us. "You sprung up like you got a rocket in your ass."

"I'm good." I stumble when I walk. "I'm . . . I've gotta go."

"Uh-huh. Sure." His laugh carries over the noise and some of the guys turn their heads our way. "Don't lose this guy we had tonight. He— you—were fucking awesome."

I laugh and hold my middle finger over my head.

"Why you leaving?" Finch shouts as I walk past another table of teammates.

"Things. Gotta do things," I say, but it has nothing to do with things.

And everything to do with someone else I want to celebrate with.

This time, when I knock on her door at one in the morning, there's a need there, but it's different.

This time, it's because I want to share in something with somebody.

This time, it's because I want her near.

55

Dekker

WHEN I OPEN THE door, I'm not exactly sure which Hunter Maddox I'm going to get. The knock alone at one in the morning was unexpected, but the sight of him even more so.

"Hi," I say. I don't fight the grin that comes at the sight of him all disheveled and glassy-eyed or the surge of emotions that hits me seeing him on my doorstep on a night that's obviously momentous for him. "What are you doing here?"

"I'm drunk." He shrugs, and it throws him off balance so he sways.

"So I noticed." I lean against the half-open door and hate that the sheepish grin on his face has me gripping the handle instead of pulling him into a hug I so desperately want.

"We won." Such a simple statement, but the emotion in his face is so pure, so relieved that it tugs on my heartstrings. It gives me hope that some of the words I said to him helped bridge the divide between his self-imprisonment and his eventual freedom.

"I know. I watched."

"And?"

"And you were *incredible*. One of the best games I've seen you play all year."

"I was? It was?" His cheeks flush red and that little-boy smile kills me in every way imaginable—all of them good.

"You most definitely were."

"I'm back," he says, and it sounds funny because he is physically back at my place but he means figuratively as in on the ice. He realizes the humor the minute it leaves his mouth and we both laugh.

But when the laughter fades, we're left staring at each other as how we left things between us hours ago replay in my head. There were no words spoken, there was nothing mentioned of where we go from here after this experience that no doubt drew us closer. There was just a bear hug that lasted so very long where words we both wanted to say were exchanged without speaking.

Thank you.

I'm here for you.

What is this between us?

Where do we go from here?

But when he left, we both had smiles on our faces—his eyes were still hollow, his shoulders still weighed down with the guilt I think he'll forever own—but I swear it was less than he walked in here with. And that's what I hope for. Each time I see him, to chip it away a little more. To lessen it bit by bit.

That he's here, tells me I might be right in my thinking. That I might have seen what I thought I saw as I sat astride him and rode him to bliss.

"Why are you here, Hunter?"

A scratch of his cheek. A lopsided grin. A rock back on his heels. "Because your bed is way more comfortable than mine."

And with that, he walks past me, into my apartment, and does a dive bomb onto my bed with the biggest whoop of laughter I've ever heard.

I stand there shaking my head at him until he notices me, grabs my hand, and yanks me down onto it with him. "Come here."

My shriek fills the room, and while I'm more than certain the drunken, chaste kiss he smacks on my cheek is going to turn into something more, it actually doesn't. Hunter pulls me against him, so his leg and arm flop over me, and pulls me in tighter.

"Mmm. I'm sleepy."

"Okay, drunk boy."

"I am drunk, thank you very much," he murmurs. "And you're just as comfortable as this bed."

And for the second time in as many nights, Hunter Maddox falls asleep beside me.

If this keeps up, I'm going to need stronger locks to guard my heart, because he already has a large piece of it.

Falling for someone is never the plan. One day, you just wake up and it's there in full-freaking, high-definition color.

How right my sister was.

56

Dekker

KINCADE SPORTS MANAGEMENT
Internal Memorandum
New Recruit Status Report

*denotes urgent status

ATHLETE	TEAM	SPORT	AGENT	STATUS
Alex Redman	n/a	Soccer	Chase	First contact
Desi Davalos	n/a/	Basketball	Chase	In talks
Harry Osgood	Rays	Baseball	Brexton	Meeting set up
Michelle Nguyen	n/a	Soccer	Brexton	Negotiating terms
*Hunter Maddox	Jacks	Hockey	Dekker	No talks. Just sex.
Vincent Young	Rams	Football	Dekker	Contract sent

I STARE AT MY response and go to delete it four times.

It's unprofessional.

It's not like me to write something like this and send it.

It's rather crass.

And while it might be true, they sure as hell don't know it. But they deserve it for razzing me over him. Between the status sheets and the ridiculous comments and innuendos over the past few Monday morning meetings, followed up by texts for juicy details, it's the least they deserve.

Let them read my comment—*no talks, just sex*—and I bet they'll either bombard me with questions . . . or leave me alone.

My dad will think I'm playing them.

My sisters? My bet's on them leaving me alone.

The question is whether they'll leave me alone because they think it's true or because they think I'm pissed.

57

Hunter

"HEY JONAH. HOW ARE you, man?"

There's a quiet response on the other end—an R sound attempted—and even though the tears well in my eyes, a smile widens on my face.

"Can you believe it? The playoffs are next week. Next week. It's surreal and I don't know, J, it's crazy." I run a hand through my hair and look out the window to where the snow is falling. It looks so peaceful, but I know it's wreaking havoc for so many. "The Titans are a tough team, but I've been studying their films and have their defense and plays mapped in my head, so I think we can do this. You know if we make it to the finals you'll be there. I don't care what I have to do."

And I mean it. I don't care how much it costs, if I have to bring a traveling medical team . . . he'll be there.

"There's something else I want to tell you and I don't know . . . it's insane, but, I met this woman. I know. Don't be too shocked." I laugh, nervous over why I'm telling him. Torn over making him feel horrible and wanting him—needing him to know and be a part of my life more now than ever. "She's everything you'd say I don't deserve, but shit . . . I think she's actually making me a better person. A better man. I've known her for years but not until lately have things really clicked. And God, yes, it's scary as shit, but it's also pretty damn awesome to finish a game and be able to shut all the outside noise off because her opinion is all that matters.

Her name's Dekker. Yes, *that* Dekker who I was having fun with a couple of years ago and who you met at the game, but, dude . . . this is a first for me. I'm at a total goddamn loss. She's . . . she's fucking everything and—"

"Hunter?"

"Mom?" I ask, startled and a little pissed at the interruption. "What—"

"What is it you just told your brother?"

"I—uh—why?" I fumble, not ready to tell this to anyone else yet. Shit, I haven't even told Dekker how I feel about her.

"Because he just got the biggest grin on his face, and I haven't seen him smile like that in the longest time." I can hear the elated relief in her voice, and my chest constricts at her words.

"He did?"

"Yes. What did you say?" she asks again.

"Some things are best left between brothers," I tell her, my own smile widening at the phrase I haven't used in years.

I hear her quick intake of a breath and know she heard it too.

And maybe, even if only for a second, we can both forget the accident, and I can revel in the knowledge that Jonah grinned about Dekker.

That's something to me.

When I hang up thirty minutes later and head to training, I couldn't be in a better mood.

58

Dekker

"WHY IN THE WORLD are we here?" I ask Hunter as he glances at me. He's wiggling a key in what looks like an ancient door lock on a place that hasn't seen any attention in years.

The parking lot has weeds growing up through its cracks, the paint on the outside of the industrial-looking building is peeling in huge curls, while some spots are in hunks on the ground.

"Come on."

It's all Hunter says and curiosity gets the better of me—though I make him walk ahead of me in case the Boogey Man plans on popping out of its depths. But the minute I pass through the entrance, I know exactly what this place is—an old ice hockey rink.

Despite the outside looking well-worn, the inside is in fair condition. The walls and stands are gray, the barrier between what used to be the ice and the stands a faded and yellowed white, but there are hints of what used to be here.

"Well, it doesn't look like you'll be getting any practice in," I say, walking onto where the ice should be as he flicks on the overhead lights to brighten what the skylights in the ceiling don't.

"Nope."

"I thought you were taking me on a date to teach me some of your mad hockey skills."

"Mad hockey skills?" he asks as he takes a step toward me.

"Very mad, above-average, beanie-wearing Hunter." Instinctively, my arms slide to the side of his waist as he leans down and presses a chaste kiss to my lips.

It's that easy, the simple rhythm we've found ourselves in. Him at my doorstep after a game when he's in town. It's never talked about, never discussed, and yet he hops on the subway from Jersey to Manhattan and is there. We never make plans, but we end up hanging out together or taking a drive or talking on the phone till odd hours of the morning despite my work schedule and his games and practice.

It's fun and exhilarating and scary and overwhelming all at once— going from thinking only of yourself to suddenly thinking in terms of *we* when we've never really discussed anything.

As he walks around the vacant arena and moves toward the rink's center, I know he's changed in the few short weeks we've been doing whatever this is, and I like to think it's for the better.

"So is this your way of remembering where you came from before you start the first round of playoffs?"

"If I were remembering where I came from, I'd take you to an outdoor rink where your fingers would be frozen before you were able to put your gloves on. The lights would flicker on and off, and there'd be a chair near the edge where my dad sat with his whistle as he ordered us to do suicide after suicide." The soft smile on his lips tells me it's a good memory. "So in a sense, yes . . . just not the cold."

"This place could use some major TLC," I say as I walk around the rink's edge, my boots echoing around the space.

"I want to buy it." His words startle me.

"You want to buy it?" I ask with a laugh, but when he turns to face me with that lopsided smile of his, I know he means it.

"Yep." He shrugs as he takes a step closer, and there's emotion clogging in his eyes.

"What is it? Tell me?" I say, stepping beside him.

"It's a stupid idea. Never mind." He starts to walk away, and I grab his hand to keep him here.

"I think it's an awesome idea." I take a step away from him and can see it through the dust and neglect. When I turn back to face him, I can sense his discomfort. "Hey, why are you embarrassed? You can tell me anything."

"I believe I already have," he murmurs, his eyes as quiet as his voice.

I nod. "Fair enough." But it's not. Nothing is fair in this life, and while Hunter knows that better than most, the fear I still have of admitting I've let him get too close is in the back of my mind.

I take a walk to the other side of the rink and run my finger along the dust atop the wall at its edge. The memories come fast and sharp and are ones I prefer to keep in the dark recesses of my mind . . . but he shared his with me. He let me in while I'm still pretending I've kept him out.

The irony.

"For the longest time after my mom died"—I clear my throat—"I thought I was the one who killed her." Even the words are hard to say. I appreciate the fact that he stays silent to let me get them out on my own accord. "We'd been playing with those blow-up plastic baseball bats. My sisters and I won them at Coney Island in those games that cost like twenty dollars to actually win things."

My smile is bittersweet as I remember everything about the day. The scent of sunscreen and fried foods filling the air. The bickering between us sisters as my parents strolled in front of us, fingers entwined, their laughter easy.

"Anyway, we came home and were being pains in the asses—probably ungrateful . . . but I refused to get in the shower. I was too busy doing who knows what," I say when I know exactly what I was doing. I was texting the boy I had a crush on, because God forbid, my parents had taken us out for some family time instead of letting me stay home and stare at my phone waiting for him to text me. "My mom came upstairs to tell me I needed to get in because there were three others waiting for me . . . and one thing led to another. What started with her picking up the plastic bat and swatting me playfully on the butt ended with me grabbing my sister's bat off her bed and hitting her back. We had a fake sword battle with those stupid bats. We hit each other everywhere—heads, backs, legs, until we were laughing so hard we had to stop." I smile. I can still hear her laughter, can still remember her calling me Dekky-Doo, can still recall the drop in my stomach when I woke up in the middle of the night to the ambulance and its sirens and my dad's frantic tears.

"What happened to her?" Hunter asks as he steps up beside me. I was too lost in my memories to realize he'd moved closer.

"She had a massive brain aneurysm sometime during that night. For the longest time, I thought it was because I had hit her in the head with the blow-up bat. I hid it from everyone, thinking they'd all hate me for killing her."

"Dekker." My name is a resigned sigh as he places his hand on my lower back.

"I know now that it wasn't my doing, but back then, I was devastated. I worried the police would arrest me for murder, that my family would hate me for ruining their lives." I rest my head on his shoulder. "It wasn't until years later that I confessed to my dad that I'd killed her."

"What did he say?"

My sigh is heavy. "There were a lot of tears and hugs and reassurances that there was no way I was at fault . . . but I still worried."

"I'm sorry." He presses a kiss to my temple, and the warmth of his breath hits my scalp.

"Don't be. It's life, I guess. You live and you think you know one thing until you learn another. Guilt can be a nasty, ugly bitch, but it can also pull people together."

A silence falls between us. One full of mutual respect and understanding that we're each lost in our own pasts, our own memories, our own reasons for our guilt.

"No more sadness," I say suddenly, needing to shake the vibe. "Sadness is definitely not what you need before the big game tomorrow. How are you feeling about the matchup? You haven't really spoken about it."

"I'd name it after my brother, you know." His words give me whiplash and it takes me a second to realize he's talking about the arena. "'The Jonah Maddox Hockey Facility.' We'd make it the premier place to train for sled hockey," he says, referring to a modified version of ice hockey for those with physical disabilities. "We'd have camps for kids who are paralyzed, so they could forget the confines of their chairs for a while. No cost to their families. I'd get some of my teammates and friends in the league to come visit them. We'd make it easy for them. The equipment, the access—all the things most kids who want to play but can't get at other places."

My heart swells, and I can't hide the tears over the purposeful thought he's put into renovating this place. And when he looks over at me, there are tears in his eyes too, and that heart of mine swells so large it virtually falls out of my chest, landing at his feet.

Not that I mind since right now, in this moment, I know it is pretty much already his.

"I think it's going to be amazing." I smile through the tears as he reaches out and links his fingers with mine. Such a simple action, but there's intimacy in the moment and it's perfect. Quiet and subtle.

"You do?"

I nod, realizing this is Hunter's way of letting his brother live on forever. This is his way of holding him close when the earth no longer can. "What better way than to let him be a part of the sport he loved while getting to be with his best friend?"

His smile is automatic. The bob of his Adam's apple reflecting the emotion that he's trying to keep at bay.

"I think you could even create a charity in his name, some kind of scholarship, or something like that. Something for your mom to be a part of. It might give her an outlet after. . ." *Jonah passes.* I twist my lips and hate that my mind went there, but I can't imagine living your whole life for someone and then suddenly having a life for yourself but a future without the person you cared for in front of you. I avert my eyes the minute my voice fades off, because Hunter knew what I was going to say and now I feel like shit.

"That's a good idea." His voice is soft but sincere.

"This place is not only going to be Jonah's legacy," I say and squeeze his hand, "but yours too."

59

Hunter

"HEY MADDOX." HER VOICE jolts me from my focus as I walk toward the locker room and stops me in my tracks.

I turn and find her leaning against a wall. She has jeans on.

"Where's your Jacks gear?"

"Where's your Stanley Cup?" she asks, her smile wide, her tone playful in the reminder of the Dartmouth game when she told me she'd only wear it when I won a Stanley Cup.

"I'm working on it." I laugh and walk over to her. "What are you doing here?" I ask, confused and surprised as every emotion in between surges through me.

"Did you really think I was going to miss your first playoff game?"

"You said you had a client who—"

"I know what I said," she murmurs as she angles her head to the side. The sunlight highlights her hair and the gold lights up like a halo. There's a thump in my chest, and Christ if this woman doesn't do things to me I never expected. "But I'm here."

"Dropping your duties as an agent, huh? Poor client."

"No, dropping an agent's duty falls along the line of Sanderson," she teases.

But it's out there. The first damn time she's brought anything up about agents or my agent or any of the shit that's Sanderson's job since that night that feels like months ago. The night when we stood outside of whatever fucking arena and she told me the truth about why she was there. About how she feared telling me would ruin whatever this was between us.

"Sanderson drops the ball?" I ask with a smile on my lips.

"So I've heard." She nods.

"And you? Do you drop the ball?"

The slow run of her tongue over her bottom lip and the devious look in her eyes tells me exactly what she's thinking about. How the last time we saw each other, her lips were wrapped around my cock as her fingers gripped pleasurably firm around my balls.

"If you have to ask, Maddox, then I'm doing things all wrong." Her voice is liquid sex, the smile that crawls over her lips not far from it either.

I groan in response.

"You win tonight and we'll see if I drop the *balls* again or not."

"We'll win. No worries there. And I'll be the judge of your grip." I glance over my shoulder and lift a hand to Katz as he walks into the arena. "Hey Dekk?"

"Hmm?"

I take a step forward and lean in. "I never brought up the agent thing because you said it was either one or the other. You as mine or you as my agent. I'm not sure if that's still true."

"Oh." Her lips shock in an O, and I take the chance to steal a quick kiss before taking a step back and smiling.

"Thanks for coming." I wink. "I've got to go."

"Good luck," she says as I start walking away. "Hey, Cap?"

"Yeah?" I turn back to give her one more glance.

"Take a moment and let it all sink in. It'll go by in a flash, and I want you to remember it."

I nod and turn back toward the door.

"Stick, skill, finesse, Maddox."

I throw my head back and laugh.

~>

NERVES RATTLE AND I'M never nervous.

Sticks tap on the ice—the only kind of clapping we can hear while we're in the zone, and yet right now I hear everything.

The crowd.

The buzz.

I look up into the stands and see the people. The little kids wanting to be in my skates someday. The dads with their daughters teaching them the ins and outs of the game. The college frat boys needing an excuse to get drunk and heckle a player. The families wanting to be entertained.

I take it all in.

The sounds, the sights, the excitement.

This is for you, Jonah. And for once, I can see your smile.

I'm going to make you proud.

So maybe . . . maybe, this is for us.

60

Dekker

ALL EYES FOCUS ON me.

Brexton lifts her eyebrows. "Well?"

"Well, what?" I ask as I glance at the notes that have nothing to do with this status meeting on my notepad, but pretend to find them interesting.

"Hunter? The client you've been"—Chase coughs—"err . . . *not talks, just sex*, recruiting."

My cheeks flush with heat. "What about him?"

They're the queens of being difficult, so I'll take pleasure in being difficult for once.

"You've written a status sheet every week for the past few months, and it seems the only thing that's going down isn't your finger to the keys to fill us in on what's going on but rather"—she looks at our dad and shrugs apologetically before looking me straight in the eye—"well, *you on Hunter.*"

Her smile is cold and unmoving while the rest of us in the conference room choke back shocked laughter.

"Seriously, Chase? Should we go through your exploits? How about when you—?"

"Ladies!" My dad's voice thunders around the conference room, and the sudden bickering approaching DEFCON 3 suddenly quiets. We all turn to look at him. "Let's keep this meeting focused, as I'm sure you're all incredibly busy. Right?"

"*Busy?*" Lennox chokes on her laugh. "Sounds to me like Dekker's been plenty *busy.*"

Another round of laughter ensues followed by me scratching the side of my cheek with my middle finger. "Screw off."

Poor choice of words . . . I realize the minute I say them.

"There's that too," Brex chimes in.

"It's all fun and games until you have to face the music," Chase says in that singsong voice that annoys me. "So tell us, Dekk . . . just what's been going on with Hunter and his stick?"

I stand and pace to the window, hating, embarrassed, and feeling on the defensive that I really don't have much to report. *The favorite child has failed.*

I'm more than aware that they're all staring at my back as I watch the clouds building across the skyline, and I wonder if we'll get to watch the thundershowers sometime soon.

"Dekk?" my father asks.

Shit.

Time to face the music.

"I'm starting my conversation by reminding all of you that while your caseloads have remained the same, I've become the guinea pig for Operation Fuck You, Sanderson," I say as I turn around, cross my arms over my chest, and lean my hips against the credenza at my back. I meet each one of their eyes.

"Just give Sanderson that look and his balls will shrivel off," Lennox mutters. "Problem solved."

But it's the "*Pretty please*" that Chase murmurs that has us all laughing again.

"I have a meeting in twenty minutes in this conference room, so we need to get through this," my dad warns, and it still takes a few moments for our laughter to subside.

"Hunter Maddox." I draw in a deep breath and vacillate between the truth, somewhere close to the truth, and letting my father down wholly. "He knows I'm recruiting him. He knows we have a vested interest—"

"Vested, my ass." Lennox laughs, but I meet Brexton's eyes and her smile encourages me to continue.

"Truth be told, he knows why I was on the road trip. He knows why I'm there, but he's going through a lot of shit. I'm helping him through it. I'm . . ." *in love with him.* My breath catches at the words I've skated around in my mind for what feels like days but I've known for longer. I blink away the tears that flood and pray no one caught them. My hands fist where they're hidden beneath my elbows, crossed because I don't show emotion. I don't—

. . . they're on your sleeve when it comes to me.

Hunter's voice floods my head from those beginning days on the road trip, and I smile, because he's right. I do.

And isn't that part of this?

I twist my lips and meet each one of my sisters' eyes as I straighten my back. "He's currently in the playoffs and I don't think changing agents is where his mind is at." And it's true . . . but there is so much more at stake here.

For me.

"But he wasn't months ago when you started this, so that doesn't hold water," Lennox says and raises her eyebrows.

I refrain from glaring. It's hard, but I do.

"True, and all that time I've spent pursuing him, on top of my regular client load, and honestly, I'm not sure what's going to happen. I'm helping the human he is before the athlete everyone wants. I'm just being there for him." I draw in a deep breath and prepare myself to meet my father's eyes. When I do, the disappointment I expected to be there . . . isn't. Instead, his eyes are questioning but quiet. "I know I'm an agent and my job is to recruit him and help us on the whole, but I'm also a person who can't push another human being who is hurting."

His nod is just as reserved as his gaze, the muscle in his jaw ticks.

"So . . ." Lennox asks. "What does that mean? When all is said and done, I mean? Should I update that status on the recruit sheet for you?"

I open my mouth to give a vague response, but my dad cuts me off. "Ladies, can you give me a moment alone with Dekk?"

Feathers may be ruffled, but the conclusion of a meeting when they all have a million things to do overrides the irritation.

"Teacher's pet," Brexton says with a wink as she shuts the door so I'm alone with my dad.

"Take a seat," he says.

"I'm fine."

"Take a seat." It's the father tone and not the boss tone, so I begrudgingly slide into a chair at the complete opposite end of the table from him. If he's angry at my failure, I have distance, and if he starts asking questions, I can hope the space might mask the emotions in my eyes.

"What did you need, Dad?"

"Nothing."

"Nothing?" I laugh. "Then why did you ask me to stay?"

It's his turn to lean back in his chair and stare at me. He fidgets with the pen in his hand as the time stretches. "What is it you want to ask, Dekk?" he asks in that way where he knows exactly what I'm thinking—*and need*—without me ever saying a word.

And I do.

I have so many questions.

Ones that run through my mind as Hunter's soft snores fill my bedroom in the wee hours of the morning. Ones that nag at me as I watch him tear up.

"How come you never got remarried after Mom died?" He startles, and I know I've caught him off guard.

"I never found someone I wanted to marry."

"But you never dated."

He nods until his twisted lips spread into the softest of smiles. "I date plenty. I had girlfriends for months at a time," he says to my utter shock.

"When? Who? How come I don't know this?"

"Because the last thing I wanted was for you girls to ever think I was trying to replace your mother." He sets the pen down. "And I went out at night. Sometimes client dinners weren't really client dinners. Sometimes business trips were a little more than that."

Oh my God. I had no idea. How did I not know this?

"I'm stunned."

"Why? Because your old man had lovers or because—"

"Because I had zero clue, Dad. None. You had this secret life as a gigolo, and here I was feeling sorry for you for devoting yourself to your family." I laugh.

"Hardly the gigolo, but you and your sisters' well-being was more important to me." His smile warms my heart as much as his words do. "What else do you have milling about in that mind of yours?"

"Did you ever love any of them?"

"A few, yes. Not in the same way I loved your mom. I mean, look at what she and I created together." His eyes fill with tears. "You and your sisters and this agency, but yes, I think I may have loved one or two."

"I don't even know what to say. My mind is blown."

"Why?"

"Weren't you scared to be hurt? Weren't you . . ." My voice fades off.

"Ah," he says, his fingers steepled in front of him, as if I finally got to the point he was waiting for me to get to.

"Ah, what?"

"Part of putting yourself out there, Dekker, is opening yourself up to getting hurt."

I stare at him for a beat and try to figure out how to put the jumble in my head at peace and turn the last key in the lock chained around my heart.

"Not that kind of hurt . . . the kind . . ." My eyes well with tears I attempt to blink away as my dad rises from his chair and moves toward the seat next to me. He turns my chair to face him like he used to do when I was a little girl, about to get a scolding or be taught a life lesson.

"The kind where the person dies and your insides feel like they're broken and your heart will never recover let alone beat again?"

I don't trust myself to speak. His words are too damn close to the truth, so I nod and when I do, the first tear slips over.

"It's always there in the back of your mind, because that's a pain someone never forgets, but Dekk, finding someone to love again is how you know you're not broken. It's how you know your heart can still beat again. It's the cure and the demise all at the same time. To be able to love again means you're still alive."

He reaches out and wipes a tear off my face like he did when I was a kid, his hands still feel so big even now that I'm older. I lean my cheek into his hand as his eyes meet mine. "Love is powerful, Dekker. It's why you're here. It's why you try so hard to please me. It's why you fight doggedly with your sisters. But it's also so very powerful when you find the one you want to give it to. Don't ever be afraid. You can't give half a heart, that's equivalent to giving someone your broken heart. No, you have to give them all of it and trust that they'll hold on to it and protect it."

The knock on the door shocks both of us apart to turn to look toward the interruption. "Come in," my father says.

And the shock that floods through me when Hunter opens the door and peeks his head in. "Mr. Kincade. Hi. Sorry for the interruption. I wanted to see if Dekker was free for lunch."

"No need to be sorry," my dad says. I wait for the shift from doting father to savvy agent as he crosses the distance toward Hunter to shake his hand. But it never happens. Instead he shakes Hunter's hand and pats the side of his shoulder. "Looking good out there. First round down, second starting, what? Tomorrow?"

"Yes, sir." Hunter nods. "We're headed to the airport in a few hours."

"Good luck, son. You're going to need it."

"Don't I know it."

My father looks back to me with something I can't read before nodding to Hunter and leaving the conference room.

I'm left to stare at Hunter as he leans against the shut door behind him and meets my eyes. He has a dark blue Henley on with jeans. His hair is styled and his grin is wide, and I'm sure the emotions I just shared with my dad are sitting on my sleeve for him to see.

For him to decipher.

For him to realize.

"You've got a lot of balls showing up here." I laugh as I close the distance toward him.

He shrugs. "Agents are a dime a dozen."

"Then switching agents should be no big deal," I tease and then am more than surprised when he tugs against my waist to pull me in for a soft kiss that steals my breath and incites my pulse.

"Hi," he says when he leans back.

"Hi." I'm breathless and my knees feel like rubber. How does he do that so damn easily?

"You look pretty." He fingers the lapel of my blazer. "Very *I'm going to bust your balls right after I suck them* pretty."

"Jesus," I bark out and laugh. "Only with you, Maddox. Only with you."

"Good to know." His hand slides down my torso and rests on my hip. "I thought you might want to catch a quick lunch before I head out."

I shouldn't feel overwhelmed by the gesture as it's quite simple, but he came here to ask me, knowing my family would see him, and that means he doesn't care what anyone thinks.

The panic I expect to ricochet through me like normal, doesn't flutter to life. No. It's too busy being soothed by my father's words and by the touch of the man whose hands are framing my cheeks.

"Lunch?"

"Yes, that meal between breakfast and dinner," he says as I stare at him, this feeling so very normal for us. "I'm hungry. I'm sure you're hungry . . . so, lunch."

"I'd love that. Thank you for asking." I take the initiative and press another kiss to his lips. "Be prepared for the shit my sisters are going to give you when we walk out of this door."

His grin is lightning quick and does things to my insides that shouldn't be legal. "I already got some, but you know as well as I do"—he winks—"I give just as good as I get."

I laugh as we open the door and Lennox is right there with her phone. "Do you mind taking a selfie with me? I think it'd be awesome to show you here at the offices on Instagram," she asks with a saccharine-sweet smile.

"Len," I warn as Hunter looks amused and confused.

"I can see the caption now. Hockey great, Hunter Maddox, touring the KSM offices." She holds her hands up as if she's reading it on a marquis.

"C'mon—"

"No, you c'mon, Dekk. You know Fuckface would croak if he saw Hunter here."

"Fuckface?" Hunter asks and then laughs when he realizes who she means. "You mean Sanderson?"

"Yes. Fuckface," Lennox reiterates, and I push her playfully away.

"I take it you met Lennox?" I ask as I tug on his hand to pull him toward the door.

"I met them all, yes," he says, and I'm not sure if I should be scared I wasn't here when they did.

"I guess that's our answer," Chase murmurs as I walk past her. I can only assume she's referring to their assumption that something more is going on between Hunter and me.

I'm just about to give a smart-ass comeback when I catch my father's eye in the back corner of the office. He's sitting with his arms crossed and the softest smile on his lips as his eyes hold mine. He gives the slightest of nods—almost as if it's approval—and my feet falter for the briefest of seconds as I hear him loud and clear.

Giving half a heart is akin to giving someone a broken heart . . . so give them your whole one instead.

61

Hunter

DAD: *Not horrible. Some of the best hockey I've seen you play, but there's still major room for improvement. You'll fall short if you keep that up. No doubt.*

DEKKER: *Get off that road and come home to me. I'll show you just how damn proud I am of the way you played tonight. You were on fire.*

"NOW THAT'S WHAT I'M talking about, Maddox." I look up from my phone to see Sanderson bearing down on me on the far side of the LumberJacks' locker room. My gloves are off, my pads still on, and fuck if I haven't had time to take a seat before I have to talk to him. "You were a fucking lunatic out there. Way to go, man."

He goes to high-five me and I just stare at his hand and leave him hanging. Funny how the high fives are flying now. Interesting how I can see our relationship more clearly—when I'm good, we're good. When I'm troubled, he's with management and filled with threats. I get it's a business, but I'm finding more and more I need the people around me who care more about me when I'm at the bottom than when I'm at the top.

"Is there a problem?" he asks.

"No problem." I shake my head. "Just tired and hungry and ready to get home. It's been a long battle, and I'm ready to win the next two on our turf in front of a home crowd."

"You keep that shit up, you're going to have deals pouring in. I already have five messages on my phone."

"Great. I've got to hit the showers." I take everything he has with a grain of salt these days but nod, trying to give him the hint I'm not in the mood. He starts to walk away when I realize something. "Hey, Finn?"

"What's that?"

"No negotiations about anything during the playoffs."

"Come again?" he says as he takes a step back toward me, his hand curved around his ear as if he didn't hear me.

"I said hold off the phone calls and negotiations about endorsements. My game is dialed. Shit is sitting right in the universe. I don't want to jinx anything."

"I feel you on that. Not a problem. I'll send over who's interested but nothing else. You're focused on the Cup. I get it. I like the way you're thinking."

And when he walks away, I wonder if he'll still like the way I'm thinking when all is said and done.

⁓

IT'S LATE AND FREEZING as I stand in the lot of the arena and wait for the rest of the guys to load the bus that will take us back to the airport with my cell to my ear.

"Hey." She sounds half asleep. Sexy. *Like home.*

How did her voice become the first thing I wanted to hear after every game? When did it start drowning out everyone else's?

"Did I wake you?"

Her sleep-drugged chuckle brings a smile to my face. "I fell asleep going over contracts." She shuffles papers, and I can picture her snuggling into that big blanket on her couch with SportsCenter on mute, and an empty glass of wine on the table next to her. Papers will be spread everywhere and her laptop will be half-charged on the pillow beside her.

"Sounds exciting."

"You gave me more than enough excitement tonight, thank you very much." She pauses. "I don't think I've ever seen you play this well. You guys are like a well-oiled machine. It was so much fun to watch."

"We've still got two games to win before we can celebrate anything," I say holding up my finger to Jünger who's waving me over.

"I'm all for celebrating every victory, no matter how big or how small."

"You are, are you?"

Her seductive chuckle vibrates through the line. "I'll show you just how much when you get home."

My balls tighten at the thought. Will I ever get enough of her? The prissy business side, the stubborn softer side, and the vixen I hope no one else knows about?

I hope not.

Because hell if I've ever felt at peace like this. I've still got a long way to go, but this—*she*—is definitely a really good start.

"I'll tell the pilot to hurry."

Her laughter is all I hear as I end the call and head toward the bus.

62

Dekker

KINCADE SPORTS MANAGEMENT
Internal Memorandum
New Recruit Status Report

ATHLETE	TEAM	SPORT	AGENT	STATUS
Alex Redman	n/a	Soccer	Chase	In talks
Desi Davalos	n/a	Basketball	Chase	Signed!
Harry Osgood	Rays	Baseball	Brexton	Contract sent
Michelle Nguyen	n/a	Soccer	Brexton	Signed!
*Hunter Maddox	Jacks	Hockey	Dekker	****
Vincent Young	Rams	Football	Dekker	Walked away

****Whatever the heck it is you're doing to him (*or his stick*), Dekk . . .
KEEP DOING IT! He's on fire.

ALL I CAN DO is laugh.

All I can do is hope he feels the same way.

63

Dekker

HUNTER'S SITTING AT THE kitchen table with the soft glow of the overhead fixture the only light in the room. He's slumped in his seat, but his attention is completely fixed on the laptop in front of him.

He's exhausted. I can see it in his eyes, in his posture, in the way he crashed when he hit the pillow earlier tonight.

So why's he up now?

This second round of playoffs has been grueling for him. With Finch out from a blown knee and Katz limping to the finish, if the Jacks can clinch a spot in the finals tomorrow, they'll have a few extra days rest while the other series still has at least two games left.

Regardless, the pressure on Hunter is tenfold, whether it's self-inflicted or not.

Not wanting to disturb him, but also wanting to be near him, I stand where I am at the bottom of the stairs and look around the common area of his house. Where my place is orderly and every piece has its place, his is an array of mismatched things that don't look cluttered when they should, and that shouldn't fit together, but do.

Kind of like us.

"Hey," he murmurs and pulls my attention to him.

"What are you doing up?" I ask as I move toward him. "You're exhausted."

"Can't sleep." He smiles as I lean my butt against the table so I can face him. My love for him is growing each and every day in ways I'm not sure I could ever have imagined. "Trying to crack their defense." His hand flicks to his laptop where he's watching film of the Eagles. "It looks so simple watching it but when you're on the ice, when you're bearing down on it, it feels fucking formidable."

"You're pretty formidable yourself, Maddox."

"I didn't feel like it last night."

I run my fingers through his hair and he lets his head fall back with a sigh. His eyes close, and I can see the wear and tear from his need and will and want and drive for this to happen.

I know it's for him, but I also know it's for Jonah too.

"You're too hard on yourself," I murmur, and lean over and press a kiss to his lips. His body jolts with awareness and his eyes flutter open. "You know, you said your dad used to train you hard for hours and hours. Does he know the game as much as you do? Would he have insight you can't see being so close to the ice? Would he have any suggestions for you on how to break the defense?"

I'm not sure how he'll take my question, but a part of me feels like this fence needs to be mended if it can be for him to heal and move forward.

"Not an option." He moves the laptop out of the way and then uses his hands to guide my hips so I stand before him, his hands dipping beneath the hem of my shirt. "How about you sit right here and let me taste you."

Well, that's a change of topic if I've ever seen one. I thought he might be angry at my suggestion or stalk off and go to bed, but this? This is definitely him deflecting, and who am I to tell him no? Hell no. Not with a tongue like Hunter's.

I scoot up on his table, my bare ass feeling the chill of the wood beneath me, lean back on one of my hands, and spread my thighs.

That sigh. That smile. I'm thinking that sex might tire him out, relax him, and get him to sleep.

"You need some inspiration, huh?" I murmur as our eyes hold and I slide my finger down between my slit. A moan falls from my lips as my eyes close. My head falls back when I rub the pad of my finger on my clit and down to find myself already wet for him.

His groan matches how I feel sitting here, bared to him and so very aroused.

"Inspiration?" he asks, his eyelids falling heavy with desire as one hand reaches out and squeezes the tops of my thigh.

"Mm-hmm." The lazy friction mixed with his hands on me and his eyes a reflection of his own desire, is extremely arousing. Even more so is feeling comfortable to do this in front of him, the vulnerability of it only making it seem so much more.

"First little victories and now inspiration?" His smile widens.

"At your service," I murmur and sink my teeth into my bottom lip. "Inspiration comes in so many different places."

"Like here?" he asks, and I suck in a breath when Hunter's thumbs slide up and down the side of my sex. It's a hint of touch, but I feel it in every nerve all the way to my toes. "Or here?" His fingers push my hand out of the way and part me so the cool night air hits my most intimate parts.

Hunter looks up at me, a devilish grin on his lips and unmistakable desire in his eyes. They hold mine on the slow descent of his head between my thighs. "I'm thinking right here is an even better place."

And when his mouth touches me, when the warmth of his lips close over my clit, and then the heat of his tongue slides down its path to my core, when his fingers join the mix in an all-out sensual assault, all I can do is brace myself on the table behind me and let him find all the inspiration he needs.

64

Dekker

HUNTER DANCES DOWN THE ice like a man clawing his way out of hell.

The clock counting down to the end of the game reads thirty seconds.

He weaves around one defender, then the next.

Twenty seconds.

He chases down the opposition, the forward heading straight for the goal unopposed by any teammate.

Ten seconds.

He swings his stick back for the shot toward the open net. Katz had tripped getting back to defend his goal and this is do or die. The opposition scores, and we're into overtime. They don't, and the Jacks go to the finals.

Five seconds.

Hunter dives across the ice the same time the puck flies. His body blocks it—a visible punch to his abdomen when it hits.

The buzzer sounds and LumberJacks Arena goes insane. The noise, the music, the cheering—they're like a symphony of chaos that has never sounded more beautiful.

But even better is the sight of Hunter being picked up by his team-mates and celebrated. Tears blur my eyes and my heart soars into a dimension I never knew was possible.

It takes a second for me to catch on to what the crowd is chanting. It starts low and then becomes the heartbeat of the arena. *Mad-dox. Mad-dox.*

I think it takes even longer for the team on the ice to hear it because when they do, they slowly lower him to his feet, and one by one, they skate back a step and let Hunter have the limelight he hates.

But something about the moment is so poignant to me. To see Hunter standing center ice looking around with an incredulity on his face I could never put words to, hearing it. Taking it in.

He turns to each corner of the arena and puts his hand over his heart to let the fans know it's them that make it worth it for him. It's them who help motivate.

When he turns my way, the distance is great, but our eyes meet, and the slightest nod as he pats his hand over his heart is all I need to know. The feelings we've never addressed, the words we've never spoken, the future we've never discussed, don't matter.

Because that right there tells me how he feels about me.

And there's no question that I feel the same in return.

65

Hunter

"I'M NOT HAVING THIS argument with you again, Mom. He will be there for the first game and God willing the last game when we win if not every game in between. The arrangements have been made. You've seen them and his doctors have approved them."

"It's very gracious of you, but—"

"You don't have to come if you don't want to, but I will move heaven and earth for Jonah to be there. I have the means and I will do whatever it takes to make it happen."

"His health though. You don't understand—"

"But I do. I understand that you want to keep him within your bubble until the day he dies and while he's still alive that way, he's not fucking living."

"Don't you take that tone—"

"We had this dream since we were kids. Since we were teenagers, and we'd sneak out late at night and break into the rink and skate in the dark. We'd laugh and drink some of the beers we'd stolen from Dad's fridge in the garage and dream about the first time he'd get to play for the Stanley Cup."

"But he's not playing."

"Yes, he is," I shout, the emotion smothering my reason and respect. "We are one and the goddamn same. Don't you see that? I'm his legs because he can't walk. I'm his mouth because he can't speak. I'm his goddamn heart, and I can feel it beating still, so don't try to kill it because you're afraid of germs. Let him fucking live. Let him come see the dream he had, but that I promised I'd finish for him."

"Well," she says in the prissiest of tones. I've upset her. "I'll have to talk to your father."

"Don't you dare rob Jonah of this." When she remains silent, I continue. "The medical team will be there at nine to evaluate and prepare him for a safe transport." Steps that are way above and beyond what he needs but I know if I do this, she can't say no. "There are three tickets at the box office for you guys."

But when I hang up and toss my cell on the middle of the bed, I know not to hold my breath that my father will show.

66

Dekker

"I'M SORRY. I WALKED in. I didn't mean to eavesdrop."

Hunter turns to my voice in his bedroom doorway and there's justifiable sadness in his expression that hurts me.

"It's just par for the fucking course," he mutters and laces his fingers behind his neck and exhales loudly. "Don't worry about it."

"But I do."

"I'm used to it." He shakes his head and forces a smile I know is masking his pain. "We still ordering food?"

"If you want." I pat my back pocket where I thought my phone was.

"Use mine," he says, pointing to the bed.

I'm distracted when I open it and it takes a second for me to believe what I'm seeing. The top of the iMessage screen says Dad, but there's no way in hell the messages on this phone could be from his father.

In just the static screen in front of me, there's word after word of negativity. Comment after comment of cruelty.

"Dekk? What is it?" Hunter asks, but when I'm so abhorred by what I see, I just look at him and hold out his phone.

"I didn't mean to. It was there when I opened it," I fumble. "What the hell?"

His sigh sounds like resignation and defeat as he takes his phone and tosses it right back to where I found it.

"I'll never be good enough for my dad." It's all he says. It's pained and raw and it rips my heart out.

"You play in the goddamn NHL, Hunter. You're the captain and have records and . . ."

"And I'm not Jonah."

Our eyes meet and hold, and so much is exchanged. So many emotions I think he's afraid to show come through loud and clear.

"Is it like that after every game?"

He nods. "I don't care. It doesn't affect me."

That has to be the biggest lie I've ever heard, because how can you play at the top of your game and your father, the man he probably craves approval from, not approve?

"You never respond to him. There's nothing from you back to him." At least not on the screen that I see.

"I did one time. I didn't get the satisfaction I thought I would from it, so I don't anymore."

I hate this. I hate seeing this the night before he's leaving for his first finals game. I hate that this is even a thing in his life when he deserves so much better . . . so much more.

"Why don't you block his number?" I ask, knowing it's much more complex than that. His parents are his lifeline to Jonah. If he cuts them off, he's cut off from his other half. It's complicated to say the least, but even harder is listening to his stoic tone when I know the words on these texts have to wreck him inside.

He chuckles. "You wouldn't understand."

"Try me."

He shakes his head, but I know he's going to tell me. "You know how you get used to something and it becomes a habit?"

"Yeah," I say, but I don't know how that can play into anything that's healthy for him.

"It's kind of become that thing I do. After I play a game, I walk in the locker room and look at my texts before I do anything else."

"But the comments are brutal. I mean, you played one hell of a game the other night and *that's* what he said to you?" My voice is rising as I realize so much of the turmoil inside him, of his long-term mental health, has to be affected by this. "My blood is boiling just thinking of it."

"*But he's watching.*" And there's something in the way he says it that stops the next comment on my tongue. It's sadness mixed with resolve, but it's something so much more. "It's sick and it's twisted and it makes no sense to anyone but me, but those texts at least tell me he's following me. It's not much." He stops when his voice breaks and another piece of me dies inside. "But it tells me he's still watching."

A scrap.

That's all Hunter wants from his dad. A scrap of love, of praise, of attention . . . anything from a father still hung up on a life that can no longer be lived the same.

I hate seeing him like this. I hate seeing him accept so much less than he deserves.

I tighten my ponytail and try to follow Hunter's logic, but God knows it's not normal. "He's watching but he's tearing you down. He's watching because he's trying to see if you measure up to your brother who hasn't played in fifteen-plus years." I get up from the bed and move from one side of the room and back, unable to shake the anger that's eating at me. "This is bullshit. You need to tell him that. But you don't need to because he can see it on his precious TV when he watches his son, the goddamn hockey star, score goal after goal."

But somewhere during my rant, the distress in his expression morphs to a soft smile. He's standing there with his shoulder against the wall of his armoire with amusement in his eyes, and it stops me in my tracks.

"What?" I ask.

"You're more mad at him than I am."

"Mad is an understatement. Mad is me wanting to pick up your phone, call him, and tell him he can take his texts and shove them squarely up his ass. Fury is—"

"Dekker." That smile. Those eyes.

"What?" I ask again.

"I love that you're so worked up about this on my behalf, but it's not going to change."

"Why not? Why can't he see you for you? Why can't he see the hours you put in studying film and the shot practice and the charity work and the way you love your brother and . . . Christ, Hunter, there are a million things that are incredible about you and a million more that I love about you . . ." My voice fades as my confession floats into the room before I have the courage to meet his eyes. This time when I speak, my voice is barely audible. A soft phrase spoken aloud, but it's been screaming in my head for weeks. "And even more reasons why I've fallen in love *with* you."

The tears that well in his eyes are blinked away but not before I see them. "That's not possible."

Months ago, he wouldn't have believed them, but not now. Not after we've spent hours talking about his past and his guilt and how he deserves the whole goddamn world.

"Yeah, it is," I say and take a step toward him. "It's more than possible because there are so many incredible things about you that it makes it hard *not* to fall in love with you."

"Dekker." He shakes his head back and forth, but there's a ghost of a smile on his lips that tells me he hears me. It tells me it'll take more time for him to believe it.

I frame the sides of his face with my hands and smile. "You don't have to say anything. Just hear me. Just know it. And while I'm sure your heart is pounding and your head is asking how this is even possible, know that mine does that every damn day I lay eyes on you. Without fail. And it feels pretty damn good."

67

Dekker

THERE'S A PALPABLE EXCITEMENT within the arena when I step into it. With home-ice advantage, it's black and red everywhere you look—faces are painted and hair is sprayed to match. Instead of going straight to the manager's box, I take my time walking through the arena to soak it all in.

I think of last night with Hunter. My confession that I don't want to take back. Of how we spent the night making love before falling asleep in each other's arms. How a man who swears he doesn't deserve love sure knows how to give it.

I think of this morning—when he found out that Jonah had come down with another chest infection and wasn't cleared to make the flight here. The fact that it was Hunter's medical staff that made the decision and not his mother added validity to the outcome, but I know it still distressed him. But the calm I saw in his expression outweighed his disappointment. It's what I saw years ago in him, an inner strength not many have. But the difference was his lack of anger. In the past few months, his temper would have ignited. Yet he accepted the news about Jonah calmly, and my heart only grew deeper in love with him because of it.

I think of how he sat in his office for over an hour on the phone with Jonah. The conversation may have been one-sided as Hunter worked through the Cyclone's defense and offense and strengths and weaknesses, but you'd never know it. It's like they had their own way of communicating.

You'd think he could actually hear his brother. Even more touching was when Hunter told Jonah to look closely on the coin toss when the cameras pan in and notice how he had written Jonah sideways in the one of his number thirteen so he could be playing with him.

And when Hunter walked out of his office and then house to join his team at the arena, I've never seen him more at peace.

68

Hunter

EXCITEMENT HUMS THROUGH ME like never before.

I can feel the energy of the crowd and the anticipation of a game I've waited my whole life to get a chance to play.

"Let's do this, boys," I yell as I walk up and slap the shoulder pads of each player on my team. "Start with a win, end with the Cup! Start with a win, end with the Cup!"

They start chanting while we sit on the bench as my adrenaline begins to surge.

I take a glance up to the box. The owners are there. The GM beside them. Finn's there too. But it's Dekker I focus on. She's in the far corner, elbows are resting on the edge as she leans forward, but her eyes are on me.

She blows me a kiss, and I smile in return with a nod.

She loves me.

Me.

Fucking loves me.

"Start with a win, end with the Cup!"

The chant of my teammates brings me back. To the here. To the now.

To the ice beneath my skates.

To the feel of the stick in my hand.

To the chill of the arena on my cheeks.

Just like when Jonah and I were kids.

I've got you, brother.

I never stopped.

69

Dekker

"WHAT'S THIS?" I ASK, as I look at the gigantic box Hunter's carrying through my front door.

"Things."

"Things?" I ask with a laugh.

"Yes, things." He sets it down on the kitchen counter and pushes it my way.

"Can I open, said, things?" I ask as I toy with its edges.

"Yes." He presses a kiss to my lips. "I can only stay for your initial reaction and then I've got to get to work."

"Okay." I draw the word out as I lift the flaps of the box and then a laugh bubbles out when I see the team colors of the Jacks. Like lots of team colors. Black and red on hats and T-shirts and jackets and koozies and pens and everywhere. "Did you mug a vendor?" I ask when my laughter subsides and my sides ache.

"Perhaps," he says with a shrug of innocence but a smile like the devil.

"And these?" I ask as I pull out a thong—if you can even call them that—with the Jacks logo imprinted on the only spot of fabric big enough to hold it and dangle them off my fingertips. "These are sold in the kiosks?"

"We like to make sure everybody's covered."

"Covered being the operative word there," I say as I hold them with both hands to show how small they are.

"I wouldn't complain to see how they cover you." He quirks an eyebrow, and I roll my eyes. "Now there's no excuse why you can't wear Jacks gear to the next game."

"And I told you I only wear it after a team wins." I toss the thong back in the box and shake my head at the gear. "Besides, why are you pushing this? I thought athletes were superstitious and never liked to jinx anything."

"We are . . . but sometimes when you feel something in your bones, you just know that no amount of superstition is going to mess with your game."

"Getting cocky now, are we?"

He takes a step toward me and grabs his crotch. "Why yes, I have a cock."

"Jesus." I push against his chest and roll my eyes, but can't say it's not a hot sight. "Besides, *a lot* of players would disagree with you."

"I'm not a lot of players." He leans in and presses a kiss to my lips that is unexpected and heartfelt and stokes those fires he's damn good at sparking to life.

"Thank you for the gear, Mr. Maddox, but while you might not be superstitious, I, for the record, am." I wink and trail my fingernail down the midline of his chest. "Only *after* you win."

"Whatever." He exhales dramatically. "*After* we win, I'll make you wear them every day for a week."

"A week?"

"A week. And especially those panties."

I smile. "Deal."

He kisses me again, his hands wandering to places I want him to not let go of. Everything about the moment is perfectly right.

The Jacks are up in the series three games to two.

The game may be at the opponent's arena, but it's only a few hours away so I've been able to make every game.

Jonah's gotten the all-clear and will be at the game tonight.

I love Hunter Maddox.

How does it not get better than that?

"So I'll see you there?" he asks when he leans back.

"Wild horses wouldn't be able to drag me away." I squeeze his hand, glad he'll have this time tonight to be with his team and see his family before the big game six tomorrow. "And I just might have something for you too."

"Me?"

"Yep," I say with a nod as I walk over to grab the legal-sized manila envelope sitting on the counter.

"What's this?"

"You have to wait to open it."

"Why?" he asks.

"Because it's a surprise and if you don't like it, I don't want to see your expression." I laugh, my words partially true.

"It's that bad?"

"I don't think so."

"Okay, if I have to wait to open this, you have to promise me to personally go through this entire box until you find the surprise I left you."

I eye him, suspicious. "Deal." I lean in for one more breath-stealing kiss. "Good luck, Maddox."

"I'm gonna need it."

"Stick. Skill. Finesse."

And it's not until after he leaves and I settle down on my floor with this massive box do I realize just how much crap is packed in there. There are hats and socks and bears and you name it, along with my most favorite thing, a Maddox jersey.

In fact, there are two of them.

But it's not until I turn the second one over that I see my surprise.

My breath catches and I stare at it for the longest of moments. Tears blur and slip over and my soul sighs in contentment. I reach out with my fingertip and trace the Sharpie block handwriting that fills the number one of the number thirteen on the back of the jersey.

I LOVE YOU TOO.

I sit and stare at it for the longest time. A confession that just made me more whole than I ever thought I could be. An admission I didn't think he realized he could make.

It takes a few minutes for it to sink in. How hard that must have been for him to pen and probably even harder to admit to. But the minute it does, I run to get my phone to call him, and of course I can't find it. After a few minutes, I locate it on my bathroom counter and when I do, there's a text waiting for me on its screen.

HUNTER: *I didn't want to see your expression if you didn't like my surprise either.*

My own laughter fills my silent apartment as I flop back on my bed and hug my phone to my chest.

My first call to him goes to voicemail. So does my second. My desperation to hear him say those words growing stronger with each second.

HUNTER: *We're reviewing film before we leave. Can't talk.*

ME: *I found your surprise. Tennis balls. Lots and lots of tennis balls.*

HUNTER: *LOL. I meant what I wrote.*

ME: *I know.*

I squeal into my apartment in elation. I probably scare the neighbors, but I don't care.

Hunter Maddox loves me.

70

Hunter

THE CHARTER COACH IS spacious. The Cyclone's arena is too close to fly and too far to get there ourselves, so we're all spread out among the seats of the bus, each of us in our own row as we make our way to what could be the final game of the series if we can pull it off.

I stare at the manila envelope for a moment, before curiosity gets the better of me and I open it. I spill the contents out onto the tray table in front of me and it takes me a second to realize what I'm seeing.

And when I do, I'm speechless. One of my dreams is coming to life before my eyes.

The renditions are in different colors with varying logos, but they're all the same thing—or rather the same place. Dekker had a graphic designer create mock-ups of looks and logos for the arena I told her I wanted to buy. *The Jonah Maddox Hockey Facility.*

I thumb through the fifteen or so versions, over and over, as chills chase over my skin at the sight of them. At the knowledge that she heard my dream and is trying to help me see it brought to life. Seeing the logos makes my idea seem that much more real, and I know come hell or high water, I will make this happen.

I grab my phone to text her, glad she understands that Coach has a no talking on cell phones rule on the bus.

ME: *I'm speechless. They're incredible. I can't wait for you to help me pick one.*

DEKKER: *See? Dreams do come true. Now, go out and achieve your other dream tomorrow.*

ME: *I love you.*

DEKKER: *I love you too.*

I stare at the text. At the three words and the weight they hold when I never thought I deserved them, and know I truly do mean them. Fuck, how can I not when it comes to a woman like Dekker?

She's everything I need and nothing I deserve.

She's strong, passionate, driven . . . and I love that she doesn't take shit from anybody, least of all me.

She's seen me at my worst and still loves me.

She champions my dreams when I doubt them, and she fights for me when I've stopped wanting to fight for myself.

How did I get to be such a lucky bastard?

71

Hunter

"GOOD MEETING YOU, MAN," Katz says to Jonah before heading out of the meet and greet room where we've been hanging out in the underbelly of the arena.

"See you in a few," I say.

"My, he's handsome," my mother says with a smile and a fluff of her hair.

"I like to think more of his hockey skills than his looks, but that's just me," I tease, the strain a little less with each minute we visit. "You too, right, J?"

My brother looks so very weak—the pallor of his skin, the hollow lines of his face, his size—but it's his eyes when he looks at me that get me. He's proud. So very proud of me, and I refuse to let him down tonight.

I lean over to his ear and whisper what feels like I've waited a lifetime to say to him. "Tonight's the night, Jonah. We're going to win that Cup we promised each other when we were kids. You pushed me to be better and fuck . . . I'd give anything for it to be you out there, for me to be rooting for you. I would." I close my eyes to fight the tears so I can finish what I need to say. "I promised you I'd get here someday and that when I did, we'd do this together . . . so this game is for you, brother. Every shot, every juke, every block. I needed you here to win, because I couldn't do this without you."

I rest my forehead against his as my shoulders shudder with the weight of my words and the chance at my fingertips. When I lean back to meet his eyes, there are tears on his cheeks. He understands. He hears me. He forgives me.

He's with me.

"I've gotta get to the locker room." I turn to my mom and freeze when I see my dad standing in the doorway. "Dad." I sound like a child when I say his name.

You came to a game. To my game.

You're here.

"Son." He nods and takes a step forward. He extends a hand to me to shake and I do so, feeling detached and uncertain.

"Sir." I stumble over words. "Thank you for coming."

Another somber nod. "Good luck tonight."

Our eyes hold, and fuck if my chest doesn't tighten. "I've got to go."

And when I walk out of the room, I stop and brace my hands on my knees for a few moments to catch my breath.

The man I've called Dad for thirty-two years used to tower over me. Add in his anger, his shame, his . . . loathing, I've always felt so small.

But not now.

Now, I feel tall, like I tower over him.

Now, I feel proud, because I earned everything about this fucking moment. I'm the one who put the blood, the sweat, and the tears in. I'm the one who has sacrificed parts of my life for this chance.

Yeah, him showing up means something to me, but tonight I'm playing for something bigger than him and his relentless criticism. His presence doesn't erase anything . . .

I have a job to do. A win for my team to produce. A place in history to make. So, I straighten and turn toward the training room, ready to lead my team to victory.

Ready to achieve my dream.

72

Dekker

THE PRESS BOX IS not where I want to be to watch this game. I want to be with the fans. I want to be high-fiving when goals are made and booing on bad calls by the ref.

Tonight's game is definitely not one I want to watch from the expensive seats.

But I've spent the better part of the last hour up here as the countdown to the face off draws near. I've visited with Carla, since apparently Hunter has told her we're dating, I've talked at length to Jonah about how Hunter's conversations on the phone with him give him more clarity than I've ever seen, and I've been introduced to Gary, their father.

He's a hard one to read, but I'm sure my anger and resentment doesn't help much.

Uncertain what I'm going to say, but more than sure of my intentions, I step up beside where he's stood the whole time, arms crossed over his chest, as he watches the teams warm-up.

He doesn't acknowledge I'm standing there and for some reason, I don't expect him to.

"Your son is a good man, you know. Incredible, actually."

He nods, but doesn't say a word or look my way.

"He's lived a life trying to make you proud, trying to make amends for fate's cruel hand in the accident that injured Jonah that wasn't Hunter's fault to begin with. I understand your lives changed forever that day. I can't imagine how angry you are over it, and I can't imagine the pain and suffering you've all been through because of it . . . but while you lost the Jonah you knew that day, Hunter lost the parents he knew that day too."

When I look his way, there are tears welling in his eyes and his chin trembles, but he gives no other acknowledgment that he's heard what I've said.

"I'm in love with your son, and I will not stand by and let him be hurt by you any further. I won't let it happen. Are you prepared to risk losing your other son too or are you going to try and find a way through your anger to treat him how he deserves to be treated?" I take a step back. "Your call."

And without another word to Gary Maddox, I turn on my heel with so much more I want to say but restraint locked in place, and head toward my cheap seats.

73

Hunter

A GLANCE AT THE clock.

Ten minutes left in the third period.

It's a tied game.

Ten minutes left to either be a hero or forgotten.

Two to two.

Ten minutes left to make something happen.

Katzen collects the puck and slings it out to me.

I pass it over to Finch then dodge around a defender. My grunt as his shoulder checks me is loud in my head.

C'mon, Hunter. Twenty bucks and me taking over all your chores if you can make this goal. Show Dad that you can.

The puck is stripped from Finch and we race back to help Katzen.

Withers cuts across the ice and intercepts the pass. We all switch gears and go back the other way.

We've been at this for fifty fucking minutes.

Our legs are tired. Our chests burn from breathing so hard.

We need to stay focused.

No more missed passes. No more checks turning into fights.

We need to focus.

We have to win.

I have to win.

Pass after pass we move down the ice. Withers to me. Me to Heffner. Heffner back to me.

A glance at the clock.

Time's wasting.

We need to score.

There is no sound.

There is no crowd.

There is no pressure.

It's me and the goalie.

It's the puck and the net.

It's Jonah beside me, pushing me to make this shot.

Daring me to prove that I can.

74

Dekker

"TEN. NINE. EIGHT."

The Jacks fans in the crowd begin the countdown to the buzzer.

"Seven. Six. Five."

To them winning their first Stanley Cup.

"Four. Three. Two."

To twenty men a childhood dream is about to come true.

"One."

The arena erupts into chaos.

The men on the ice even more so as they pile on top of each other in an ecstatic frenzy.

Frozen in excitement, I stand in the midlevel seats in the arena with both hands covering my mouth in a state of shock myself.

They did it.

They really did it.

I can't take my eyes off Hunter as he breaks free from the pack and skates over to the edge of the rink that's closest to the box seats where his parents are seated. He stands there and points to the booth where Jonah sits in his chair, and I don't have to see Hunter's face to know that tears are streaking down his cheeks are elation, relief, and everything mixed in between.

He won Jonah his Stanley Cup. The one promise he could fulfill . . . he did.

I don't even realize tears are sliding down my own cheeks as I watch Hunter begin to search the arena, his lips moving as he reads the huge section numbers painted on the walls until he finds mine. It takes him a second but when he finds me, the look he gives me is one I'll never forget.

"We did it," he mouths, and all I can do is nod and watch him shine in the moment of his life.

He's quickly engulfed by reporters and teammates and his attention is diverted, but my heart is full beyond measure.

My attention shifts to the box seats where Hunter's family is seated. To where it's ventured numerous times tonight. To the man standing at its edge with his arms crossed over his chest in a formidable stance, but with a hand that's lifted a white tissue to dab beneath his eyes.

My anger is still there at Hunter's dad, it still burns bright. I don't think I will ever find it in me to forgive him for the years of agony Hunter experienced at the hand of his father. Perhaps a better woman would forget and forgive.

I'm not her.

But where does that leave us? By protecting the man I love and this man—his father—taking a step forward, when for so long he's refused to budge?

I'm not sure how to process his presence tonight as I make my way down the edge of the rink, but one thing keeps repeating in my mind. He showed up. He took a first step. He's the one crying, watching one son reach the pinnacle of his sport and fulfill a promise he made to his twin.

Maybe my words hit home.

Maybe this might change things.

Only time will tell.

I make my way to edge of the rink, wanting, needing to be closer to Hunter. Closer to the man I love.

Just as I get there, when I'm as close as I can possibly be while the TV networks are getting everything set up for the presentation of the Cup, Hunter skates over to where I am.

"You," he shouts and points to me as he climbs on the team bench so he can reach over the plexiglass partition. "Let her down here," he says to all the fans screaming for his attention.

It takes a few moments before fans realize what he's asking, so I can make my way to the seats right by the team bench. I climb up on the seat of the stands so I'm tall enough to be pulled into the arms that Hunter engulfs me in. His lips are on mine in a kiss that is one of pure jubilation.

"We did it, Dekk! We fucking did it!"

He reaches down to the back of his pants where he's obviously tucked something and produces a LumberJacks hat and places it squarely on my head.

I throw my head back and laugh, and then have to hold it to my head when I almost lose it.

"It's a good look on you," he shouts above the fray.

"I'm so proud of you," I tell him and kiss him one more time. "Now go celebrate with your team."

He steps down off the bench but his eyes still hold mine, and the goofy grin on his face tells me he's struggling to take this all in.

"I love you," he mouths.

"I love you more," I say, my words drowned out by the roar of the crowd as the Stanley Cup is carried out onto the ice.

75

Hunter

DAD: *Congratulations.*

I STARE AT THE text just delivered to my phone and then back across the room where my dad is standing against the wall with his cell in his hand but his eyes locked on mine.

I wait for the criticism to come. For my phone to alert another text where he tells me what I did wrong or what I could have done better. I expect the negativity that I've lived with all my life to come roaring in.

But he doesn't send another text, he doesn't say a word. He only gives a nod, but it's a nod that says more than I could ever ask for. It says things I've longed to hear for far too long and now that I don't need to hear them, I can probably appreciate them more.

But it takes me back. It challenges me to remember a time when there wasn't something negative to weigh down anything positive that has happened.

And still, the text doesn't come.

I struggle with how to feel. Relieved. Confused. Uncertain. At a loss. I'd think one of them would stand out, but it's been so long since I've been given a chance to have an emotion other than shame and anger when it comes to my dad, that I don't know how to feel.

And then there's the fact that he's over there staring at me but can't voice the word.

I should be angry at that. I should expect more . . . but I lost hope over that so very long ago.

So what now? How do I proceed?

While Jonah's body bears physical scars, mine are within, unseen, and just as devastating.

Some scars may never heal, but for the first time, it seems I've accomplished what he never thought I could. I won the Cup. I lived up to his ridiculous standards.

And a part of me suddenly feels free.

While I shouldn't give a fuck that I made my dad proud or happy because he stole or dominated so many years of my life, I have more to be thankful for than angry about right now.

I did this for Jonah.

I did this for me.

I did this for my team.

I've found Dekker.

Now I can really live.

A dream has been won. My heart is full because of the love of a woman I never thought I'd deserve.

I'm a winner in more ways than one.

And fuck . . . I'm thankful.

76

Dekker

1 week later

HE'S IGNORING ME.

Plain ignoring me.

Chase, Lennox, and Brexton are all out pursuing new clients, and I'm sitting here trying to figure out why he keeps getting up and shutting his door every time a phone call comes in.

Is it the doctor? Isn't that how this all started to begin with? My dad asking me to accomplish something and all of us in a panic that something was wrong with him?

I glance at my dad through the glass window of the conference room, but his back is to me as he talks to whoever has called him this time.

And it's not like phone calls are uncommon. That's all we do in here—talk and talk and talk some more.

So why am I on the defensive without him saying a word? Why am I panicked to talk to him and desperate to as well?

It's because he knows. It's because I failed him and his request. Sure, the status reports were cute and my sisters and I went back and forth with our facetious comments, but I failed to bring Hunter to the firm and now he's trying to figure out something else to keep this place afloat.

Overthink much, Dekk?

Jesus.

I blow out a breath and walk to the door, my hand ready to knock when he opens it.

"You got a sec?" I ask when he just stares at me. He looks frazzled. Hair mussed from his hands running through it, and cheeks flushed.

"What do you need? I'm kind of in the middle of something," he says, striding back to his desk and shuffling through his papers.

"Dad?"

"Hmm?" he says, completely preoccupied. "I have an appointment. They should be here any moment."

"*Dad,*" I say more firmly.

His head comes up and sees me for what I think is the first time. "Sorry. Yes." He stops shuffling. "What is it?"

I shift my feet and stress over asking the question, a grown woman reduced to feeling like a little girl who's about to disappoint her father. "It's been a week since they won the Cup. Why haven't you asked me about Hunter's status on switching agents?"

Especially since you know I go home to him most nights.

He stares at me with an intensity that unnerves me. "I need you to sit down a moment."

"It's not a big deal. Forget I asked. I can see that you're busy."

I'm practically walking back toward my desk when he says, "Sit."

So, of course, I do.

He takes his own seat, his eyes flicking over my shoulder to where our receptionist Marge is speaking to someone, presumably his client.

"How do you think the Jacks won the Cup?"

What?

"The best team won?" I sound uncertain, even though I know my statement is true. The Jacks were the best team in the Cup. They peaked at the right time and the distractions and outside noise faded away. "This isn't about the Jacks. This is about Hunter and how I failed you."

His laugh is a low chuckle. *He knows more than I do.* "I'll ask you the question again. How did they win the Cup?"

I pause. I can see it in his eyes. This is one of his life-lessons moments. The last time we had one, he pushed me to find love—to give my whole heart. And I did. I let go of my fear, and I believed love was possible. I realized it was worth the risk.

And that's when it hits me.

"They won because they believed they could. They won because they played as a team. They won because they trusted their captain and wanted those endless hours of pain and hard work to count for something. They let go of their fear of losing and believed in themselves."

My dad's smile isn't something he gives quickly, but right now, I see my favorite one. *Pride*. He's proud of me, and somehow I don't think it's simply about my answer.

"You're right. They played as a team. Just like we do here. What you drop, another will pick up. What I drop, same goes. We'll survive without Maddox . . . but you're missing my point."

"What is your point then?"

"His point is that he sent you to recruit me."

I gasp at the sound and then the sight of Hunter standing in the doorway to my dad's office. He's leaning against the doorjamb, his thumb hooked in one belt loop of his jeans, and he has a sheepish smile tugging on the corner of his lips.

"Because he saw more in me than I could see in myself. He saw potential through my anger and skill through my antics. He saw something that most dismissed. He knew if I could get my head in the right place, that would be to my benefit. He knew that you'd see me as more than a hockey player when that's all anyone had. He knew that you'd help me see through the pain because like me, you were fighting your way through it too."

I stare at him as my jaw falls lax and my heart swells. And there are tears. For some reason, tears are welling when there's nothing to be sad about.

Because I'm not sad.

No.

I'm so damn happy, so fulfilled, that I never knew this feeling was real or possible or something I wanted to feel.

"Is that right?" I finally ask.

"Yes. That's right." I turn to face my dad and shake my head as I try to process what he means. "I didn't realize it at first." He chuckles as he stands and leans his hips against the credenza at his back. "I thought you were the right one to go after Hunter because you were dogged, and I didn't think you'd take any of his shit, but the more I talked to you, the more you questioned me, I realized everything Hunter just said was true. That you two were more alike than I'd ever thought. Funny how fate is that way."

I eye my father. I see the moisture he blinks away in his own eyes and can feel his pride for both me and Hunter.

He nods his head and smiles softly. "If you'll excuse me, I need to get ready for my client." He holds his hand out to shake Hunter's when he approaches him. "Good to see you. Congratulations, again."

"Thank you, sir."

"It's Kenyon."

Hunter nods as my dad walks down the hallway toward his office.

"What are you doing here?" I ask, rising from my chair.

A sly smile crawls onto his lips. "I wanted to make sure you were fulfilling your end of the deal."

"My end of the deal?" I ask and raise my eyebrows as he steps inside the conference room, shuts the door behind him, and proceeds to turn the blinds closed.

Just what exactly does he think we're going to do in here?

He puts his hand on the small of my back and tugs me into him. His lips find mine in an instant. He's warmth and arousal and comfort . . . and home.

Isn't that what I've come to realize over these past few months? That even though my dad sent me to find Hunter, I also found me?

I know I should be worried that I'm in my office—in the conference room—and being totally unprofessional, but it's so damn easy to get lost in Hunter.

In his touch. In his humor. In the way he makes me think about things other than the day-to-day. In the way he makes me feel.

My body heats from his touch, despite it only being hours since I slid out of bed beside him to come to work.

It's only when his hand tries to slip inside the waistband of my slacks that I push my hands against his chest to stop him. "Whoa, tiger." I laugh and press one more kiss to his lips. "Not here."

"Just trying to make sure you're holding up your end of the bargain," he says and wipes a thumb over his lip in case any of my lipstick transferred.

"My end of the bargain?"

"Mm-hmm." His eyes say he wants to devour me. "My LumberJacks gear?"

I laugh and take a step back. "Perhaps." I'm acting coy on purpose, because playful Hunter is always so much fun.

"Perhaps?" he asks.

"Maybe you'll just have to wait and see when I get home tonight if I have my Jacks panties on."

"Is that so?"

"It is."

"What if I have a way to let you out of your end of the promise." He angles his head to the side and studies me, humor mixed with mischief on his expression.

"I'm thinking I'll wear the panties." I sit on the top of the desk behind me. "I never trust someone who changes a deal midway through."

"Says who?"

"Says me." *What in the world is he getting at?*

There's that slow smile again that tugs on every part of me. "You're an agent. You know full well that negotiations shift. Change. Realign."

"Should I worry about what exactly it is you want to realign?"

"More like I want the terms to change."

"You're talking in circles, Hunter," I tease, and his grin widens.

"Good thing you're familiar with how to follow circles."

"True."

But he is talking in circles and it's making zero sense.

"What is it you want now?"

"*You.*"

Thud. My heart on the floor.

"Oh." I don't hide the shock or the stupid grin on my face from his unexpected comment. "In that case . . ." I grab the sides of his shirt as he takes a step toward me before framing my face and dipping down so he can meet my eyes. His are intense and alive with emotion.

"In that case?" He brushes his lips over mine.

"New terms accepted. Negotiation successful."

He laughs as I pull him against me, wrapping my arms around his waist. He rests his chin on top of my head and I revel in the feel of him and the knowledge that he's all mine.

Who would have ever thought I'd say that about the only man who ever truly broke my heart?

"I've been doing a lot of thinking, Dekk," he murmurs, his chin moving on the crown of my head. "Scary, I know."

"About?"

"Things."

"Like?"

"My career. My life. What I want from it." He leans back and our eyes meet again. "All of this—the clarity, your belief in me, you pushing me, the Cup—has me looking at things in a different light."

"I don't see how I had anything to do with that."

"How can you say that?" he asks. "You heard what your dad said. That it's your belief in me that allowed me to be my best me."

"I was just doing my job."

"No, you were being you." Those lips of his meet mine again in a kiss that lacks intensity but is loaded with tenderness. "I'm madly in love with you, Dekker Kincade. Maybe I always have been, but you helped me see the me I had lost. You allowed me to be the me who had hope. You allowed me to tell my darkest truths and instead of walking away, you held on tighter. You loved the me I hated."

"And I love the you that you now love too."

"I know." Tears well in his eyes, but he blinks them away just as quickly as they appear.

"If there's one thing I learned with everything, it's your next tomorrow is never guaranteed. I don't want to miss any tomorrows with you. I think we should take the next step. I think we should move in together and start building that tomorrow and the day after that and the week after that together."

"You do?"

"I do." He laughs. "I'm getting confused where my toothbrush is and whether I'm coming or going from your house or mine. It's so much easier if I know I get to come home to you at the end of the day. That's all that seems to matter anymore."

"Says the league MVP."

"Exactly." He squeezes my hand. "We never made a bet on what I'd get if I won MVP and I did . . . and so"—he shrugs—"cohabitation."

"Cohabitation?" I laugh.

He nods. "I know I'll screw up. I know I'm stubborn and frustrating and will sometimes shut you out when all you want is to be held close . . . but I can promise you I want to do right by you. For you. For me. For us. I want to make this work because Christ, I'm miserable without you."

"But you haven't been without me for a while now."

"Exactly," he repeats, his voice softening, "because you're where I want to be."

I'm having trouble swallowing over the love that his words create, wrapping around my soul and taking root.

"Hunter."

"Don't cry." He wipes my tear that slips over. "No more tears."

"Just tomorrows."

His smile returns. "Just tomorrows."

I'm not sure how long I stay wrapped in his arms, settling into this idea of getting to wake up every morning next to him and getting to kiss him every night—but it's not a hardship to accept.

Not by a long shot.

There's a knock on the door and we jolt apart like kids getting caught.

"Dekk?" My dad peeks his head into the conference room.

"Yeah?" I pull the door open all the way.

"Can I have my client back now? You're messing up my schedule."

"What do you mean your client?" I look from my dad to Hunter and his stupid, wide grin and laugh that vibrates, then back to my dad.

"What you drop, another one of us will pick up," my dad says.

"Hunter?" I ask, confused but hopeful.

"He means *his* client. You once told me I could only have one or the other with you, and, Dekker, you sure as hell know which one I'm going to pick."

"Me?" I ask, an incredulity in my voice as my world comes full circle.

"Did you not just hear anything I said?" He laughs. "Of course, *you.*" He gives me a chaste kiss on the lips. "And then him."

He squeezes my hand as he stares at me, and I don't care that my father's there watching—I wouldn't care if the whole world was—because when Hunter looks at me, everything else is just background noise.

"I'll be in my office," my father says, leaving us alone.

"'Kay," Hunter says, but his eyes never leave mine.

"You sure you want to do this?"

"Do what?" he asks.

"This. Me. Us. KSM," I say with a nervous laugh, "because this is your only chance to bail. You know us Kincades, we never walk away from negotiations."

"Lucky for me, because I already let you walk away once, and I'm sure as hell not making that mistake again."

He leans in and kisses me with a kiss that's equal parts emotion and heat. But when he pulls back, the look in his eyes is one hundred percent emotion.

"What?" I ask softly.

"Just trying to fathom how you're here. How I'm here. How life happens."

"Skill. Stick. Finesse, Maddox."

He throws his head back and laughs.

And it's the best sound in the world.

EPILOGUE - 1

Hunter

6 months later

I ABSENTLY TOY WITH the edges of the letter. It's light, but the weight of it staggers me.

Unable to bring myself to look at the words typed on the page yet, I sit on the old dock and watch the lake sparkling in the sun before me.

"We'll own a cabin here someday," I say to Jonah. He looked over at me and skipped a rock across its surface. We both count as it dances five times on top of the water before sinking.

"Maybe." He leans back on his elbows and holds his face to the sun. "We might own a cabin and come here with our families. We might not. But this is where I want to die someday."

"Dude. That's fucked." I laugh. "Why do you have to get all morbid and shit? We're sixteen. Let's not think about that yet." I lift the beer we'd swiped from the cabin's fridge and take a drink.

I still think it tastes like piss, but I'm trying to acquire the taste.

And not get caught.

We'd be dead if we got caught.

"It's life, little brother. We live. We die. The earth moves on."

"You should drink that beer before Mom and Dad get back from the store or

we're going to practice that theory when Dad finds us."

He laughs and takes a sip. I'm relieved to see his wince and that he doesn't like it much either. But guys like beer, so we'll figure out how to like it.

"Just think about it, though. What better place to be when you die? You're surrounded by everything that we love here."

"I guess."

"Right here on this dock. That's where I want to kick the old bucket."

My eyes blur from the memory.

My chest aches in a way I never thought possible.

My life missing a piece I have to figure out how to navigate without. *God, I miss you, Jonah.*

My thoughts are filled with a million memories about this place. About that conversation. One I had completely forgotten until Jonah died and his lawyer told us his wishes were for some of his ashes to be spread here.

Just like his wish was for the lawyer to give me the letter I hold in my hand. The one he dictated to him over two years ago.

I'm not sure what my fear is. Is it that this is the very last piece of Jonah I have left? That if I read it, then this is real and he's truly gone? Is it because a small part of me feels guilty that I'm grateful he's gone so he's no longer in pain? Is it because I miss him and reading this will prove to me how goddamn much?

I shove the tears away and take a sip of beer. It's the same cheap shit we drank all those summers ago, and I laugh because it still tastes like piss.

With a deep breath, I look at the letter.

Hunter,

There's so much I've needed to say to you for so long, but I've known you wouldn't listen. You're a stubborn and determined little shit (yes, you'll always be little to me, no matter how old we get) and would probably walk out of the room if I told you any of this.

If you're getting this, I'm gone. Fucking sucks on both our parts. This wasn't how our life was supposed to go. We were supposed to be old, grumpy men on that rickety dock at the lake when we kicked the bucket. We were supposed to be Stanley Cup winners with kids of our own. Ones we'd teach how to play hockey if they wanted to. We'd argue over whose grandkids were the cutest before we'd fill them up on sugar and send them home. We'd have wives who were best friends.

We would have lived our lives to the fullest and without regret.

I no longer can, but I need you to promise me that you will. That you'll live for you. Every second. Every minute. Every day. Every year.

To do that, you need to hear this: what happened to me wasn't your fault. I've had a lot of years to think about this and plenty of time to play out all the scenarios that could have happened that day. Bottom line is, I'm at fault.

I drank. I got behind the wheel. I killed that woman. I did this to myself.

And I'd do it all over again if that meant protecting it from happening to you. That's the job of a big brother. Even now, I want to protect you. And the only way I can do that is by telling you I never blamed you, and the accident was not your fault.

I should have told Dad to go to hell that day, and that you were going to junior prom with us. I should have stood up for you—that time and so many other times—but I didn't. I failed you.

I've come to terms with that, and I hope one day you can forgive me for it.

I couldn't have asked for a better brother. You sat by silently while Dad put me on a pedestal when you were just as skilled and talented as I was. You cheered me on while being slighted. I see that now. Time has given me that opportunity to realize how wrong that was. I'm sorry. You are every bit as good as I could have been. I watch you playing now on the TV, and I'm so damn proud of you.

It's more than hockey though. It's about you. About how you've tried so hard to live for both of us. How you've made sure to include me in every step. How you've called and talked for hours when I know you had so many other things to do.

So what happens now, Hunter? I know you'll miss me as much as I'll miss you.

You live.

For you.

Without regret.

And every once in a while, go to that dock, crack open that cheap, shitty beer, and take a sip for me.

You were the one true thing I held on to all these years.

You were the one who kept me going.

You were my inspiration.

I love you.

Jonah

I hang my head as the sobs hit me. As the words my brother wrote crack every last chain of guilt I've grown so damn used to wearing.

It's just like him to know what I need to hear.

It's just like him to know that I'm struggling with how to move on in a world without him, and how to throw me a lifeline.

It's just like him to have one final say so there's no doubt in my mind how he felt about me.

In time, I know the ache will go away and the sadness will fall dormant, but fuck if it's not going to always hurt.

I let the tears fall, and when they subside, when I'm all cried out, I lift that crappy beer and take a swig.

My laughter is unexpected, but I can't help but remember him here that last summer before his accident. How crazy and carefree he was. How much we laughed. How much we loved.

I take the small container sitting beside me that holds my portion of his ashes and slowly pour them into the lake.

I give him what he wanted that day.

To be here when he dies.

To have the sun and the water and the memories.

I'm not sure how long I sit here, but I know she's here. I know she's been sitting here this whole time, giving me my space to grieve how I need to, giving me the time to figure this out.

But when I'm finally ready to go, when I get to my feet and turn around, I'm so very grateful to see her here. The blonde hair flying from the breeze and the compassion in her smile.

I know I'm leaving my brother here today, but I'm so very grateful to be walking toward her when I do. And I plan on carrying out my brother's final instructions.

I'll live.

For me.

Without regret.

EPILOGUE - 2

Dekker

1 year later

EXCITEMENT FILLS THE AIR.

I take it all in. The people milling around. The clusters of people sitting in the stands. The special staging area for kids to lose their wheelchairs and gain their sleds so they can skate. The staff in their bright blue shirts helping anyone and everyone who needs assistance.

And then I see him.

Hunter's standing on the far side of the rink. He's in the parking zone—a spot he created where parents park their kids' wheelchairs and then walk away to the stands. It's where kids can feel like kids. Where they can be entertained by clowns or talk hockey or anything really and have some autonomy. His grin is wide as he sits on his haunches talking to a little girl.

Everything I love about him can be summed up in this one moment—his passion, his drive, his kindness, his love, and his devotion.

The past year has been a hard one for him and so to see this—him—this alive as he immortalizes his brother's memory, is so heartwarming.

Someone comes over and taps him on the shoulder and hands him a microphone. The opening ceremony is about to start.

People hoot and holler as he walks out onto the rolled-out mat to center ice. My father's whistle being one of the loudest.

"Thank you for coming today," Hunter says and clears his throat. "What started as a dream of mine about eighteen months ago is now, today, officially a reality. *The Jonah Maddox Hockey Facility* is now officially open."

Applause fills the arena, but it's Hunter's eyes that find mine. There's a soft smile on his lips, and I'm sure I'm the only one who notices the tears welling in his eyes.

"This arena is for you. It doesn't matter what abilities you do or don't have, all that matters is that you want a chance to play and learn hockey . . . and I'll do everything in my power to give that to you." Another round of applause. "My brother was an incredible person and through this program, he will live on." Hunter bows his head momentarily to collect his emotions before looking up and finding me again. "Dekker, will you come out here and do the honors with me?"

I startle at his request but shouldn't be surprised by it. The two of us have been working side by side, nonstop, to get this place ready for today.

It takes me a few seconds to cross the carpet and make it to him. He links his fingers with mine and gives me that devil-may-care grin.

"In a lot of places, they cut a ribbon to officially kick off the start of something. But here at the Jonah P. Maddox Arena, we like to start things a little differently." Hunter glances at me. "You ready? Do you remember what we talked about?" Hunter asks the kids all around the ice. "Five. Four. Three." The arena counts down with him while I look around confused, as if I'm missing something. "Two. One."

And the minute one is said, the kids around the ice and the people in the stands, all start tossing tennis balls onto the ice.

"Tennis balls?" I laugh.

"Yep."

I laugh as I watch kids of all ages, ethnicities, and with differing disabilities toss tennis balls onto the ice. There is laughter and giggling, and chills chase over my skin at the sight of Hunter's dream coming true.

At this lifeline anchoring him.

I glance his way, fully expecting to catch his profile as he takes it all in, but I'm startled when he's looking straight at me. His eyes are serious, intentional. But his grin, wide and gorgeous, is a funny contradiction.

"What?" I ask just above the noise.

"Nothing." But the expression on his face dares me not to look away.

"I thought you hated the limelight," I tease as tennis balls bounce against our legs and feet.

"I do."

"Then why are we standing here in the middle of all these tennis balls," I ask.

"Because some things deserve the spotlight."

"Your brother most certainly did." I squeeze his hand.

His smile softens, his eyes sadden, and he reaches out to run a thumb down my cheek. *"So do you."*

I go to refute him when I see the tennis ball in his hand. Except it's not a real tennis ball—or rather a useable one—as it's been cut in half. And when Hunter lifts the top off it, my mind goes blank. I have to remember to breathe.

Nestled inside is a diamond ring. I'm sure it's gorgeous and sparkly and everything, but what it looks like doesn't mean a thing. It dims in the shadow of the man who's holding it.

"Hunter?" I ask in reflex.

"Some things most definitely deserve the spotlight. And you, Dekker Kincade, have made every part of my life shine since the moment you walked into it. With your defiant will and your fiery temper. With your need to help and your love to fix. With just you. We've been through so much already, and all I can think about is how there's no one else I'd rather go through life with than you. Will you marry me?"

"Is this a negotiation?" I ask, fighting back my own smile and my urge to jump in his arms and kiss him a million times.

"No. This is one thing I'm not negotiating on."

"Whew. I taught you well, then."

"And?"

"Yes. Of course, the answer is yes."

And then I give in to what I want.

I jump into his arms and kiss him senseless.

With a whole arena watching.

Because today is a day for spotlights.

Today is a day for dreams coming true.

COMING SOON

DID YOU ENJOY DEKKER and Hunter's story in Hard to Handle? Stay tuned for the rest of the series and exploring just who Dekker's sisters—Brexton, Lennox, and Chase—might fall for in Hard to Hold, Hard to Score and Hard to Lose. All books are available for preorder HERE.

And if you're looking for something to read in the meantime, check out Kristy's next book, Flirting with Forty, late summer 2020.

ABOUT THE AUTHOR

Photo © 2017 Lauren Perry

New York Times Bestselling author K. Bromberg writes contemporary romance novels that contain a mixture of sweet, emotional, a whole lot of sexy, and a little bit of real. She likes to write strong heroines and damaged heroes who we love to hate but can't help to love.

A mom of three, she plots her novels in between school runs and soccer practices, more often than not with her laptop in tow and her mind scattered in too many different directions.

Since publishing her first book on a whim in 2013, Kristy has sold over one and a half million copies of her books across twenty different countries and has landed on the New York Times, USA Today, and Wall Street Journal Bestsellers lists over thirty times. Her Driven trilogy (Driven,

Fueled, and Crashed) is currently being adapted for film by the streaming platform, Passionflix, with the first movie (Driven) out now.

With her imagination always in overdrive, she is currently scheming, plotting, and swooning over her latest hero. You can find out more about him or chat with Kristy on any of her social media accounts. The easiest way to stay up to date on new releases and upcoming novels is to sign up for her newsletter or follow her on Bookbub.

ACKNOWLEDGMENTS

HARD TO HANDLE WAS a chance to write my three favorite tropes all in one—sports, enemies to lovers, and second chance. I truly hope you enjoyed Dekker and Hunter's story as much as I did writing it.

I want to give a little shout out to my crew that keeps me on track: Christy for keeping things straight. Chrisstine for the honest feedback for that first 20% of a book where I'm constantly saying, "This book is horrible." Ali, Steph, Annette, Val, and Emma for keeping things running in the VP Pit Crew. Marion for polishing my words and cutting out all the repetition (and there's *a lot*). My proofers—Karen, Kara, Janice, Michele, Marjorie—for making sure my errors are few and far between. And lastly, to the readers . . . thank you for picking this book up and for all of your continued support over the years.

CPSIA information can be obtained
at www.ICGtesting.com
Printed in the USA
LVHW051520290423
745673LV00002B/384